Blood In The Bricks

Edited By Neil Williamson

Blood In The Bricks

Edited By Neil Williamson

NewCon Press
England

First published in the UK October 2025 by
NewCon Press
41 Wheatsheaf Road,
Alconbury Weston,
Cambs, PE28 4LF

NPN353 (limited edition hardback)
NPN354 (paperback)
10 9 8 7 6 5 4 3 2 1

ISBN:
978-1-917735-11-7 (hardback)
978-1-917735-12-4 (paperback)

Cover art by Vincent Chong
Cover layout and design by Ian Whates
Edited by Neil Williamson
Typesetting by Ian Whates and Neil Williamson

Table of Contents

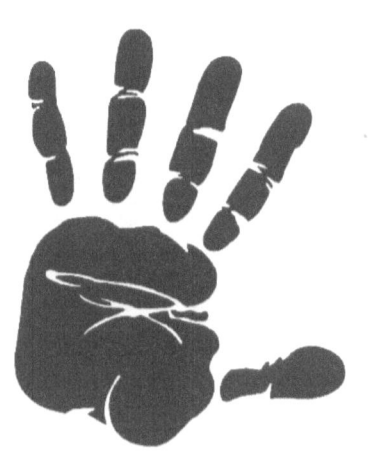

Introduction

Neil Williamson

With the growth in popularity of Folk Horror over the last decade, there's an argument to say that the subgenre's landscape has grown, ironically, familiar. As readers and viewers we've come to know what to expect when we venture down those remote and unwelcoming country lanes: an isolated community with somewhat skewed beliefs, a penchant for ritual, and a flare for violence. A beguiling formula, that was first recognised by the critic, Adam Scovell. Strangers entering these here parts are assured a cold welcome (or an exceptionally hot one), but still we come in our droves.

But have we had our fill of bloodthirsty fields? Ten years into the boom, is that great dropped *uh-oh* beat when we open the door of the Slaughtered Lamb just a bit predictable? If we've outstayed our welcomes out in the sticks, where else can Folk Horror be found?

Though I live in a city, I grew up in a country town and I can say definitively that there's nothing intrinsically weirder about rural communities than urban ones. Scovell, himself recognised this not long after he coined the famous *Folk Horror chain* referenced above. Our towns and cities have been around for a long time after all (Glasgow, where I'm writing this introduction, celebrates its 850th anniversary in 2025, but has been a site of settlement for millennia). Our urban centres' histories have been constructed over centuries. Foundation upon foundation, brick upon brick. Their secrets long kept and buried deep. Their cycles and rhythms governed by a different set of needs.

And there are other types of isolation than simple geographical remoteness. Urban environments are rife with no-go areas and Keep Out signs. Think stumbling into the wrong pub. Think exclusive members' only clubs and gated communities. Think industrial wastelands, derelict factories and crumbling tower blocks. Think abandoned hospitals and sealed off subway stations. Think the ultimate weirdness of … *suburbs*!

Cities are naturally alienating environments. They're not built to human scale, unknowable in their entirety, and those of us that live in them generally limit our city lives to the size of a village as a result. Recognising narratives that played on this innate alienation but were lacking the other elements he'd attributed to folk horror, Scovell coined the term *Urban Wyrd*. But if we venture out of our familiar neighbourhoods and cross to the other side of the tracks, might we not find that the people who live there have some odd beliefs? A hint of the dangerous about them? That we're not welcome over there, and it's too late to turn back?

And what of the ones that live among us, in plain sight? What do you really know about your boss, your barista, your bike-fit instructor? For all the pleasant regularity of your interactions, who knows what they get up to the rest of the time?

In *Blood In The Bricks* we seek out the strangers in the darker parts of town and reveal what secretive superstitions our neighbours practise behind closed doors. From the risks of riding the London tube late at night to the sinister secrets of rare motorcycle aficionados; from eager-to-share artistic collectives to what finds mudlarkers dig up along the Thames; and from what you've got to do to get by after the fae invade to what happens when you return home and find that you've outgrown the tribe.

Ever wondered what those crumbling old bricks were made from or what that utility pole is really for?

Read on and find out.

– Neil Williamson
Glasgow, July 2025

Down Street

James Bennett

Rats in London are far from rare, but there's a giant one standing on the eastbound platform of Hammersmith Tube station. Cherry, in no mood for pranks, almost trips over her heels as she comes down the steps and sees the man in the scruffy bomber jacket and jeans, the mask in question over his head. *Idiot.* It's eleven pm on a Tuesday night and if the guy is heading into the city for a knees-up then he must be either a tourist or late. Doubtful, judging by the state of his clothes; grime covers him, marking him out as homeless, a member of the dishevelled tribes that haunt every station entrance, doorstep and corner in the capital. Still, she can't fault the craftmanship on display, the moulded pelt of grey hair, the blank glass eyes and ragged, pink-lined ears under the strip lights. A glance at her phone tells her she has a five-minute wait for the next train to Holloway, but even that feels like forever considering that her, a kid in a baggy tracksuit and Rat Man are the only ones waiting.

I should get a better job, Cherry tells herself for the umpteenth time. Regularly working late in the office with only a long commute as a reward isn't where she thought she'd wind up at thirty-three, let alone the prize at the end of it all being a cramped back bedroom costing her a grand a month. Every evening commute is a risk, as any woman would tell her. Weirdos in London are far from rare.

"Got a light, love?"

The kid can't be older than seventeen, but she's "love" to him all the same. With a shake of her head, the unspoken code of the city, she waves the vape in her hand and ignores his subsequent pout. What he thinks a blonde in a business jacket and pencil skirt, her handbag clutched tight, wants with the likes of him is beyond her. The rat looks on unmoved. But she's shaken anyway and it isn't his fault.

9

Damn you, Masters. She gives a sigh when the youth retreats, perhaps noticing her eyeliner, the smudge of recent tears. Or he's wary, thinks the rodent might intervene if he tries anything. Cherry doesn't give a shit about fancy dress, accountancy and even less for her boss, but she needs the job if she hopes to make rent. It's a temp position and that means that David Masters' odorous breath whenever he leans over her desk and the occasional brush of his hand on her backside in the canteen will be a brief ordeal. He makes her skin crawl, but she can put up with it, she tells herself. And most days she can. But today, of all days, the last thing she needed was him cornering her to ask her to do overtime in yet another bid to get her alone. To go on about football matches and past package holidays, which he seems to think of as flirting. He's trying to see if she'll overlook the fact of his wife; just how desperate she is to keep her shitty job, the potbellied, pisshead bastard.

Cherry has had her fill of men.

It's late, but because she can't help it (and to show the rat and the kid that she's not completely isolated), she calls Claire for the tenth time that day. For the tenth time, she gets through to voicemail.

"Claire, we need to talk." She keeps her voice low so she won't be overheard. Sneered at. "Please call back."

Cherry doesn't know what she'll say if she does; her drunken confession hasn't left much room for a chinwag. She's taken it as read that Claire has no interest in continuing the relationship, such as it is. Sure, she made her position clear from the start. Cherry likes men and women both, but she tends to take them one at a time. That's what she'd said anyway, hoping it helped Claire to feel secure. Then she'd shat all over it when she'd jumped into bed with her ex, Stephen, after the Camden gig last month. Why, oh why, had she let guilt gnaw her down to the bone and decided to own up? Had she really believed that Claire would forgive her?

It's been a hell of a day. Typical that it ends with a man-sized rat staring at her on an all but empty platform on a wet August night. Has the freak moved closer? When he steps away from the wall, she notices the graffiti there, lurid loops of red. A Celtic knot, she thinks. Snakes entwined. The spray paint drips, but she can't see whether Rat Man is the culprit or not. And the mask makes it unclear whether he's even staring at her, though she senses it. He confirms it by raising a hand – *ah, red on his fingers* – and gives her a nod.

"Praise the Gaf," he says. "Bless the tithe."

That earns him a glare from Cherry. Will she have to draw on her box-fit lessons to make the point clear?

Stay the fuck away.

Like a knight in filthy armour, the train arrives, a swirl of fumes and damp gusting into the station. A loudspeaker barks out unintelligible instructions. Passengers disembark, shoving. Faceless. Though her destination is a microwaved meal followed by a cold bed (and further bullshit tomorrow), Cherry boards the carriage, eager for the Picadilly Line to plunge her into the bowels of the city.

Rat Man and the kid get into the same carriage as her. *Of course.* It's a fifty minute ride home. Fifteen stops. Hopefully, the weirdo will get off well before that. As the train lurches off, she takes her place on the frayed and sagging seat and adopts the customary blank stare of all London passengers, gazing at her reflection in the window, superimposed on the shimmering city. It gives her something to look at, even if it's her own annoyance and guilt. The kid sniggers at his phone, EarPods in. Rat Man stands at the end of the carriage, holding onto the pole. His whiskers bob. The tips of his ears brush the plastered adverts. Insurance. Tourist attractions. Pleas to quit smoking and photographs of missing people. Unnerved by his continued attention, Cherry reads and learns that a hundred thousand people go missing in the UK every year, the equivalent of forty passengers per single rush hour on the Tube. Not much comfort.

At Baron's Court, a woman gets on, wrestling with a push buggy, shopping bags and a screaming child. *Great.* Cherry feels bad when the woman, bulging from a Primark dress, rolls her eyes to convey her nightmare. She offers the ghost of a smile and returns to her reflection as the woman crouches, chiding her son in a language that Cherry can't place. Polish perhaps. London is a melting pot and she's the last person to judge, what with having cheated on her girlfriend. But she doesn't know how people can put up with kids.

When she dares a glance at Rat Man – because what does he make of the uproar? – she sits up a little straighter. His back is turned and

11

he's busy with the wall, can of spray paint in hand. A jerk of the track reveals the same red and looping lines, the knotted serpent, albeit rendered smaller than the one in the station. His *Gaf,* some arcane symbol born of mental illness or too much meth. *Poor bugger.* It's vandalism, not that she'll report it. Too much hassle. She'd move carriages if that was possible on the Tube. There's just the five of them heading east, the disparate souls of London forced into proximity, uncomfortable and wordless.

Her phone buzzes in her pocket. Snatching it out, she sees that it's Claire. *Claire!* Putting the device to her ear, Cherry only catches a sniffle, some hissed imprecation but then the train plunges underground before Earl's Court and she loses signal.

London swallows her whole, rehearsed apology and all.

There's no announcement, no crackle of driver's spiel to speak of problems on the line. Cherry only realises that something is up ten minutes later, the train rattling along at speed, the lights stuttering and stations flashing by. A blur of tiles. The familiar red circle design. The odd bundled figure. Gloucester Road. South Kensington. Knightsbridge. Cherry knows them like the pages of her planner, the daily slog of riding to and from misery. The lion's jaws of harassment. All go by with no sign of slowing, no expected halt to disgorge and take on passengers. *Eh?* As far as she's aware, none of the stations have been closed for building work. The rain isn't hard enough to suggest flooding. She'd be glad to be getting home earlier, but a worm coils in her stomach, accompanied by the same wave of nausea that she's experienced since breakfast this morning, neither relating anything good. Rat Man and the kid seem oblivious. But the woman with the buggy is frowning.

"Odd," she remarks from the space by the doors. "It better stop at Hyde Park or – shit!"

The station in question flashes by, a larger smear of people on the platform. Sparks scatter past the windows. Wheels screech. Then the train plunges onward into Central London.

"Must be an electrical fault." It's all Cherry can offer the woman, repressing a shrug that she doesn't feel.

12

The child, catching its mother's distress, renews its aria with gusto. The kid remains hypnotised by Snapchat or whatever. Cherry gives an inward tut. The man in the mask could be thinking anything, his glass eyes dark, inscrutable. Red paint drips on the wall, an ugly symbol of unease.

"Fuck that. Where's the emergency – ?"

The carriage jerks, cutting the woman off. Even as Cherry sighs in relief that the train is slowing, the wheels screaming under her, the lights go out. *Typical.* The kid looks up, the one who's providing the light now. His features look sallow in the glow of his phone. There's the sense of the track turning, the carriage bucking, and Cherry assumes that they're entering a siding, one of the many tunnels that run under the city. Everyone knows it's a labyrinth down here. Old and deep enough to sprout urban legends. Ghost passengers. Unaccounted for screams. Even a rampant mummy over by the British Museum. All rubbish, of course. There's nothing down here but dirt, rats and –

The train shudders to a halt. Again, without announcement. The doors slide open, eviscerating her scepticism. Fumes waft into the carriage, the tang of diesel and damp bricks. Her flesh prickles in the chill. *What the hell is going on?*

It's enough to see Cherry onto her feet. To her alarm, she finds herself looking out at a platform lit by pools of feeble sodium. The roof shares its curve with the tunnel, just like any other station in the city. There's concrete. The same mired tiles. A faint urine smell. The walls are a patchwork of brown and beige, tugging at some distant classroom memory of wartime Britain, grainy photos of the Blitz. Dust and debris speak of abandonment. No adverts line the walls, promising wealth and eternal youth. An arrow points to a way out, but it isn't one she's prepared to take. The adjoining passageway lies in darkness.

Down Street, she reads on the platform wall. The name means nothing to her. The station isn't on her daily commute. She hasn't seen it on a Tube map, not that she recalls. They must be somewhere under Green Park, judging from the journey so far. This might've aroused her curiosity, even a sense of adventure, but then she sees the

13

graffiti under the sign. The coiled serpent, a washed-out pink, appears to have been there for some time.

"What the actual?"

This from the youth, EarPods out and finally noticing that all isn't well in Tube-land. The three of them are on their feet now, gawping.

All mundane concerns fly from Cherry's mind when a pair of figures emerge from the shadowed passageway, stride across the platform and board the carriage at the far end. Intent informs their movements, a stiff-legged purpose. Their clothes, nondescript, look ragged and soiled, caked with grime. It's their faces that arrest her, push her in retreat down the gangway.

Fuck.

Both are wearing masks. One, a fox. The other, a rabbit.

Before Cherry can do so, the other woman steals the chance to scream. Instead, she turns to find Rat Man, the harbinger of this strange, subterranean circus, looming behind her. The masks all bear the same craftmanship. The same glued whiskers, woven fur and dark bauble eyes. A carnival indeed. None have any business being on the Tube, she thinks, her head spinning. The carriage has no place at this station.

Nor do the knives the strangers bear, glinting in the half-light.

Cherry has stopped complaining by the time that the strangers usher them into the passageway. Partly it's the jab of Rat Man's knife, promising her injury if she doesn't shut up. Partly it's the train. The engine rumbles and she turns to see the carriages sliding off into the tunnel, most of the light going with them. *On to Picadilly and home beyond, along with anyone to hear us...* Why it's dumped them here, the kid, the woman and her... well, it's far from normal. Only means bad news. And she'd thought that Masters and cheating were the worst of her worries. Tuesday has become a horror show.

Thinking this, she fumbles in her pocket, hoping to tap out an urgent message. A missed call. The police. Anything. Not that she has reception. Rat Man notices, however, and plucks the phone from her. He shakes his verminous head. *Try it.* The kid is swearing for England, having undergone a similar mugging. The Fox gives him a shove, the lad stumbling ahead. The woman clings to her buggy, sobbing. But

14

the child, amazingly, has fallen silent. At the head of the freakish procession, Rabbit leads them through the gloom and emerges onto another platform, one for the westbound trains – not that any have stopped here for years as far as Cherry can tell. The station has been abandoned. Forgotten. At least by anyone sane.

"What… what do you want?" she manages. She doesn't expect Rat Man to answer her. As her eyes adjust to the dimness, the orange glow of several LED construction lamps placed well apart on the platform, her pleas dry up in her throat.

There are other animals down here. Other masked strangers. Badger. Otter. Frog. Crow. The place has become a Halloween parade, the lot holding knives and clubs with nails hammered into the end. One, she notices, is holding a rifle. That's enough to chase thought of flight from her mind. Whoever these people are (*terrorists*, her nerves whisper), they mean business.

But it's the others on the platform – passengers, she assumes – that reduce her to a trembling wreck as Rat Man waves his blade, insisting that she get down on her knees like the rest of them. There must be thirty of them at least, shivering, muttering and crying (quietly) on the narrow concrete surface. Men and women. Young and old. Business suits. Casual dresses. Cheap deodorant can't compete with the pall of sweat and fumes. If the general air of alarm is anything to go by, none of them have been here that long. How many trains pass by in an hour? How many have the freaks kidnapped? *Shit*, she thinks. *The driver must be in on it.* It doesn't offer any explanation for the hostage taking. Rat, Fox and Rabbit aren't about to tell her either. The tunnel beyond, a gaping mouth leading into blackness, turns their combined noise into a susurration of dread.

"No. Please."

This from the woman, the one from the train. She's clinging to the push buggy as Frog tries to wrench it from her, child and all. Cherry can't help but cry out when the woman scales towards violence and Frog gives her a slap in return. Then a kick. Drags the buggy from her. A Cat in a floral skirt steps forward and shoves the woman to the ground, following up with a thump of her cudgel for good measure. The woman, cowed, groans in the dirt while Frog, all business, wheels the buggy away, the child whimpering, echoes fading into the passageway.

Cherry has a brief, horrid thought that she's never going to see Claire again. Never get to say sorry. A microwaved meal and a cold bed have never seemed more appealing. Then a man in an owl mask appears up ahead, suited, booted and mired like the rest despite his bizarre avian appearance. Owl steps up onto a crate to address them, his captive audience.

"Blessings, Tithe of the Gaf," Owl says, his voice muffled but resonant. Confident. As if they're some congregation in the unseen church of the London Underground and not a bunch of helpless prisoners. "Rejoice! For you have been chosen and your sacrifice shan't be in vain. It's you who ensure the continued health and safety of our city and that is no small thing. Tonight, we gather to –"

Sacrifice? Cherry drinks in the word, her heart yammering. But that's when the kid decides that he's heard enough and makes a break for it. Leaping to his feet, he lurches away from her side, heroics the last thing on his mind. He gives a yell when Cat Woman steps up to bar his way, prevent him from ducking into the passageway, but he's the taller of the two and doesn't refrain from lashing out. The woman in the mask gives a grunt and stumbles away from him. Badger shows less reserve, pitching forward to grab the youth, his curse muffled.

The youth struggles in his grip.

"Get the fuck off me! Twat!"

And it should end there, Cherry thinks. She *wants* it to end there. The vague purpose of hostages goes swimming through her skull from a thousand stupid TV shows. This is all temporary. A ransom will be paid. They'll emerge blinking into the light, their images splattered across the front of every paper and news channel in the country. Claire will come round out of sheer relief. She'll take a hundred pats on the backside from David Masters if that's how it's going to turn out. Anything but –

Steel glints in the murk. The kid wails. Then something wet and warm splashes Cherry's face. The taste of iron is on her lips, rank. In a puff of dirt, the kid crumples to the concrete beside her. Jerking. Gargling. The same substance that coats her chugs from the mess of his throat. Then his eyes drain of shock, joining the blank stare of Badger. The kid falls still. Some drag him away.

No. We're going to die down here.

"Praise the Gaf!" The Owl-priest says, his hands spread.

The other animals, the masked captors, raise their own and murmur in response.

All their palms are stained red.

Badger's most of all.

How could this happen? Half an hour ago, Cherry was just another London commuter among three odd million of them, running on the daily hamster wheel of the city with all her humdrum needs and concerns. A cheated girlfriend. A creep of a boss. Rent.

Fuck you and your overtime, Masters. Should've called in sick.

Now she's a shivering jelly of a woman shuffling down a pitch-black train tunnel, her arms held over her breasts regardless. The strangers, the masked disciples of the fucking Gaf, forced the lot of them to strip, discarding clothes, shoes, jewellery, watches and spectacles on the abandoned platform of Down Street. You don't argue with knives, clubs and a cocked rifle. Then, the animals (and animals they were) had taken up flashlights and cattle prods – cattle prods! – by the station wall. Along with Owl, their apparent leader, they'd ushered their captives down a ramp and along the tracks, into the cold belly of the Underground. Men shout and sob. Promise money or retribution. The women are mostly silent, resigned. Cherry can't see any children and she wonders at that, she does, but her queasiness has returned and the scream she so dearly wants to vent seems lodged in her throat, a thick, hot ball. She holds a hand out to Rat. Staving off the crackling of his prod, she staggers over to the wall and disgorges her lunch, a cheap baguette from Greggs. Chicken mayonnaise salad – so ordinary in the face of her abduction, whatever gruesome end awaits her ahead.

"You okay, love?"

The woman, recently robbed of her child, actually asks this. The kindness pricks tears from Cherry all the same.

"Not really. No."

17

The woman gives a wet-sounding snort. Humour in this place, though it's obviously from shock. And murder is likely the punchline. Still, she lets the woman take her arm and lead her on, out of Rat Man's reach, the carnival bringing up the rear. Making sure they go on, into the stinking tunnel.

"My boy. My boy," the woman says.

After a few minutes, a dampness thickens the air, setting Cherry's skin crawling. There's a warmth to it too, a rankness that threatens to choke her, her breath coming in ragged gasps. The stink, diesel, smoke and sweat, has soured into something deeper, an earthy, bitter pall. It reminds Cherry of opened cesspits. Withered vegetables in the back of the fridge. And the foul August weather outside. How she yearns for it, the world above with all its trials and indignities. What she wouldn't give for tedium now, stumbling along under the city streets, the teeming shops and the hooting traffic. For all the urban myths, who'd imagine that such dangers lurk beneath their feet? In turn, that tells Cherry that whoever happens to raise the alarm about the missing passengers – eventually and way too late – an abandoned station on the Tube is the last place they're going to look.

The equivalent of forty passengers per single rush hour... The advert wings back to her like an omen, begging a question that she doesn't want answered.

It's the woman who notices the weirdness first. At their backs, the strangers have halted. A glance over her shoulder confirms it. The bastards are a line of masks behind their flashlights, allowing the captives to proceed. Moisture drips from above, globs of some oily substance plopping into puddles on the ground. Spongy, this ground, the concrete no longer biting at her feet. The stench has grown even thicker, a foulness that sees every hand over nose and mouth. An old man splutters and coughs. A youth gags, his profanity stark in the murk. A general ripple of unease travels through the throng, an acknowledgement of the shift in atmosphere, the sodden terrain. But it's the woman who screams, her head turned to the lightless roof, her grip hard enough to hurt. Echoes spiral in the cavern, falling leaden in the dark.

With a hiss, Cherry wrenches herself free, following the woman's wide-eyed gaze. Up there in the glow of the flashlights, she makes out a row of hand-sized shapes, each a pale diamond set in the roof. Then another, and another, ranks that arch from on high and down the glistening walls. The ordered design does nothing to dispel a sense of the bestial, an impression bolstered by the dampness, the fetor. The black throat down which they walk.

Teeth.

The thought has barely formed when Cherry hears a yell up ahead, a primal roar of terror. Human, nevertheless. The rest of the crowd join in chorus as confusion erupts, a flash of struggling limbs, a naked form plucked aloft in the gloom. Dumbstruck, rigid, she sees a man rise up to the cavern roof (what she now doubts *is* a roof), some dark, rubbery length coiled around his waist. He flails, balls dangling, turning helpless above. At last, her own scream breaks from her, joining the woman's beside her. The man, entangled, hits the roof with a wet thud, his cries a discord of pain. In a slick, horrible moment, the tendril drags him across the gleaming surface, the sharp, serrated rows. Blood showers down, speckling her face, her shoulders, her breasts. In no time at all, the man comes apart, a leg, his head torn from him by the fangs, scattering into the murk.

"Jesus."

"Holy fuck."

Someone is muttering a prayer, but Cherry has no appeal of her own. At once, the procession has become a stampede, the crowd turning, desperate to return to the tunnel behind them, the relative safety of concrete and cold. The known. To avoid a trampling, she spins, warbling, her hands held out. The light is failing, meagre as it is. There's little in the way of radiance back the way she's come, the masked strangers dwindling behind their flashlights. The tunnel mouth – an impossible sight – is closing by degrees. If only she could ignore the stalactites that bar her way, pale spindles of bone that draw together with the shrinking ring of the aperture, eager to shut them all in.

Is this punishment? she thinks, drunk on dread. *Haven't I had enough?*

Or perhaps she's suffered a psychotic break, her mind caving in under stress, the daily round of abuse in the office… Something whips past her ear and it's all too real, some black, gleaming tendril shot from the depths. Hands out, futile, Cherry can only watch as the

19

appendage snaps around the throat of the woman from the train, a slick, tightening coil. There's a hiss of heat, followed by the stench of burning flesh. The woman gags, her eyes bulging. She claws at the tentacle that grips her, stiff with the sting of acid. Then the woman is gone from her, plucked away like the other, a morsel for the ravenous dark.

Cherry screams, her throat raw. Her skull threatens to split wide, sundered by panic and madness. Then the crowd crashes into her, desperate for the last of the light, the closing maw up ahead. The wind knocked out of her, she sprawls onto her stomach, splashing in the muck, the surface an ever-steepening incline. Swallowed, frantic, she claws at the ground – what she knows isn't the ground – her fingers seeping with gobbets of grease, unable to find purchase. But the collision has spared her, it seems. There are several tendrils now, a river rippling overhead, questing forth to snap up the passengers, suck their scrambling forms into the depths. Some godless, cavernous gut. Wherever the tentacles fall – on shoulder, around limb – flesh bubbles and seethes, the screams become a symphony, wild and unhinged. Further scraps, the steaming remnants of the digestion underway, thump and splash down around her. There's no getting out of here. The fact slams into her, a runaway train. She has made her last commute.

The snake. The Gaf. Breathless, she pictures the graffiti on the station wall, dripping in red just like the poor sods around her. *It feeds…*

Cherry stiffens, too lung-punched to scream, as a tendril snakes around her thigh, hot as a poker. Her own undoing wafts to her nose, a certain sweetness. Gross. The nausea that's troubled her all day surges in her belly again, her throat, a tide come to claim her.

Oh, Claire.

It's all that she has for a farewell. An entreaty.

Then the darkness drags her down.

"… shunned."

When Cherry opens her eyes, she's surprised to find the construction lamps, the unwelcome glow of orange. The platform under her. Cold. She's naked still, filth covering her, a thick slime that adds to her discomfort. Her skin burns, scalded. Hair straggles in her face, but she can make out the pair of shoes by her head. Feel the press of metal against her skull.

"I say we kill her. If the Gaf don't want her –"

"No!"

Footsteps approaching, fast. Groaning, Cherry tries to shut out the echoes, the pictures in her mind. Scattered. Broken. Her last memory makes no sense at all. It flashes and rattles, a train heading into nothing. Vaguely, she recalls some presence above her. Segmented. Hulking. Large enough to fill the tunnel. Tendrils make a curtain of its mouth, all dripping with slop. Pale orbs, countless. Eyes. Insectile. It had whispered something, hadn't it? Some voiceless call in her skull. A demand. A need.

Then blessed silence.

Blearily, she looks up. Badger stands over her. Rat Man too. The former holds a rifle against her head. The sign on the wall tells her that she's back in Down Street, not that it offers her relief.

"You know the law." It's Owl. Owl has appeared above her, his beak lending him a hollow command. "If she's spurned meat, there's a reason."

"Cancer?"

"Or…" Owl nudges Cherry with his boot. Obliging him, she rolls onto her back, too weak to do otherwise. Then he places his hand on her stomach, his palm clammy. "Maybe. The worm won't eat the young, if experience is anything to go by. We *need* them, don't we? Gotta keep the mill turning. None of us will outlast the Gaf…"

There's sense in this, of sorts. Cherry recalls the Frog, wrenching the buggy away from the woman. *Poor bitch.* The strangers have shown no mercy, but there must be a reason why they spared the child. A terrorist group – no, a *cult* – will need its recruits, perhaps. The thought brings a shiver, a recollection of her night with Stephen after the Camden gig last month. Her fuck up. Had they used protection? She can't remember now. But she can grasp what Owl is getting at. What it might mean.

"Listen to me," Owl says and she realises he's addressing her, his face close to her ear. "The Gaf must feed. The Tithe is all we have –

21

a handful a month. If not, then that thing is going to go hungry. And when it does, it will rise. Do you understand?"

Cherry gives a groan. Owl seems to take it for assent.

"We're guardians," he tells her, nigh on apologetic.

"Yeah. And the law is the fucking law," Rat mimics, clearly pissed off. "The number is inviolate, shunned or no. One was already spoiled thanks to Badger and his knife, and will need a stand in. You can't just let her go."

"She won't go alone," Owl says. "I'm not daft."

Despite herself, Cherry thinks of Claire. The fleeting hope of it. The open air. Holloway. A chance. But the gun against her head suggests otherwise. Spared or no, she is far from free.

"So how about it, love?" Owl seems to think that they're discussing business, some mundane matter, the way he talks. "Are you willing to make up the Tithe? One to stand in your stead. We don't have a great deal of time."

To her surprise, Cherry laughs. She laughs because she's aware that her wits have left her, down here in the labyrinth. And because this part is easy. Bad breath and hands on her backside have made it so, the daily ordeal of the office. She knows Masters' schedule as well as her own. The pub after work. His space in the car park. How he goes home to his wife every night, shameless. How hard will it be to invite him back to her place? Get him onto the Tube?

She's part of the carnival now. The Gaf must have its share. She knows that.

She fixes Owl with her smile, his glass eyes as blank as her own.

Danse Macabre

Kim Lakin

Stepney, London - July 1922

The lavatory is overflowing. In the smeary darkness of the outhouse, with the evacuations of all the other tenants who share that rancid hellhole polluting her every breath, Mary struggles to balance above the pan in a half squat.

Footsteps sound heavily from the backyard. A hand pulls roughly at the door, the tiny latch just holding.

Mary drags at her backside with a fistful of newspaper and yanks up her drawers. Hooking the handle of her lamp over the crook of her arm, she steels herself against the newcomer and unlocks the door.

Outside is a docker who lives in one of the two attic rooms and has a young wife only a few years older than Mary. The woman seems to have a babe eternally at the breast but never a child survive past infancy. Mary knows those attic rooms; they were once occupied by Miss Eliza Joseph, an ex-chorus girl forced into retirement after a savage case of pox, and who had taken Mary under her wing for a time. When the world was at war, Mary would escape to the very top of the house and listen to Miss Joseph's tales of prima ballerinas, crowded dressing rooms, the burn of stage lights, and the roar of the audience.

But Miss Joseph has been dead five years, killed alongside the gent she had led down a back alley where the bomb struck, and here instead is the docker. The man in the yard sways from foot to foot, reeking of stale beer as if oozing his own peasouper. He blocks her way and gives a low wolf whistle.

"Ain't you the pretty picture? I've watched you kicking up your skirt by the water pump. How'd you like to dance in my lap?" He makes a grab for her, but Mary ducks beneath his arm, nerves firing at the fear of getting trapped with no one to call for help.

Mercifully, the need to defecate exceeds any thrill to the docker's loins; she hears the slam of the outhouse door, and, almost immediately, the watery gush of loosened bowels.

Escaping the yard, she hurries in through the washhouse lean-to with its peculiar aromas of dank, mildewed walls and tarry yellow soap. A narrow passage looms beyond, her lamp casting greasy pools of illumination. Mary knows which broken floor tiles to avoid; she skips between them, toes pointing instinctively as she jumps. In her mind's eye, she dances in limelight, her shift transformed into a tutu as the ghostly faces of admirers haunt her from the stalls.

She takes the last door on her left. In that festering house, with three floors, attic and even a lightless cellar carved up into pitiful dwellings for seven families, noise is a constant. All the same, Mary tiptoes inside and quietly locks the door.

A low ceiling bows overhead, the laths in the walls showing through in patches where the plaster has deteriorated. On a single iron bed, Mary's twin brothers sleep on. Stripped to their under things, the four-year-olds' pale, thin limbs poke out at all angles. Mary thinks of a stack of boiled bones at the knacker's yard. She shudders, and, in that moment, hates that her parents brought all their young lives into existence.

The lamplight flickers. Mary's shadow dances across the walls.

"That you, Mary?" Her mother rocks on the edge of the bed, digging fingernails into her knees.

"Leg playing up, Ma?" Fetching a tiny, dark blue glass bottle and some rags from the windowsill, she kneels at her mother's feet, unstoppers the bottle and tips some iodine onto one of the rags.

Peeling the fouled linen from her mother's ulcered ankle, Mary starts to clean the wound. But her mother reaches down and clamps her wrist with a damp hand.

"I'll be dead soon. The rot's burning me up on the inside. You and your brothers will be put out on the street, and who will save you then, when you have nowhere to go? London don't take care of its poor, you know that for a fact. It spits our bones into that black stinking river. And the do-gooders and the rich? They watch from on high with the likes of us playing out our misery below for their entertainment."

Mary peels her mother's fingers back, a little cruelly. "Settle down, Ma. It's gone midnight. The pain's making you maudlin." She winds a fresh rag around her mother's leg, sealing in the canker. *I have to get away from all this decay*, she thinks bitterly. *Like the great Russian dancer, Karsavina, I've flower bouquets to be gifted, ballet slipper ribbons to be laced so tightly they'll never let me go...*

Her mother goes back to rocking. Mary takes the lamp and returns the iodine bottle to the windowsill. Retrieving a small tin from beneath the pile of rags, kept safe there from prying eyes and sticky fingers, she sits at the table. She prises open the lid of the tin and takes out the square of folded paper which lies inside. With great care, she opens the theatre bill on the table, using the flat of her hand to ease out the creases.

The poster had been tacked to a wall in the attic rooms until Miss Joseph noticed how it enchanted Mary and insisted the girl take it as a gift. All these years later, it is dog-eared and fragile from too much handling.

Mary uses a fingertip to trace the fluid illustration of a dancer wrapped in flames. 'The Firebird,' proclaims the elegant font: *'A Ballet in One Act. Presented by The Ballets Russes. Music by Igor Stravinsky.'* And then Mary's favourite line of all, *'A Night of Enchantment, Magic, and Mystery...'*

Three sharp raps strike the door – sending Mary's mother crawling up into a corner of the bed like a frightened animal. Mary's shaken too. It's a queer hour for visitors. She quickly folds the bill back up, tucks it safely away and shoves the tin back under the rags.

Tiptoeing over to the door, she slides the key from the lock and bends down. Putting an eye to the keyhole, she sees a swish of luminous white skirt, then a long-lashed eye staring back at her.

Mary bolts upright. "Who's there?"

"My name is Sister Clara Ashwell." The woman has the crisp, cultured accent of the rich and the well-meaning. "I'm sorry to call so late, but it has taken me the best part of the evening to locate your address." A pause, then, "I've come to help you."

"We don't need no help." Mary spits the words. Even as part of her wants to throw the door wide and shout, 'Yes! Come in. Let me leave in your place!'

The silence stretches as she senses the woman's continued presence. Cursing under her breath, Mary unlocks the door.

Standing in the passageway is a younger woman than Mary had pictured. She is wearing a uniform of sorts – a straw boater with her dark hair fastidiously pinned beneath, a taffeta burgundy dress with a high stiff collar, and a long, starched white apron. A dark grey cross, with arms of equal length, is embroidered across the woman's apron bib. Each arm of the cross ends in a spike stitched with scarlet thread.

Mary has heard of The Salvation Army's 'slum sisters', pious women from good homes who lend the poor a helping hand in return for sermons about their sins and derogation. She also knows they forgo their uniform for civilian dress, the better to blend with the destitute and lowly. Standing at the door in her crisp apron and straw hat, Sister Clara strikes Mary as belonging to an entirely different religious order.

She nods at the red leather book in the woman's hand. "We don't need saving."

"Oh, I offer nothing so pedestrian," Sister Clara scoffs. "Disciples of The Bloody Cross shouldn't behave like sheep. They must earn their admittance to the hallowed kingdom." She raises one eyebrow, exuding a haughty elegance. "I am here to extend an invitation for you to entertain our church patrons tomorrow evening. You are Mary Carter? Aged fifteen? Daughter of Lucille and William Carter?" She opens her bible, takes a card from between the pages and holds it out.

Mary hesitates. How has she come to the woman's attention? Has she been watched in secret, dancing out by the water pump maybe, turning in stockinged feet as her brothers bark and howl at her ankles like little dogs?

Her palms itch where the skin is ridged and hard. For all her dreams of a gilded life, six days a week she tears rags for a pittance at the factory on Heneage Street. Her mother's ravings repeat in her mind: *They watch from on high with the likes of us playing out our misery below...*'

Tentatively, she takes the invitation between two fingers. She holds it up to the weak lamplight. The card is embossed with a black, curlicued frame and headed with the spiked cross. Below is an address: *The Jubilee Club*, Land of Promise Street, Kingsland Road, Shoreditch.

A pang of hope gnaws at her. Is this the moment she gets discovered? "You're inviting me to dance? On a stage?"

Sister Clara snaps her bible shut and smiles prettily. "The Bloody Cross holds a special place in its heart for gifted children. You and your family will be appropriately rewarded. As I understand it, during the war, your father was granted exemption from conscription on account of your mother's ill health, and has suffered his own hardships these last four years, failing to secure casual employment on the wharf…"

"You'll find my Pa rotting in drink at The Ship. Ma's just rotting." Something about Sister Clara standing so pristine in the doorway makes Mary feel spiteful.

She waits to see a look of excruciating sympathy cross the woman's face. Instead, a gleam of exhilaration lights Sister Clara's eyes.

"Since The Jubilee is some distance away, I will arrange for a motor car to collect you at six pm. A costume will be ready for you to change into upon arrival." Her gaze flicks past Mary, who shifts uncomfortably, knowing the woman can see the bed and the state of its occupants. Sister Clara takes a small, cork-stoppered bottle from her apron pocket and holds it out. "For those who suffer. The blessed gift of sleep."

Mary grabs the bottle. The label is a scrawl, but one word stands out. *Laudanum.*

The Sister turns as if to leave, but then she stops and glances back over her shoulder. With breathy excitement, she adds, "I, for one, cannot wait to see you dance!"

There, she walks away and is swiftly absorbed by the shadows.

Mary doesn't hear her nocturnal visitor exit the front door onto the street; she's too absorbed by thoughts of riding in a motor car, unboxing a spectacular costume, and her glorious stage debut. How she longs to run up to the very top of the house and brag to Miss

Joseph that she is destined for the bright lights! "I'm leaving all this ugliness behind!" she longs to tell the one person who might understand. "You just watch. Everything will change after tomorrow night. I will enchant them all when I take to the stage and not a living soul will dare to look away!"

But there is no Miss Joseph to tell, not any more. A tiny chink opens onto the howling grief Mary keeps tucked deep within her, hidden away like the dogeared, fragile theatre bill inside its tin. She seals the pain back inside by picturing how elegantly she will dance for her audience tomorrow evening, and she forces her mother to swallow a spoonful of the precious laudanum. Watching her mother sink down into oblivion, Mary imagines that it is Miss Joseph's ghost who haunts the room instead, full of praise and sharing so many stories of the theatrical wonderland that awaits her young protégé.

Only later, when she's tucked into her own narrow spot on the bed, does Mary's mind settle enough for her to recall what she glimpsed inside Sister Clara's bible when the invitation was held out. Rather than the usual cramped lines of scripture, the pages, fine as insect wings, were inked with morbid illustrations – on one side, a crucified man, and on the other, a monstrous devil.

Mary might be feasting on swan and champagne for all the notice she takes of her share of the bread and dripping. All day she floats, whether chasing her brothers in from playing soldiers in the gutter or quietening her mother's fever with the laudanum. By the time the bells of St. Dunstan's ring out at five o'clock, though, the twins have burned through their meagre reserves of energy. Dozing on the bed beside Mother, their pale, bony chests rise and fall. Mary hums and practices her attempts at twirls and arabesques in front of the overshadowed window.

When the bells strike six, she shakes her little brothers awake and tells them with a squeak of childlike excitement, "I'm going to dance The Firebird like a Russian girl." They fall back into the sleep of the dead and she kisses their heads. "Sleep well all," she whispers, and locks the door at her back.

A gleaming black motor car is waiting on the street and has already attracted a crowd of admirers. Mary notices the crude docker is among the number, and his fragile young wife cradling her swollen stomach. Next to the grand machine with its sleek hood, whitewall tyres and brass headlamps, into whose limelight Mary steps, the pair look desolate.

The driver gets out. He is a tall, thickset man, with a white walrus-moustache and a spiked cross pin attached to one side of his collar. Mary is surprised to see he has on a Service Dress uniform – and it is as if she is a child again, watching the young men in pristine khaki say goodbye on their mothers' doorsteps. Some had returned after the war, prematurely aged and hollow-eyed. Most did not.

"Miss Mary Carter. Our esteemed dancer. I am Colonel Emory Williams-Moore." The driver shakes her hand with a firm, almost painful grip. He opens the car door, and with a smile in the wiggle of his moustache, waves his hand to indicate she should climb in.

Running her rough fingers over the soft leather upholstery, the sprung seat buoying her up, Mary imagines herself one of the great prima ballerinas, travelling in style to give her next acclaimed performance.

Colonel Emory Williams-Moore talks all the while.

"...of course, usually I'd have sent my man, Jones, to collect you. But church events are so splendid and always over too soon, so I like to join in from the outset, as it were. Say, do you like the car? British engineering at its best' He raps one of the highly polished brass dials in the walnut dashboard. "It's important to have instruments which work, don't you think? Back in Flanders, the mud swallowed the dead whole and buried the living calf deep – not that you can imagine such a thing! But the grime got into the guns and jammed the mechanisms. Yes, I've always believed a thing should work as designed, people included. I remember, one afternoon, I got word the men required geeing up on account of the rain being so bloody ceaseless and them losing faith, out there in the quagmire. I insisted on being taken down to the front line, shells blasting around us like the spit of the goddamn almighty. One man had his face blown off in front of me. Can you believe it? The bugger kept up his salute though, even with one eye dangling from the socket and the jelly of his brain showing through his shattered skull. Oh, they were brave men, only boys, really. Would it have been too much to ask for everything to work as it should? No

29

seizing up of rifles or worn-out boots letting the gangrene fester. The Fallen. By the end of the war, they numbered 880,000 British forces dead. It's hard for the rational mind to comprehend! Such a damnable waste…" The colonel's eyes are bright now. "Well, anyway. The Bloody Cross picked up the slack, gave those poor dead bastards a path to retribution…"

Mary watches the narrow rat runs of Stepney give way to wider bustling roads, and all she wants to do is bask in anticipation of what is to come. But as the colonel drones on with his brutal tales of an old and finished war, it's as if the London outside is no less a battlefield. Everywhere, a mania of wagons, motor cars, pedestrians crossing, workers on bicycles zigzagging in between. A piercing whistle from a tram sends children scattering. Workers spill from the gates of ironworks and mills, the tall chimneys pouring so much heat and smoke into the atmosphere, the sky looks as if it is on fire.

"Is it much further?" She winds down the window. The air is stiflingly close.

The colonel snorts from the front seat. "Eager to dance, hey?" His wrinkled fingers flex and curl around the steering wheel. "I admire your commitment to one's duty, Mary. Much like our Sister Clara. Fine woman. Just twenty-three when she volunteered as a nurse in the field hospital at Rouen. On her feet twelve days straight during the Battle of the Somme, doing her damnedest best to soothe the dying and save the wounded who kept on coming. It's a miracle the woman can ever scrub her bloody hands clean of all that gore and guts!" He guffaws at the notion, even as Mary struggles to feel anything except revulsion. The man seems determined to share the war's grim details, and, at the same time, displays the flippant disregard for suffering she associates with the wealthy.

Fortunately, the colonel turns his chat back to church matters. "Nowadays of course, Sister Clara is so adept at locating those in need of our ministry. She found one family in Summertown, Oxford, residing in an affluent Arts and Crafts villa, can you believe it? The father was a high up in the Great Western Railway throughout the war. Mother was a clerical assistant. Their boy had quite a talent for dramatic Tragedy."

The motor car turns off the main thoroughfare and onto a tiny side street. 'Land of Promise Street' declares a grubby sign. Mary feels a rush of excitement, but also confusion. The motor car pulls around and to a stop, and she finds herself peering up at a dilapidated building crammed between dark, rundown terraces at the dead end. She has been picturing an imposing, ornate theatre on a grand promenade. Instead, The Jubilee Club looks abandoned. Its painted signage is faded, its poster boards bare, with only their weather-splintered backings on display. Shallow dirty steps lead up to a set of broad double doors.

A shiver of homesickness prickles Mary's skin and she hugs her arms around her waist; she is not so sure she wants to go inside. But then the colonel is there, ushering her out of the car and up the steps with his prattle and bluster. And when he guides her through the double doors, she barely notices the bleak atmosphere inside the foyer or its flaking gold. Because here is Sister Clara, crisp and efficient in the electric glow from the wall sconces.

"Mary, we are so delighted to have you. We attract an intimate congregation, but like to think we do our part to honour the Fallen. Now, Colonel, you must head backstage and get ready – it is so good of you to volunteer this year. Say goodbye to Mary. The next time you see our guest will be on stage."

The man gives a snort of delight and strides away; Mary doesn't watch him exit, being distracted by Sister Clara's reference to an 'intimate congregation'. With a pang of disappointment, she realises that performing for a church congregation may not prove to be the grand debut she pictured. However, Sister Clara is smiling down, and as Mary is quick to remind herself, even a prima ballerina may have humble beginnings before their star rises. What matters is that, tonight, she gets to dance on stage, in a theatre no less, and an intimate congregation is still an audience!

Sister Clara holds up a rouge stick.

"Makeup exaggerates the performer's features, does it not? We don't want you to look washed out under the stage lights. You are quite a pale girl and it is so important that our patrons get to appreciate the full range of your expressions."

"You said there'd be a costume?" Mary is staring up at where the bare walls meet the high ceiling and a single tiny window is fenced behind bars. Her surroundings have the *smell* of a dressing room – the candied perfume of grease paint, the lingering whiff of cigar smoke, the woodiness of dust burning on the lightbulbs. But there should be rails heaving with drapery and shimmering wired wings, alcoves crammed with tiaras, flower crowns, turbans, and ballet slippers. Instead, the room is empty except for a threadbare velvet chair which sits in front of the small table and its tarnished mirror.

Sister Clara empties a black tin of colourful pan sticks, laying them out in a row on the dressing table, like shiny bullets in their gold paper. "I couldn't quite recall your size, and things must fit as they should to serve their purpose." She steps back and eyes Mary. "I have the measure of you now."

"I'll paint my face like a firebird if it's all the same to you." Mary swallows at the faded memories of Miss Joseph teaching her to apply make-up, how the woman would hold up a hand mirror and Mary would see a fantastical face reflected in place of her own...

Sister Clara stops at the door, the rim of her straw hat shadowing her eyes. "I could not suggest a more perfect fit."

From the passageway comes a low scraping noise, like the sound of something weighty being dragged. Mary hears the colonel's distinctive droning voice say, "Keep going, gentlemen. Not far now, then you can hoist the bugger up onto the stage."

Sister Clara blocks the doorway, nodding at those beyond. "Captain Milford, Lieutenant O'Connor. You are doing a sterling job." She glances back to meet Mary's eye and puts her hand to the key in the door. "I will lock you in. Every young lady needs her privacy. And we don't want to spoil the surprise."

Mary tries to imagine that her hands are Miss Joseph's and that, together, they are just playing dress up once more. Using a carmine grease stick, she draws dramatic flicks either side of her eyes, and in a charcoal grey, shapes her brows into elongated dark arches. Across each cheek, she paints lines of crimson and gold to represent feathers. Her mouth, she outlines with black, then stains her lips with bloody rouge.

32

Muffled voices occasionally sound from the passageway. Once, Mary distinctly hears a woman exclaim, "Oh, you do look the part, Colonel! This promises to be the most glorious Retribution for The Fallen." The term *retribution* strikes Mary as most peculiar. Miss Joseph's tales of the theatre had always been so magical and full of life and precious colour. They had conjured up a world of glorious possibility and paved gold, along which a girl might dance her way to freedom. But instead here she is, locked inside what feels like a sterile cell, listening to the peculiar talk of these strangers beyond the door, and all she can sense is her growing unease.

The key twists sharply in the lock and Sister Clara returns through the door, carrying a small trunk. Observing Mary's painted face, she gives a visible shiver of delight. "My goodness, Mary. Our worshippers will adore you. You really have captured the atmosphere of the piece. Now for your costume…"

Placing the trunk on the floor, she unfastens and lifts the lid. Mary catches a flash of feathers as the woman works to pull the garment from inside, wriggling the white form as if aiding the passage of an afterbirth. Finally, she shakes it free – to reveal a corseted bodice covered in tiny white feathers and layers of soft white net which billow out into an ankle-length skirt.

"Christ Lord Almighty." It is all Mary can think to say.

"And still there was silence." Sister Clara presses a palm over the embroidered cross on her apron bib. Then she puts the heel of that hand to her mouth and bites down – a quick snap of movement, like a Catholic's reverential kneel before entering a church pew.

Mary isn't sure what has just happened. She stumbles over an apology for blaspheming. But as if time has stitched back upon itself, Sister Clara makes no acknowledgement of the act and simply kneels and indicates that Mary should step inside the skirt. When she stands to help Mary slip her arms through the bodice, Mary sees a crescent of dark red indents on the woman's palm.

Sister Clara turns Mary towards the mirror as she laces the bodice. "Now you look the part!"

Taking in her reflection, Mary forgets the niggling disappointment and unease, the locked door, the weird talk from the passageway, even the Sister's self-inflicted bite wound. Seeing the shimmering colours of her painted face, how the tiny white feathers cling to her body and the netted wings of the skirt enfold her as if she were born a bird, Mary feels as if she might burst with happiness and self-adoration.

"One more thing…" Sister Clara reaches back into the trunk. She takes out a pair of ballet slippers.

The very fantasies instilled in her by Miss Joseph helped Mary cope with the emptiness inside after her friend was gone. Always, it is her dreams of frothing tulle and shell pink ballet blocks which soothe Mary in times of fear and anguish. They kept her safe when she was eight years old and the bombs had dropped over London. She had seen the huge German zeppelin pinned to the night sky – so low she could make out the officers in its three gondolas – and then watched the craft fold and burn, the noise of machine guns ricocheting from the rooftops of the nearby factories. And ever since too, when her father stumbled through drink, or her mother wept in pain, or her brothers wet the bed and they had to sleep, all five of them, on the hard, cold floor.

Standing backstage, she runs her hands down the tickling feathers of her bodice, the flowing net of her skirt, and tries not to feel scared. It is so very dark. She can just make out the backdrop – a fall of silk painted with the Bloody Cross symbol – and across the empty stage to the blackness of the wings on the far side. The audience, she senses, as a hushed collective.

Sister Clara whispers by her ear, "I will give the evening's address, then the entertainment will follow. Listen for your music."

Mary opens her mouth to ask what she should do when her dance is done, but Sister Clara is already striding out onto the stage in a crackle of taffeta and starched linen. The lights go up in a blaze and the curtain rises.

Waiting in the wings, her heart fighting to escape from behind her ribs, Mary watches Sister Clara give her own grand performance. Stage lit, the woman is all shadowed folds and carved features. She could be a marble archangel, except in place of a flaming sword, she wields a red leather bible.

"… And the prophet Habakkuk cried of that falsifier of covenants, 'How long, Lord, must I call for help, but you do not listen? Or cry out to you, *Violence!* but you do not save? Why do you make me look at injustice? Why do you tolerate wrongdoing?' And still there was silence.

And Habakkuk cried again, 'Why then do you tolerate the treacherous? Why are you silent while the wicked swallow up those more righteous than themselves?' And still there was silence.

So it was when the fire blazed and ash fell and our bodies were put to ruin. Only the seal of perfection walks with man among the fiery stones of pestilence and of war. He who is also fallen said, 'Do not suffer the weak or the wicked, but rise up on the pyre of their bones. For I will sit enthroned on the mount of assembly, on the utmost heights of Mount Zaphon. I will make myself Most High…'"

To Mary, the words have a strange, unpleasant sound; they make her want to cup her hands over her ears to block them out. She concentrates on the boards at Sister Clara's feet, how the wood sparkles with a thin layer of dust. The drapes around her give off the same mildewed smell she knows from the washhouse back home, and it is as if everything around her is mouldering.

Her eye goes to the backdrop as it softly undulates. Narrowing her gaze, Mary tries to make sense of the fall of silk, how the painted image of the cross appears at once a part of the fabric and yet apart from it. Unless… can it be a physical prop, staged behind the backdrop and showing through the watery silk? Her breath hitches. For a terrible instance, she thinks she sees the silhouette of a human head in profile to one side of the cross.

The face is gone in a flicker of footlights. She feels slightly dizzy. Sister Clara's pitch has risen to a shrieked command, as if calling men to arms, and it seems Mary's mind is determined to conjure nightmares out of the gloom. In the shadows of the wings opposite, a monstrous figure looms…

But that is when the music starts and there is Sister Clara, signalling that now is the time to dance.

All horrors evaporate beneath the halo of the spotlight. Mary has no idea if the crackling music coming from a gramophone offstage is The

Firebird score. But the air is so pretty with soaring strings and bursts of gilded brass, and she does her best to dance with grace.

When she glimpses the shadowed audience, so very still, she feels momentarily at odds with her element. Who is she to dance for these silent strangers? Do they see through her pretence? Judging and finding her wanting? Here on the boards, she is meant to find her charmed life, to finally know freedom. But the stillness of those souls beyond the apron of the stage threatens to dim her courage.

She finds unexpected solace in imagining she is dancing at home. Back in the oppressive hallway of that festering villa, skipping to avoid the broken floor tiles as the rats run through the walls. Back by the communal water pump, feeling out each bow and crest of her arms, each stretch and lift of her legs, each flex and point of her toes. Her body finds and slips seamlessly into the emotions of the music, matching the airy swirl of the woodwind, the battle cry of drums and horns. Finally, she is the dancer she'd always dreamt of being...

The music cuts off abruptly. Mary staggers, mid-step, and gulps as if she has taken a punch. She stands, blinking dazedly against the glare of the lights. Silence hangs. The hot prick of tears threatens. *Where is my applause?* In confusion, she drops into a low curtsy.

With an audible click, the stage lighting switches from cream to deepest indigo. Mary wobbles in her curtsy – and is suddenly aware of no longer being alone upon the stage. No shadow falls. Instead, she senses the presence a few feet behind her: otherworldly, hulking, and transforming the quiet into a reverential hush.

A fine wire of fear slices the length of her spine. Tears hang tremulous on her eyelashes. *Do not look*, her mind implores – even as she is already straightening up and turning around...

Her gaze rises, trying to make sense of the horror her eyes are taking in – the huge cloven hoofs, a sheath of rippling leather draped at the groin, pendulous, fur-covered breasts, and fold upon fold of flesh at the broad neck. The figure has the elongated head of a goat, with a glistening nose, cavernous flaring nostrils, and two thick horns twisting up either side of the skull. Into the muscular brow is sliced a five-pointed star.

In the beast's liquidly black, slitted eyes, Mary sees herself reflected as a cowering girl, dressed in sacrificial white. She opens her mouth to cry out, but no sound comes.

"The Bloody Church welcomes you, Mary, daughter of Lucille and William Carter." A resonating masculine voice emanates from the creature, although its mouth doesn't move. "Did not the deceiver say, 'Do not take revenge, my dear friends, but leave room for God's wrath, for it is written: It is mine to avenge; I will repay'?"

"And still there was silence," the audience murmurs as one.

"On this sacred eve, I call for retribution against all those who hid in ivory towers or lay like fleas in the mire at our hour of need. Bring the coward into the light!"

The clips of her heels ringing out when they strike the boards, Sister Clara walks briskly across the back of the stage. Arm outstretched, she draws the silky curtain of the backdrop aside.

With a shudder of revulsion, Mary sees the true extent of what she had glimpsed when waiting in the wings ahead of her performance. To the back of the stage is erected a nine-foot-tall version of the church's cross, the bottom spike driven into the stage floor like a stake. A man hangs suspended on the cross. The sinews of his arms strain against the ribbons that bind his wrists and ankles, his head lolling forward onto his bare chest.

A crucified man on one page, a monstrous devil on the other... the illustrated plates from Sister Clara's bible flare luridly in Mary's mind. *Now will you run?* screams the voice inside which she has been ignoring ever since she arrived at The Jubilee Club. It was the beautiful dream of dancing and acclaim, and escape into another life, that prevented her from listening before, but now terror burns in the depths of her bones.

She tries to flee the stage. But hands materialise out of the blackness of the wings and thrust her back. She tries the opposite way. More hands repel her, harder this time so that she is sent tumbling backwards and lands painfully on her hip at the foot of the cross. In wild panic, she glances up at the crucified man – and it is as if she falls away from her own soul. Under the subterranean half-light, Mary sees, not just any man, but one whose familiar eyes roam in turmoil, and whose haggard face she knows.

"Pa?" The seconds stretch, knife-thin, as she tries to find meaning in the nightmare of all that is happening around her. This evening was never about her talent. Instead all these pretenders in their Good Samaritan guises have made her their plaything, with her weak, desperate, drunkard father strung up to bear testament!

The beast moves closer, each lumbering step resonating through the floor. "The coward will die many times before his death, but the valiant taste of death but once." Towering above her, it holds something in its clawed hand. The metal shaft of the object glints under the blue twilight and Mary shuffles back, crab-like, on her hands and slippered feet when she sees it is a rifle with a bayonet.

The flashing tip of the bayonet drives in at her father's side, is pulled back glistening with gore. The gag-stifled cry from her Pa makes Mary sob aloud.

"880,000 British forces dead. William Carter is in debt to the Fallen. The Bloody Church demands retribution. Shall he die with valour so that his child shall live, or will the child cleanse the father's iniquities through fire?"

The beast reaches out and pulls the gag down from her father's mouth. "Choose."

His face glistening with snot and tears, a rabid terror in his roaming eyes, William Carter rasps, "Please…I don't want to die…"

"And so the coward makes his choice." The gag is forced back up.

Sister Clara is suddenly besides Mary, encouraging her to stand even as her trembling legs threaten to give out. The woman guides her to the front of the stage, where Mary is horrified to realise the congregation is made up of soldiers and slum sisters in uniform, who all sit enrapt.

"I want to go home," she says in a desperate whisper, imploring Sister Clara to offer some aid.

The woman pulls her in tight and speaks hotly by her ear, "You want to go back to that rancid slum which will be torn down at any moment, to be replaced by a tenant block with higher rents your family will never afford? Back to ripping rags as your life drips away like so much rat piss in the gutters? Back to mopping up the vomit of that coward up there on the cross, or hearing your mother's ravings as she rots? Back to mothering boys whose destiny is already written in filth and squalor. Is that your glittering career, Mary?"

Mary hears the savage words as if from far away. The Passion Play of her performance unfolds around her as two soldiers haul a rolling metal tray to centre stage, faces straining against the billowing heat. They exit immediately; in their wake, the fire pan gives off white heat from a bed of sparking red embers.

A single, high tinnitus note fills Mary's fractured mind. A memory flickers across the back of her eyes like shadows playing over walls – the too generous spooning of the laudanum into her dying mother's mouth, the same administered to her twin brothers out of mercy before she kissed them goodnight and locked the door on her way out.

Her Pa didn't wade through filthy trenches, but her mother got sucked down into the mud of madness, her brothers gassed by poverty before any taste of opium met their lips. Mary, though, she refuses to be reduced like Miss Joseph, forced to turn tricks in back alleys until her light is snuffed out. She will fight, scrap and claw her way up into the Gods. *She* will be the one to watch from on high!

"Ma said no one would save the likes of us, but I did. And I'll do it again." Mary juts her chin. "Pa? He's always had a way of cheating death."

"The Bloody Cross will always provide a stage for a resourceful young woman, especially one who understands the meaning of sacrifice and how important it is to do one's duty." Sister Clara releases Mary from her grip. In her starched uniform with its violent, godless emblem stitched across the apron bib, she flashes her pretty smile. "But first, Mary, we are all so eager to *really* see you dance. You are our Firebird, after all."

The ballet slipper ribbons squeeze Mary's ankles, tied agonisingly tight. The white feathers of the bodice prickle the tender skin of her inner arms.

So many eyes – turned upon her now, as she has always dreamt they would.

Mary tiptoes lightly across the boards, and as she takes her first trembling step onto the coals, the music swells once more, and the applause is rapturous.

Hagstone

Tracy Fahey

I'm reading the Saturday paper – *Celtic Tiger Boom Continues* – when I hear the shouting. It's the hottest day of the year; only eleven o'clock and already the temperature is climbing. Twenty-four degrees now, according to the radio. The oven breath of a baking day wafts in the Portakabin window. The air smells of warm plastic.

The yelling is louder. I sigh, fold over the page of the sports section, and get to my feet, grunting out a *whoosh* of air as I do. Outside, the stark new shapes of industrial units tower over me. The digger is in front of the old half-demolished factory; a rotten tooth in the slick industrial estate. A boy jumps off the digger and runs towards me. Even though the sun beats steadily down, I shiver suddenly; a quick spasm. *Goose walking over my grave.*

I don't know it at the time, but it's the beginning of the end.

"Mr Boyle." It's the young McAllister lad who was taken on last week – *George?* I think it's George anyway. His face is pale and slick with sweat.

"You don't look good, son." I offer him the bottle of lukewarm water I hold, but the boy ignores it.

"Mr Boyle, I need you to come with me." He presses his lips together, but they still quiver. "I need you."

And when we get to the raw site of the building, I can see why he does.

It's an untidy job, and the boy has dug up exactly the wrong patch of ground on the estate. I blink in irritation at the jagged hole of brown earth yards away from where it's meant to be; the rubble of the original foundations. The McAllisters. *Pay peanuts, get monkeys.* But

41

that's Field all over. No matter how rich he's gotten, still the poverty mind-set, pinching pennies till they squeal. The old stone, the one with the hole in it that's stood in front of the factory ever since I can remember, is lying at the bottom of the pit. I click my tongue. The kid's made a bags of it.

"Look, Mr. Boyle." I follow the lad's finger. Under the stone, a creamy flash in the dark earth.

"Look at it." It's bone. A curved spine, unless I'm mistaken, knobbed with pale vertebrae. Glints of ribcage bloom underneath. Beside it, some spikes of brown metal. It looks for all the world like the yellowed plastic skeleton Dr. Evans keeps in his office to frighten children. For a second, I think – *Is it?* – then shake my head in swift dismissal. No. This is real.

"I've called the police." Young McAllister – I'm *almost* sure it's George – is white and defiant, clutching his mobile phone.

"Aye." I pat him on the arm. "Go on now, over to the cabin. Make yourself a cup of tea. I'll stay here."

The boy nods. He's trembling, glad of direction. As he walks off, I take out my battered old Nokia.

"Mr. Field? Jim." I pause. "There's some trouble here up at the industrial estate."

It's Gemma they send. Guard Evans, that is, but I can only think of her as Gemma. Even as I watch her hoist herself out of the garda car, belly-first, shirt stretched over her huge bump, there's still that vivid flash of herself and my Lisa screaming with laughter, two dirty-faced kids in the backyard. There's a lot to be said for a small town; knowing the locals.

"Well now, Mr. Boyle, how are you?" Lovely manners, as always. "Looking well."

I'm not, and she knows it. The neon light over my bathroom mirror reveals the truth each morning.

"How's your father keeping?"

"Grand, grand. And sure I don't have to ask how Lisa is, I was talking to her last week on the phone." She wipes a moustache of sweat from her upper lip. "Can you believe the heat?"

"Twenty-four degrees, and hotter later they say."

"Oof." She grimaces. "So what have we here? A George McAllister" – *aha*, it is George – "called it in, said he found something…"

She peers into the hole.

"I sent him to the Portakabin. He's a bit upset."

"As you would be." She produces a torch, shines it around. Her face changes.

"Right." She's all business now, beckoning at the car. A tall, dark-haired man gets out and nods.

"Kevin." She straightens up with a groan. "Looks like he was right. You've got a job of work to do."

Always a nice girl, that Gemma. Her daddy raised her right. She's soft with young George, insisting he drink his tea with sugar, quietly asking him what time he made the discovery, and if he touched anything. She calms him down enough to come back out and join us.

All the while, the other fellow, Kevin, is down in the shallow pit. He's got the white gear on you see on police shows. It makes him look like a paper astronaut. He strokes dirt gently off the bones that gleam out of the dirt.

Gemma's still asking questions. "What's that stone in the hole?"

George stares at her and shrugs.

I clear my throat; it turns into a cough. That crackling sound. Gemma waits patiently.

"It's the old stone that used to stand in front of the door. It must have fallen in when the digging started." I can't help myself. "George dug in the wrong place. It was the remains of the foundations he was meant to dig out. Mr. Field did a map for him and everything." Young McAllister bites his lip, but I don't care. Carelessness like that annoys me.

"Is that right?" says Gemma. Her voice is bland, but she's writing everything down in her black notebook with the elastic band. "Do you have it, George?"

George produces a battered map from his back pocket. Sure enough, there are the areas for demolition circled in black, and the area we are standing in marked in red, not to be touched.

"Grand." She folds it, slides it into her notebook.

A black BMW swings into the estate. The new car gleams like oil. "That's Mr. Field now. You probably know he was the owner of the old factory; now he runs the estate."

"Right you are. Did you ring him, Jim?"

I shrug. "Aye. Have to if anything happens. He has it drilled into us."

"That's fine." She snaps the elastic band back over the notebook. "Well, why don't you make us all a cup of tea, Jim? I know I'd murder for one."

I come back with the tea in a variety of stained mugs. Gemma is interviewing my boss, John Field. Field is pompous as ever. Even though it's a Saturday, he still immaculately dressed in a black suit with a dazzling white shirt. My neatly-mended lumberjack shirt and jeans look shabby by comparison. He's pleasant but definitive. *Terrible thing to have happened.* No, he doesn't know anything about a body, how could he? Gemma is her usual friendly self, but I can tell by the little frown-line over her right eyebrow that she hasn't taken to him.

"Why was the factory knocked, Mr. Field?"

"We have a new American company who wanted the site. Very desirable place to open a business, here." He smiles; his teeth white and even.

"And the old factory wasn't operational?"

"No." He waves in dismissal. "The old building wasn't fit for purpose any more. It was the site of his original factory. Fields." He gestures at the faded sign that still stands in front. "My father bought the site, built the factory, and from then on his business flourished."

"So that's how you made the millions. Rags to riches." I look at her but her face is innocent. "And you kept the old factory as a lucky token?"

He clears his throat. "My father would never sell it. For sentimental reasons. I respected his wishes."

"Until someone offered good money for it?" Gemma's voice is bland, but Field flushes.

"I suppose."

She changes tack. "Is there anyone you can think of who might have gone missing here?"

Field pauses, shakes his head. "No one. I'd know if there was anyone." He smiles at me. "And if there was, Jim here would know. He worked in that factory for my father when the site first opened."

"Is that so?" She is steadily writing.

But I'm watching Gemma's face. It's shiny with perspiration and her hand has moved to the small of her back.

"One second." I duck inside the Portakabin re-emerging with the old blue fold-up chair. I set it down and Gemma lowers herself into it with a little gasp. She still looks a bit pale, so I retrieve my paper, the one with the Celtic Tiger headline, and flap it in front of her. Field's been tapping away at his phone, oblivious. He looks up and flashes a smile.

"Now if there's anything else I can do for you, don't hesitate to let me know."

"Thanks Mr. Field. You've been very helpful."

See? Lovely manners.

"Jim, if you're not needed for anything more, you can go home now." Mr Field's face is tight. "George, you too."

I open my mouth in dismay – *what about my double time?* – then stop myself.

"Grand, so." I look back in the hole. There's a long bone emerging now, like a photo coming out of developing fluid. I shiver, suddenly cold. *Goose walking over my grave.*

I can't stop thinking about it later. There's not much to distract me at home. I iron my clothes for tomorrow, sweep up the clean floor to the background noise of the TV. The banks are in some spot of bother, and the TV pundits seem very exercised about it. But as I fold up the ironing board, all I can see, over and over, is that dark hole, those pale bones.

Were they here all this time? Were they here while I worked in Field's old factory, back in the seventies, putting together agricultural machinery in the din and noise of the assembly line? I picture the hunched body, slowly decomposing under our feet, shiver.

For the first time in a long time I crave a drink. Maybe a beer, the cold liquid frothing as it pours, the sides of the glass damp with condensation. I cough and rub my chin. Or a whisky, glowing amber, a latent fire.

I lick my lips.

No.

To distract myself, I get out the old photo album. The album is worn now, cracking a little at the sides. I've looked at the images so many times; they've lost their original connotations of memory. I thumb through. Janey and me at our wedding. I touch the photo, amazed, as always, at our youth, the hopeful happiness of the grins. Lisa as a baby. I smile at her fierce eyebrows, always frowning. More images of Lisa; her First Communion, resplendent in white dress, prayer-book held aloft like a talisman. Photos of her and Gemma, their cheeky faces split in identical grins.

I sigh and close the book.

It still hurts. Not Janey. Memories of her are washed-out as the photographs. When Fields was booming in the eighties, I was making good money, better than most. Easy to make as much as you wanted, working overtime. And easy to spend it too, I found, especially in the pubs. I cough again, shift in my chair. Those days are hard to remember – uncomfortable, but mostly just difficult. Too many nights of staggering home, a blur of alcohol, the raging hangovers only subsiding with the hair of the dog the next day. And it got worse. I can't pinpoint the time exactly, but it was when the drinking got grimmer. Trips to the local off-licence instead of the pubs. The bottles on the top shelf, the smirk of the young one behind the counter.

Janey left first, years ago. She went to England, to be with her sister. Lisa told me last Christmas she had a boyfriend. I chuckle anew at the idea, the youthful sound of it; a *boyfriend*. I don't begrudge her this new life. But Lisa –

I get up and put the kettle on. I don't even want a cup of tea.

Lisa didn't exactly leave. She just faded out. Got a grant to go to university, and then never came back home to live here. The town lost its allure, I guess, once she got to the city. She still visits, every Christmas, but she's adrift from me now. She got married a while ago and I was awkward for the day; Janey looked so different, and I didn't know any of Lisa's new friends. Not even her husband; we'd only met once or twice before the big day. I know it's my fault. It's *all* my fault. She doesn't want me in her life, even if I've stopped drinking.

It hurts. I can't bear to think about her memories of the olden days; the fights, the late nights, the endless, miserable spin-cycle of the drunk.

All in all, I'm glad when the old house phone rings.

"Mr Boyle? Gemma here. Apologies for calling late."

"No bother at all. And it's just Jim."

"Jim." She tests out the word hesitantly. "Just wondering if you know anything about that old stone in front of the factory."

I pause, thinking. "No, I can't say I do. Old Mr Field put it in front of the factory when it opened, like a decoration I suppose. It was in the early seventies, after they'd come into money and bought the site. It's proper old. I can ask around for you if you want, see if anyone remembers anything more?"

"That'd be great, Jim, if you could."

"Are you still above on the site?"

"That we are." I can hear voices in the background. I picture the estate, normally so quiet and dead at the weekend, stirred into life, washed by the lights of the squad cars.

"Any joy on the body?"

She laughs. "Sure we can't release details yet, you know that. But no, still working away."

"Take care, Gemma." I cough, splutter into my old hanky, cough again.

Her voice is troubled. "You don't sound so good, Jim. Would you not pop in to see my dad in the surgery?"

I shake my head, even though she can't see me. "I wouldn't bother him for a cough. How's he keeping?"

"Ach, he's looking forward to being a grandad, to seeing his first grandchild. Sure you'll know all about that soon, what with Lisa being pregnant..." Her voice tails off.

I say nothing. My insides are a sick whirl.

"Jim?"

I put the phone down so she can't hear me crying.

They're still there Monday, the guards. When I reach the entrance, I'm stopped. It's a new guard, officious. He examines my ID closely before stepping back and letting me drive forward. There's a tent up in front of the old Field's factory, white-clad figures dipping in and out of it.

Field is standing by the Portakabin. It's the first time I've seen him here that early. Even though I've arrived on time, I feel vaguely guilty as if I've been caught out in some way.

"Morning Jim." Field has his phone in his hand, checking it. His perfectly shined shoes are clouded with dust.

"Mr. Field. Grand day. Looks like another hot one later."

"It does, it does." He looks at me. "This crowd here should be finishing soon. We have a big meeting in later, just so you know." He slips the phone in his pocket, hands me a list of car registrations. "Hopefully the guards will be finished by then, but if they're not, don't say anything to the businessmen, just let them in."

"Right you are, Mr. Field."

"Oh and Jim? Things like this are bad for business." He flicks a glance at me, pauses. "Best not to talk too much about this." Sometimes Field sounds just like his father. He takes my loyalty for granted, and he's right. After all, it was him who gave me this job as caretaker, my second chance.

"Right you are." I'm eager to get the kettle on, get started with the day. In the distance I can see Gemma, her bump unmistakable.

Field follows my gaze. "Best not to talk too much about this," he repeats. "Not to anyone." His meaning is clear. I dip my head, slightly, in acknowledgement,

He walks away, phone already to his ear.

Even if Field wanted to contain the news, it's impossible. It's always impossible in a small town.

"Here's the man now who can tell us all about it!" My neighbour, Joe, waving me forward to my usual seat at the counter of my local bar, Caseys. I still come here a few times a week. "7-up, please Rosie."

"The usual, so." Rosie smiles at me. She already has the bottle on the counter. I smile back and slide onto the worn leather of the barstool.

"So Jim, what's going on up above in the industrial estate? Word is that George McAllister found a body!" Joe's face is red and expansive with drink.

"Aye." I take a long drink of the 7-up, and burp discreetly.

"Well now, that's shocking. Shocking. We were talking about who it could be, you know. No one from round here, that's for sure. Any idea when the poor soul went into the ground?"

Those bones looked fresh, but Gemma told me they were probably older. "The ground here is sandy, bones last a long time." I sneaked a quiet look in the tent when they were on their tea-break. Before I heard the footsteps return, I had time to see the exposed skeleton, furled around itself. The head was beside it; as if it had fallen off, two shards of metal either side of the body. It stays with me now, the image of those bones, arched in a curve.

I know better than to gossip to Joe, though. *Be a listener not a talker*, was what I was told as a child.

"Not a notion."

"And it was beside the old Field factory they knocked down because of the asbestos. I heard there's a big deal going down there? Americans coming in?"

I'm on safer ground. "That's right." I remember the convoy of cars, mostly black, mostly new that pulled in that afternoon after the guards had folded up their tent. Men in suits with strident American accents.

Joe lifts his glass in a toast. "Grand man, Field. After they got that pull of money, he and his father have kept this town in business since the seventies. Hope this sad business doesn't derail the deal."

Behind him the TV blares into life with opening headlines of the six o'clock news. Joe's attention drifts.

"And now they say the banks are in trouble. Sure, they should be grand, they have enough of our money." He turns away from me to another of our neighbours. "What d'you say, Sean?"

I drain the last of my glass. "Another there, Rosie, when you have the time." I look around and see her. The person I came to find. "Mairead," I say. "It's yourself."

"Jim." Mairead sits down beside me. Mairead the Scholar. Or she was a scholar once, she taught archaeology in Lisa's university in Dublin before she started drinking.

"And a Jameson with that 7-up."

"Thanks Jim." Mairead's eyes are watery; she's had a few before the pub.

"I wanted to catch you tonight. Ask you about the old stone up there on the industrial estate." I clear my throat. "Gemma Evans asked me to find out about it, and I thought, well, you know plenty about that sort of thing. Archaeology."

Mairead nods, adjusting her scarf. "Nice girl that Gemma. Friend of your Lisa's, I remember."

I nod; throat tight. I don't talk too much about Lisa. The town sees her infrequent visits, I know they talk about me and my failures. "So, the stone?"

Mairead doesn't speak for a moment, takes a swallow of her whisky, and then wipes her lips. "Aye, I know the one you mean. The hagstone."

"What's that then?"

"It's a magic stone, or so folk believed, back in the day. Any stone with a naturally occurring hole in it often has protective powers. People used them for cures, for warding things off, for protecting property, livestock, that kind of thing." She pauses. "Folk believed that only good fortune could pass through a hole formed by water, so it made sense that it kept out bad luck."

I nod, slow and thoughtful. *That makes sense.* I'm from a generation whose mother threw dirty water outside the house, who put a saucer of milk down in front of the door. Simple, protective charms that her mother had performed, and her mother's mother before that.

Mairead pulls out a chain. Something glints black on the end. "I have one myself. A hagstone." She laughs, raises her glass. "Not that it worked for me."

I don't know what to say, so I take a sip of the 7-up, clear my throat.

"Why did Gemma want to know about it?"

"They found the body under the hagstone," I say quietly, not wanting to be overheard.

Mairead puts her glass on the counter. "Did they?" Her lined face is alive with interest. "You didn't happen to see it, did you?"

"Aye." The memory of the bones is still vivid. I describe them. Mairead listens, lost in thought. She peels back the advertisement on her beermat and takes out a pen.

"So, like this?" She's drawn a rough map of what I've told her; a curled spine, bones hunched in a protective huddle.

I nod. "And the head was beside it, not on it."

"Right." Mairead slides off her stool, her glass only half-drunk. "I'll be off. Going to look up this one." I haven't seen her so animated in a long time. It suits her.

"Right you are." I turn back to the TV.

Later that night, I cough. I cough so hard and long I have difficulty catching my breath. I think about the asbestos in the walls of Fields. I'd heard about that before. Sometimes when I cough at night I wonder if that's why.

Sometimes when I cough and the spit is red, I *know* that's why.

I wake with a knocking at the door. I blunder up in a tangle of sheets, heart thumping, grabbing my watch off the nightstand. Six o'clock in the morning? *Lisa?*

But when I open the door, it's Mairead. Her hair is rumpled; she's still wearing the same clothes as last night. She has that intense look I remember from when we were kids together at school.

"Jim." She's sober too. "Tell me one thing. Were there –" she swallows, "– were there spears beside it? The body?"

Confused, pause, then remember. "There were bits of metal there. One each side of the bones."

Mairead seems to shrink a little into her jacket. Her face is pale. "Jim, I think we need to go to see Gemma."

If Gemma's surprised to see us, she doesn't show it. "Come in and have some tea." She's in a towelling dressing-gown, her sizeable bulk anchored by a stoutly knotted cord above her bump. I think *Lisa* for a sad moment before I can help it.

"Sorry if we woke you, Guard." Mairead clasps her bony hands together, awkward.

51

"Just Gemma. And you didn't." She pats her bump affectionately. "This little blackguard did."

"It's about the stone, Gemma." I get to the point. "Mairead here has some information."

Gemma looks at Mairead again. "You're an archaeologist, aren't you?"

Mairead nods. "I was. Back in the day."

Gemma fills the kettle at the sink, clicks the switch and sits down. Mairead tells her about the hagstone.

Gemma has her black notebook out, writing. "Is that it?"

Mairead clears her throat. "No. It's also about the body."

"So Jim told you about that, then."

I flush. "I had a wee look on Monday before the tent came down."

She sighs. "You could get in trouble for that. Don't worry, I won't tell. But you owe me a favour, Jim."

Mairead's face is strained. "Does this look familiar, Gemma?" She takes out a piece of paper from her pocket and unfolds it. It's a photograph of a bog body from the National Museum. The brown, creased leather of the flesh folded in a circle, shattered head resting beside it. Two broken spears poke from the ground on either side.

Gemma looks at her sharply. "It was exactly like that."

Mairead draws in a deep breath. "It took me a while to put it together. It's been a long time since anyone buried a body like that. But experts reckon that in the Neolithic era it was to do with the crowning of a new king."

She swallows. "They reckon it was a sacrifice."

Gemma tells us to stay put while she gets dressed, so we stay put, drinking tea in the sunshine of the quiet kitchen. The surfaces are clean and sparkling, and I wonder how she manages it all.

Before she leaves, she has one last question. "And you're *sure*, Jim, you're altogether sure that George McAllister was told not to dig there?"

I think of red circles around the entrance. I'm quite sure. "The map Field gave us it was clearly marked – George gave it to you."

"Right," she says. Her shirt already has sweat patches under the arms. "I'll head back up to the station and get it. Wait here. I might be a good while."

And she is. My mobile rings once at seven o'clock, the time I usually arrive in work, then there's a flurry of calls an hour later. Field. I itch to pick up, but I don't.

Just as the last call rings out, there's the unmistakeable wail of police sirens outside. They sweep by the house and up the road, up towards the industrial estate. We look at each other, eyebrows raised.

"Reckon Field has a few questions to answer." Mairead pours more tea. She looks at the wine-rack, looks away. I feel a stab of sympathy.

"She probably won't be much longer."

Mairead shrugs. "It's okay. It's nice to be helping." She seems brighter, somehow, crisper, more organised.

I wonder, not for the first time, how things might have been different if Mairead hadn't started drinking. I remember her when she was working; her neat suits, a smart car. My sigh transmutes into a cough.

"You okay, Jim?"

My eyes water with the effort of drawing breath. "Just an old rattle, hard to shake." Mairead nods, looks away.

I think about my job for a moment. *Have I lost it?*

The bones surface in my mind, their pale shapes a silent reproach.

It's afternoon before Gemma comes back. Myself and Mairead eventually dug out a pack of cards from behind the radio. We're playing pontoon for matches when the door opens.

"Well now." Gemma sits down with a sigh, puts her hat on the table.

"What's the news?"

Her face is pink and shiny with heat. "Thanks both of you. You've been a major help. Mairead, you can go now. Just mind what you say. Everything's still under investigation."

"Grand. Call me if you have any other archaeological questions." Mairead's chair scrapes back. She pauses, suddenly shy. "Thanks Jim, for asking me. Here, I have something for you." She picks up my hand, presses something into it.

We wait for the front gate to close. I open my hand. Mairead's hagstone in my palm. A silver chain shivers over it.

I'm touched. "She'd be great at forensics, wouldn't she? Mairead. Pity."

"She would." Gemma takes out a tissue and blots her forehead. "God bless her, if it wasn't for her, we'd be still looking for evidence."

"Is Field at the station?"

"You heard the cars go by?" I nod. "Well, yes he is, and we sent another up to his house." Her face clouds.

"Was there anything there?"

"Jim." She draws her chair closer to mine. "I shouldn't say, but Jesus, the stuff we found in his basement. Mostly his father's, I'd say." A muscle jumps at the side of her mouth. "And stuff belonging to a builder. A young fellow from the city, we've looked him up in the archives. He was reported missing in Dublin in the seventies."

I open my mouth but only a series of coughs comes out.

"I can't believe someone would do something like that. And for what? The money they got? Success or protection or whatever? How could they?" Her eyes are red. I'm not sure if it's emotion or exhaustion.

"I'm sorry you had to go through that."

She pushes her hair back. "Don't be sorry for me. This is my job. And now, Jim, you owe me a favour.

I know what she's going to say. Like father, like daughter.

"You're going to get checked over in the hospital."

"Well now Jim, good to see you resurface." Gemma. She folds over the paper. *The Celtic Tiger: Beginning Of The End.* Not that I care. It all feels a million miles away.

"Good to see you too." My voice is croaky from the endless procession of tubes they stuck down my throat. There's a bowl of glowing green grapes by my bed. I struggle to sit up in the bed; the white sheets pin me firmly to the mattress. A cold jolt slithers down my front. The hagstone. Someone must have hung it round my neck.

There's a missed call on my phone. *Lisa.* I press a button, the screen dims. I see myself in the black screen – hair wild, face pale and lined.

"We got Field," Gemma moves her chair forward. "Well, we're holding him. Gonna be hard to make it stick, though."

"Don't you have the evidence?"

She shrugs. "Yeah. But he's well connected. That lot always are. They genuinely think they're above us. That normal rules don't apply. Just because they have money."

I know it's true. We're all just so much collateral to them.

We're both quiet for some minutes. Then she says carefully, "How're you doing, Jim?"

"Aye, not so bad." My voice is still scratchy. "It's cancer, though. I've known for a while."

"But it's the early stages. I asked my dad, and he said if it hasn't spread –"

I put up a hand. "We'll see. It just feels…"

"Feels like what?"

"Feels like this hasn't been worth anything. Me." I'm amazed at my own honesty. "I'm afraid…"

Gemma reaches over me and pulls a grape off the bunch. "You're alive right now, aren't you?"

"But I don't know how long I've got."

Her eyes are steady. "None of us do. That what makes life so important."

I shrug, as much as I can under the tight sheet. "Ah, I know. Just sometimes I think, what's the point." My voice is steady, devoid of self-pity, a statement of fact.

"Don't say that." She frowns. "You have friends around you. Like Mairead."

"Aye." I think that one over. It felt nice to work with her, right enough. And Gemma too. But that's not enough.

Her phone buzzes, startling us.

"Got to take this." Gemma steps out.

"Thanks for the grapes."

She turns in the doorway. "Not from me, Jim. Must be another admirer."

And she's gone. I hear her voice in the hallway, raised in excitement, her footsteps tapping away in the distance.

I'm tired. I close my eyes. She means well, but I don't want to think about it; those dark cells multiplying inside.

The door opens again, and I look up. "Gemma?"

But it's not Gemma. It's her. Lisa. She's crying, that awful, frozen look she wore at Christmastime is gone. Her coat is open. I can see it, the small, incredible bulge of the future.

Everything recedes; the sounds of the hospital, the sickness in my lungs, even the memory of the lonely bones in the dark earth.

I raise my arms, veined with tubes. "Come here to me."

I hug her tight, the hagstone hard between us, as if we're trying to compress this miracle through it.

Gerädert Fühlen

Steve Toase

We all have our own versions of a city, especially as a visitor, and mine was very different from that of the usual tourists. The ones who visited to traipse between Tripadvisor highlights or buy trinkets in the gift shops near the train station.

I was there for work, writing an article about old motorcycle manufacturers. At one time the city was home to hundreds. Most were small enterprises, set up in home workshops, building a vehicle every couple of weeks. There were larger concerns, of course, with vast factories that expanded into other towns and other countries as their success grew, but they didn't interest me. I was searching for slivers of a world long disappeared. That's when I found the tattoo studio.

The building I was interested in was across the road, the tattooist behind me. I didn't even notice they were open until I finished taking my photos of the small block of apartments that once housed the SilberRaben Motorrad Werke.

I turned around and winced. The day's constant drizzle hadn't done my leg any good. It ached as if the moisture in the air was constantly seeping into the old wound. Soaking in where the pins once held my bones together, freezing my ankle in place. Looking through the dull window, I saw sun-faded flash lining the walls, each design marked with a price sepiaed until they were unreadable.

I tried the door, more out of curiosity, and startled a little when the bell above me rang out. The silence that followed the sound was unsettling. I had more than my fair share of tattoos, and I was used to studios with the sound of rotary machines and the music playing constantly in the background. This felt different. This felt reverent. This felt holy.

Once inside, I stood in the middle of the room and looked around. The reception felt more like a museum than a working studio, the art all at least thirty years old, and most much older. I peered close at some of the designs, holding my breath so I didn't disturb the silence.

"Darf ich ihnen helfen?"

I hadn't heard the man come in. He leant on the counter, staring at me, not unkind or threatening, but it suddenly felt to me with a certain knowledge of why I was there, even if I didn't know it yet myself.

"Es tut mir leid," I said. "Meine deutsch is nicht so gut."

"Then we will speak in English," he said. "I learnt all my English from the nearby American base. How can I help you?"

"I'd like to get a tattoo," I said. That had never been my intention. Never been on my mind, but somewhere between walking into that peaceful room and the tattooist interrupting my reverence for the art on his walls, I now had the certainty that I would be leaving with a new design.

"And do you know what you want?"

Between each sentence, the man fell quiet, a stillness and presence that sucked all the sound from the room. I began to search the walls for the right design.

He did not rush me. While I looked, he did not even acknowledge my presence, though he did not leave. I moved around the walls in a circuit.

Most of the sheets of flash were older than me. Some were older than the walls they were pinned to, their colours faded by time, light, and the eyes that scanned over them looking for the right tattoo.

There was nothing in particular I was searching for. The colour schemes were all similar, reds, greens, yellows and blues. Touches between thick lines that echoed through the ages. I had no theme to my ink. No deep meanings or memorials. I just got tattooed with what I liked, though I had never been so impulsive before. Normally I booked appointments months in advance, design ideas agreed weeks ahead in emails, with the final sketches shared a few days before. There was knowledge and anticipation. Now, this was a different feeling. A lack of certainty. A commitment made on the spot. A chance to be impulsive. A chance to make a choice, when so much choice had been taken from me. When the pain was really bad, every step had to be planned in advance. So often my body controlled me. Stood in that studio, I knew I could turn the tables for once.

Avoiding all the nautical designs and those showing women who were showing more, I spotted the one I wanted nestled between a pair of swallows. The wheel was side on, with fat spokes and red dripping off the bottom of the metal tyre. More carriage wheel than anything else, it reminded me of the first motorbikes, little more than primitive bicycles, and by the time I turned around to the tattooist, my mind was made up.

He hadn't moved. It was hard to tell if he had even taken a breath while my back was to him.

"Made a choice?" he said.

"Number fifty-seven," I said, pointing. He walked around and unpinned the flash sheet from the wall.

"Go take a seat," he said, nodding at the curtain behind the counter.

I walked past him, through the shroud-like barrier, into the studio itself hidden from the main reception room.

This too was like a museum. In the centre of the room was a cracked leather chair for the customer, beside that an old wooden dining chair, and above it a single-bulbed light. A metal trolley was covered in kitchen roll, and spread out on it, an old coil machine, the barrel and several soldered needles of different sizes and configurations in sterile packets, waiting to be fitted.

Lowering myself down, I sat in the leather chair and leaned back, staring at the ceiling, studying the cracks in the plaster, the scars of a long forgotten flood from the rooms above.

"Where do you want it?" I hadn't even noticed him come in and sit down beside me. Up close, I could see the nicotine in his moustache and the watery glisten of his eyes. He picked up the glasses hanging on a string around his neck and fitted them in place.

Slowly, I rolled up my sleeve, exposing the skin of my forearm. Nodding, he reached into the hidden bottom shelf of the trolley and brought out a razor, shaving the arm clear of any fine hairs, then, running a stick deodorant over the skin, pressed the transfer in place.

59

"Happy?" he said.

I twisted my wrist, looking at the purple lines on my arm, marking out the limbed wheel, and nodded.

"Give me a moment to set up the machine, then we'll begin."

When he started I felt the music of the coil machine pressed into my muscles and through my bones. Of course it hurt, but not constantly, an intimacy that was revealed in discomfort as the percussion of the needle sang the colour into my skin.

I'd forgotten how loud coil machines were, and when the tattooist started talking to me, I missed his words at first.

"Why are you here, in the city?"

"I'm working. I'm a freelance writer," and as he worked ink into my arm, I talked about the stories I too wrote in ink. About the commission to write a series of articles about the lost motorbike manufacturers. About my love for that pioneering time of engineering. Of all that knowledge lost, all that experience lost, with conglomeration and retirement. The evaporation of experimentation.

"The loss of the city's soul," he said.

I nodded, and carried on talking. The room smelt of blood and disinfectant, both intensifying as he ran the needle back and forth, finding places where there was no sensation at all, and others where the buzz of the needles went from my arm up into my shoulder and into my throat, before he moved the tip once more.

I did not watch, instead turning the other way. It wasn't through any squeamishness. We all approach the modification of ourselves in different ways and I liked to wait to see.

"And have you found many of these old places?" he asked, pausing to change the needles for a shader.

"Not as many as I'd hoped," I said truthfully. The war had changed the city, the peace even more. The splinters of the past were harder to find than I would have liked.

"Maybe I can help you," he said, wiping down my arm with a liquid-soaked piece of paper towel. "My friend has an old garage, and that garage has a long history. Too small to be blown up, too hidden to be developed. Above the door he found some paint. Drehrad Motorrad."

"That sounds promising," I said. The name was not familiar, but I had not been able to memorise all the manufacturers that flourished and faded in those first few decades of the twentieth century.

"I can take you there," he said, pausing to change needles again. "But not today. Two days' time. Meet me here."

For the rest of the tattoo he worked in silence, and only when I heard him say, "Fertig," did I look down. The tattoo was perfect, the wheel rolling down my forearm to my wrist, in reds and blacks and greens. He gave me a few minutes to admire the work and compliment his skill, before he wrapped it with a medical pad and clingfilm.

We walked through to the reception room, and once more the silence embraced us as I paid him, the cost of the tattoo and a generous tip.

"Danke," he said, sliding the cash into a metal box below the counter.

The rest of the day was spent eating and watching TV in my hotel room, the sound of the street draping itself over the programmes. I don't know when I went to sleep, but when I did it was shallow. Every time I rolled over and caught my arm, I woke, and when I did drift off the dreams were vivid, as they often are close to the surface of the pool of rest.

I can barely remember them, despite how real they felt. Cobbles beneath my feet, the sound of chattering and the sound of sobs distended by shivering. Occasionally screeching and a sudden stop, then blood, before looking down and seeing bone splinters. I knew that one though. I'd dreamt of broken limbs every night since the accident, baby blue paint scraped along the tarmac, the crumpled Triumph tank leaking petrol to pool on the road. I hadn't yet found a way to fix my memory like they'd fixed my legs. Or maybe I had. Maybe the dreams were the aching scars. That first night was not restful.

In the morning, I got up and walked through to the bathroom, cleaning the tattoo and applying the ointment to help the healing. My finger ran around the wheel rim and down each spoke. Only then did I realise the design wasn't quite the same as the one I'd chosen. The metal tyre had split away from the wooden rim, and a couple of spokes were broken, not lining up. At first I thought the tattooist had messed up, but I checked it over with an obsession you can only have for your own skin, and each difference was definitely intentional. Maybe he just got bored of tattooing the same design over and over, though I wished he had checked with me before making the alterations. Still, I liked it, and it fitted with my other ink.

I was late to breakfast, filled my plate at the buffet and sat down in a far corner, facing a painting of a city that was not this city.

The owner of the hotel walked past, toward the kitchen door, and stopped.

"Looks sore," he said, nodding toward my arm. I'd left my sleeve rolled up to let the tattoo get plenty of air and heal.

"A touch," I said. "Only got it done yesterday."

He nodded, and leant in closer to have a better look, taking a pair of glasses from his top pocket and slipping them on.

"A permanent reminder of your visit."

"More just a spur of the moment thing," I said.

"A Catherine wheel," he said, then shook his head. "A breaking wheel."

"Yes, it is broken," I said, taking a sip of my coffee. I wasn't caffeinated enough to deal with conversation at such an early hour.

"No, though the wheel does look broken. A breaking wheel is not a description, but a function. One used for breaking people."

He walked off, saying nothing more, and I ate my breakfast in silence, my arm hot from the new ink. I did not think about what he had said. Conversations in hotel breakfast rooms were often strange.

I had no plans for that day, and after carefully sliding my coat over the tattoo, I checked my map for other workshops I wanted to find. So few of the hundreds that had existed survived that at times I felt more like an archaeologist than a motorbike journalist, teasing the past from the present.

Rain came down in torrents, cascading between cobbles before making its way into the drains beside the street. Pain flared and I ran my hand down my thigh and calf as if that would make it go away. Or maybe just to remind myself that I still had a leg, despite the collision. I walked, stopping occasionally in shop doorways to check where I was going, and make sure I was at least heading in the direction of some of my targets for the day.

By lunchtime I'd achieved nothing. The scouring away of the past in the first two neighbourhoods had been total. I cut my losses and found a cafe where I could grab a coffee and food, and regroup. I spread the map out in front of me, looked at my route, and tried to decide where to go next.

It was a modern place, a takeaway bakery really, with the cafe a few tables to one side, where customers could eat their purchases. Sometimes it was nice to find old places with history and other times I was in the mood for anonymity.

"Are you lost?"

I looked up at the shop assistant standing beside me. The presence of the map and my camera bag must have suggested I was a tourist, bypassing the usual attempts at communication in German, something that didn't improve my mood.

"No," I said. "I'm a photographer, but I can't find any of the places I'm trying to photograph."

The man was younger than me, and I could see his own tattoos cresting out of his uniform shirt collar.

"Then you are lost, yes?"

"No, you misunderstand," I said, trying not to sound as annoyed as I felt. "I can find the locations, but when I get there, the places I'm looking for are no longer there."

The shop assistant nodded in understanding. I'd not seen him behind the counter, but maybe he had been in the back. My arm felt stiff, and I still had no clear leads for the afternoon.

"Yes, the city is more interested in renewing than preserving its traditions and identity."

"I'm not sure about that," I said. "The part of history I'm interested in was itself a break in the past."

I saw the expression pass across his face, and quickly corrected myself.

"I'm researching the motorbike manufacturers of the early 20th century."

"You ride yourself?" he said, pulling up a chair, even though I hadn't invited him.

63

"I do," I said. "A 2022 Royal Enfield Interceptor. Electric start. Can't kickstart an old bike any more."

"Here?"

"No, back home in England."

He nodded, considering this new information.

"My grandad worked for one of these motorbike manufacturers," he said. "I can show you."

"I'm not interested in the big companies. Not this time."

The man shook his head, smiling. I took another sip of my coffee, already cold but worth finishing for the caffeine.

"No, he worked in one of the small workshops nearby. I can show you."

I finished the dregs of my drink and made a decision. Much as I found the waiter's eagerness irritating, I'd had no luck by myself in that part of the city. Maybe some insider information would be useful.

"I'll meet you outside," I said. "I'll just freshen up."

Inside the customer toilets, I rolled up my sleeve and checked the tattoo. Too early for it to scab, it seemed healthy, though sore.

Back in the cafe, I slid my tray away and met the man on the pavement outside.

"Matteo," he said, holding out his hand. I shook it and told him my name.

He walked fast to beat the weather and I followed, the rain robbing us of any conversation.

Rainwater softened the world, running colours together, turning the city to ink as we walked down narrowing streets, and more than once I thought he was setting me up. Taking me out of the way to mug me. My camera set up wasn't expensive, but desperate people can see value in their lack of knowledge, and really desperate people can make anything pay.

We rounded a corner into a narrow alleyway, cobbles beneath revealed through abraded tarmac. Either side were wooden doors, too old to fit properly. I knew the feeling.

"This one," he said, walking down to the end of the small street. Bracing a foot against the floor, he lifted and dragged the door, stepping aside to let me in.

The building was one vast room, still a workshop, untouched for years. A chapel to a forgotten industry. A forgotten world that only existed in slivers. Only visible to the few who knew where to look. To the few who were allowed to glimpse behind the curtain. A layer of dust had accreted to the pools of oil and other fluids. Somewhere in the rafters a bird took flight, finding an exit through a broken skylight.

I walked across to a pile of tarpaulins in the corner. Whatever colour they had once been, they were now grey, the dirt of work ground into the heavy material. I wrenched one back with a flourish I hoped would bless the unveiling, but there was no bike beneath. Just a stack of broken wheels, beading dented through use.

"Over here," Matteo said. I followed the sound of his voice. "We used to play here as kids. Not much survives. When the mechanic died, the workshop got looped in a confusion of ownership. No one claimed it. Maybe it belongs to the city now. This might be the sort of thing you're looking for."

The stack of order books had been untouched in decades, dust settled on the unevenly cut pages.

"May I?" I said.

"More the city's than mine, though not many people know this is here. Even fewer are able to show an outsider," he said, standing to one side.

"Do you know what's here?" I said.

"Don't really care," Matteo said, though there was something in his expression. An eagerness, even as he voiced his disinterest. I said nothing and leant forward to look.

Most of the books seemed to be old workshop manuals, for models I did not recognise but standard enough, but amongst them were other volumes, similar in size, their spines covered in text I could not read. I'd encountered similar difficulties before. The German fondness for blackletter fonts well into the 20th century made some texts almost unreadable to the British eye, but these were different. More pictograms than letters.

Once I'd taken photos in situ, I opened the books and shot some of the pages. The first couple were manuals, with beautifully rendered diagrams showing engines dissected. I put them to one side and folded back the cover of the next. Inside was a density of text interrupted occasionally by patterns precisely drawn and bearing no resemblance to any engineering I'd seen in my time, but maybe they were a different style of mechanical drawing. My guide was no longer paying me attention, fixated on his phone. I ignored him. Left him to his ignorance, not understanding how someone could be so uninspired to be surrounded by such a rich collection of history. I flicked through a couple of pages, the drawings more like medieval woodcuts. I photographed them anyway. Maybe one of my contacts would be able to describe their relevance to motorbike maintenance, because I have to confess, I was a little lost and didn't understand what they had to do with bike building. They looked out of place, and their presence amongst the technical volumes unnerved me, but I couldn't explain why.

Only then did I notice the plans pinned to the wall, a motorbike in profile with time faded measurements alongside in engineer's pencil. There was an article to write on that single room. Maybe I'd get a chance to go back. But I had to focus on my current commission.

"I'm done," I said, but I was alone, the rain outside finding its way in and bouncing off the worn concrete floor.

Sleep was a creeping creature with too many legs that did not visit that night. I felt it at the edge of my vision, but it would not approach.

My arm ached from healing, and I ached from my own wounds. Unable to rest, I got up and stared out of the window at the street, a cup of tea going cold by my hand as the world slid from night to dawn and the time came closer for me to go and meet the tattooist.

I didn't have nerves. What was to be nervous about? I felt I was keeping vigil. A holy observance, though I had no religion to frame myself in. I was a photographer who found the world and froze it, while trying to keep outside its debates and decisions as much as possible.

Sometime after dawn, my body must have decided it couldn't hold on any longer and I slept, dreams coming thick and fast. The smell of burning meat, crumpled wheels to one side. Shattered bones. I woke, hand going down to the scars on my leg. In the low light of the morning, running down my skin like morse code. There was no secret message hidden there. I knew exactly what history was indented into my flesh. I looked at my latest wound, full of colour and no real meaning. The broken wheel. Already, it was starting to scab. Beautiful fine lamination. A reiteration of how the body can adapt. If only the mind could heal so easily.

Getting dressed, I went downstairs and ate my breakfast in silence, my phone on the table in front of me, though with the dining room in the basement there was no signal. I had no interest in connecting with the wider world right at that moment anyway. Instead, I listened to the room breathe, the footsteps of the other diners as they went back and forth to the buffet. The scent of the coffee cooling as it was put to one side in favour of planning and conversations. The murmur of a radio in none of the languages I could speak. I felt it all around me, and yet it lacked something. It lacked the discomfort I felt as my arm healed. It lacked the memory of the pain in my leg as the surgeons bolted me back together. The failed mission to get my old bike rebuilt and ride it again, and from there find a reason. A reason for something.

The tattooist stood inside the doorway of the studio, huddled against the rain. By the time I reached him my leg was reminding me that I still had it, and I was struggling to see the positives of that, considering whether it would have been better to deal with phantom pain than real discomfort. At least I could take painkillers. There were no cures for the ghosts of agony.

"You brought your shit British weather with you," he said.

"Oh, I think you concocted this all on your own," I said. He spread his arms.

"We like to make you feel welcome. How is the tattoo?"

"Sore," I said. He did not ask to see it.

"But not as sore as your leg, yes?"

"Old war wound." I shifted my camera bag so the weight was on the other side of my body.

"We are too young for wars. I think roads are the only enemy we have now."

"The roads are fine. The cars? Not so much," I said.

"Live long enough and we're all broken," he said. "Shall we go?"

Reaching behind, he pulled up his hood against the rain. I hadn't noticed before how the years of bending over people's skin had given

67

him a slight stoop, or the way he punctuated every step with a cough he tried to hide, but I was grateful he wasn't as fast as my companion from the day before. I felt my foot drag a little the longer we walked, and the scar that ran from my nose, bisecting my lip, began to ache in the cold.

"You find it easier on a motorbike?" the tattooist said.

We were threading our way through tourists as we crossed the city, having to pivot between them in their distractedness, each step at risk of twisting my knee as my body went one way and my foot didn't turn.

"Ironic, isn't it? But yes, I can balance myself fine. The weight is off my injuries and I can let the bike do the work. Open roads are better, of course. Not so much gear changing."

"Open roads are better for many reasons," the tattooist said. "But there are no open roads here. Everything is crowded and enclosed. Narrowing and getting smaller. They call it progress."

We walked on without speaking further. Around us the sound of people faded as we entered a more industrial area. Old buildings with plastic signs bolted through crumbling stone. Most were obscured by dirt and grime, as if these small firms were a secret the city didn't want to show. I could tell the tattooist was walking slowly so I didn't fall behind. Underfoot, the surface changed from tarmac to stone slabs, damp and treacherous. I took more time. I was in no rush.

The sound of people faded completely, and there was a period of silence, as if we were pressing through some membrane into another world. Breaching the blood-brain barrier of the city. Gloving our fingers into a world few saw any more. Silence left and was replaced by the sounds of machinery, the scent of welding, scorched ozone in the air.

I glanced to my side and saw a plumage of sparks arc into the air, drifting back down to a cold death on the workshop floor. There was life here, in this hidden place, but it was a life of grease and searing hot metal. A place where scars and accidents were a fact of life. The tattooist never turned to see if I was there, just kept his pace so the gap between us never got too large. We turned another corner and the noise fled once more, this time replaced with the silence of the monastery or grave.

"We are here," he said, still not turning.

In front of us was an alley, the buildings on either side empty and shuttered. Even in the dull light I could see 'Drehrad Motorrad' in peeling paint on the wooden panel across the front of the building at the far end.

"Shall we go in?" The tattooist said, turning and smiling. "My friends are waiting." A sensation went through me, from my still healing arm to my long-healed leg.

"I'm just going to take some photos of the front, if that's okay," I said.

"Of course." The tattooist spread his arms like a king granting a boon.

Taking my time, I photographed the building, making sure the sign was clear, and searching the front for any details I'd missed.

"You can go in," I said, pausing to change lenses. "No need to wait for me."

"We go in together," he said, watching me work. "Better that way."

I took a few more shots, then packed my camera away.

"After you," I said, and stepped aside as the tattooist opened the door.

Once you've smelt burnt live flesh, you never forget the scent. There's a sweat to it that you don't get when cooking meat. A salty tang to the air. The tattooist led me behind a stack of tyres. Above us a fluorescent tube turned the air the colour of dull glass. In front of us stood an arc of men. Each one had a tattoo on their arms, all different, all in the same style as mine.

I looked at the floor to see what was the focus of their attention.

Matteo was bracketed to the concrete, wounds on his arms and legs already festering while they still smoked. His face was a mess of gristle, jaw shifted to one side, loose in the skin.

The room was too warm like the heat from all the welding and cutting over the years was trapped as ghosts of heat in the workshop. I felt sweat sliding over my tattoo, making my own wounds itch and I struggled not to scratch the fresh ink out of my skin.

"The city is old," the tattooist said. None of the other men moved. "And sacrifices have to be made to keep it living. We all have our own roles in keeping the city alive, and you do too. You were brought here for a reason. You chose that tattoo for a reason."

He paused and for the first time, I noticed the old wooden wheel leaning up against the stack of tyres.

"Why him?" I said. Matteo was trying to speak and as his mouth opened I saw the bloodied stump of his scissored-off tongue.

"He showed you places you shouldn't have seen. Not before you were ready."

There was a certainty in that workshop. A knowledge. Glancing up to the ceiling, I saw something hanging from the rafters on heavy chains. A baby blue triumph, rust showing through where the petrol tank had once crumpled against the tarmac. Oil dripped from the abraded engine.

I had found what I was looking for, or it had found me. I was part of the city now. Part of this society of ink and wounds. In the corner of my eye, I caught a glimpse of my tattoo. It was healing and so was I.

I picked up the wooden wheel, feeling the splinters claw at my hand, cold iron rim leaving rust on my skin. Shifting my weight to compensate for my leg, I rolled the wheel across to the prone figure on the floor.

"Cities drink blood like broth," the tattooist said. "We need to feed it spoonful by spoonful, to keep it healthy."

I pictured Matteo's shattered limbs threaded like cotton through the spokes. Like my own netted into surgical steel. It didn't matter that he wasn't responsible for my injuries. There was balance here. A palindrome of pain. Matteo was trying to speak again but his lungs were compressed beneath shattered ribs. I brought the wooden wheel down hard on his right thigh. It seemed fitting to start there.

The Inverse Nurse

Ian Whates

Day 1 After Surgery

"I'm Doctor Ahmed, one of the surgeons who operated on you. I'm pleased to say that the procedure went well…"

I lie on my back, the air mattress beneath me vibrating as it inflates and deflates, apparently with a mind of its own. I don't care; sufficient anaesthetic still courses through my veins to keep things pleasantly mellow. Tubes lead from a cannula in my left wrist and from a line in my neck to transparent bags on stands and mysterious monitors with unfathomable displays. An oxygen tube runs from my nose: twin grips in my nostrils, the loops around my ears holding it in place already threatening to chafe a little.

I'm alive. I made it through surgery. With the elation of that fresh in my mind, I drift back to sleep.

"I'm Ellie, one of the nursing team, and I'll be looking after you today."

"You're a sister," I note, seeing her badge.

"I'm the *other* Ellie," says her colleague, "also a nurse but not a sister…"

"So she has to do as I say." The two exchange grins.

"If you need us at all, here's the alarm – just press this button." She places the grey lozenge by my right hand, having looped the cord through the bed frame to prevent it falling off. "And here is your PCA – Patient Controlled Analgesia." Another plastic lozenge with attendant cord. "If you feel in any pain or discomfort, just press the red button and it will administer a shot of morphine. Try not to over-use it."

I won't.

71

"I'm Martin. I'm here to check your blood sugar levels…"

"I'm Sarah, one of the physiotherapy team. It's important we get you active, as much as you're able. Can you sit up yet…?"

"I'm Donna. Is it okay if I carry out your observations – blood pressure, pulse rate, blood oxygen levels…?

"I'm Helen, senior anaesthetist. I just wanted to check in to make sure you're not experiencing any lingering effects following the surgery…"

"I'm Dorcas, here to take your bloods…"

"I'm Sam, one of the diabetes nurses; we'll be administering your insulin intravenously for now."

"I'm Rachael. Sorry to wake you in the middle of the night, but it's time for your obs again…"

Day 2 After Surgery

"Would you like anything to drink? Tea, coffee, fruit juice?"

"I'm Agnes. Here to change your sheets and give you a wash. Can you sit up? Don't worry if not, just roll over onto your right side, as far as you can. A little bit further…"

"I'm Carrina, part of the nursing team." Her badge identifies her as 'Junior Sister'. "This is Maz, he's shadowing me today. Would it be all right if he did your blood sugars?"

"I'm Lisa, part of the pain team. On a scale of one to ten, how much pain would you say you are in right now?"

72

"I'm Doctor Kerrigan, one of the surgical team who operated on you. The procedure went well and you're making good progress. If I press here, is there any discomfort at all?"

"I'm Nadia." Her name badge is upside down. "Here to take your bloods."

"What's a physician's assistant?" I ask, reading the words stitched onto her russet uniform.

"We help the surgeons in various ways."

"Such as taking bloods, I presume."

"Yes, but we do a lot of other things as well," she says quickly, defensively.

"A sort of phlebotomist with go-faster stripes, then."

She grins. "Yeah, I can live with that."

"I'm Maria, here to check your blood sugars."

"I'm Kai, here to do your obs…"

Second Night After Surgery

"I am Ursa, your Inverse Nurse."

It's dark. Being woken up in the middle of the night is hardly a novelty by this point – it's happened plenty of times: by torchlight, by nurses bearing blood pressure pump and cuff or lancet and blood sugar monitor, but this is somehow different. For one thing, I don't recall falling asleep. For another, the light doesn't seem right.

"My what?" I ask, focusing on the here and now.

"Inverse Nurse."

"And what do you do?" I say in my customary jovial fashion, attempting to make a connection. I sense nothing coming back. I try to make out her face, but the features remain obstinately indistinct in the limited light.

"It falls to me to determine who lives and who dies."

"I'm sorry, I think I must have misheard you." Am I hallucinating, suffering some sort of after-effect from the anaesthesia, a delayed reaction? Am I even awake right now?

"No, you did not."

"What does that even mean…? *Who…?*"

"We are the oldest branch of nursing." She speaks calmly, precisely, unphased by my stuttering question. "Our calling predates your hospitals and your Health Service, reaching back to older lore, to a time more attuned to the heartbeat of the land that has dictated the rhythm of life since long before the advent of your people; a harmony that accommodated the discord of your kind, embraced it even. When you moved from forest to farm and then from farm to village, we were there. When you established your urban sprawls, stifling age-old custom beneath the weight of stone, concrete and neglect, still we were there. Waiting, watching, for those moments when our services are called upon. Such as now."

"What 'service' exactly?"

"Enough!" The word crackles in the air. "Time is pressing and the brand of care we administer takes a very specific form."

I suddenly feel over-warm, the atmosphere grows thick and claustrophobic, as if the darkness is taking on a physical presence.

"Paul Bishop!" She seems to swell, filling my vision, and my name rings out like a verbal slap, focusing my attention, impossible to ignore. "Do you wish to live or do you wish to die?"

"Well… live, of course." What else am I supposed to say? "But…"

"So it shall be. Your Choice has been registered, completing the sacred binding."

"Registered where exactly and what do you mean by 'binding'? And given the options you offered me, *what* choice?"

She ignores my questions, posing another of her own. "Who do you wish to see die?"

This is swiftly sliding from the absurd to the ridiculous. "Now hang on a minute, I don't want to see *anyone* die. What is this, what's going on here?" It has to be a dream, but I never remember my dreams and this feels so vivid, so real.

"I have identified myself as etiquette requires. While other nurses promote life and assist recovery, it is an Inverse Nurse's lot to designate death. The time is now 2.18 am on the 28th September. Your heart rate is elevated beyond its capacity to cope. One second from now you are set to suffer a fatal coronary. Death will be quick but painful."

Death? I let that sink in, and now recall reaching for something; half tumbling, half pushing myself out of bed in making the attempt. The strain, the shortness of breath…

"It has been determined that you may yet serve a greater purpose and so should be given the Choice. You need not die; not now, not yet, not unless you choose to," she continues.

"What does 'determined' mean? Determined by whom?"

"That has no relevance to this moment and is not for you to know. All that matters is that an intervention has been arranged – you can only ever have one, a privilege most will never be granted. I have been assigned. You were offered the Choice and have chosen to live. However, balance must be maintained in all things. For you to continue living, someone in your life has to die. A friend, a relative, a colleague. As part of the Choice you have the right to select who this will be."

"I can't do that! Sentence someone to death? I just can't." Yet my mind is already working, considering and rejecting possibilities, frantically taking inventory of everyone I know. I freeze on one face: my cousin, Peter, whom I rarely see and have always clashed with. Appalled, I refuse to think of him, turning my thoughts elsewhere, to an image of idyllic meadows – Grantchester, a picnic from a couple of years ago. Belatedly I dismiss the whole process, feeling angry, ashamed that her words have sent me down this path.

"I won't," I say firmly, bracing myself, wondering if by doing so I have just ensured my own death, no matter what might have been 'registered'.

"Very well, then it is up to me to make the decision for you."

"What? But you said *I* had to choose."

"That is the optimum course, but in the face of your unwillingness to accept the responsibility I am bound to assume the role. Balance must be ensured."

She pauses for a moment and I find myself unable to speak; horrified and yet no longer disbelieving.

"It is done," she says. "You will live."

"Who... but who have you just...?"

"You will find out soon enough."

Her voice sounds fainter, as if spoken from a distance. I try to focus, to ask again, to scream the question at her, but already I feel myself slipping into unconsciousness, her presence fading.

I awake in darkness, but a different darkness, a *normal* darkness. Lights come on. I'm in a bed, *my* bed, in the hospital; it feels mercifully grounded and I feel alive in a sense that contrasts starkly with the recent encounter. Two figures hover over me.

"I'm Simon," the closest says, "and this is Stefani. We're both doctors in the ICU outreach team. You gave us quite a scare there for a moment. Welcome back."

"Who... who's died," I croak, my voice cracked and dried.

The other one, Stefani, chuckles. "Don't worry, you're fine now," she assures me. "No one has died."

But I know deep down that she's wrong.

Open Studios

E. Saxey

Feeling sorrow without an obvious cause or a cure, Ruth started running. Cheerful friends told her that running had saved them, and in the dark winter Ruth was hungry to be saved.

At first, unfit, she was tethered to a dismal circumference, ten minutes of jogging out and slogging back past the same suburban terraced houses every night. She willed her legs to grow stronger to take her further, but her mind to grow calmer so she could drop the running altogether.

When she'd seen everything in her neighbourhood a hundred times, Ruth discovered the alleyways.

The first had looked more like a driveway or an overgrown garden, but Ruth feigned ignorance for the space of ten steps or so, and discovered it was a footpath. It was an alleyway bisecting a block of houses, running between the foot of one private garden and another.

And there were many alleyways to discover, ducking under a traffic barrier or slipping between hedges. Most were mud paths with rough grass, others had a sprinkle of gravel. They were hemmed by wooden sheds which peeled and leaned, and scruffy brick garages with corrugated roofs. Were they private land? Dogwalkers had passed the same way, she knew by their horrible mementos. Ruth might be trespassing, but at least she wasn't shitting.

Having found several alleys on foot, Ruth checked for more of them on maps. Hilariously, many were called 'mews', which suggested elegant living, not abandoned cars with weeds growing under their wheel arches. Some alleys were a proper assault course: stacked up bricks, wheelie bins and piles of planks with protruding nails. Ruth hopscotched the obstacles, relishing the challenge.

One evening in April, Ruth spotted a haze of light above a garage roof: a skylight. She crept close to the scratched-up wooden doors. From within came a racket of music, sporadic screeches. Someone was operating machinery. A rattle of metal, a burst of laughter.

The alleyways were not uninhabited, after all.

The running itself was doing nothing for her mood, but curiosity made her stick to her regime, spotting more lit windows, hearing thuds and hammering. She moved from jogging to sprinting to cover more alleys each night. The doors of the sheds remained closed, even as the weather grew warmer.

Ruth's patience was rewarded a month later, on a long Sunday afternoon. A cluster of limp balloons dangled from a garage door handle, and the door stood ajar. Ruth stopped dead, her sprint cut short.

"Come in!" The voice from inside the garage was posh and rather weedy. "Welcome! Have sweets! I'm Adriana."

Ruth entered and found that the garage had been partially converted. There were windows, and a workbench where an older woman presided, her silver hair heaped into a messy crown. "Welcome! Have you come from the other studios?"

"Others?"

Adriana passed Ruth a piece of printed paper: *Open Studios: Spring Weekend.* A map of the area was dotted with a dozen numbers, all of them clustered in the alleyways, nothing on the main roads. The numbers corresponded to names in a list. This woman must be *Adriana Rutter (Engraving).* A few doors down lived *Henrietta Styles (Watercolours).*

The flimsy leaflet transformed Ruth's sense of her neighbourhood. The sounds and lights in the sheds had a marvellous explanation: artists were working inside. And all those frustrating closed doors, Ruth realised, would be open for her today.

She looked eagerly around Adriana's studio. Where was the art? Over there was a visually pleasing cluster – no, that was a kettle and some mugs. What about that bowl of small spheres, metallic green?

"Do have one," said Adriana. "They're milk chocolate."

Ruth finally examined the stuff piled up on the workbench, like old stripped wallpaper.

"There's quite a range of styles," Adriana said. "Eugenia's been helping me to find my direction. Dig about."

This, then, was the art. Beige paper, scarred with rusty lines like scratches from a bird's claws. Ruth was sweating from her run, and began to prickle from embarrassment as well from viewing the art while the artist sat watching. But Adriana Rutter (*Engraving*)'s smile remained mild and made no demands.

Ruth followed the scratchy lines until they suggested shapes: the angle of a crouching leg, the dented circle of a flat bike tyre, a pigeon's wing car-crushed into tarmac.

"What are they?"

"Abstracts."

Thank goodness they weren't actually still life, or dead flesh. Although that meant that Ruth's own mind had provided the uncomfortable angles, the mangled animals.

"What were they inspired by?"

"Oh, this and that! Organic forms and processes."

Ruth looked for price tags, because if this one cost £50, and that one £1000, she'd know which was best. "How long have you been making them?" It could have been an accusation: *Why aren't they better?*

But Adriana relished the question. "Almost five years, now! I worked as a paralegal. But Eugenia – her studio is very close to here – she helped, she gave me permission."

Following the lines with her eyes had given Ruth a kind of motion sickness. "To do what?"

"To give *myself* permission. To be an artist! And do you, are you…?"

"I can't draw."

"You could, you know," said Adriana, confidingly.

"I should go. But thank you!"

"Wonderful to meet you! Go that way!" Adriana pointed, off down the alley. "You must look at Henrietta's sunsets. And Eugenia's studio – at the end of the day, she'll be hosting the afterparty."

Once outdoors, Ruth blotted her face with her T-shirt, printing a dark butterfly of sweat on the fabric. She saw, further along the track, a child's blackboard with a chalk arrow steering her into a shed. *Henrietta Styles (Watercolours).*

According to the leaflet, there were two hours to go before the end of Open Studios. Ruth resolved to visit as many as she could.

One aspect of Ruth's awkwardness was quickly relieved: there was never anything to buy. Starting with Henrietta's misty landscapes, the artist would explain that an item was "just a sketch for a larger piece". A souvenir would be offered instead: a sweet, or a postcard from a previous exhibition. Tessa the fabric designer had floppy blue cloths showing mushroom rings. But again, they were samples, nothing you could purchase. The oil painters "couldn't possibly sell *that* one", which was great, because Ruth couldn't possibly buy any of them.

The art was terrible.

It mirrored the dereliction of the alleyways outside. *Organic forms and processes*, Adriana had said, and the other artists echoed that notion, but these were not joyful processes or pleasing forms. Webs of rot, swelling growths. So many circles but instead of harmonious orbits, they resembled the surfacing of unwelcome bubbles. Bad sculptural art, too: prolapsed glass lumps, vases with dry crevices cracking open in their sides. Did you not need to be more skilled, before they let you near a furnace or a kiln? But Ruth kept moving across the pamphlet map, kept looking into different sheds and outhouses. She'd longed for something to happen, and this was certainly happening.

Despite running faster than ever, Ruth couldn't reach all the studios that afternoon. At five minutes to closing, Ruth entered a final property, a sun-bleached summerhouse. The walls were covered by huge canvases. More circles, these ones in murky brown pastel, overlapping to create tangled nests. Imagine how they were produced, the endless swooping scrawls, repetitive movements like a maddened zoo animal...

"That one took thirty hours, you know." The artist was another pale woman in late middle age, this one with henna-red hair. She smiled wanly at Ruth from a garden chair, a sketchbook on her knees.

How long had it taken to make all the works Ruth had seen that day? Motion sickness swept over her again at the idea. "It must be very satisfying," she said, with desperation. "To make something."

"Well, I'm part of a very nourishing creative community," the pastel artist said, sounding undernourished but contented. "Do you know, it's been five years since I started doing this. I was an estate agent, before, if you can believe it! Eugenia organises all this. She helped me to take my art seriously."

Ruth stooped to examine some sketches, to show she also took the art seriously.

"Speak of the devil!" cried the artist.

A young man had popped his head round the studio door. "Hi! Mum says: see you at the afterparty? Fifteen minutes?"

"Of course! Have a button, Tim!"

He snatched up a chocolate button from the plate of visitor treats. "The stuff looks amazing, totally amazing, Mum'll love it!"

"Excellent! Tim, which piece do you think...?" But the young man had gone.

A sudden splatter of colour on the artist's lap. The artist's nose was bleeding. She hadn't reacted, so Ruth pointed as politely as she could.

"Sorry, you're –"

"Oh!" The artist clutched at her face, bright blood smearing on her waxy skin. The drips had contaminated the sketchbook. "My goodness. So sorry. And do you draw?" The artist was still making polite conversation around her pinched nose and a paper towel.

Ruth shook her head. "No, no. I used to do linocuts."

"Wonderful! Do you think you'll make them again?"

Ruth recoiled. The artists had opened their studios to her, but she wasn't prepared to open up to them in return. "I should go, you're closing."

"You should try it!" insisted the pastel artist. "It freed me, it really did!"

Ruth had already stepped outside. She started to run but her legs wobbled. She'd have to walk home, her sweat pooling and cooling.

As she walked, artists emerged from the alleyways, alone or in pairs, all trotting north. Each one carried a piece of their own work, the sketches and samples and canvases they couldn't possibly sell. The red-haired pastel artist came too, carrying her sketchbook showing rust-coloured spots. She saw Ruth watching, smiled and waved, then hurried onwards in the dusk, heading for Eugenia's afterparty.

*

In months that followed, Ruth kept running the alleys to study the studios and ponder what she'd seen. The doors were shut again and she never saw the artists out and about, or the young man who'd invited them to the afterparty.

Ruth's memories began to smudge. So what if the art had been as shabby as the abandoned furniture in the alleyways? Think of the scale and the vigour of it, works springing up like nettles. So what if the artists had been listless? They'd spent the whole weekend sharing their work, baring their souls!

More persistently, Ruth remembered the insistent questions from artists: *Do you draw? Will you draw?*

It didn't feel like a creative urge. It felt like an itchy scab. But it prompted Ruth to excavate an old cardboard box from under her bed and bring out the red-handled cutting tool. The thick sheets of grey lino were so flawlessly smooth they made her nervous to begin, but the cutter still fit her palm.

Her mother had called it a horrible hobby, with its sharp tools and dark inks, but as Ruth set her cutter to the surface she remembered what she loved about it: it was drawing with light. Every track she gouged out of the lino would eventually be a white line, crossing a black page. She'd been a happy enough child, perhaps this was a route back to that happiness. She'd shut away her creativity, but she could fetch it out again and nourish it, like Adriana had. Well, perhaps not exactly like that.

Her favourite technique, she rediscovered, was to keep the tool moving forwards and turn the lino instead: pivoting, swiveling, forcing the groove to bend round into a circle. Like a starling in a murmuration, turning and turning until the circles filled a whole sheet.

Suddenly her cutter careened off the sheet. It nipped the index finger of Ruth's other hand then chewed into the tabletop.

Ruth pinched her injured finger and held it above her head. The cut was trivial, but she realized her arms and back were also aching. She'd been working for hours. Was this creative flow? Was this why the other artists had been so weary?

82

For a while, dots of her blood were the only pigment on the lino because Ruth's tubes of printing ink had all dried up. The images remained only a potential, invisible in direct light.

New ink was expensive but Ruth took the plunge. Running hadn't saved her. Art was worth a try. She bought fresh ink to make the print, to find out the truth.

When the ink arrived, Ruth rediscovered the gratifying hiss of the roller crossing the ink tray. Roll on thin layers, press on thick paper, lift off and view your new design.

The smudgy, squidged rings were as bad as anything she'd seen in the open studios. Utter frogspawn. Ruth didn't wait for the prints to dry. She bundled them into the bin, washed off the ink tray and cursed the way it blackened the bathroom.

But she didn't put her tools back under the bed. Maybe the next one would be better.

She found herself rushing home from her job to return to the work. This was what she'd wanted when she'd started running: movements that felt natural, and a repetition which soothed her mind. The accidental cuts to her fingers were just part of the process. She kept printing, and the prints got clearer, stronger.

Something had woken in her. Was it self-expression? Like a bulb breaking through dry earth, a bone breaking through split skin, it was a sensation after a long spell of numbness, and therefore very welcome.

A leaflet for the next Open Studios slithered through Ruth's letterbox in September. Ruth started immediately to pick out her best pieces, which were still bad. She had no idea whether the artists could help her to improve, or put her work in front of an audience, or *give her permission* to *take herself seriously*. She had a sudden guilty recollection of how poorly she'd judged them: crones in sheds with dabs and doodles. But now she understood them better, she knew how hard art was, and how satisfying. She wanted to share that understanding with them.

She packed several sheets of her circle-art into a satchel, and set out. Strange to be walking slowly through the alleys in a linen dress, not speeding through them in lycra.

Open Studios: Autumn Weekend. It struck Ruth, as soon as she picked up the leaflet map, that there were more studios this weekend – as many as thirty. And the artists, she found, were even chattier than last time.

"Do you have your own practice?" asked a stone sculptor with a wispy ponytail. "Have a mince pie, I know it's a bit early."

Ruth shyly brought out her work, setting her inks next to the artist's granite boulders. Straight away, the circles in both pieces stood out. Also, their matching injuries; the cuts on Ruth's hands, the sculptor's more ambitious scars.

"These are wonderful pieces," said the sculptor. (Ruth was learning to call everything 'pieces'.) "You should show them to Eugenia! You really should."

The praise made Ruth's spine tingle, and sent her off in search of more appreciation. Artist after artist offered up their craft, then enquired after Ruth's own. She showed her pieces. Honeyed words flowed from their lips. After an hour of being admired, she went to find Adriana, to shyly tell her: *you gave me permission.* But her shed was all shut up, and she wasn't on the map.

Ruth questioned a nearby textile artist. "Do you know Adriana? Is she still making pieces?"

The two of them stood before a blanket of grey lint. It was adorned with circles – no, with holes, which gaped as it rippled in the draught.

"Oh, I expect so! She was Eugenia's favourite, at the Spring opening, you know."

"Great!"

"You should call at Eugenia's studio." Maybe all the circles in the art were actually holes; maybe all the artists, herself included, were only tracing around the edge of huge gaping gaps…

She'd missed a question from the textile artist. "Sorry?"

"You're coming to the afterparty? Eugenia would be so happy to see you!"

Ruth had been wondering how to get an invitation. The expectation that she'd attend was even better than praise. She fumbled with the map, checking the blots on the grid.

84

She'd not visited Eugenia's studio last time. It stood at the end of a graveled *cul de sac*. As Ruth crunched along, she gripped her satchel and tried to feel the moment as deeply as she could. She was being welcomed into a creative community.

The studio was robust, not a converted shed but a brick building like a small storehouse with fairy lights dangling in the doorway. Inside, the high gloomy space yielded no clues as to its original purpose. A few massive metal tables stood by, ready to shriek against the concrete floor if they were moved.

The art pieces were big as well: huge twisted shapes in industrial materials. The scale was greater, but they shared the other studio's obsessions: organic forms, empty spherical shells, ringworm conjured up in pitted chrome. Rust everywhere, or rust-like stains. Many holes.

"Hello!" Someone hailed Ruth from the back of the studio.

It was the young man from the first Open Studio, Tim. His unsteady stance made him look even younger: hands shoved deep into his jeans' pockets, he struggled against his self-imposed straight jacket. "Bit cold in here. Have a look, though."

Every other artist had been an older woman. Not seeing how she could politely ask about his age or gender, Ruth stuck to the usual question. "Are these your work?"

"Not mine, my mum's. Eugenia. But I can tell you about any of the pieces, just ask." That explanation opened more questions. What was it like, having a mother who created these monstrous blobs, and left you to chat to the potential customers?

"Here, have some more light..." He pushed at the curtains and they slid aside to reveal tall windows, and through them, the alleyway. The *cul de sac* had a wide turning circle at the end which hosted a pile of tyres and a splintered ladder. Half under a tree, a slumbering skip could not contain its load of rags and paper. Ruth thought: If I was a proper artist, and my studio looked out onto that view, I'd clean it up.

The extra daylight did not flatter Eugenia's art. Ruth could now see the frail details: fraying things trapped between panes of glass, and thin wires resembling long hair straggling down a plughole.

"And she does commissions!" The words struck Ruth as a horrible truth. Eugenia could take something from Ruth, some idea

85

or impulse, and trap it in an object like these. She almost spoke out in protest, but instead looked away, looked aside.

In the dim evening light, the other artists were coming down the alleyway. Each held in their hand a piece of paper, a canvas, a boxed-up object. Ruth glimpsed things she'd seen earlier that day: thunderclouds and puffball growths. Each artist had brought the finest piece of work from their show. They were heading for Eugenia's studio.

The boy nodded at the procession. "Oh, right, they're here. Are you staying for the party?"

"I'd like to."

"Did you bring anything?"

"Here." She pulled a print from her satchel.

"Oh, this is good! She'll like this!" His tone was fervent and relieved. He walked to the window, presumably to see the design in better light. "She could really use something like this. You got blood on it." He pointed to an ochre smudge on the reverse.

"I'm so sorry, I didn't notice –"

"No, she'll like it. I'm in a band, I *was* in a band, but that doesn't work."

"What doesn't work?"

"She can't do anything with music. It needs to be something physical."

The artists' conversation and laughter drifted in through the open studio door, but they didn't enter. Ruth saw them passing on down the *cul de sac* and gathering in the shabby clearing. The party would be an outdoor affair. Eugenia would arrive with drinks and snacks and shower them with praise.

Twenty or so women stood in a ring, like an amateur choir, formal but excitable. Each held up their art with both hands in front of her chest.

Then the granite carver stepped forwards, hefted her work – a fist-sized spiral like an ammonite – and popped it carefully into the overflowing skip.

"Oh! That'll wake her up," said the boy.

Something stirred inside the skip, dislodging more papers which drifted across the grass. Ruth saw they were sketches, oil paintings, watercolours. The rusted skip was full of art.

At the centre of it, an elongated figure raised itself. It seemed human-sized but heron-shaped, detritus from the skip adhering to it like a great cape. It stalked to the metal edge, stepped down onto the heap of tyres. No haste, no stumbling. It moved with the gait of a patient predator.

The artists fell into a soft reverent cooing. A few of them murmured her name in welcome. They awaited her attention.

It could be a cape and a mask, Ruth told herself. A cloak from the textile artist, and a *papier mâché* mask made by another woman, in another studio. This could be a performance, another form of art.

Now the creature was on the ground but Ruth still found it hard to make out its exact form. It was the drab colour of old tarpaulins and brick dust. Its head swung round on a long neck to examine the artists and their art. The wicked beak of the mask pointed first at a sketch, then at a canvas. Before the red-headed pastel artist it paused longer. It nodded as though hypnotised by the rings and loops of her artwork. The artist no longer clutched the paper to her chest but held it at arm's length. Her hands were shaking.

With explosive speed, the creature's head darted forward and its beak-mask stabbed through the paper. It pulled back almost as quickly, ripping the art away from the artist. She dropped to one knee, clasping her forearm where a red blot bloomed, calling out: "I'm all right! I'm all right!" But none of the other artists had moved to help her.

At Ruth's side, the boy murmured: "Watch."

"What —"

"She's always interested in new talent."

He tapped on the glass of the studio window. With his other hand, he held Ruth's print up to the glass, waggling it to and fro.

Eugenia's head swung towards them. She approached the window, step by long-legged step. She could be a woman. Those legs could be bleached wooden stilts, she could be crouching at the top of them. The bends of knee and hip could be hidden by the cloak.

"C'mon," coaxed the boy, giving Ruth's print another twitch.

Eugenia ran at them in a flurry of grimy cloth.

"Jesus!" The boy grabbed one edge of the curtain and flung it across the window. Eugenia thumped against the glass, just as the curtain shut out the sight of her.

Ruth staggered backwards. She hit tables that screeched and exhibits that toppled and smashed.

"Don't worry!" called the boy. "Don't worry, it's fine! She likes your work!"

Listening in the dark, Ruth sensed the thing outside had not recoiled after its impact. Sure enough, a moment later, fingers or claws squeaked against the window. The same squeak, over and over. Ruth thought about her own hours of lino-cutting, the careful satisfying arcs. Obsessive movements, endless patience. What had this creative community nourished? What had its art freed?

"Is there another way out?" asked Ruth. "Another door?"

But the lad would be no help. He was listening to the scratching sounds, and smiling, and stroking Ruth's print.

Ruth let the satchel slip from her shoulder, but kept her hand closed around her prints. She could drop them behind her, one by one, to slow Eugenia down if she followed.

She had run so much through the spring and summer. It had done nothing to help her mind. But it had made her legs strong, and today at least, running might save her.

Through the open metal door of the studio, Ruth ran.

Escape Notice

Tim Major

There's no harm in asking, Adam told himself. *She'll be pleased at somebody showing an interest.*

He had been summoning courage for the entire ten minutes he'd been standing on his driveway, trimming the border. In truth, he didn't know whether the plants from which he'd lopped the heads were weeds or more legitimate growths. He had a blind spot for such things.

He placed the secateurs on the low wall and strode across the road. The construction worker stood at the end of the cul-de-sac, her back to him, looking up.

"Hi there," he said, waving, even though she couldn't see him.

The construction worker turned. Her yellow helmet matched her hi-vis jacket. Long vertical lines framed her mouth, which made her appear stern even though her expression was otherwise placid.

"Can I help you?" she asked.

Adam pointed at the telegraph pole. "I was just wondering about that."

"Oh yes?"

"It was installed a couple of weeks ago."

The woman hesitated. "That's right."

"I just wondered why."

"Why what?"

"Why it's there. Surely telegraph poles aren't needed nowadays. Isn't everything underground?"

She shook her head. "It's a misnomer. Telegraph pole, I mean. Utility pole is the preferred term. The wires could be electrical, communication, anything. Poles are quicker to install and more convenient than digging. The fibre network's supported by the copper network, and will be for years yet."

"Okay. But…"

"I really do need to get on, sir."

Adam frowned. What *had* she been doing before he came over to talk to her? Just looking upwards, staring at the upper reaches of the pole.

"Yes, but –" *There's no harm in asking*, he repeated internally. "But there *are* no wires."

The woman gazed at him blankly for several seconds, then looked up again at the bare wooden pole that rose to a height greater than the second storeys of the houses in the cul-de-sac.

"No, there aren't," she said.

"Will somebody be coming along to attach wires?"

"Why do you ask, sir? Have you been having trouble with your connection?"

For the first time, it occurred to Adam to wonder who she worked for. The symbol on her hi-vis jacket revealed little: a black square containing the white outline of a wavy circle, like the corona of an eclipsed sun. Below it were printed words which at first he took to be a Latin phrase: *COMM TRANSIT POWER*.

He shook his head. "My broadband's fine, thanks. No, I'm just curious, that's all."

"You have time on your hands."

Adam blinked. "I suppose so. The freelance work's flowing less freely than it used to. Perhaps all the work offers have got stuck in the cable – ha! It'd be wonderful if you could just unblock it, like a plumber."

"I'm not a plumber."

"No. Of course not. Anyway, my desk's just up there –" He pointed vaguely at the upper bay window of his semi-detached house. "And I often find myself gazing out at the street, and I've been wondering about the telegraph pole."

"Utility pole."

"Yes, of course."

The woman nodded slowly. "Most people don't tend to notice them," she said.

Adam smiled. "I'm a noticer. Always have been."

Those vertical lines either side of her lips became more pronounced: this was genuine sternness. She nodded again, then moved towards the van parked on the kerb.

He hadn't seen Hiram for months. They were due a catch-up. Hiram clearly felt the same way, because he responded to Adam's text message immediately, suggesting they meet that same afternoon. Adam's instinct was to put it off, in order to demonstrate that he was busy, that his time was precious. But he had nothing on.

Adam's glasses fogged as he entered the Micklegate Social. The place was full, the noise almost overwhelming after the silence of his house.

Hiram had secured sofas by the window. He stood as Adam approached, and they performed an awkward mixture of handshake and one-armed hug.

"How's it going?" Hiram asked.

"Good. Good."

"Yeah?" Hiram's head tilted.

Adam smiled. "Really, it's fine."

"I'm sorry I haven't checked in on you."

"It's not like I'm in any danger, Hiram. My life's very much the same, only a little quieter."

"A lot quieter, is my guess."

"Oliver does come back every once in a while, you know. It's not as though the house will never again echo with childish chatter."

But it wasn't often. He and Becky had begun the separation with clear rules about the frequency of Oliver's visits, but the gaps had become longer, the number of overnight stays fewer. There was no animosity, no manipulation. Adam had been guilty of letting things slide. And Port Talbot was a world away. If only kids these days made phone calls. Quite sensibly, Becky didn't allow Oliver his own smartphone, so WhatsApp chats were off the cards for another few

91

years yet. Adam only hoped that he and Oliver still knew each other by that point.

Hiram reached out and squeezed Adam's arm. "That's the spirit, mate."

Adam moved to the counter, partly to avoid having to respond to Hiram's condescension. He ordered a double espresso even though he shouldn't, at this time of the day. By dinnertime he'd be wild-eyed, unable to eat, unable to process coherent thoughts. Not like it mattered.

"I'd been wanting to ask you about something," Adam said when he returned.

"Shoot."

"Telegraph poles. Utility poles. There's a new one in our cul-de-sac."

Hiram groaned. "Mate, I'm not wearing my uniform." He tapped the rucksack at his feet, which was emblazoned with the York City Council crest. "When my uniform's stashed away, I'm off-duty."

"But it's work hours."

Hiram snorted softly. "You've got me bang to rights there, I suppose. So. This pole."

Adam hesitated. "Actually, never mind. It was already explained to me. I'm sure a team will come and install the missing wires at some point. But something else came up, just as I was leaving the house. Marks on the pavement. Spray paint."

"Yeah. Yeah, we do that."

"Why?"

"Because us council workers aren't mind-readers, Adam. We're a team, working on projects at different times. Us electricians need to do our bit at the right point in the process. Same goes for pipes and road markings. The survey team sprays marks on the pavement – not on the road, if that's going to be dug up. Think of it as a to-do list written in the most visible place possible. Think of it as somebody marking up a document that needs editing."

"So my road's going to be dug up?" Perhaps that was why no wires had been attached to the pole. A change of plan. The thought of construction noise directly outside his window was galling. He'd never get anything done.

"Depends. What are the marks?"

Adam took the napkin from his saucer, then patted his pockets. Hiram conjured a pencil and handed it to him. Adam drew an arrow with the arrowhead touching a vertical line. Then he drew a mirror image of the same symbol, the verticals inmost. In the gap between them he drew a circle and within it an X.

Hiram studied the symbols thoughtfully.

"Where were they?" he asked.

"The pavement, directly outside my house. Actually, the arrows were in front of each of the neighbouring houses. Those vertical lines matched the boundaries of my property."

"What colour?"

Adam frowned as he tried to recall. "The circle with the X was red."

"Yeah. That's my guys. Blue's water, yellow's gas, green's cables and comms. Red represents power. Nothing sinister there, Adam. Just a street lamp."

"But it's directly in line with the window of my home office."

Hiram shrugged. "Then you'll be able to work into the night, without needing to turn on your lights. Just open the curtain."

Adam groaned. "I think I'm being victimised."

"By the local council?"

"By a woman who didn't appreciate me asking questions. She thought I was a nuisance. I pointed out to her where I worked, and… I swear she's arranged for extra construction work to be carried out, just to get back at me. And she wasn't from the council. Some sort of contractor."

Hiram's eyelids flickered, but his gaze was still fixed on the symbols on the napkin.

Adam tapped one of the arrows. "What about these, though? Don't tell me it means more disruption."

"Okay."

"No, *do* tell me. I want to know. What do arrows either side of my house mean?"

"Dunno," Hiram said quickly. "Honestly, no idea. Just shorthand. Most people don't tend to notice them."

"That's exactly what the woman said."

Hiram shrugged.

They lapsed into the usual exchanges. Hiram described family holidays on Greek islands. Adam recounted the most interesting books he'd read recently. Hiram had recently taken up taekwondo and screen printing. Adam had platinum-trophied *Elden Ring*. At school they had seemed to have a lot in common. Now, not so much.

When their conversation dried up, Hiram said, "Mate, I gotta get back to it."

Outside the café, they faced one another. Goodbyes were always awkward.

"Which way you heading?" Hiram asked.

Adam pointed at the upper reaches of Micklegate Bar, the huge medieval gateway that interrupted the city walls. "I'll go back along the walls," he said.

"Nice view, if you're not in a hurry. I'll head up there too. Take the scenic route back to the office."

As they climbed the steep steps, Adam said, "Actually, I often take this route just to see the chessboard."

"The what?"

"There's a chessboard, near Victoria Bar, carved into a stone paving slab. I like to imagine the Roman soldiers sitting there on the city walls, playing chess between shifts. If you've never seen it, you should. I always notice it. I'm a noticer."

Hiram scoffed. "Noticing isn't knowing. Yeah, I've seen it, mate. It's not Roman. Hardly any parts of the walls are. They're medieval, then repaired in the seventeenth century, then again by the Victorians."

"Still, it's definitely a chessboard," Adam said defensively. "It must have been carved by somebody wanting to play chess, and that person must have been guarding the walls."

"Nope. The slab was taken from the prison when it was demolished. Your chess player was a criminal."

"Oh." Adam considered this. It was a very different mental image, but no less fascinating.

"You know what a palimpsest is?" Hiram asked.

"Not really."

"A manuscript with writing that's written on top of other writing. Reused parchment. Layers on layers. Like when they do X-rays of paintings and find other paintings underneath. That's what this city is, Adam: a palimpsest. But it's way, *way* more complex. More like a living creature, and what's beneath are veins. Those pavement markings you're so interested in, they're just a hint at the nervous system beneath your feet. You're best off leaving the decoding of them to the experts."

"The surgeons, you mean. If it's a living creature."

"Yeah. The men in white coats. Whatever."

They had reached the head of the steps. Now the suburbs to the south of the city walls were visible, laid out like a detailed relief map. In the foreground, directly below the walls, a strip of road had been stripped of its tarmac surface, and a yellow backhoe loader was scraping away the rubble beneath. This was part of the ongoing works that would improve the approach to the railway station; the old flyover had already been demolished some months ago. In the early stages of the project Adam had read about archaeological finds: glaze pottery and animal bones. The area had once been used as a dumping ground. History had been underfoot all that time.

Adam stared down at the construction area. Beyond the chugging JCB he could see symbols spray painted onto the rough ground: two overlapping rectangles, a symbol like an web-browser bookmark icon, five circles describing a pentagon.

"It's a whole other language," he murmured.

"Seriously, you need to let it go," Hiram said.

"I can't. I notice things. That's who I am. And I follow up on interesting finds."

"You're *determined* to see things that others don't."

95

"That's right. I refuse to be blind. I'm a noticer."

Hiram sighed and nodded. His torso twisted as he peered into the pocket of his jacket. Checking his phone, probably.

Then Adam jolted with shock as Hiram emitted a sharp whistle.

Far below, the backhoe loader drew to a halt. Its driver craned his neck to look out of the cabin. From a nearby portacabin emerged another construction worker. Both of them shielded their eyes to gaze up at the city walls.

Hiram waved an arm slowly in a wide arc.

He placed his other hand on Adam's back.

"What are they –" Adam began.

"Colleagues."

The construction workers didn't wave back. They just stared. From this distance Adam couldn't be sure, but he felt they were looking not at Hiram, but at him.

Adam paused at the chessboard for a long while, crouching beside it and tracing the X shapes that represented the black tiles. This flagstone was greyer than the surrounding ones. The fact that it had been taken from the prison made it more interesting than he had supposed, not less. The prisoner who had carved it would have been astounded at the idea that the board would be exposed to the elements, hundreds of years later.

On Bishopthorpe Road he crossed at the lights in order to examine one of his favourite local sights: a brick wall in which were embedded a double set of metal doors, half buried by the relatively new paving which rose up a shallow embankment. The metal was green with rust. The doors looked like one of those aged electrical cabinets you saw on street corners. But they would never open, having been blocked shut. Adam liked to imagine that the cabinet and the wall had sunk over time. He'd mentioned the sunken doors to several people in the past, but nobody else had noticed them.

He took several photos. When he turned away, he realised he was being watched. An elderly woman leant on a crutch, staring at him. She shook her head slowly, as if admonishing him.

Adam hurried away.

As he passed the hardware shop, he caught his reflection in the wide window. There was something on the back of his Peter Storm raincoat. He took it off.

It was a symbol drawn in red chalk. A circle with an X in the centre.

He felt the ghost of Hiram's hand on his back.

By the time he reached his house, dusk had fallen. Perhaps a lamp located here would help relieve the gloominess of the cul-de-sac. The council knew what it was doing.

And Hiram's chalk mark had been only a good-natured joke.

Adam glanced down at the pavement, then froze.

The red symbol was harder to make out in the dim light, but it was still there. He held up the coat he'd been carrying in a bundle. Yes, the symbols matched. He had tried to rub off the mark on his raincoat, but the chalk was surprisingly durable. It'd need a proper wash.

The other pavement symbols were more concerning. Earlier, the two arrows had been drawn at each end of the low brick wall that marked the edge of his property. Now they were located directly below the circled X. The two arrows still pointed inward, but the vertical lines were now barely a centimetre apart.

What could it mean?

Adam moved to and fro before the low wall. He could see no trace of the earlier white marks at all. Surely spray paint couldn't be cleaned so effectively.

If this was another joke at his expense, it no longer seemed good-natured.

He'd ring the council tomorrow, ask about the mysterious contractors and complain about the conduct of the stern-faced woman. He paid his taxes. He didn't deserve to be terrorised, however subtly. If Hiram got caught up in an inquiry, so be it. They had little in common anyway.

He shuddered. It was getting colder.

He jogged the few paces to his front door, retrieved his key from the pocket of his bundled coat, then fumbled with it in the lock.

It wouldn't turn.

Seconds passed. A minute or more. It was difficult to accept that he was still out here, failing to enter his own house.

He stood back, looked up. The windows of his house were dark, of course. The place was lifeless. None of the windows were open, and there were no drainpipes to climb, and there was no access to the rear of the house.

He bent to peer into the keyhole, but saw no evidence of tampering.

The key must have been damaged somehow.

Inspiration struck. He returned to the pavement, then turned sharply to stride along his neighbour's keystoned driveway. Becky had once given their neighbours a spare key.

He knocked on the door.

No answer.

"Excuse me?" he called. He couldn't remember the names of the couple that lived here.

He knocked on the window. The curtains were drawn, but through them he could see the flicker of a TV, and movement on the couch opposite it.

Adam took out his phone. To his surprise, he found the number of his neighbour's landline in his contacts list.

The ringing from inside the building echoed the tinny ring that came from the speaker of his smartphone.

The silhouettes on the sofa shifted. But neither rose to answer the phone.

Utterly disheartened, Adam returned to his own driveway.

He tried the key in the lock again. He clenched his teeth, then wrenched the key more forcefully. Its head broke off in his hand, the shaft still embedded within the lock.

Adam slumped to the concrete.

He shivered. He unbundled his coat and put it on.

What now?

A shuffling sound. A young man was moving along the street. It seemed unnaturally slow movement, until Adam saw the Jack Russell on a lead, sniffing the ground.

"Excuse me," Adam said as he stumbled from his driveway, "I was wondering…"

The man didn't look up. He watched his dog as it plodded towards the spray-painted arrows on the pavement, sniffing cautiously. Then it backed away, whimpering.

"You see, I'm locked out," Adam said.

The young man rubbed his chin as he examined the marks on the ground. Finally, he raised his head. He didn't look at Adam, though. He studied the house to the left of Adam's home, then the house to the right. In between, as his gaze passed over Adam's house, his eyes were glazed, as if his brain had momentarily disengaged. As if he simply didn't notice anything there.

Adam looked again at the arrows. When he had left his house to meet Hiram, the arrows had bracketed his building. Now that the arrows met, it was as if they negated the existence of his home entirely, like the marks of a proofreader requesting a deletion.

"I don't know what to do," Adam said weakly.

The Jack Russell whined.

The young man nodded sympathetically – at the dog's plight, not Adam's.

Without looking at Adam, he lifted his right hand, and with a shaking index finger he traced a shape in the air: a circle, then two intersecting lines making an X.

Then he walked away.

Larking

Phil Sloman

Evan sipped from his pint as the gulls swooped over the ditch-dark waters of the Thames, their wings arced, harrying back and forth with an elegance lost on most seated outside the pub. Ruddy turnstones pottered along the foreshore with equal anonymity. Squat in stature. Feathers sleeked back. The eager mud sucking at their feet as if sensing sustenance only to be disappointed in taking fleeting imprints of their passing.

Evan watched all this with casual disinterest while he waited for Justin to return from the pub's toilets. He leant against the embankment railings, intrigued as the turnstones meandered between rotting wood jutting irregularly from the mud in their search for worms. The saturated wood reminded him of decaying teeth, blackened and irredeemable, the Thames ready to swallow any unwary trespassers. In years gone by, the wood had formed the staves for the fishing boats used by the locals who sold their catches at early morning markets. Now, lorries came from across the country to Billingsgate Market in the east of the city filled with vast hauls from the North Sea and beyond.

Ignorant to this history, the gulls changed flight patterns, their attention drawn to a slow-moving barge, its length filled with waste from across the city. The boat forged ahead, keeping to the middle channel where the water ran deepest. Ripples echoed out from its passage to create a miniature tide which lapped at the foreshore several feet below the embankment and Evan. The more emboldened of the gulls began landing on the barge, their strong beaks digging into clumps of rotting food before the gulls took to the air again.

Beyond the barge, on the far shore, were offices converted from an old warehouse. A mixture of seventeenth century architecture combined with what modern city planning regulations would allow. It was a Saturday so the buildings themselves were quiet, yet something on the foreshore below them caught Evan's eye. Close to the point where the water met the exposed banks of the river. The glint of sunshine on… he wasn't sure… something metal perhaps. And there was movement. Like a lumbering creature… a seal perhaps, one which had drifted too far up from its more familiar estuary habitat. But a seal wouldn't be so upright. Maybe a person?

The railings held firm as he leant forward, pint in hand, eager to get a better look. He was right. That's what it was. A person. But not apparent immediately to the passing eye. Obscured as they crouched down in the mud. No, not quite crouched. More that their legs were part-submerged in the dark mire beneath them, the tide mark coming up around their calves.

Christ, were they in trouble? Should he call for help?

Except they weren't struggling. More searching. A bucket of some sort in one hand, a trowel in the other. He now realised that's what had caught the reflection of the sun. He'd have missed the person otherwise. Unintentionally camouflaged in mud-coated clothing, their forearms covered in filth.

Every now and again they would bend forward, reaching into the mud, their arm deep within the sludge. Then they would stand upright, squidging muck between their fingers, examining the contents of their hand before either dropping a selection into the bucket or bending forward once more.

But what exactly went in the bucket?

Instinct made him lean further forward, one foot off the ground, as if he would be able to see the detail of something so small from this distance. And yet…

The slap of a meaty hand connected with his back. Caught unaware, he dropped his pint, watching it tumble end over end until it squelched into the wet mud below. Evan whipped around, his fists balled, cheeks reddening, only to be greeted by Justin's beaming face.

"Careful, buddy. You wouldn't want to fall in there. Chances are you wouldn't be seen again."

"Fuck's sake, Justin," said Evan, unclenching his beer-free hands. "Do you know how much that cost me?"

"You should have been more careful," Justin smirked. "Come on, I'll get you another."

"Larking."

"Larking?" asked Evan taking a sip from his fresh pint.

Justin had found them a seat at the rear of the pub away from the tourists. A menu on the table listed a whole host of ales. All with pretentious names like Dutchman's Delight or The Dog's Nads.

"Mudlarking. That's what they call it. Loads of folk do it. Or they used to before the licences got stopped."

"What? You need a licence to go grubbing around out there in the mud? You're making it up."

"Scout's honour." Justin held up his hand in a mock salute. Not that he'd ever been in the scouts or anything else with levels of organised authority. "Too many people needing rescuing by the river police cos they got themselves stranded. Far too interested in what treasures," Justin threw up a couple of imaginary quotation marks with his fingers, "they could find. Most of it's old bits of tatty pottery that the Romans chucked away back in the day. That's if you're lucky. Mainly broken Victorian chamber pots, to be honest."

"Well, why do people bother then?"

"How many lottery winners do you know?"

"What?"

"How many? Simple enough question."

"None."

"Exactly. And yet I see you week in, week out buying yourself a ticket or a scratchcard just in case. Same principle. See, those shards of pottery are your lucky dips or now and again a fiver on your scratchcard. But what you're hoping for is a bit of jewellery or if you're really lucky a purse of gold coins that Richimus Maximus dropped overboard from his sailing vessel a couple of thousand years back. Now if that comes in, there's your winning lottery ticket, right there."

That had all been a month ago.

Since then Evan had fallen down a rabbit hole of obsession. Online first to find out what gear he would need. Wellies, thick black rubber gloves, a trowel and a bucket seemed the main things to get

103

him started. Those had all been easy enough to get hold of though he had minimal space to store them in the postage stamp of a suburban flat he could barely afford to live in. That was all going to change for the better when he struck gold. No more getting by any more with the odd extravagance now and again. He deserved better than that. Much better. And why not sooner rather than later?

A life of luxury and excess was well within his grasp.

He could feel it in his bones.

Now he needed to get out there and go hunting.

Some folks used metal detectors but he didn't have the cash for anything like that. He'd realised early on in his research that he was going to have to rely on blind luck and dogged determination in sifting through the silt.

One thing he hadn't reckoned on was the tides. Tides were what you had at the beach, ebbing and flowing at the whims of the moon. Associated, perhaps falsely, with some long distant memory from being in his dad's car listening to the Shipping Forecast with its ridiculous names. Viking, Dogger and German Bight were the ones he could still just about name. To his way of thinking, rivers were long bodies of water which were simply there, every now and again flooding when the heavy rains came, but otherwise just there.

He now knew different.

The Thames was a tidal river. Rising and falling throughout the day to expose its rich banks and his path to gold and glory. It also explained the bodies.

In his research, he'd read about the pagan rituals which used to take place. People sacrificed by drowning in appeasement to the gods to keep the waters bountiful and the bank dwellers safe. There were also tales of sewer pigs, or Black Swine, which had tormented those foolish enough to delve into the sewers which emptied out into the Thames in their search of treasure.

Evan didn't put much store in any of those tales. He was more interested in what was concrete and likely to bring him some wealth. The perfectly preserved corpses from the fifteenth and sixteenth centuries, for example. He'd seen photos of leather boots still clad around the feet of one poor soul who had foundered in the river, their body stunted by osteoarthritis from what the scientists could tell. Or that's what the press had said. And if their boots were still on then so would be their purses and the jackpot that he craved. How the bodies ended up there would always remain a mystery, but what he had learned was that the Thames revealed her treasures when she wanted to. When the tides were right.

"What do you think you're doing down there, son?"

Evan cursed under his breath.

Earlier that day, he'd grabbed all his gear, downloaded a tidal app on his phone and snuck out of the flat around 6am. The smell of urine and vomit from the London nightlife was still fresh on the breeze as he'd walked past empty chicken shops, vape stores and nail bars on his way through the early morning city. Clomping along the pavements in his wellies, he got a couple of funny looks from some of the late-night revellers only just now emerging from whatever dance till you drop club they'd ended up in. But he hadn't cared. He'd still walked with a spring in his step. The air had been warm, the summer sun rising and he'd had a confidence that he was going to strike gold from the off.

The one thing he hadn't accounted for in his preparations was the police.

"I asked you what you're doing down there," they'd barked from up on the embankment. Evan had shaded his eyes from the sun as he looked up from the riverbank below.

"Just walking."

"Just walking, is that right?" The officer's gaze had gone from Evan to the trowel in Evan's hand to the bucket on the foreshore. "Often take your gardening gear with you when you go walking?"

And that had been that. Conversations about licences or the lack thereof. That he had to pay his dues. Oh, how Evan wished he'd listened to Justin back in the pub.

Loads of folk do it. Or they used to before the licences got stopped.

Filth halfway up his arms and legs plus a bucket full of slop, he'd been sent packing and told not to return in no uncertain terms unless he fancied a night in the cells along with a fine for his troubles.

And that felt like the end of it until he met Marie.

*

Part of him had considered giving up, yet he couldn't escape those thoughts of opulence and decadence which were due to him all for the sake of getting his hands dirty.

Lurking in an online forum, he'd seen her message pop up.

Partner in crime wanted for licenced larks

He'd skimmed through the rest. Fifty years' experience. Slowed down by poor health. Mainly arthritis. Her brain and enthusiasm were still sharp though. Plus a seventy-thirty split in her favour. He figured he could negotiate that if he needed to. For now, he had a route back in.

Marie was short. Under five foot and half bent over to go with it. There was a whiff of the river about her. Subtle hints of mud and brackish water. Her cheeks and palms were mired with dirt to the extent that Evan imagined no amount of hot showers would ever get them clean. The unruly tangle of hair on her head looked like a bedraggled heap of straw all tinged with green.

"Used to be more boats out here, back in the day." Those were the first words she'd said to him, looking out across the Thames as the rising sun reflected off the glass buildings on the banks. "But that's progress for you, I guess. Or that's what they'll tell ya."

Her accent confused Evan. While he was used to the melting pot of London culture, there was something in her tone he hadn't heard before. Something old. A mixture of the West Country combined with a hundred versions of that distinct uneducated lilt of street urchins he had seen and heard in a smattering of Dickens and Kingsley tales brought to the small screen.

Marie held her hand out.

"A smacker."

Evan looked at her, wondering what he was meant to do. Was there some secret handshake he hadn't been made aware of? Some hand slapping ritual to perform?

"A smacker. A nugget. A quid. Some dosh."

"Oh. Oh right."

He hadn't thought he'd need to pay her but a pound was nothing in the grand scheme of things. Not when there was treasure to be had. Evan rooted around in his pocket, feeling a mixture of lint, a half-

106

used pack of gum, and a few random pieces of shrapnel. He took the coins out, a mixture of silvers and bronze, spreading them out in his palm.

"Seventy-two pence, I think," he said, poking at the loose change.

Marie bit gently at her lip, digesting the information as if there was some complex calculation to be had. A small flock of gulls floated by on the water, the silence disturbed momentarily by the subdued chimes of St Paul's in the distance, as Evan waited for some epiphany to come to her.

"It'll do," she said eventually. "Give it here."

He handed over the cash reluctantly, dropping it into her outstretched hand. She didn't even look at the money. Simply closed her hand around it to form a fist. Holding her fist to her ear, she shook the coins in her hand like an expert gambler at Vegas about to shoot craps, listening to the jingle, before pulling her arm back and launching the money into the Thames.

"What the hell," exclaimed Evan, his voice louder than he had meant it to be. "Why on Earth did you do that?"

"Tithe."

"What?"

"It's a tithe. Got to pay your dues, otherwise…"

"Otherwise what?"

"Simply the way it works. You've got to pay 'em. Your dues."

"And what if you don't?"

"Then on your head be it," she said touching two fingers to her forehead.

And no matter how much he pushed, that was the matter closed.

Marie had made them walk another twenty minutes. Evan carrying the gear. Marie stopping every so often. Assessing the foreshore as she sought to find what she eventually decided was the perfect spot.

They had dug for the best part of two hours. Or rather, Evan had dug and Marie had barked out instructions. Coaxing him along the different tidemarks. Pointing out where there were likely to be richer seams of finds. Identifying anomalies in the mud which to his untrained eye looked like nothing more than puck marks yet seemed to call out like sirens to the five-decades of experience Marie carried with her. By the end of it, they had a half-bucket of loot to sift through.

"What's been your best find to date?" asked Evan as they sat on the jetty, his legs dangling over the edge.

"Eh?" asked Marie, their finds spread out across two pieces of cloth. One piled high with items yet to be determined, the other a mixture of coins and other small metal items she had already cleaned and assessed.

"Your best find? What's been the most valuable thing you've uncovered to date? I bet you've seen some incredible pieces over the years."

Marie continued sorting through the day's finds. Rinsing the muck off in a bucket of water they'd filled from the Thames. The pieces she fancied, she put to one side. The others, the dross as Evan imagined it, broken shards of pottery and chamber pots, she slung back onto the mud flats.

"Well," ventured Evan again, "what *was* your best find?"

Marie stopped sorting and looked his way.

"Nothing as would interest the likes of you," she said and went back to her work.

Evan raised an eyebrow.

"Really?"

"Really," replied Marie, never taking her eyes from the task before her.

"And what would interest me?"

"Anything shiny. Like a magpie. Nowt with true worth."

"A magpie? Yeah, right."

"I been watching you. There's a twinkle in your eye the moment summat with a bit of shine comes out the ground. What you should be looking for is connections."

"Connections?"

"To past. To your roots. Like this." She held up the bedraggled remains of an old cloth doll fished from the pile. Its features warped. The eyes too big. The dull clothing coarse and ruined. "We ain't nothing without that connection."

Evan looked at the doll and scoffed.

"Well connections won't pay my bills."

108

Marie put the doll to one side and faced Evan.

"You got it all wrong. All of it. You hear me. This stuff here," she said pointing at a scattering of coins laid out on the cloth, "ain't worth nowt. Not to me at any rates. Not in real terms."

"Aren't those silver?" asked Evan..

"You ain't listening to me, Magpie. You think you have it all worked out. Know what? This lot," Marie swept a nonchalant hand in the direction of their haul. "It's yours. All of it. See what it brings you. A few notes to spend. Something nice to eat. Nothing that'll last. That stuff ain't worth as much as you think. So go on. Take it. All of it. Take it and see if I care. All of it, 'cept this and this."

Marie held up the doll and a small unadorned cross, barely bigger than the palm of her hand, the metal puckered and blistered green over time from sitting in the water. A crude circle connected the arms of the cross to the central beam with tiny holes punched across its circumference. "These, now these is mine."

Pound signs lit up in Evan's brain. He was no fool. If she were willing to let him have the silver then how much must the cross be worth? The doll? The numbers kept increasing the more he thought about it. One thousand pounds. Five. Ten. A hundred.

"Perhaps I should take them too?"

She laughed.

"Think you're the first person to threaten me?"

"Might be the last," said Evan, standing. *She really is quite small*, he thought, his shadow darkening the spot where she sat. "Though we don't have to do things the hard way…".

Evan reached out a hand in expectation.

"Magpie," she hissed and spat at his feet.

"Hard way it is then," he said, forming a fist.

Marie stared back, unflinching. Waiting.

"Oi! You all right there, love?"

Six foot plus of tattooed muscle shouted out from a way down the promenade, arms straining to control two pit bulls tugging at their leads.

Evan grabbed the cloth with the coins, then ran.

*

109

Marie had been right about the coins.

Evan had pawned them earlier that day, walking into one of the less discerning pawnbrokers near where he lived. Discreet was what he was after and discreet was what he had got.

"How did you come about these?"

"Aunt passed away."

And that had been the extent of the questions. No offer of condolences or sympathy. Just a simple grunt before the broker took out their loupe to inspect the coins. One hundred and seventy pounds, give or take, was what Evan ended up with in the end. All paid in cash. He had hoped to get more but it proved right what the old lady had said to him.

A few notes to spend. Something nice to eat. Nothing that'll last.

Better than nothing but a long way from anything remotely close to bringing about the life of luxury he was owed.

So, the question was how to build on this. On his own he didn't have the knowledge or the expertise. And he'd burnt the one link he had to someone who did in a moment of greed.

He could reason with her. Make her realise she had mistaken his intentions. A foolish misunderstanding. And if she didn't believe him then there were other ways to get what he wanted from her.

The next few weeks he ventured to the banks of the Thames on a daily basis, asking around about Marie. Any larker he came across, he always got the same look of bafflement. No, they didn't know anyone by that name. Didn't know anyone who fitted that description. Even the old-timers he happened upon dismissed her as a myth. Someone Evan must have imagined.

The same when he went searching online. The initial post he had seen was no longer there. Vanished. Like Marie herself. He couldn't even remember her username to hunt for her. Though he suspected that would be fake anyway.

It was only when he was ready to give up that he got a lead.

While hunting for Marie, he had continued to work the shoreline as best he could. Keeping an eye out for local police before scraping at the surface of the mudbanks. Each time nothing. As if the Thames were punishing him for his actions.

"*Connections,*" was what she had said. "*Got to pay your dues.*"

Just words. Nothing that was going to stop him striking gold. It was all superstitious nonsense. Plain bad luck on his part for now. Luck which was about to change.

"I've been hearing about you."

The conversation had been unexpected. Sitting on his own in the pub where Justin had spilled Evan's pint, contemplating his next move. The girl had settled down in the chair opposite him without asking if she could join him. He wasn't sure she was even old enough to be in the pub on her own but that was another matter. Evan was about to tell her to piss off when…

"Folks say you've been asking about for Marie. Those folks in the know, that is."

"Go on."

"Well, I might be able to help you out."

"Might you now." Evan leant forward. "And just what will that cost me?" He knew a shakedown when he saw one and this was as blatant as they came.

"Morgan's Wharf," she said, ducking the question. "You want to find her; you'll have to look there."

"Morgan's…"

"…Wharf. Out East. Not what you'll call on the beaten track. Or not for the likes of you at any rate. Here." She passed a folded slip of paper across the table. "This'll see you right."

Evan unfolded the paper. A crude map scrawled in a heavy hand showed where he needed to head with a date and a time. Much further than he had ventured in his searches and definitely a long way off the tourist trails.

"And what, now I pay you for this… this drawing?"

"Oh, mister, it's not me you'll need to pay. Really it's not."

It was early morning when Evan spotted Marie near Morgan's Wharf. He'd half expected a fool's errand or a trap of some kind. Blind obsession had driven him to come when common sense had told him not to. Yet now, as he watched her hunched shoulders and reduced stature in the distance hobbling along ahead of him in the morning shadows all alone, he realised he'd struck gold.

Morgan's Wharf was in an older part of town out to the east and away from the City. The buildings in the local area were in stark contrast to the renovated waterfronts cultivated along the tourist hotspots. This was the land of tower blocks with metal gates across front doors and bikes padlocked to balconies forty feet in the air. Broken windows were common across long since abandoned estates where graffiti tags provided a rainbow of colours to break up the grime-coated walls.

The scream of gulls rose up as he followed Marie along rubbish-strewn streets, her steps taking them inevitably towards the river. Evan kept his distance for now. Curious as to what brought her out here and what she might lead him to. Maybe to where she kept her treasures. Hidden away from prying eyes and sticky fingers. Well that would make things easier for him if that were the case.

As the morning sun rose higher, the architecture changed. The tower blocks giving way to a more industrial landscape of mesh fences, portacabins and scrap metal dealers. These in turn opened out into a semi-wasteland filled with old shopping trollies, husks of burnt-out cars and edged by large metal freight containers double-stacked to tower over him. Weeds found life from deep within the cracks formed across the open expanse of concrete. Yellow-headed dandelions and white-crowned daisies added splashes of colour to the desolation. Even in the least likely of places, nature never lost her foothold.

The remains of a warehouse rose from the rear of the expanse. Buildings like this were commonplace in the more industrial stretches of the Thames. Perfectly situated to send materials along the river to wherever they were needed. Though that was long in the past. The roof had collapsed in on the upper floor years ago leaving more of an iron-wrought skeleton silhouetted against the sky. The lower half was more substantial. All four walls standing though the main entrance was blocked by fallen masonry and metal. It didn't matter. Along the main wall, mortar had given way in places creating gaps large enough for someone to squeeze through where the bricks had been pulled aside.

Marie walked to the warehouse with the confidence of familiarity. Side-stepping broken bottles and impromptu burn sites without a second thought. More strident in her step now as if her aches and pains were a forgotten memory. Evan hung back, watching from behind the wreck of a car, curiosity spurring him on now as much as the thought of what treasures she might lead him to.

She stopped at a gap in the wall, placing her hand on the flaking brickwork. Here, among an array of tags and swirls scrawled across the building, someone had graffitied rudimentary depictions of people on the exterior walls. Each image near life size. Perhaps those who used to work the river in years gone by. Except the drawings were off. Like the doll Marie had shown him. The eyes of each person that bit too large, a bit too round, a bit too dark; sunken within pale worn faces topped with thin wispy hair. Crude brown trousers coupled with matching tops. Barefoot. All of them. The artist struggling to capture their feet accurately. Each one's toes interconnected like carnival freaks.

Marie stepped inside.

Desperate not to lose sight of her, Evan followed, quickly covering the distance to the warehouse. It took a moment for his eyes to adjust as he climbed inside the building.

Shafts of sunlight speckled the floor, dust motes dancing in the beams. The room was spacious, with debris from the floors above scattered throughout. Makeshift shelters formed from sheets and boards or whatever materials seemed to have been to hand dotted the perimeter. *Probably old homeless dens* was Evan's initial thought. Probably. He didn't fancy staying too long to find out. There were enough places to hide all sorts of things around here though. And if this was where the old crow had her stash then he could help himself and be gone quick sharp.

An external door clanged shut at the far end of the room.

Marie.

Evan picked his way across the floor, stumbling on fallen masonry momentarily before regaining his balance. Lost in the shadows before, he could now make out more graffiti on this far side of the building. The same images of people. This time they stood together on a riverbank. Arms outstretched with palms face up. Like worshippers witnessing a baptism.

Normally he might have stopped, taken his phone out to grab a picture, but not today. Marie was on the other side of the door and that was where he needed to go. He wasn't about to lose her now.

Emerging, blinking into the daylight again, he wasn't ready for the drop. First there was ground, solid wooden boards, and then thin air. Slipping and sliding, he tumbled helter skelter onto the exposed mudflats of the Thames. The thick, glutinous surface pulled at him, coating him with its filth. Fighting, he twisted himself around, struggling to regain his legs as his feet slid beneath him.

Slowly, cautiously he managed to right himself. Almost immediately, a cold chill gripped his ankles as his feet sank into the mud.

"You received my invitation then?"

There she was. Positioned on the edge of the mudflats, one hand resting on the rungs of a ladder leading back to safety.

"Invitation?" he asked, raising his voice to be heard as he strained to free his feet.

"Think the girl found you by chance?"

Memories of the pub days before dredged up from the recesses of his brain as the mud clawed at him further. Swallowing him up to his knees.

"Fuck's sake."

A lump of metal landed in front of him. The cross he'd tried to steal first time around.

"This what you came for? Perhaps hoping for more loot like it?"

"Don't want it. You can keep it," he shouted back, pushing with his hands to try and free himself.

"Oh, I can keep it can I, Magpie?" Marie chuckled. "Ain't that why you're here? To take it from me? By force?" Evan saw movement over her shoulder as she spoke. "Thing is, ain't mine to keep. Was just bringing it home."

Behind her faces appeared. Seven or eight of them. Clambering from the building. From the banks.

"You asked me what my best find was. Back then, when we met."

Young and old. Short and tall. All barefoot and dressed in coarse materials.

114

"When you tried taking what you hadn't earned. Like the magpie you are. Except it was the wrong question. Or asked in the wrong way."

More joined what was now a throng on the wharf. Each face sallow and drawn as if deprived of the sun.

"Connections. I told you but you didn't listen. Connections is important. Was never *what* was my best find. Was always w*ho*."

They stared from the wooden promenade high above him. Dozens of them now. Their dead eyes fishlike; cold and bereft of emotion. All watching in silence. An air of expectation hanging unspoken on the breeze.

"Help me," he implored, changing tack as Marie turned her back to him. Climbing the ladder to join her people. "Please, help me."

The mud pulled at him in response, fetching up around his hips. A dark part of his mind imagined this was the quicksand he'd been warned about as a kid on old tv shows. The ones with the sepia tones and hollow-eyed children.

Except this was London. This didn't happen in London. Did it?

"I understand now," he said, trying to push himself free, feeling a little give beneath the surface as he did so. "I really do. One more chance. That's all I need. Just one."

Breathing deeply, he concentrated on his legs, moving them slowly while his arms pushed against the upper surface. Movement, followed by counter movement. A shift to his advantage. One leg seeming to come loose, met with frustration as the other leg sank deeper. Back and forth, back and forth. On his own he might free himself, eventually. But what time did he have until the tide changed?

If only one of them would show some humanity!

"Will you just help me!" he yelled, not caring for the desperation woven within each syllable, all caution in his struggles abandoned. "Help me! Why won't you fucking help me?"

Nothing.

All they did was stare as he lost purchase once more and the mud dragged him in further.

Nothing, until one of them broke free. Small in stature. Smaller than Marie. A child. Clambering down the bank with the simplicity of youth. A doll clutched under her arm. She stopped when she reached the foreshore. Cocking her head, like a blackbird, watching the man caught tight ahead of her. And as she watched, and he pleaded, and, oh how he pleaded, she crept ever closer, and he sank ever deeper, until his arms were secured and all that remained surfaced above the tidemark was his head.

Closer and closer she approached. Watched by her elders. By Marie. By her family. The mud supporting her weight. Happy with what it had been offered.

So close until she could touch Evan's head if she chose. Could peck at it like a rabid gull. Instead, she reached forward to the ground in front of him and took the cross to her breast. Then held it high for all to see.

As one, the gallery raised two fingers to their foreheads and bowed in recognition.

Satisfied, she turned ready to scurry back. Except there was one thing she needed to do. One thing she needed to say. Twisting once more to face Evan. Her words a whisper.

"Should have paid your dues."

And then she fled.

From deep within the mud, cold bony fingers grasped Evan around the ankle, their grip burning his skin like ice. He looked up to the gathered crowd one final time. Marie surrounded by her people. Her treasure. And now he understood. Far too late as the fingers gripped tighter and Evan was dragged beneath the mud; forever to be larking.

When The Blood Runs Dry

Lyndsey Croal

The temperature plummets as soon as Chloe crosses the abandoned mansion's threshold. She tells herself it's just a cold evening, with winter not too far around the corner. She wishes Lucie hadn't refused to come with her. This podcast is supposed to be a two-woman operation after all, but she'd chickened out. She should be dying to visit this place, to experience its grisly history, up close and personal. This one is sure to be the hit they need to keep the podcast going, to really boost their audience.

Chloe moves further into the building now, her phone torch illuminating the rooms in disjointed bursts of brightness. It's a strange pieced-together place, built from the remnants of a 13th century sandstone castle, once a mansion, then a children's home, then abandoned at the southwest edge of the city. She moves through the entrance hall, finding moss and mould nestled in every nook and crevice. In one gap, she spots a spider so big it surely belongs in a tropical country, not the dark corners of Scotland's capital. When her torchlight lands on it, the creature retreats quicky into a hole in the wall, to lurk in shadows, unseen. She shivers and walks quickly on.

Holding her digital voice recorder up to her mouth with her free hand, she begins. "Redhall mansion has seen a lot in its time, and of course the castle it was built from was the site of a bloody battle, besieged by Oliver Cromwell himself. But, dear listeners, we're not here for a history tour today." She says the next part slow, savouring the words on her lips, letting her tone soften and lilt. "This is the site where, three years ago, Red Cameron began to take his victims."

She's memorised the route from the news reports, through what was once a grand entrance hall, past empty and blocked off rooms

117

with boarded up and broken windows. The décor displays a mish-mash of styles from the building's various uses over the past century, though some of the grand original features still creep through attempts at modernisation. Panelling and intricate cornicing adorn the walls and ceilings while characterless modern doors hang from rusted hinges, creaking as Chloe walks past them. The wallpaper is slick with black mould or graffiti, peeling and torn at every edge, while any woodwork appears rotten and damp. This journey was likely the last thing the victims saw before their demise – a dark thought, but she feels a certain thrill in imagining it. If Lucie were here, she'd probably accuse her of being morbid – her friend was more interested in ghost stories and tame local mysteries, but Chloe knew that listeners would be drawn to more gruesome ones. When she found out about Redhall, she couldn't pass up the chance to come here.

After passing the kitchen, she winds her way to an ornate, red-stained wooden staircase. She looks up into the darkness above – somewhere up there, the murders happened. She holds her breath and starts the ascent, up past more mould-ridden halls, rooms blocked off with scrap metal and wood, a crumbling fireplace that looks too big for the room, then finally, at the top of the third-floor, winding stair, there's a grand room with tall ceilings, and carpets stained red-brown. She knows straight away that this is the place. At the door, she steps over the torn and muddied police tape and shines her torch into the dark space. A foul smell greets her, and a whistle of wind sweeps inside from another falling-apart fireplace, before making a break for a gap in one of the half-boarded up broken windows. Like the mansion is letting out a sigh. She surveys the rest of the room. All along the walls, paint bubbles in diseased formations, blistering and peeling, as if it's in the process of melting.

Chloe takes a breath. "Red Cameron of course claimed he wasn't responsible for the deaths of the residents he tricked and lured here." A sound echoes behind her, and she stops narrating. She turns. In the furthest corner, she's sure that a shadow just moved. She stares at it for a long moment before deciding it was probably just a tree or bird outside casting movement across the floor.

She shakes the tension loose from her shoulders and continues. "In this room, Red Cameron slaughtered his victims. He sliced them up with a weapon that was never found. Though when he was questioned about it, he only smiled, mumbling under his breath, words that no one could decipher." She speaks quietly now to build atmosphere – listeners lap this stuff up, the horror of the act, lingering on every dark and dangerous detail. "After he killed his victims, he soaked their clothing in their own blood. Only parts of the bodies were ever recovered, their remains scattered around the abandoned corners of the mansion." She can't help the chill that runs down her spine as she recounts it. "A trail or a puzzle to solve? If the police had a theory, they never shared it with the public. With the investigation now closed, we may never know for sure why Red Cameron acted the way he did. Though, dear listeners, that doesn't stop us trying to answer these questions. To come to the place where this all happened, to get inside his mind. It's hard not to wonder what was going through his head, what drove him to commit such horrific acts." She holds the voice recorder up, lets it record the sigh of the wind.

She moves further inside the room. She looks up, and the ceiling suddenly feels dizzyingly close. It's speckled with cobwebs and more creeping mould, and the remains of wires and rusted hooks that must have once held chandeliers. She's never really been claustrophobic, but she feels it now.

I shouldn't be here.

A primal instinct, but she tries to ignore it, swallows down the bile rising in her throat. This episode is going to be a hit, she knows it. "There's definitely an energy in this room. It feels like something very, very bad happened here. Regular listeners will likely know the history of Red Cameron." She pauses for effect. "That in his trial he claimed a demon at Redhall made him do it."

As she says the final sentence, her recorder screeches with sudden static and something moves in the corner of her vision. Turning to face that dark corner again, an image appears there before her: A twist of mangled limbs, melded together, a seeping jumble of exposed bones and bloody muscle. Too vivid to be real. They almost look like they're moving, writhing, stretching out, reaching for her.

She closes her eyes. When she opens them again, the image is gone. It's just an ordinary shadowy corner, with a crumpled pile of curtains, bunched up in a grotesque formation. Her mind is playing tricks on her.

Then there's a clatter from below. *Footsteps.* She's sure of it. Chloe tiptoes to the doorway, and hunkers down, listening carefully to what can only be the sound of someone walking around downstairs. They stop directly below her, and she holds her breath. She could sneak down to see who it is – maybe Lucie decided to come after all... Instead, she pulls out her phone and types a quick text to her, *"are you here?"* The message fails to send, no signal.

For a while, there's silence beneath, punctuated by the sound of Chloe's breaths and the whistling wind. Then, comes a scraping sound. Piercing, loud, as if someone is carving into the ceiling below her. As this is happening, her voice recorder shrieks again with static, then it's playing her own words back to her, *"in his trial he claimed a demon at Redhall made him do it."*

She taps the buttons on the device as her own voice grows shrill from it, repeating the words over and over. Louder and louder, until her voice becomes a scream. A screech. Then there are other words.

"What happens when the blood runs dry? What happens when the blood runs dry... the blood runs dry... the blood runs dry... the blood runs dry."

Words she never said. Panicking, she throws the recorder to the ground. It breaks apart and the recording stops. So too does the scraping sound below.

She slumps in the doorway. Lucie was right and she should have listened to her gut when she entered this room. She shouldn't have come here.

She pulls her knees to her chest, keeping her breathing as quiet as possible, waiting for whatever is below to find her. But nothing comes, no footsteps moving up the stair. No sound at all, like the mansion is holding its breath. Could she have imagined the sounds as well?

Finally, regaining feeling in her legs, she heads past the police tape and into the winding stairwell. Part of her, the sensible part, wants to run straight to the front door, out of the mansion, and down the street to her car. But she can't stop thinking about the footsteps below, the scraping, the static on her broken recorder. She came here for a story, and maybe this is all a part of it. Either way, she wants to find out, so she tiptoes down the creaking stairs, down into what once must have been a dining room below where she'd been standing just moments ago. She thinks of the scratching she heard and looks up. Etched roughly into the ceiling are four words:

The blood runs dry.

She looks around the room and drags across a chair, then a sturdy side unit beside it. She positions them carefully, making sure they're stable before she climbs up until she can just reach the ceiling. She traces a finger along the freshly carved marks, but when she tries to take a photo of them with her phone the words on the screen appear to merge into a red blur. Then she notices something else: She has signal again. Jumping down, she scrolls to her contacts and calls Lucie.

"Chloe?" Her friend answers with a sigh. "What's up?"

"Were you at Redhall today?" she asks.

"No. Chloe, I told you that I didn't want to, and your obsession with the place is –"

"Yes, I know, too gruesome, morbid," she cuts in. "But like, you didn't decide to come anyway, last minute?"

Lucie lets out a breath. "No. I'm at home." A pause, then, "What's going on? Are you okay?"

"I'm here, at the mansion. I came to record the podcast."

"What?" There's an edge to her friend's voice as she says it. "You went on your own? It's the middle of the night."

Chloe shakes her head. "I didn't exactly want to get seen sneaking in. Plus I thought it would make the atmosphere better. You know that's important for our listeners, not that you seem to care." She glances to the windows, no light now coming through their cracked edges. It's pitch black outside. Even the moon seems like it's been snuffed out.

121

"Are you still there?" Lucie's voice sounds tinny, distorted. "I don't think the signal is very good."

"I… there's someone here. Or there *was* someone here. They left a message, and I just…"

Chloe stands on the side unit again and looks up at the markings, shining her phone torch up, she brushes her hand over the words. In the indent, her finger catches something sharp. A shard of what looks like bone broken off in the gap. She snatches her hand away. Her finger is bleeding. When she looks up again, the bone shard and letters are turning red, gleaming blood spreading into the gaps.

"The blood runs dry," she whispers. *"What happens when the blood runs dry?"*

"What?" Lucie says. *"Blood?* Okay, you're really freaking me out now."

"The blood runs dry," Chloe says again, a coldness running up her arm, from her finger all the way to her chest. "Lucie, you need to come here. You need to come to the mansion. Please, won't you come?"

"I can't just trek out to the other side of the city in the middle of the night. I told you, I can't do this anymore," Lucie says. "This podcast… your obsession with this case, it's too much, don't you see?"

"I know, but please, just come. We can do this episode, one last time together. Then it will be over. Please."

"You're worrying me, okay, so just leave now and call me when you're home?" Lucie says. "We can talk about the podcast tomorrow."

"I can't leave," Chloe says. "Not until… not until you come here. It'll all make sense then. Please, Lucie, don't leave me alone here. I need you."

There's a long pause, and Chloe stares at the four words again, the letters seeming to writhe together, just like the disjointed limbs in her vision from earlier. There's a rush of air from behind her as if a door has been opened, and her phone buzzes with static. It stays on long enough for Lucie to reply, "I'll be there soon, okay, just don't –" It cuts out, and Chloe lets the phone drop to the floor. She doesn't need it anymore.

She feels the figure's presence even before she turns to see him. He looms, half in shadow, half in torchlight, pushed into the corner of the room as though he's part of the peeling wallpaper. He has long limbs, joints gnarled like they've been stitched together. A patchwork of fabric tangled with long wet hair hangs down his back. It's dark red, the colour of dried blood. He's holding something like a staff, but on closer inspection she sees it's a long bone, sharpened and stained red. She finds she cannot look away from him, this creature, brilliant and bloody, with a deep red glow in his eyes.

"The blood runs dry," the figure says in a rasping voice. "It must not be so. You will fix it."

She nods, mesmerised by the patterns in his patchwork clothes, and the *tap, tap, tap* of his bone-hewn staff on the hard floor, rhythmic like the dripping of water. Or of blood. He holds out the staff, and she takes it from him.

"Yes, I will fix it," she says, and they share a smile.

Then he retreats back into the darkness, leaving her standing in the cold, damp room, staring at the carved words until they're all she can think about. She understands them now.

The dark shroud of the ruined mansion is later pierced by a flash of headlights – Lucie has finally come to her. Her four-wheel drive stops on the quiet street outside, and she steps out. She's in her pyjamas still. As she walks up the driveway, towards the mansion's embrace, her blonde hair billows in the wind, straw-like.

Before Lucie can see her, Chloe heads inside the building, leaving the front door open. She heads upstairs, to the top floor, the grand finale.

Lucie calls her name when she comes inside, but Chloe doesn't answer, she just waits, tapping the staff on the floor, rhythmic and ready.

When Lucie finally arrives, torch in hand, following the tapping as Chloe knows she must, Chloe is standing there in the centre of the

123

final room. She's barefoot now, toes curling into the red-stained carpet.

"Chloe? Why are you just standing there?" Lucie asks as she comes inside the room. She's shivering. Chloe doesn't feel the cold anymore.

She doesn't reply, only tilts her head a little, takes in the vision of her friend better. She came here to learn the mystery of the mansion, and now is the time to solve it. Lucie will help her with the first part of the puzzle. This was always supposed to be a two-woman operation, after all.

Lucie has frozen, a few feet away from Chloe. "Is that … what the hell… is that a bone?"

Chloe looks down at the staff held tight in her hand. It's light and smooth, sharpened at the end, reflecting crimson in the glare of the torch. She steps towards her friend, holding it aloft. A waft of cold air sweeps up from below as all the doors in the mansion slam shut.

"Thank you for coming," Chloe says. "The blood runs dry. But it must not be so."

Behind Chloe, hidden in her shadow, the red creature follows with a bloodthirsty grin.

A Tiding
Timothy J. Jarvis

On the evening Mark was to go with Colin to the dank garret in Kentish Town where dwelled the King of the City of Paste and Tin, it was warm for late November, but dreary – the gibbous moon overhead leered down from out of a scum of cloud. The two men had arranged to meet on the High Road, out front of the underground, at closing time, but when Mark got there, a few minutes late, there was no sign of the nervy odd fellow. He waited, stood leaning against a wall next to the entrance to the tube, watching huddles of drunks who'd been kicked out of the pubs stumbling down the street, squabbling. Then it began drizzling, slicking glistering reflections to the tarmac, hunching folk into their coats, and he took shelter in the entrance to the station.

After a short while the rain eased. Mark was considering leaving when he saw Colin standing at a bus stop over the road. Whether he'd just alighted or had been standing there some time, Mark couldn't be sure. He seemed even more agitated than before, clutched his carrier bag in his left hand. Mark attracted his attention by waving. Paying no attention to the traffic, Colin hopped down from the kerb and crossed over. A taxi driver, forced to brake, sounded his horn.

Colin grabbed Mark's arm, started to pull him back into the road. Mark set his heels. "What's going on?"

"I was followed. I think I've lost him, but he'll know where we're headed! We need to get there before him. And before the moon sets. That was made very clear to me. Hurry up!"

And Colin ran back into the road once more, darting in front of a white van.

Mark had met Colin only a few days before. It had been the evening of his fortieth birthday, though he'd not felt inclined to celebrate. He should have had a lot to raise a toast to: promotion to Associate Professor at the London university where he taught Cultural Studies and Sociology; the eight-year anniversary of his marriage to Natalie; his daughter, Cecily's first parents' evening. But two months previously, he'd got hold of some tabs of acid for one of his PhD students, Genevieve, a young woman who was writing a thesis on psychedelics and counter-culture. She'd not heeded his advice about taking them in a safe space, but had instead dropped two that night at the student union bar, on the top floor of the university building, had had a bad trip, and flung herself from the terrace. Mark heard she'd taken two days to die, drifting in and out of tortured consciousness.

Somehow the whole thing came out, and he underwent disciplinary proceedings and was suspended from his job. Natalie initially stood by him. But then the tabloids got hold of some texts between Mark and Genevieve, presented them in the most sordid light, and Natalie left him, taking Cecily with her, and filed for divorce.

At that time then, seeing censure on every face, he tended to avoid company when he could, preferring to spend his evenings alone, solacing his woes with whisky. That day however, feeling he ought to at least mark the occasion in some way, he decided to go to his local, the Saracen's Head, for a meal and a pint or two.

The sky was clear, and it was colder than usual for the time of year. Shed foliage, drifted by a strong breeze, was banked against front garden walls along his street, and he kicked through the heaps, sending flurries of dead leaves into the air.

On reaching the pub, he ducked under the low lintel, into the warm, and his sullen temper, already improved a little by the bracing walk, brightened still further. The Saracen's Head is a convivial old boozer. Many of its appointments are relics of its Victorian origins. Wooden screens, inset with panes of etched glass, partition the space; the bar is mahogany and pine, ornately carved; and a lapis-tile dado runs round the walls. After dark the place is lit only by a few dim standard and table lamps, with just cracked and fly-spotted mirrors to multiply the light, but the effect is homely, not dingy. The landlady is justly proud of the array of real ales she stocks, and her husband, of the simple, but delicious, traditional fare he cooks.

There was a group of regulars drinking at the bar, an Irish wolfhound slumbering at their feet. When Mark crossed over to buy a beer and peruse the menu, they greeted him warmly, though he was a stranger to them. He ordered the special, pigeon pie served with buttered greens, took his pint, and found an empty table in a nook in the saloon bar, at the front of the pub, by a window which looked out on the street. He got out the book he'd brought with him: a trite, poorly written work of sword and sorcery, a genre he'd found himself turning to for salve in the preceding months. It was entitled *Ferule of the Preceptor*, and was part four of the *Rule of the Decepter* saga (the publishers insisted on the rhyming titles, thinking it a strong gimmick; the author, under contract, but increasingly disgruntled, came up with some awful names for later instalments – a nadir was reached with that of the seventh volume, *Drool of the Elector*, whose contrived plot did indeed centre around a ballot paper spoiled by slobber). On the book's cover was a depiction of the eponymous instructor: a severe man, with a grizzled beard, who wore a robe, and was standing before a blackboard on which were scrawled some arcane ideograms. In one hand he held a stick of chalk and in the other the titular ferule, from which a greenish glow emanated. A magpie was perched on his left shoulder, its head cocked inquisitively. Superimposed on the image were the author's name and the book's title, embossed, silver, in a sham-runic font. Mark sat enjoying his beer and his book, and his temper continued to improve.

Engrossed in his reading, it wasn't until a savoury aroma rose to his nostrils that he realised the landlady had set his pie down before him. The dish was delicious, chunks of tender pigeon flesh and smoked lardons in a rich gravy, encased in shortcrust pastry. The good food lifted his spirits still further. When he'd finished eating, Mark pushed his plate from him and, slouching down in his seat and stretching out his legs, gave a sigh of contentment. Taking up his pint, he took a draught, returned to his reading.

On finishing his drink, he went up to the bar to get another. As he waited while the landlady pulled it, the regulars engaged him in conversation, canvassing his opinion on a celebrity scandal that had recently provoked the censure of the tabloids. Their warmth towards him finished the work the book, beer, and tasty pie had started, entirely dispelling his gloom. Which is why, when Colin approached, a short while later, after Mark had returned to his alcove, waved vaguely at an empty chair and mumbled, "Mind if I join you?" Mark did not rebuff him.

Colin was short, paunchy, jittery – turning his head with jerky movements to look about him all the while – and dressed in threadbare, rumpled, and dun-coloured garments, dull green chinos and a brown corduroy jacket with leather elbow patches, his only flash of colour some bright red and blue knitted socks; he looked a city sparrow that had somehow found its way inside the pub, but could not then find a way out – plump from feeding on scraps, but mangy and fraught. In his right hand, he clutched an orange plastic supermarket carrier bag.

The two men introduced themselves, then chatted generally, discussing the unseasonably bitter weather and the Saracen's Head's range of ales, but their conversation was awkward; Colin seemed distracted, and Mark had the impression he was building up to broaching a topic of some significance to him, that the grotesque little laps at his beer were to stoke his courage. But then, sighting a dartboard in the corner of the pub, he launched into a tedious monologue on the game, and Mark thought his intuition had been awry, and that, whatever the cause of Colin's agitation, the man was merely a pub bore, that breed of lonely individual whose lives lack anything of interest, and who, desiring companionship, haunt watering holes in the hopes of snaring strangers in the toils of politeness. Mark groaned inwardly, let Colin's chatter blur to a dull drone in his ears and considered how he might extricate himself.

But Colin had been nerving himself up to raise a matter of great moment to him after all: in the midst of his rambling, he said, without preamble, "I see you're also collecting…"

Here he paused, winced, and kneaded his nape with his right hand. Then took a sip of his beer and choked, sputtered – his chest heaved, his face turned red. Over Colin's shoulder, Mark could see the antique clock on the mantelpiece over the pub's hearth and, uncomfortable, stared at it, watching the jerky gyring of the second hand till the fit had passed. Then Colin hawked noisily and spat into a handkerchief taken from the breast pocket of his shirt. After peering at the clot of sputum a moment, he balled up the cloth and returned it to his pocket.

"...collecting for the King of the City of Paste and Tin," he continued finally. "The Lord of the Devil's Blood Drop."

"The Devil's Blood Drop?" Mark echoed after a moment's pause.

He'd taken to carrying around with him an antique silver locket, a keepsake of Gen, something she'd left behind in the hotel room when they'd last met, and which he'd planned to return to her the next time he'd seen her, which had never happened. He had, without thinking, taken it from his pocket and was fiddling with it, pressing the catch to open it, then snapping it shut, again and again. Its chain lay whorled on the table top.

Colin pointed at the locket, then at *Ferrule of the Preceptor*, which Mark had left splayed, to keep his place, on the table, before looking at Mark and raising his eyebrows.

Mark put the locket back in his trouser pocket.

Colin continued to stare at him. "You should be more careful. There are those who'd steal rather than make their own collections."

"What?"

"Don't worry, though. I'd never do that."

Mark drummed his fingers on the table. "I'm sorry, but I've not the faintest idea what you're on about."

"I came over here because I noticed the book. The locket made it certain. But really I saw it as soon as I came into the pub. There's a haunted look of desperate hope. Marks us out."

Taking up his book again, Mark feigned reading. When, after a minute or so, Colin had not left, he sighed and looked up. "My only desperate hope is that you'll bugger off, leave me alone."

Colin tugged each of his fingers in turn till the knuckles cracked. Mark cringed.

"How close are you to completing your tribute?" Colin asked.

Mark rubbed his eyes with the thumb and forefinger of his left hand. "Oh Christ."

Picking up his carrier bag, Colin thrust it at Mark. "I told you, you've got nothing to worry about from me. Look, I'm nearly done."

129

Mark took the bag and looked inside, glimpsing some lurid stuff before Colin snatched it away again.

"See?"

"See what?"

Colin pinched his nose, looked quizzically at Mark, then, his finger at his lips, breathed in sharply.

"Sorry," he said. "My mistake. I'll be on my way."

Pushing back his chair, he got up and began to walk away from the table.

Mark tapped his temple. "Fucking lunatic," he muttered.

But Colin heard, turned back. "What? You think I'm mad?"

The regulars at the bar looked over. Colin eyed them warily, then sat down again and went on, now in a low voice. "I'm not. What do you know of tutelary daemons?"

"Tutelary daemons?"

Colin looked intently at Mark. "Protective spirits. Before the world fell into ignorance and greed, people believed certain places were watched over by powerful entities."

"And?"

"Those beings exist. London's, or maybe only one of London's, can be found in a garret bedsit in Kentish Town, in the guise of a sickly old man. Offerings made to him, of shiny things, can propitiate, and those he's favourably inclined towards may experience a change of luck."

Frowning, Mark leant back in his chair. As he did, he happened to glance out the leaded window and saw there a jowly man, with a shock of red curls like a clown wig, his nose pressed against the glass. He was staring intently at Colin. Mark flinched, and Colin turned to look. On seeing the flabby face at the window, he got to his feet, grabbed his carrier bag, and fled the pub.

The man at the leadlight turned away, moved out of sight.

Mark got up and headed outside. There he saw Colin's carrier bag lying on the pavement, split open. Bizarre junk was strewn about: an LP of the show of an unpleasant, liberal-baiting stand-up comic; a sheeny centrefold cut from an old pornographic magazine, the women's breasts and loins obscured by thick hatchings of black biro; an old deck of playing cards with photographs of the victims of lynchings on the back; a gaudy glass sculpture of a clown; a diamante-studded Alice band; and, weirdest of all, a merkin spray-painted bile green.

Once Mark had taken in this motley, he looked up and, in the cone of light cast by a street lamp, saw Colin tussling with the man who'd been peering in at the window. He was hulking, a giant, and wore a wool three-piece suit too small for him and strained at the seams, and black patent shoes with large buckles.

Mark hung back, watching them scuffle, unsure what to do. Then the big man flailed with his fist, splitting Colin's cheek, and Mark shouted, ran forwards, barged the giant with his shoulder. Staggered backwards, the man tripped, landed heavily on his back, and lay winded, rolling his eyes.

Colin shook his head, blinked, crossed to the giant, kicked him hard in the groin, then fell to punching him. Unable to get up or block the blows, he wallowed groaning. Mark ran over, threw his arms round Colin, and dragged him off the other man's sprawling bulk.

Grunting, the giant rose ponderously to his feet, then staggered away down the road.

Mark let Colin go, and he, pulling another orange plastic bag from his pocket, dropped to his hands and knees and scrabbled for his things. Once he had gathered them all up, he stood and glared at Mark.

"What?" Mark said.

"I was going to stave in that vat of guts and lard."

"If I hadn't knocked him down, he'd have flattened you."

"Sod off!"

Mark groaned, then kicked a stone along the gutter, before sitting down on the kerb and slumping forward, elbows on knees, chin cupped in hands. Colin stood peering down at him, absently dabbing the cut on his cheek with a handkerchief.

"I wasn't wrong, was I? That wretchedness I saw in you."

Taking his asthma inhaler from his pocket, Mark took a puff; the exertion had got him out of breath.

Colin sat down on the kerb next to him. "Don't you see? I can help, or rather the daemon I was telling you about can. I've nearly finished my collection now. I hope to be able to make my offering in a few days. Why don't you come with me?"

"Leave me alone."

"Suit yourself," Colin said, then got up and walked away.

And Mark went back into the pub and sat morosely drinking till closing time.

The next day he woke with a sore head. When he went out in the afternoon to the local supermarket he saw, walking towards him, a colleague, Angela, a professor in the History department, who'd been second supervisor on Genevieve's project and one of the most vociferous voices against Mark following the girl's death. He darted into a bookshop, but she'd seen him and, following him in, drove him outside again with her harangue.

"You miserable shit."

"Leave me alone. Please. It wasn't my fault. You know that."

"Fault?" A bitter laugh. "I've seen those texts. I know what you did. That poor girl."

A small crowd had gathered. Mark pushed Angela away, tried to force his way through, but was tripped and fell, grazing the heels of his hands. Angela crossed to him, spat. The mob dispersed. After getting to his feet, Mark wiped the spittle from the nape of his neck, went home, hunched into his coat.

That evening, he drank the best part of half a bottle of whisky. Then called Natalie.

"Hello?"

"Natalie, it's me."

"Are you drunk?"

"No. A little."

"What is it?"

"I was wondering if I could see Cecily this weekend, take her on a day trip."

"You know what the court said."

"Please, I'm begging you."

"You really are a self-pitying shit. What did I ever see in you?"

"What? Why are you being such a bitch?"

Natalie sighed. "Mark," she said, wearily, "don't call here again."

"Sorry, sorry. It's just…" he began to whine, but she'd already put the phone down.

The following evening he went back to the Saracen's Head. Colin was there. When he saw Mark, he beckoned him over.

"I've finished my collection. I'm going to present it to the daemon tomorrow night. Coming?"

Mark shrugged. Then nodded. So they arranged their meeting at Kentish Town tube.

That night, after Colin had run back out in front of traffic on the High Road, Mark followed, though more warily. On the other side, Colin scampered off into a ravel of streets scarred by a low viaduct, where 1950s council housing, Victorian terraces, warehouses, and small factories jostled. Mark was forced to break into a jog to keep up. After ten minutes or so, Colin ducked into the maw of a railway arch. Mark hesitated a moment, then followed. They passed beneath a vault of dank brickwork and emerged into a small square of grey tenements. The syrupy neglect furred Mark's teeth. Overhead was a pale and bloated moon which seemed to glisten as if damp. Colin crossed the square, Mark followed. Underfoot was a slurry of mouldering flyers, newspapers, cartons, used condoms, smeary brown paper bags, and fast-food scraps. Going up to one of the buildings, Colin waited in front of the door; it was wood, there was a window set in it that had been boarded up, and the bottom panel had been kicked in. Catching up, wheezing too hard to speak, Mark put his hand on Colin's shoulder, then took out his inhaler, pulled on it till his breathing eased. Colin peered at him the while. "You all right?" he asked. Mark nodded. "Fine now." Shrugging, Colin then opened the door with his foot, entered. Mark steeled himself, then went in after.

There were two doors leading off the hallway – both fastened with padlocks. Flocked paper covered the walls, its paisley design cankered

133

with mould. Ahead there was a wooden staircase. Colin started up it, Mark followed. Many of the treads were rotten and they had to pick their way with care.

As they climbed, they passed several doors on landings; all were, as those on the ground floor, secured by padlocks. The place was silent, save for rodents scuttling in the walls. At the top of the staircase there was a doorway from which a weak light spilled. On reaching the threshold, Colin paused a moment, crossed himself, then entered. Mark also hesitated before going in after.

The room was cramped, a garret with a slanting ceiling and just one window, a sash, in front of which a filmy curtain the colour of milky tea and stinking of stale smoke hung. It was meagrely furnished. Under the window was a bed with an iron frame. Beside it, along the wall, were ranged a bedside cabinet, wardrobe, and chest of drawers in chipboard with flaking pine veneer. On the cabinet, a mug and a Gideon Bible rested. The mug was tannin-stained within, emblazoned with a photograph of the Royal Pump Rooms at Leamington Spa without. To the front cover of the Bible had been glued a collage of snips – a brawny bare-chested young man, with pendulous dugs and tiny Jack-o-lanterns for pupils, hefting an ichthyosaurus over his head.

The odours of camphor, cold tea, and lavender mingled on the air; underneath there was a reek of urine. And then, very faint, cheap vanilla – a cloying scent that put Mark, with a pang, in mind of Gen. The room was drear and stark: a naked forty watt bulb dangling at the end of a long flex was the lone light source; there was a hearth, but no fire burnt in it; the walls were papered a drab olive; and the floorboards were bare, unvarnished. The sole vivid hue was the blowfly green of a satin counterpane which lay crumpled on the floor beside the bed, and the only ornaments were six taxidermy magpies, variously mounted and posed, four displayed on the chest of drawers and two on the mantelpiece above the grate. One of these latter was perched on an old-fashioned Bakelite telephone, beak cruelly agape.

A draft stirred the bulb; in the skittering light the stuffed birds seemed animate.

"The magpie," Colin whispered, "is the daemon's familiar."

A cranefly listlessly circled the light, whining low; nodding towards it, Colin said, with great solemnity, "Daddy longlegs. They don't bite, you know."

Mark, staring aghast at the bed, did not hear him. There, on stained sheets, lay a withered old man, in blue-and-red-checked pyjamas too large for his scrawny frame. His skin was thin and brittle as an onion's and his greasy white hair stuck up from his head in a coxcomb. The sleeves and legs of his pyjamas were rucked up, exposing spindly, pale and mottled limbs, garnetted with weeping bedsores. He lay still, save the shallow rise and fall of his ribcage, staring vacantly up at the beaten egg-white peaks of the Artex ceiling.

Taking Mark's arm, Colin pulled him towards the bed. As they drew nearer, Colin pointed out the quilted coverlet on the floor.

"Look. The mysterious quincunx."

At that moment, the old man gave a sigh, the breath rattling in his throat. Pulling free of Colin's grip, Mark stepped away from the bed. Colin fell to his knees, upended his carrier, tipping out its contents, then held each one up in turn, muttering the while.

Mark crossed over to the window. In the narrow alley below, he could see, by moonlight, a one-eyed fox scrabbling in slop spilling from an overturned bin.

When Colin had finished, the old man moaned. Seeming to take this as a sign of approval, Colin began chuckling and nodding. The old man indicated the fireplace with a trembling hand. Nodding, Colin gathered up his things, took them over to the grate, and threw them in. He got down on his haunches and heaped them, balled the playing cards, took the vinyl record out of its sleeve, which he tore in half and crumpled up, and shattered it in the hearth. Then he ripped the magazine page into strips, which he twisted into spills.

Mark looked over at him.

"That won't catch."

Colin smiled, took a lighter from his pocket, lit the spills. He poked them here and there into the pile. In moments, it was aflame. Turning to Mark, Colin bowed low.

"Ta da!"

135

He crossed back over to the bed. The old man said something to him that Mark didn't catch. Then Colin beckoned Mark over.

Mark shook his head. "Look, I want to leave. How do I find my way back to the High Road?"

"What?" Colin said.

"I'm going to go."

"But he's agreed to help you."

"I've problems enough already."

Mark began to walk out, but the old man, raising himself on his bony elbows, fixed Mark with a glare, and said in a high nasal voice, "You really are a self-pitying shit."

Mark started; even the intonation was uncannily reminiscent. He stood pale and feeble, hanging onto the doorjamb, staring at the old man over his shoulder.

"Come here," Colin said, kindly. "Listen to what he has to say."

Mark staggered over.

Reclining once more, the old man began to speak. "I so love shiny things. All kinds of things that glitter, or glisten. And brightly coloured things, gaudy stuff."

He grinned.

"Handkerchief," he demanded, looking up at Colin.

Colin took one from his pocket and offered it. Reaching out a liver-spotted claw, the old man snatched it, took several wheezing breaths, hawked, and, holding it to his mouth, spat. When he took it from his lips, a dark clot clung to the cloth. After peering at this for some time, with the air of a crone scrying in tea leaves, he swaddled it up, threw the balled handkerchief from him.

Then he turned his head, gazed upon Mark once more.

"As you can see, I'm old and feeble now. It wasn't always so. Once I walked abroad and men quailed at my approach."

He dug in his nose with a filthy fingernail. "But now I can't leave here, so I'm always on the lookout for people to act as my proxy."

"Proxy?"

"To go out on his behalf," Colin answered. "Gather the offerings the city makes him."

136

"That's right," the old man said. "You'll be directed to these gifts. There'll be seven, there's always seven. All you need do is collect them and bring them to me, and I'll reward you with a peck of good fortune."

He drubbed the mattress with his heels, raising a haze of dust, clawed the air, shrieked, "Shiny, shiny, shiny!"

At first Mark cringed back, but then he sniggered, turned to Colin, and tapped his temple. Colin frowned, looked away, hissed, "Be respectful."

"Well, it's up to you," the old man said.

He shifted slightly in bed, grimaced, and farted. It stank of rot.

"Now leave. If you choose to collect the offerings, return when you have them all. You won't find me here in the daytime. Come after seven in the evening. And no later than ten thirty. At ten thirty, I sleep."

Turning his head, the old man looked at Colin.

"Colin, you have done well by me and will be rewarded."

Colin gave a crow of triumph and broke into a gawky jig.

"Cease that," the old man said, "or I might think to withdraw my favour."

Colin stopped cavorting, cast his eyes down, and began to scratch, frantically, the side of his head, above his left ear. A habit, Mark realised – there was a bald patch fretted there.

The old man slouched back onto the mattress, broke wind again. Mark tugged Colin's sleeve.

"I think we should leave."

Colin nodded. "He'll need to sleep," he murmured. "We need him to sleep, the whole city needs him to sleep, for his dreams sustain the place."

They left the room, descended the stairs, went outside, and began returning, the way they had come, to the High Road.

When they emerged into the open again, after passing under the railway arch, Colin stopped, tilted back his head, and stared at the sky.

"They've never seemed so dazzling!" Colin exclaimed.

Mark looked up, saw the sky was overcast. He strode on ahead, and after a moment Colin noticed and scurried to draw close once more.

"So…" he said, a little breathless.

"So, what?"

"Will you collect for him?"

"He's a senile old man."

Scowling, Colin kicked at a pile of leaves. Then, catching sight of something, he bent down, hollered with glee.

"A twenty-pound note. Things are looking up already."

Mark gave a low whistle. "Twenty pounds, eh? All your troubles are over."

"Well, it's a start, isn't it?" Colin said weakly.

Looking into his face, Mark felt a pang. "No, no. You're right, of course. Sorry."

"There's no need for envy. Do as he instructed you and your luck'll change too."

Just then the giant came barrelling out of the dark mouth of an alley, flung himself at Colin. He swung a wild blow with a mole wrench, which would have caved Colin's skull had it struck, but he tripped and staggered, then went down hard, hit his head on the kerb.

Colin started to cackle. Mark crossed over, and went down on haunches beside the man on the ground. A trickle of blood ran in the gutter, into a storm drain. Mark felt for a pulse.

"Christ! I think he's dead." He turned to Colin.

Who rubbed his hands together in glee. "See? What did I tell you. Things are looking up for me!"

"What are you talking about?"

"Come on, leave him. Let's go."

Mark took out and brandished his mobile phone. "I'm calling an ambulance."

"Do what you like," Colin said. Then he scarpered.

After watching him flee, Mark started to dial 999. But then thought better of it. He'd seen a phone booth on the way to the tenement, so he found that, and called the emergency services from there, before running off and catching a bus home. He hadn't given his name. When he got back in, weary, he undressed and threw himself down on his bed.

On being roused by his alarm clock the following day, Mark felt sluggish and gut-sore, as if he'd been bingeing.

His day was uneventful. He went out walking the streets of London, drifting, not caring where his feet took him. He scanned graffiti for hidden messages, sought other worlds in the reflections in puddles. Returning home in the evening, he discovered a message on his answer machine from Natalie's lawyers; she was taking out an injunction against him.

So he went out to a local newsagent's, bought a packet of cigarettes. As soon as he left the shop, he lit one, his first in nearly ten years. He choked, felt a little sick, but it calmed his roiling brain, and he smoked it to the filter, lit another right away. Then wandered back to his flat. His way took him along a road that followed the spine of a ridge, a vantage offering a prospect, to the south, of the river basin from the City to the Isle of Dogs, and on a clear day as far as the television transmitter at Crystal Palace – one half, with the mast that bristled to the north at Alexandra Palace, raising hairs on the nape of anyone taking in the view, of an oneiric dipole that flung a net of dreams over the city.

The night was cold and misty, and the office towers were hazed, as if seen through a scrim. As Mark stood, smoking a third cigarette, he happened to glance down at the ground and read, chalked on the asphalt, the words, "Look up". Reflexively, he did, and saw, twined around a tree branch overhanging the pavement, a length of silver tinsel.

So he ended up collecting for the old man after all.

The second tribute was a plastic spleen taken from an anatomical model in a public library. It was iridescent purple. He knew it for, on the table in front of the model, there was a children's biology textbook with a magpie-shaped bookmark marking the page describing the functions of the organ.

The third of the city's gifts was a seven-inch single by a dull and short-lived indie band, which Mark came across in a charity shop. He took its title, 'One for Sorrow, Two for Joy', as a sign. When he got home and drew the record from its sleeve, he had confirmation of his hunch – it was pressed in silver vinyl.

The fourth was a paperback crime novel he found in a second-hand bookshop on top of a stack waiting to be shelved. He was attracted by its cover – a pink sports car driving along a desert road beneath a lurid sky. The author's name was emblazoned in big blue foil-embossed letters, but the title was in a more modest type, so it wasn't until Mark got closer that he made out, 'Jaybird'. He reached for the book. Another customer made to grab it at the same time, and their hands struck, flinched away. Mark stammered apologies, looked up.

Stood before him, wincing, was a woman about his age.

"Sorry," Mark said. "Wasn't paying attention."

The woman made no reply at first, but picked up the book, then looking at Mark slightly askance, one eyebrow raised, read from its back cover. Her voice was lilting, gently accented.

"'Things were not going well for Alex O'Malley, P.I. Her most recent client had lost his head – literally. His killers were hunting her down. And worst of all her new shoes were giving her blisters…' Blah, blah, blah. 'A sexy thrill ride…' Blah, blah. I don't think you're the target audience for this, you know. What do you want with it? Are you making a collection of the most garish trash you can find?"

Mark paled.

She laid her hand on his shoulder. "You all right? Something I said?"

Mark collected himself, fixed his face in a grin. "Fine. Had you worried though, didn't I?"

Bemused, she shook her head. Then smiled. She had a large gap between her front teeth, a pretty flaw.

"Really, what do you want with a book like that?"

"Gift. Why do you want it?"

"Actually, I don't. I just wanted to skim a few pages. To sneer at it."

Then she pinched her lower lip between her thumb and forefinger. "Gift for who?"

"A friend who appreciates trash."

Nodding, she handed him the book. "Fine. Well, perhaps see you."

"All right."

She turned, walked towards the door of the shop. Mark gazed after her. Then she wheeled about, caught him, smiled. He reddened.

"So," she said. "Drink?"

Mark peered at her, rubbed his eyes. "What?"

"Drink?"

"Oh. When?"

She shrugged, pursed her lips.

"Now?" Mark asked.

She laughed. "Fine. I'm Marguerite, by the way."

"Mark," Mark said.

"Mark," she repeated. "Okay, buy your book, Mark, and let's go. There's a nice pub just down the road."

Marguerite was French, from a small town near Paris. She'd moved to London in her early twenties and lived in the city ever since. By coincidence, she was also an academic, taught fine art at a small private university in Kent. Mark and Marguerite found they shared many interests, and they struck up a friendship. Over the next weeks they went on some long walks together, visited art galleries, saw films, grew closer and closer.

Marguerite was nothing like her namesake flower, with its open bright face, thick stem, and clumsy bobbing, being small, dark, and having a dancer's taut grace. But when Mark mentioned this, she told him that the name actually meant 'pearl'. "They come in all colours, you know. There are even some from Tahiti that are black." Then she pointed at a brooch she wore. "Look." There, in a silver setting, was a single greenish orb. It shimmered.

"That's beautiful."

"It is, isn't it? My parents gave it to me when I left France."

Mark went on collecting the city's offerings. He wondered if his luck was looking up because his efforts had met with the old man's favour.

The fifth item was a gold umbrella, left behind on the tube.

The sixth was the calling card of a dominatrix (professional name Raven, clad in black-and-white fetish-wear in the photograph, and, most tellingly, with six gold studs through her lower lip). Mark chanced upon it, one spring evening, while walking from work to meet Marguerite and some of her friends for drinks in Islington. As he passed by a telephone box in Russell Square, a dazzle of sunlight off the panes of its door attracted his notice, and glancing over he saw, through the blaze, the tart card stuck up above the phone inside.

He opened the door, then, before reaching out to take the card, looked about to see if he was observed. There, on the other side of the road, leaning against the black-and-white pole of a Belisha beacon, was the burly man who'd attacked Colin, twice, and who, Mark was sure, had died after cracking his skull open on a kerb in a backstreet in Kentish Town. He was staring at Mark. He smirked, waved, then capered grotesquely out into the road.

Mark watched transfixed with horror. The wattles on the brute's neck quivered. He gestured obscenely.

Then a black cab driver, waiting at the crossing, sounded his horn. The man roared, reached into his pocket, drew out a coin or stone, flung it at the taxi's windscreen. The glass whited over. Spinning on the ball of one foot, he crowed, head thrown back.

The driver got out of his cab. Darting at him, the giant butted him in the face, then turned and ran off. Groaning, the cabbie sank to his knees. Mark's pent-up breath escaped him in a rush and he crossed over.

He helped the cabbie to his feet, then supported him as he staggered over to the pavement and sat down. His nose was bloody, but other than that he seemed merely dazed. Still, Mark waited till a small concerned group had gathered before sidling off.

He crossed back over to the telephone box, picked up the calling card, and went to meet Marguerite and her friends. He remained watchful the rest of the evening, but did not see the giant again.

Mark's flat was small – the ongoing cost of the divorce had depleted his savings – the bedroom cramped, the furniture packed tight, and one night his and Marguerite's writhings in bed jolted his wardrobe, juddering to the edge and over a cardboard box that was on top, the box in which he kept the tributes he was collecting. It turned in the air as it fell, tipping its contents on their twined bodies. The crime novel struck Mark on the brow, the tinsel floated down and settled round Marguerite's neck like a trashy boa. After a moment's perplexity, she broke into cackles. Mark joined her, though he wasn't quite sure what was so funny.

Once her mirth had waned, she looked about, frowned at the tart card.

"What is all this stuff? I thought that book was a gift."

"Oh right. Sorry, I lied about that." He thought quickly. "It's a project I'm working on, an analysis of this kind of superficial cult of gaudy that has taken hold of society. It's just an idea at this stage really."

"I see..."

"What? You don't sound convinced."

"Nothing. Really."

"No, tell me. I won't mind, I swear."

"All right. It's just I find your research, your thinking, odd somehow. My work, you see, I engage with it wholeheartedly, throw myself in, but your discipline calls for distance, an unimpassioned stance..."

"What do you mean?"

"I'd have made something out of all this stuff, you, you'll just analyse and archive it."

"Hmm... It's called intellectual rigour."

Marguerite, ignoring him, spotted the seven-inch and clapped her hands together and cried out. "I used to love this band. Where did you find it?"

"In a charity shop."

She dipped her head, looked up at him through her fringe. "Do you really need it?"

"Well..."

"I'd really, really like it."

Mark, chary of letting Marguerite see his panic, told himself he could get hold of another copy of the record.

"Okay. I'm sure we can come to some kind of arrangement."

Marguerite grinned, then looked at him coy. "Yeah. Maybe you could give me a lesson in that 'intellectual rigour'?"

They were woken later that night by a siren. Marguerite nestled into Mark.

"I was having a really strange dream. I was…"

Mark cut her off. "No, don't tell me."

"Why not?"

"I don't dream," he said. "When other people tell me their dreams I feel this… This lack, I guess."

She turned to him, took one of his hands in hers. "Hey."

He looked at her. "Sorry. That was stupid. Go on, tell me about it."

Letting go of his hand, Marguerite pulled her hair back from her face, tying it in a loose knot at her nape.

"Are you sure?"

"Yeah, of course."

"So, in my dream I was the first living thing to walk on land. I swam to the shore, was cast up on the beach by a breaker, and lay there, gills gasping, on the black sand. It was night, and there was a storm raging overhead. At first I thought I would die, but then felt a set of lungs grow within me, and I could breathe. My fins became stumpy limbs and I began to crawl up the beach towards the treeline. I felt elated, but also sad to abandon the sea."

Mark shook his head, then reaching out to cup her face in his hands, kissed her.

Marguerite pulled free.

"Is it really true you don't dream? You must dream as much as anyone else. Perhaps it's only you don't remember your dreams?"

"I suppose so. Though to me it really seems as if I don't dream at all."

"Strange."

He looked askance at her. "I'm strange? Really?"

She glowered, reached behind her for a pillow and landed a blow on him with it. Then they fell about, laughing.

Mark found a replacement for the seven-inch online, on an auction site, the following evening, was relieved to have tracked it down so easily. When it came in the post, he discovered the record wasn't silver, was just the ordinary black, but he figured it was still fine, it was still shiny, that vinyl beetle-carapace sheen.

One night, a week or so later, it being a warm evening, Marguerite and Mark went to a pub which had tables out front. They chatted, drank continental beers. Then as the sun sank low in the sky, a shaft of light, striking obliquely down between two limbs of a pollarded elm, limned Marguerite's face.

"You do realise," Mark said, "your dream got things the wrong way about?"

"What dream?"

"I wandered lonely as a tetrapod. That dream."

"What about it?"

"Evolutionary biologists don't now believe vertebrates first crawled up on land then later gained the adaptations that enabled them to live there. It's thought legs and air-breathing lungs were developed in aquatic creatures long before the first terrestrial animals."

Marguerite yawned, then rolled her eyes. "Hmm. Very interesting. I think I know why you don't dream." She dipped a forefinger in her pint and anointed his forehead with beer. "I hereby dub thee Sir Pedant Pettifogger."

Mark grimaced, wiped his face with his sleeve. "I think it *is* interesting. I think it's weird and really fascinating."

She smiled softly. "You know, I guess it is."

At that moment, a magpie hopped up onto their table. Mark startled and Marguerite cackled at him, scaring the bird off.

"You know Scottish folklore has it they carry round a drop of the Devil's blood under their tongues?" she said.

Mark shuddered. "What?"

"Strange, isn't it? I've always thought they were a bit sinister. I much prefer rats."

He grimaced at her.

"I know they've got a reputation for being filthy and disease ridden, but I think they're quite cute."

"Yeah, they're not. They're disgusting. And no one is forcing you to choose between magpies and rats anyway."

"I guess not."

Then Mark thought he saw Marguerite smirk, but the light was failing, and her face was in shadow. They drank some more, went for a meal, and the notion fleeted.

The seventh and final item for Mark's collection was a plastic top with LEDs that flashed when it was spun, bought in a toyshop. As the girl behind the counter counted out his change, it occurred to him he shouldn't wait to take his offerings to the old man – that hanging on to them was fraught. He decided to pay tribute that very evening.

The light in the sky had dwindled to a faint glow in the west by the time he arrived at the grey square in Kentish Town, clutching a carrier bag containing his collection. Wary, he looked about him before crossing over to the old man's tenement. The front door stood open. Mark hesitated on the threshold.

Then he heard a cry. He pelted up the stairs, but when he ran into the garret room, saw the old man sitting placidly on the edge of the bed, gazing at a postcard he held.

He looked up, beckoned Mark to approach. Mark did so, and the old man held the postcard out to him. On it was a photograph of a young woman wearing a bowler hat and scanty Union Jack underwear. Behind her there was a red double-decker bus.

"Welcome to London," Mark said.

The old man shrugged, began turning the card over and over in his fingers, rapidly, so the image flickered. As Mark watched, it seemed the pretty flesh fell from the girl's face leaving a grinning hollow-eyed skull. Then the old man stopped spinning the postcard, folded it in half, and put it in the breast pocket of his pyjama shirt.

"What have you brought me, Mark?"

Mark looked about him, instinctively furtive, and saw over in a nook, by the fireplace, a large canvas holdall, full, lumpy, and with something he couldn't make out sticking up, where the zip had not fully closed.

"Your offering?" the old man prompted, but Mark ignored him, crossed over to the bag. Nearing, he could see it was a leg and an arm that jutted up, both wrenched into sickening shapes. He recognised the sleeve of a brown corduroy jacket and a flash of brightly coloured sock and realized Colin's luck had not held for long.

Turning back to the old man, Mark gestured behind him at the holdall. "Why?"

"Oh that. Well apparently Colin was flighty, went to seek the favour of another god, a god of flies who's holed up somewhere east of here, and I think hopes to claim this patch. And if there's one thing that really ticks me off, it's disloyalty."

"Who told you?"

"That's my business."

"But –"

"But nothing. Now come over here and show me what you've brought."

Mark went over to the bed and held out his bag.

"Empty it out on the floor."

Mark did so, then watched as the old man picked up and scrutinised each item in turn. When he came to the seven-inch he held it up, shrieked, "What's this sham?"

He flung the record at Mark. It just missed, arced passed him, smashed against the wall.

"Treachery! I suspected as much. Just as well I had Harris watch you. He'll bring the missing item to me."

Mark just stared.

"He'd been trying for years to get a tribute together," the old man continued, "but due to bad luck and, well, idiocy, could never do it. Never learnt to read the signs. You picked that up quickly, I'll give you that much. Anyway, Harris never did, so I've offered him another way to gain my favour. Now he acts for me whenever there is violence to be done. He might be a bit thick, but he's good at violence, is Harris."

Mark then had a vision of the giant pirouetting in the living room of Marguerite's flat, crowing up at the ceiling.

The old man spat a clot of sputum on the dusty boards and stuck his tongue out.

Mark turned and ran.

Forty minutes later he arrived, gasping, outside Marguerite's building. Blue-and-white police cordon tape was threaded through the iron railings out front. A small crowd had gathered. Mark spotted Marguerite's downstairs neighbour, Ellen, and went over to her.

"Oh Mark," Ellen said.

"What? What is it?"

"Mark, I'm sorry."

"Tell me!"

Ellen looked at him helplessly.

"Please."

Ellen sobbed.

"There was someone hiding in her flat when she came home from work. He... They've taken her to the Whittington, Mark. You should go to her."

Mark went straight to the hospital, but was told by a nurse he couldn't see Marguerite that night. She couldn't have visitors until her condition stabilised, till she was 'out of danger.'

It was past eleven by the time he arrived back at the Kentish Town tenement. He found the old man asleep in his bed with the light on, that dim bare bulb. Seizing him by his shoulders, Mark shook him awake. He opened his eyes, looked blearily about him.

"Why?" Mark yelled.

The old man grinned, belched in Mark's face. Mark cuffed him.

Rubbing his cheek where the blow had struck, the old man sneered.

"You're good at reading the signs, but other than that not too sharp. She worships another god, a god of rats and filth, with whom I've been skirmishing these past thousand years. That entity knows I recover a little of my strength with every offering presented to me, so had her compromise your collection."

Mark groaned.

148

"What? You didn't actually think she liked you, did you? You realize she knows what you did to that girl, don't you? The whole of London knows."

Mark hit the old man again, harder this time. The side of his head struck the wall. He lay there, unmoving, eyes open, but dull, like those of a fish on the slab. From his right ear ran a trickle of yellowish ichor. Mark turned and ran down the stairs.

On the pavement outside, he crouched, retched. A one-eyed fox with mangy fur, perhaps the same he'd seen when he first visited the place with Colin, padded by, chicken carcass in its jaws.

When, the anger and sickness passed, remorseful, he went back up to the garret, the bed was empty. He searched the building; the doors to the other flats were all securely fastened with padlocks as before, and there was no sign of the old man.

Returning again to the garret, Mark noticed a stuffed magpie he was sure had not been there before – now three leered at him from the mantelpiece. The new magpie was posed with a silver brooch in its beak.

He crossed over, wrenched it free, and looked for a moment at the greenish pearl set in it. Then he turned it over, and found 'Chère Marguerite' written there, in cursive script, as he knew he would.

Mark felt leaden, weary. His chest was tight. His gaze fell on the bed.

Winking at the magpie, he said, "I think I'll just have a little lie down."

After switching off the light and pushing the filthy bedclothes to the floor, he stretched himself out on the mattress and fell asleep. And he dreamt. In his dream he woke in that squalid bed, in that dank garret. He sat up. A crescent moon hanging in the sky, skull down, horns up, in rut, shone in through the gauzy curtain. By its baleful light he saw a woman dangling naked, by her ankles, from a rope tied to an iron hook set into the ceiling rose. Seven magpies flapped about her, rending her with beak and claw, taunting her with their harsh chatter. She flailed her arms, seeking to fend off the birds, setting herself swinging at the end of the rope. As she swung, she was sometimes Marguerite, sometimes Genevieve, and sometimes Natalie. She was steeped in blood, black in the wan light, trickling from many shallow wounds. And blood was flicked from the gory snaking ropes of her hair to spatter the floorboards with arcane sigils. Getting out of the bed, he made to go to her aid, but the magpies flew at him, pecking, clawing, drove him out the door, down the ramshackle staircase, and outside. He found the Victorian tenement stood alone in the midst of a waste strewn with the scattered skeletons of birds – skulls like bone callipers, vertebrae like dice, rib cages like the frames of elfin coracles, pelvises like elfin ploughshares. Mark fled from that place, pounding the brittle bones to bone dust underfoot as he ran.

When, a little further on, he collapsed, sputtering, gasping for air, his lungs two flaccid carrier bags, he reached into his pocket for his inhaler and found it wasn't there.

Our Sister Of Blackthorn

Dan Coxon

So, a huge shout-out and thank you to everyone who's subscribed since the last episode. If you haven't done it yet, please do – your support is what keeps us going!

This week I'm going to be touching on something more personal. Those of you who've met me outside of this podcast will probably know that I started Presumed Missing *because of something that happened when I was sixteen. If you listened closely to our first episode, you'll have heard me dedicate it to Emma Lawley. It's Emma's story that I'm going to tell today.*

Where to start?

With the important part, I guess. Emma was my best friend. We'd been friends since she came to our school in… year eight, I think? It was one of those immediate friendships that form when you're young – the kind of friendship that encompasses your whole world.

Emma's mum had got divorced, and they'd moved from Coventry. They lived one street down from us, on the edge of the Blackthorn Estate. A little maisonette, but plenty big enough for the two of them. I remember listening to music together in their back yard, the great concrete cliff of Speedwell House casting a shadow over their scrap of lawn. I spent more time there than I did in my own house, which makes everything that happened later so much more difficult to talk about… But yeah, we were besties, me and Em. Emma and Sophie, two peas in a pod.

Emma Lawley disappeared on 7th June 2013, a Friday. Me and her were meant to hang out at The Rooster, *our local, with a couple of boys we were seeing: James Berry and Simon Orton. Simon was my date – we'd gone to the Odeon in town a couple of times, but nothing serious. James and Emma had more of a history: six months the previous year, followed by a messy break-up when she caught him snogging someone at a party (I won't name them here, they know who they are!), then a couple of months back together before she vanished.*

And yes, of course the police looked into James. He was the first to be interviewed. Emma told her mum she was going to his flat on the Blackthorn

151

Estate, and that we were meeting up later. She left home about five p.m., but according to statements given by James and his dad, she never showed up. He came to The Rooster at seven, expecting to find her there…

Anyway – you know what we do here at Presumed Missing. *Revisit the statements, talk to the witnesses. In Emma's case, I'm heading back to Blackthorn to talk to James. My train was cancelled, so it's been a long journey to get here – but three bus rides and a thirty-minute hike later, I'm finally standing on the streets where Emma and I grew up. I won't lie, it feels strange being back.*

And James Berry? Well, we'll see.

Jim lifts the kettle from its stand and waits while the hissing dies away. Pours the water in, then adds sugar – and another, for good measure.

None of this is going to be easy.

He'd recognised Sophie's name as soon as the email landed in his inbox. Of course he had – they'd been close, the four of them, before everything that happened with Em. He rubs at his eye with the heel of his hand. Blinks away the tears. They'd had a few good months there. Maybe the last good months he had, before it all went to shit.

Taking his coffee through to the living room, Jim stares at a photo of his dad on the mantelpiece until he realises the mug is scalding his hand. Placing it down, he turns the picture to face the wall.

Fuck him. Fuck the lot of them.

Beyond his door the estate whispers and groans in the wind, plastic sheets snapping like sails.

Like lungs taking a laboured breath.

I'm standing now on one of the balconies at Speedwell House. This is the block that James Berry lived in, back in 2013. Right slap in the middle of the Blackthorn Estate.

It's exactly as you'd imagine it, really. If you've seen one block of council flats, you've seen them all. Blackthorn was built in a U-shape, with a small patch of grass in the middle – as I look down on it, it's mostly mud. There are clusters of litter here and there, packets and cans… I think I can make out a couple of abandoned pizza boxes too, their corners chewed off by foxes or rats. The balcony itself is a solid concrete ledge jutting out from the cliff of the building, the railings rusted and – Oh. Okay, so a piece just came off in my hand as I said that! Moving swiftly on…

152

No one really looks after these old council estates, do they? I can see two doors that are boarded up, the flats presumably empty. Broken windows. They all have that wire mesh in the glass, to keep them from shattering? Well, I can see one on the floor below where that doesn't seem to have been enough – it looks like someone has gone at it with a hammer.

Back in 2013, I didn't come here as much as Emma did, but I don't remember it being like this. We… Well, we were better off than the families here on the estate, I guess. Even the maisonette that Emma and her mum lived in was nicely kept, a proper home. Blackthorn always felt… edgier. The kids weren't exactly rough – James was one of the politest guys I knew – but we weren't supposed to go onto the estate after dark. Had Emma been here at night? Almost certainly, I'd say – but I'm not sure her parents knew. We did plenty that our parents didn't know about back then.

Right, I'm at James Berry's door. Before I knock, just to explain – I haven't seen him since a year after Em went missing. I've been to this flat a few times before, maybe four, or five… not many, anyway. I met his dad – a tall man, thin. He looked ancient to me at the time, although I guess he must have been about fifty. In his emails, James told me he passed away five years ago.

I can't believe… standing here, it's all coming back, you know? I'd better knock…

James? Hi. Hi, it's Sophie? Good to see you after so long. Shall we go in?

Jim watches as she taps at her phone, opening some app or other, connecting to the mic she has perched between them on the sofa cushion. Sophie hasn't changed with the years, not really. Not to look at. Her face has filled out a little, sure, her hair thicker and cut short – but it's like having the old her sitting in his living room again. He half expects Em to follow her in through the door.

Placing his hands beneath his thighs, he tries his hardest to keep them from shaking. The coffee's bitter at the back of his throat, refusing to go down.

"Okay…" Sophie draws it out, her manicured nails still tap-tapping at the screen. "I think… yes, looks like we're all set. Are you good? To talk, I mean?"

Jim grunts in the affirmative. He's very far from good.

"So, can you explain for the people listening what your relationship was with Emma, at that time?"

153

He shakes his head. "You've not told them?"

"I'd like to hear it in your own words, if that's okay. What were things like between the two of you?" Sophie leans towards him, trying to get closer to the microphone. "I remember you being on, then off, then on again, but you seemed... well, I'll let you tell it."

"Things were good. I mean, she were annoyed with me still. Over, y'know, with Jackie. But we were okay, yeah. We'd been making plans for the summer."

"Really? What sort of plans? I didn't know that."

Jim stares at the mantel, and the photo turned to the wall. "Just – just planning, y'know? Thought we'd maybe go to Europe backpacking or something. To get out of here, mainly. Do something fun. It hadn't got far, and anyway – well, clearly nothing came of it. Just stupid stuff, really."

"And she seemed okay to you? Happy?"

"Em? Yeah, always the brightest spark, she was. She burned brighter than most – you know that." He pauses. "She seemed happy to you too, right? In those days before?"

"She did."

"Well, you were as close to her as anyone. Honestly, I don't really know what you're hoping to get out of this, Sophie. You know as well as me that they never found nothing. Better forgotten, my dad said to me. Forget about her. Move on."

"And have you?"

He's suddenly very aware of the low-level noises all around them: the whisper of breeze beneath the front door, the skittering of litter in the corridors. There's a bang from somewhere deep in the building.

"Not really, no. Not completely. It's good of you to come back and see me, though. You're looking well. Not like this place. Fucking council leaving it to rot, hoping we'll all move out so they can knock it down. We won't, though. This is our home, right? I want to say that, if I'm going to be on your podcast: the Blackthorn Estate is our home, and we ain't moving. Not after everything we've done to be here, everything we've sacrificed. It wouldn't be right with Emma's memory, would it?"

Sophie shifts even closer to him. Close enough for him to reach out and grab her, if he wanted. "What do you mean by that?"

"Just… just what I said. It's our home."

"But it wasn't Emma's home, was it? Did she come here often? I didn't realise her disappearance hit the estate community so hard."

Something snaps. He stands, knocking the microphone off the sofa. His hands still won't calm down, so he thrusts them, hard, into the pockets of his jeans. "I'll fetch us some coffee – sorry, I should have offered. You want a cup? Or tea?"

"Sure – but can you tell me about Emma?"

Jim shouts through from the kitchen, his smile collapsing as soon as he's out of sight. Reaching for a clean mug, he can't help clattering them against each other, the noise like crashing cymbals in his head.

"Of course, yeah, of course. Just need a cuppa first…"

I've nipped out for a minute to record this. James is still making our drinks in the kitchen, and I told him I needed to make a call. I'm amazed by how rundown this place looks. The rust, the damage. There's a thin layer of dirt on everything. And the stains… I don't even know what they are, but some of the walls have these dark brown stains on them, almost like something is seeping through the concrete. There's a big bloom of it in James's hallway, a brownish damp patch on the wallpaper. Maybe it was always like this, and I've just forgotten – but I don't think so.

As for James himself, he looks old. Clearly the past decade hasn't been easy for him. I can't imagine what it must be like, still being here, stuck in Blackthorn. It makes me aware of my own privilege, if that doesn't sound too… well, privileged. I'm so used to the bustle of the city now.

Hang on… yes, he's calling for me. I'd best get back inside.

"Thanks for the coffee, this is perfect."

She has set the microphone back on the sofa as if nothing happened. When Jim hands her the mug, she places her phone on her lap, and he notices it's already recording.

"S'okay."

"You were saying something about Emma, before we stopped? How did people take her disappearance, here on the estate?"

He stares at the undissolved coffee granules floating in his cup. Gradually getting smaller and smaller, until, at some unmeasurable moment, they cease to exist completely.

"Em? She was… she was liked, right? I mean, you knew her same as me. She wasn't from round here, but she still had time for everyone. I lost count of the afternoons she spent here, with me and my da. Like she was one of the family, y'know? He loved her, he did, which made it all so much harder."

Sophie leans in again. "I had no idea she came here so often… was that just when you were dating?"

"Yeah. You know what it was like, being that age. We were together whenever we could manage it. That's why I never… Just some things need doing, right? You don't have no choice. I didn't approve of what happened – that wasn't me."

He's said too much. He knows it as soon as the words leave his mouth, but what did they expect? He's sacrificed more than the rest of them, hasn't he? This has been his burden most of all. His hands are shaking so badly that he has to lean forward and place his mug on the carpet.

"Sorry," Sophie is frowning now, her hand automatically drifting to her phone, making sure she has all this on the record, "do you mean you know something about her disappearance?

"I shouldn't speak to you." Jim shakes his head. "I knew I shouldn't, but they said…"

"James, is there something you're trying to tell me? It's been a long time since she disappeared, but we all want answers still. Emma's parents – they need to know what happened. Is there something you didn't tell the police?"

"The Bizzies?" He almost laughs. "Nah, wouldn't tell them the time of day. They didn't care about her – still don't care about us. Mikey spent a week in hospital after that run-in with them, didn't he? Them and the council, they'd have used Em disappearing as an excuse to pull this place down. And we couldn't have that. The estate… it's part of who we are. It's more than just the flats, you know. We're a community."

There's a pause as he watches her processing what he's told her, the questions and confusion written on her face.

Finally: "What did you do, James? Was it you?"

He lifts a hand to wipe his eye without realising what he's doing. "I loved her. You should know that better than anyone. We were in

156

love, me and her. I thought we'd spend our life together. Only, decisions had to be made."

"Is she dead? Is that what you're saying, that Emma died here?"

Jim knocks his mug as he jolts to his feet, splashing milky coffee onto the carpet – but he doesn't care. Not any more. He knew this would happen, didn't he? He told them all – and they'd told him not to worry, that getting her here was the important thing. Sophie Ward, the girl who got away. Only she hadn't, not really. No one ever left Blackthorn for good.

"Why did you have to come digging all this up? Hey?" He's shouting now but he can't help it. His hand scratches at his eye like he wants to pluck it out. "It ain't good for us, and it ain't good for you. Can't do Em any good now, either. It's just the way things are – can't be stopping that, or changing it. She's gone, but she's not gone. She's always here with us still. You don't understand, but you could, if you open your eyes, if you accept the way things must be. It's what I had to do. I loved her, and she's still here with me."

Sophie coughs. Her eyes flick to her phone again.

"James, let me get this straight – are you saying Emma died here, on the Blackthorn Estate? That you and some of the other residents covered it up, back in 2013? Can you prove this?"

"I can do better than that. I'll show her to you."

So, I haven't got much time, but I wanted to record this before James takes me to what he claims is Emma's last resting place. I never... When I approached Berry to do this interview, I never thought it would lead me here. We've had a couple of cases reopened thanks to this podcast, but this... I mean, if she's really buried here, on Blackthorn, then there's proof of an actual crime, of a murder or... covering up her death at least. James hasn't told me exactly what happened yet, but he says it'll all make sense.

Anyway, I've only got a few seconds. He thinks I'm going to the loo... I can't believe where this has gone, so I just wanted to get this down. I think... I guess he feels guilty in some way? I don't know – maybe he is guilty, maybe he did this. I have a can of pepper spray in my bag, just in case things go south, but I'm not getting that vibe from him. He just looks... sad? Resigned? Tired, too. Like this whole place. Hang on, he's coming back...

157

*

It takes them almost ten minutes to gather Sophie's things and head along the balcony and down the concrete steps, winding their way to the bowels of the building. Sophie's still recording as she goes, and she keeps stopping to narrate an observation into her phone, or describe the utter disrepair of everything that surrounds them. The microphone has been stowed away somewhere, and Jim is glad. None of this should be on the record. It was all so much easier back then, but now, in this age of amateur broadcasters and video bloggers… More than ever, Blackthorn must hide in plain sight.

Her phone they can deal with later. It won't be the first time.

The concrete grows darker as they descend. Jim doesn't know why – it's as if the building is a gigantic sponge, soaking up water from below, gradually, over the decades. If that's true, then it has soaked up so much more besides. Like a plant, or a fungal growth, the Blackthorn Estate needs to feed.

When they reach the ground floor, he pushes open a stained metal door at the base of the stairwell, and they descend again, down one flight of stairs, then another. The steps are worn in the middle by the procession of feet over the years, polished smooth by shoes in their thousands. Dim strip lights cast shadows on the concrete. The air catches in the back of his throat like fine particles of rust, scratchy and metallic on his tongue.

Jim senses Sophie tensing beside him, but he says nothing.

It's as they reach the bottom landing that she speaks, her voice thin and weak in the near darkness. There's another door in front of them, once green but now stained red and brown around the edges, like something has leaked through from the other side. It's cold, and an electric shiver runs through his bones.

"What… what is this? James? Did something happen to Sophie down here?"

He can hear the other question in her tone; the one that wonders if she is safe here, if she has maybe bitten off more than she can chew. He knows the answer to that, and her other questions, but there's no point in telling her. The time for words is long past.

158

"It's best I show you," he says, pushing the door open so she can step through. "You'll see. It'll all be clear soon."

The basement room is as big as the footprint of the estate, running beneath the tower blocks like a dry lake. The ground is packed earth, unfinished but trodden down over the years; the ceiling above is dark, featureless concrete. There's an unsettling sense of the weight above them, pushing down, the room itself little more than a trapped bubble of air that might pop at any moment.

There are no light fittings, but the occupants of the room have brought their own. Sophie can see some of the faces beyond the torches and phone screens, held in front of them like beacons. Was that Mikey Strickland? And Jackie, who Jim had cheated on Emma with, back in the day? And –

"Simon? Is that you?"

There are others too, faces she remembers but couldn't name. Fifty of them, maybe sixty, packed into the wide darkness like a congregation at church. The room stinks of wet dirt and sweat.

"What is this?" Her doubt has turned to panic now; Jim hears the fear as she tries to shine her own phone on some of the faces. "Why are you all down here? Did… what did you do to Emma?"

Jim doesn't look at her as he speaks.

"I'm sorry you had to hear it like this. It's not right. But Em – she died here, in this room. We're not proud of what we are," there's a murmur around the room, "but we do what we have to. The Blackthorn has its ways, and there's nowt we can do to change that. If it makes things better, she died helping us to live, Em did. It didn't mean nothing."

Sophie turns back to the door, but the crowd has closed behind her. Her hand is shaking so badly that the light is bouncing around, throwing shadows across the floor. Jim can see the app is still recording – not that it matters. None of this will matter soon.

When her phone light hits something uneven in the floor she staggers forward, abandoning any attempt to retreat. Jim knows what she's discovered: the outline of bones poking through the dirt, arms spread so that the ribcage cracks wide, the skull, jaw broken, half-submerged where the heart – Emma's heart – should be.

159

"I'm sorry," he says, as she vomits in the dust and four of the men move forward to pin her down. "Really I am. But you've seen what the estate's become. The council, they don't help. We have to look after ourselves. If we're to have homes to live in, then the Blackthorn needs fresh blood. Em knew that, in the end."

As the men pull back Sophie's head, Jim takes his father's knife from his pocket and steps forward. Somewhere, beyond the concrete walls, he can hear singing.

I should have thought twice before doing this... You can probably hear from my voice that I'm getting all choked up. It's strange being back here, on the Blackthorn Estate. Revisiting old haunts is always unnerving, I guess. They're never quite the way you remember them – familiar but different.

Maybe I'm remembering things wrong, but growing up, I always felt like there were people all around me, a real sense of community. Even on the Blackthorn, there were always familiar faces, folks saying hello. But something's changed – to me or to the estate, I can't say. All I know is that I'm not one of them any more. I have everything they don't.

I'm the outsider now, aren't I?

One Of The Rotten Ones

Matthew Hopkins

You'd think she'd do this when it's dark out. When it's colder. But it's July, petrol-slick iridescent heat, sky blue through the kitchen window, great swathes of plastic hanging from the ceiling, lining the floor tiles. Mum's never been one for hiding. It smells sharp and dizzy, disinfectant and lemon, surgical clean, tang of sweat, warm flesh. Our Lark will take her clothes off, fold them into a neat pile, underwear on top, she will clear the table then wrap it in clingfilm.

Mum has her back turned, a keloid scar crawling up the nape of her neck, sleeves rolled up, sterilising sharp things in boiling water, sweat even behind her ears. No, never been one for hiding. She does what needs to be done.

Our Lark is unplaiting her hair with stiff hands, a tremor. Now, she hops up onto the table, clingfilm sticking to her thighs, shifts around and lies flat on her back like a good little lamb. She thinks about how meat expands when squashed under clear plastic, what she'd see if she was underneath herself, looking up. Her left elbow feels like a detuned radio. There is an X on the ceiling and she is to keep her eyes fixed right on it and only stop when Mum says she's done. But, glancing out the window, the sky blues. It arches, buzzing not like fluorescent light but a distant swarm. Something that promises to get closer, promises future.

Today, her hands are restless. The tremor, yes, but something like an itch in the marrow. A marching line, outwards. Like her bones carry on past her skin. Like she could squeeze the tip of a finger and the nail would *pop* right off. They will not stay at her sides, flat, like they're meant to. They crawl to her thighs, they pick at the stitches on her knees, little black lines, ants following. They tug her hair, trace scars, brush across stubby eyelashes, feeling the way the itch ripples in her eyelid as much as it tickles her palms. They touch her throat, they touch her jaw, they feel it open, close, open, close, open. How grateful she is; how ungrateful the body is. These keloid scars, these yellow-brown bruises around the stitching.

Mum turns and our Lark's eyes snap to the ceiling. She looks at X so hard she stops seeing it. Mum runs a latex-gloved hand from her clavicle to her lower stomach, a trail of corpse-cold in her wake. Our Lark feels blind. She feels empty, bloodless. Mum presses down. She feels what she feels, flipped. Flesh yielding to a hand, a hand to yield flesh. A knot of fear in the womb. It should hide but it wants to be found. In our Lark's periphery, she sees the whites of Mum's eyes.

The cuts are clean. The room fills with smells red and animal. Our Lark knows what insides look like, how we're all thick and runny like egg yolk underneath. She wants to know what hers look like. What's different.

Mum taps her small intestine and she makes her mind go flat. Thinks about other things, outside things. Cloud cover. Feathers. Steady moving cars and what makes them stop. What makes them stop. What makes them, stop.

Another two taps, irritated. The organs respond to our Lark thinking about them and big feelings. It's important to keep calm or Mum can't do what she has to do, not with all the noise they make. Dogs all howling. Flat-minded and pliant, our Lark stares at X. It is nothing but itself.

Mum said to get some rest so our Lark lies on her bed. Stands up. Lies back down. Stands up. Lies on the floor. Stands up again but there is no place further down. This, here, is the bit she hates the most. After. Trying to figure out what's changed and what's missing. The last liver made her hate the texture of meat, the top of her stomach skimmed and she was made a bad liar, a new spleen made her hands quick enough for knife tricks. She's tired, yes, but in that electric sense where the body's flagging but the mind is on fire.

The curtains are drawn, thin for the half-dark hushing over the small room. White walls, grey carpet, hoover tracks all towards the doorway, dark flowery duvet on a single bed, rubber mattress. Bedside table: lamp, yellow-white bobbles, baby Sylvanian Families rabbit with cuts of meat marked out, plastic cube alarm clock. Phone charger in an extension cord under the bed. Empty vanity, circle mirror. Lemon smells. Painted-white wardrobe, everything neat inside. She is clothed, clean things, fabric brushing against the gauze taped to her stomach. Her skin is cold despite the heat. Her teeth feel glued in. That she would be seeing anything but this again, after.

She peels back the curtain, a flap of skin opening, peers out but it feels like looking in. She can see into next door's garden, see the grass and the flowers and the dog and the woman wearing white denim shorts over a red swimming costume, lying on a deck chair. Her skin is unevenly red and brown and her thighs look like orange peel. Our Lark wants to touch them, feel the texture and know the blood beneath. An ocean kept in tissue paper. Next door's hair shines in the sun. Mum said once hair is a dead thing, only alive under skin, then turned our Lark blonde. Long, blonde princess hair, like she wanted. She remembers her mousy brown hair, scalp, burning in the sink, the fire unsubtle, the smoke thick and acrid. Meat crisping. You could taste it. And not next door and not next door but one and not one person across the way asked about it, the fire the smell the daughter suddenly a waist-length golden blonde, just started calling our Lark Rapunzel and still never touched her hair the way they did everybody else young. Like they can tell. She doesn't touch windows and she folds her clothes and she brushes her hair sat in front of a mirror, sprays perfume in it when it's wet so on drying she leaves a trail of white flowers. And still.

Close the curtain. Open the wardrobe. Split an invisible seal: blood surging forward, spongy yellow beans of fat lining the wardrobe doors, organs, hundreds of them, glistening hot in the half-dark.

Everything opens and closes.

Our Lark does not own white denim shorts or a red swimming costume. Sifting through her clothes, best she can do is faded blue jeans, pink vest she used to sleep in. She's not supposed to wear light colours so soon after, harder to get the blood out – and she's not really supposed to wear anything that shows the scars. Thick, white or red or purple lines looping around her joints, scored deep on her chest, her back, her stomach, too uniform to be accidental and too sure to not make people worry, or at least think things they shouldn't.

163

She undresses and redresses herself, movements weighed down. Tired. Mum said to get some rest. She looks at the body in the mirror across the room. The outline of the gauze is faint under fabric and it rustles when she moves. She'll keep the cut clean and change the dressing and it will scar again. It's ugly. Great ridged thing right down her middle. Look: this is where she cut me open the first time, you can't even see it any more.

Our Lark dreams in the steady crushing of shells, juices bursting. The house moves, twisting and turning in the earth like a wisdom tooth, tired of waiting, ready.

"Something bothering you, love?" Mum asks her as they eat breakfast off the same table they cut her open on.

She glances up, lining up crusts like soldiers on her plate. She shrugs. *Weird dream.* Then, *oh.*

That's what changed. Her voice. It's a quiet, wispy thing now. She used to talk like everyone else. What changed that? Why change that?

"It's only temporary," Mum tells her.

Imagine a body. What do you do to it? She used to want wings. Less skin. Veins royal blue and closer to the surface and thick as worms. Sharper teeth when she was going through a phase, triggered by that three-quarter kidney rejecting. Her patchwork insides to be made whole again.

I don't want —

"It's not your choice."

A knock at the door.

They look at each other. Mum stands, our Lark stands.

"Don't."

When she goes, our Lark follows, teeth clenched.

There is a man she's never seen standing in the doorway. Mum blocks most of him, but she sees shoulders, dark hair, hint of sunburned forehead. He's introducing himself, he's new, Mum moves to conceal our Lark but she dips around: they make eye contact.

He smiles. At her. He has a nice face, she thinks, everything in its right place.

"That's just our Lark," Mum says, trying to push her back, "she's shy."

"Hi, Lark! It's nice to meet you."

She gives a little wave.

"How old is she?"

Mum says "twelve" at the same time our Lark says *nineteen.*

"At that age," Mum says, "always showing off."

He laughs. "I hear you. Anyway, so sorry to be a pain, but I was wondering if you had a drill we could borrow? My partner lost the toolbox in the move and we can't get this fu- flipping table through the door."

Yes, she says.

"Thank you, sweetheart." Her voice is strained. "Why don't you go and get it for the nice man?"

She goes up the stairs on all fours because, steep, and more fun. There's a toolbox on top of Mum's wardrobe, if she climbs on the bed she can get it down. A quick-scrabbling second and it's in her hands. Easy. Mission: successful. As she goes to leave, she catches sight of herself in the mirror. This is her reflection. She doesn't get another one. Long sleeves in the summer. Twist this way, just a bit, and she can see the very top of the gauze through the material, an unbroken line. The light catches a darker patch right in the middle. Busted stitch. You'd think it'd hurt. You'd think it could hurt. Something's building, the way dogs growl low from their chests before snapping. She doesn't look herself in the eye. *Ungrateful.* Fuck you.

From downstairs, Mum shouts for her.

On light feet she runs to her bedroom, pushes the toolbox under the bed. Downstairs, kitchen, tool drawer, bone drill. It's the closest thing to an heirloom they have, antique-dull, long-nosed with a hand crank.

To the door, moving fast so Mum can't stop her, she shoves the drill into the man's hands.

"Wow!" He turns over the steel, painfully obviously medical, admiring. "Some piece of kit."

165

The glare she fixes our Lark with could melt brick. "We do a lot of DIY."

That's definitely one way of putting it, our Lark doesn't quite say, but likes the thrill of the thought.

"I'll have this back soon as," he says, smiling even as Mum shuts the door in his face.

With him away, any bravery fizzles out.

I don't move on feet or hands, don't slither or crawl. But I am coming closer. Growing like roots in the dark yet quick as flies. What am I?

Our Lark doesn't always believe in God. Hard to, when Mum does what she does. Still, there's no one else to turn to. Mum has the scars and Nan had the scars, the family tree carved up until it became tradition to reach for the knife. Our Lark sits in her dark bedroom, back against the wall, and asks *why?* What did she do? It normally stays tight as stitches inside herself but it... it's unravelling – Is it this house? Is it her? Because it wasn't always like this, was it? Cascading down: I'd take out my heart and give to her to show her I do love her, to make her understand I have one, to make it stop. She can't cry because her tear ducts are fused shut but her body sobs all the same. She hits her head against the wall, again, again, stills, staring up at the ceiling, ears ringing. From the wall, a hand cushions the back of her head.

She stops breathing.

Mum has never touched her fear, not her capacity for it or her response, maybe she's just intrinsically damaged, she is scared, terrified, but her trembling hand smooths out along the carpet until it lifts, turns, fingertips ghosting up the wall and her palm settling flat against it.

She shuts her eyes. Forces breath even. She's dreaming. Wake up.

Papery fingers interlace with hers. A thumb rubbing in her hair. Despite herself, she leans into the touch. She stays there because she wants to. It almost feels like the real thing.

A hand at her elbow, wrenching the joint out –

She screams, shock without pain.

– back into place. Mum's footsteps down the hallway, the hands back into the wall as if slipping underwater.

Our Lark experimentally stretches her arm out. The static feeling in her elbow has gone. Her hand feels loose, not bad loose, just the opposite of stiff, and doesn't shake.

The door sweeps open. "What's wrong?" Mum, backlit by the corridor, a stamp of light falling through.

She stares at her hands. Fixed. She's been complaining about this for so long but Mum said there was nothing she could do. *Remembered something scary.*

"You're a very bad liar."

Everyone knows I am. Her hands, latticed by surgery scars, old and new. *What would they do if I told them the truth?*

Her face is hidden by darkness. The house takes a breath. "You're more than welcome to."

She's right. She always is. There's nothing stopping our Lark but herself. It's only what comes after. Say they believe her, and they want to do something about it, what happens to Mum? Where does she go? Say they strip our Lark for parts and start again. Suppose the house shakes the dust and becomes somewhere to call home. Suppose the girl becomes a girl again, not just a vessel for the wound. Why wouldn't she be human, and whole, and loved. And why not now?

It's the smell that gets her. Wet like cottage cheese, fur, melted butter. They used to have a dog like this, big eyes and big energy. Border Collie mixed with something smaller. His name was Smiler. Mum said he ran away and our Lark believed it until she didn't. Smiler's a runaway in the same way these organs are runaways. They have to come from somewhere, and end up somewhere else. If she thought about it, she'd never sleep again.

This dog at full tilt comes in through the open front door, too excited to run without bouncing around, straight for our Lark. Huge smile on her face. She forgets to think this is a bad thing, forgets about consequences. He jumps up, licks her face, she gets a second of mussing his fur before he jumps back, tail wagging so hard his whole body wiggles back and forth. Barks. She feints forwards, he jumps back. She feints forwards, he jumps, barks again, tongue lolling. Then she runs. They run.

Straight out the door, out the open gate – what's a gate to a racing dog if not where to start – our Lark unsteady on her feet but getting bolder, strides longer, arms pumping, keeping pace with the dog even if he is holding back for her. She's quick, sky's huge and blue, the ground steady beneath her feet, she's quick and this is what it feels like, running. She might never have known.

Distantly, a shouting of names. The dog stops sharp, so does she.

Race you? The burn in her lungs feels good. When the dog doesn't answer, she barks. He barks back. She nods.

The running feels like flying.

The dog's name is Rudi. He belongs to the new neighbour and he says he's so grateful our Lark brought him back.

"You must be very fast," he says, Rudi sat panting at his side.

Yeah, she says, pride welling, *I am.*

Mum is tersely quiet until they get back inside, door shut, door locked.

"You're not supposed to run after dogs. They think it's a game."

I was running with him.

That night, she sits on the doorstep looking up. The night sky is so full, and so far away.

The next day, the man presents her with a teddy bear. "To say thank you for all your help with Rudi."

The bear's an awkward size, not big enough to be ostentatious but too big to hold comfortably. Our Lark grips it by the scruff, nails digging in, Mum standing behind her like an irritated shadow.

"His name's Willoughby." Over our Lark's head, the man says, "we've had him kicking around for a while and my partner said, why not give him to next door? She was great yesterday, Rudi's been going a bit crazy with the move."

"That's working dogs for you. Say thank you, Lark."

She does. Teddy bear. Like she's a child.

Mum struggles to shut the door, little fingers from the carpet pinching at it, wanting him to look closer. Our Lark sees, nobody else does.

Later, Willoughby sits big and doughy and out of place on her bed, her stood at the foot of it like a doctor with bad news. He won't look her in the eye. Things like this lose their meaning. It all happens so often it wears down into dust. Maybe our Lark is worn out. The body will never change in any meaningful way. Won't grow up, won't ever shake this free, stuck from the first time Mum cut her open. Look: you can't even see it any more, the scars so built-up they don't mean anything. The first no different from the most recent, and you can't even say *last* because this will never end. When freedom is running but still coming back when called, what do you do? Where is she meant to put all this rage, this flat black energy?

A cross-section: under her feet, the kitchen, Mum listening to the radio, maybe reading. Between them a thick line of dark. It moves, anxious as rabbits.

Our Lark takes two steps forwards and crouches down. From under the bed, she reaches for the toolbox. As she starts pulling it towards her, fingertips come up from the carpet and brush her wrist.

ss SsTO P

A thought but not hers. It just appears in her head. Layered, echoing. Different voices, all girls. She shakes it off. Hard to care. Feels like a natural progression, ants marching in a line ever forward. Everything opens and closes and nothing ever ends.

She pulls the toolbox out. The carpet grabs her wrist proper but she twists free. She takes the sharpest-looking screwdriver bit and sits in front of Willoughby, pushes him onto his back, trails a finger down the seam on his front.

We match, she softly tells him.

Again, with a fingernail. Every other stitch snags. Again, with the screwdriver bit, pushing harder. A stitch snaps. A rush, something breaking its borders. The house holds its breath.

Steadily she saws a two-inch opening into Willoughby's chest, his fibres loose and frayed. She slips two fingers inside, moves them around.

169

Does that feel good, do you like it?

Willoughby stares at the ceiling, eyes glassy. He is nothing but himself.

Our Lark's bottom lip quivers, pressure building around her eyes. *I said, I said do you... like it? You're meant to. Say yes.* She hits him. *Sorry, I didn't...* She hits him again. *You don't know how good you've got it. You don't* – and she rips his chest open. Breathes shaky and shallow at his white pure fuzzy insides. She snatches him up, takes a bite of his filling, fibres getting up her nose, chews itchy and dry and choking and has to spit it all out. Hands throw Willoughby across the room. Body crying without tears. He hits the wall and the wall catches him. Our Lark screams at it. Should've ripped his stupid little head off his shoulders. She wants to go home but she's never lived anywhere else.

sS oRRy

She thinks, the fuck are you sorry for?

INS iiDEsS

Like a firework went off in the dog pound: cacophony. Organs baying, blood baying to be let out. They jolt around inside her, furious, knocking her to her feet. Acid rises in her throat as her stomach squeezes and she vomits blood, spraying across the carpet.

The house has roots like teeth have roots, held in place like teeth are held in place. Little fibres clutching. When they break, the tooth comes out.

I didn't take them. Blood coating the inside of her mouth, rich and metallic.

From the carpet, a thumb runs along the long, ugly scar down her arm and the skin splits apart cleanly, down to the bone. No blood, no anything.

A voice from her throat, not hers, *theirs,* "We Know."

She sees them behind her eyes: the girls, the bodies, their organs, hot and pulsing in gloved hands. Their lives were so big. Too big, to end here, for her.

Their Lark says, "This Isn't Your Fault."

170

Their Lark says, "Just Go."

If she leaves, she can stop this. Stop everything. She wants to. She wants to be good. They make her crawl then walk then run, movements broken-bone jagged, toss her down the last half of the stairs. She lands in a heap but they pick her up. Hundreds of hands in hers when she reaches for the door handle, urging her on.

Door open. Nothing but blue skies, thrumming like the biggest swarm. One step out. They keep pushing her forwards, she keeps going forwards, she can do this, she can end everything. It will stop with her. Their hold on her steadily lessens the further she gets from the house, and she finds the strength to run.

Slowing to catch her breath, she looks over her shoulder. No shouts, no one coming running after her. Good. To get blood out, you have to shock it. Enough water will clean anything. Just keep going. She thinks about other things: shoes at the door, clean clothes, shoes they never wore again –

Hot food, white flowers, something clean, something's changed. She could get the bus, change her name, change her hair, sell bricks in Jesus' name. There's a whole world out there and no one else has to die. Just keep going.

She looks over her shoulder one last time.

The girls try to push her back out but they're dead and nothing will change that now. They said *this isn't your fault* but it is. Mum tried dead intestines, huge coils of them, and she coughed up grave dirt for weeks. So she knows. So she has always known. But rather them than her: despite everything she wants to be alive. The cost of her living is too high for any good person to accept, but she does because she is a selfish, stupid incomplete patchwork who can't cry can't hurt can't grow change or be anything but what she is now. She is a haunted house.

Mum stands in the kitchen, unsurprised.

171

Our Lark grabs a coaster from the table and hurls it at her mum. Mum ducks just in time and it hits the window without either thing breaking.

Fix me! FIX ME!

"How? I've tried!"

A different brain, just take it out I don't want to think any more I don't want to be me or, or change my heart I'm so sick of mine –

She says, "it's Smiler's heart."

She says, "I love you."

She says, "I didn't want you to leave."

The house could fall, the ghosts could go with it, swallowed up by the dirt. Our Lark would still be standing here, doghearted and never safe.

The Rope Swing

Penny Jones

Jess lay on her bed and tried to ignore the choking feeling of claustrophobia that clawed at her throat. Her mum had told her that work was putting them up in a swanky apartment, but instead the flat was a tiny grotty hole stuck up at the top of a crappy tower block. Her bed might as well have been in the cupboard in her mum's room for the space she had. And even here, in this tiny space, her mum was always coming in and telling her to turn down her music, or to put her headphones in – as if the local druggies would be over to have a go at them about the noise. But her mum seemed scared of everything these days.

It wasn't even as if Jess could go and watch telly if she wanted to. Her mum had turned the living room into her office. The dining table covered with files and her laptop. Jess wanted to ask why, if her mum was going to work from home, had they had to move down here for the new job anyway? But knew her mum would be full of excuses about having to go in for meetings, or being in the office more once she was fully trained. Jess thought that was a load of shit. If they didn't need her in before she was trained, it was unlikely that they were going to insist on it once she actually knew what she was doing.

Pulling out her phone Jess tapped once more at the photo of Emily smiling on the rope swing as Seth, Jess's ex, stood moodily behind. Jess wondered how long it had taken him to persuade Emily to go down to the rope swing, or if it had even been his idea. Maybe Emily had instigated it. To be fair there wasn't anything else to do in her old village. The parents thought everyone congregated on the green, pissing about around the Maypole, but that was only a front. As the hour got later, the younger kids knew when to leave. The groups dwindling down, replaced by couples, all with only one thing on their minds. They took turns covering for each other sneaking down to the rope swing, the trees hiding them from the prying eyes of the village.

Whereas the rope swing was big enough to sit in, Jess never had. She'd stepped straight in, balancing on one foot as Seth had pulled her back then released her to swing out across the drop. The treetops falling away below her as she arched up, soaring over the cliff face. The catch as the rope reached its pinnacle and twisted, ever so slightly beneath her, threatening to release her foot from its grip, and drop her down into the trees and brambles beneath. Then swinging back, making Seth hop out of its way before grabbing the rope and twisting Jess into his embrace.

"Dinner's here."

Jess heard the buzzer and then the sound of her mum's voice, worry causing it to rise as she snapped at whoever was on the other end of the intercom. That was unexpectedly followed by the flat's front door slamming shut. Jess slid off the bed and made her way into the living room. It was empty, as was the kitchen. Jess filled the kettle and put two teabags into mugs. The kettle had boiled before Jess heard the sound of the front door slamming once more.

"Bloody waste of time ordering takeaway if I have to go down and get it."

Jess opened the fridge and grabbed the milk, but other than a small splash the carton was empty. "The removal men must have finished it. Shall I go get some more after dinner?"

"No. It's too late to be going out. I'll get some tomorrow." Jess's mum plonked the pizza boxes down on the table. "Apparently, it's company policy. None of the takeaways will come in to the tower block."

Jess was about to ask why, then decided against it; although her mum had said that the area they were moving to was posh, it appeared anything but to Jess, and her mum obviously agreed. She didn't want to add any more fuel to that fire. Otherwise, her mum would get a bee in her bonnet. And Jess didn't put it past her to forbid Jess from leaving the flat at any time, day or night.

Jess stood in the rope swing. She could feel the rope digging into the arch of her foot, as someone dragged her back. She looked down, expecting to see her shoe, but her foot was bare. A strand of grass peeked out where the rope dug into her anklebone. The swing pulled higher, Jess tightened her grip, entwining her legs around the taut rope. Glancing down to ensure her foot was still tightly nestled within the loop she saw her legs were also bare, her knees dirty, grit embedded in the skin. Naked, Jess could feel the rope digging between her legs. Hands on her waist, thumbs digging in to her buttocks as she was pulled back even higher. 'Stop!' She tried to call, but her voice wouldn't come. The words choked in her throat. She wanted to cover her nakedness, wanted to know whose hands she could feel. Surely, they must be Seth's; but no, he was shagging Emily now. She twisted, trying to see who held her. Her grip loosening, though whether to pry away the fingers that now dug hard into her hips or to try and cover her body, she didn't know. Suddenly the hands were gone, free her body swung. She turned, wanting to see whose hands had been on her naked body, causing the usual gentle pendulum of the swing to twist. She grasped at the rope with her free hand, no longer caring about her nakedness. The swing reached its pinnacle. Her body continuing for a moment before it caught, pulling against the swing. Her hand missed the rope, her body dropped. The loop which a moment before had dug tight into her foot now seemed too large, her body slipping, the rope burning her thighs and breasts. Her hands grasping at nothing before the rope caught around her neck.

Jess woke with the scream trapped in her throat. Her sheets drenched, wrapped tight around her body. She pushed them off and made her way to shower away the sweat and remnants of her dream.

Jess made her mum a black coffee. Leaving it next to the kettle, she waited until her mum entered the bathroom and she could hear the shower running. "I'm just off down to the shops to grab us some milk." Jess opened the door and hurried out without waiting for a response. She practically ran down the corridor towards the stairs, hoping the fact that her mum was wrapped in nothing but a towel was enough of a deterrent to stop her coming out after her. Jess pulled open the door to the stairwell and made her way downstairs. Trying to ignore the smell that hung in the air as if something or someone had died in here overnight.

Pushing open the heavy metal door downstairs, Jess took a deep breath and coughed. The air tasted dusty. The hot summer's day

175

already lying heavily, a fug coating the morning and her skin. Around her, standing sentinel, were block after block of flats. Each one surrounded by a small strip of sunburnt grass. The area was dead.

Jess got her phone out and pulled up the map function, but even here in the city the signal was terrible. The tower blocks hanging over her must be blocking it out. Jess raised her arm up, blinking against the bright sun that snuck between the high-rises. In the distance she could hear the sussurence of cars as people headed out for work. But Jess couldn't see any sign of a road through the maze of tower blocks.

Passing along the cracked path Jess dodged round bin bags. Their sides ripped, their insides scattered by whatever scavengers had nosed their way in, not caring if they held bones or bottles. Jess wondered whether this was from just one night, or was it a gradual build-up of detritus that would mount and mount until the pathways were unpassable? Jess stopped and checked on her phone again, still no signal. If anything, the road noise seemed further away than before. She couldn't have got turned round. The blocks were square. The paths between them following in straight lines. It wasn't like wandering in the woods back home, following rabbit trails that seemed to lead nowhere and everywhere. These were purpose-built – well, she supposed the rabbit trails were purpose-built too, but she wasn't a rabbit.

Jess stared around her, but all she could see in any direction were tower blocks. Each one so big it blocked out sight of anything else. She had no idea how she would tell which was hers. She lived in Barrett, but any signs indicating which block was which, had rotted or been stolen years before. There was nothing on the side of the block she stood by except for what could have been either a crudely sprayed dick or a noose on the door.

The sound of the road came from Jess's right now. She'd walked for ages and hadn't found her way out. Stay on the path, she'd kept repeating to herself, but still there didn't appear to be any end in sight. It was stupid, she must have got herself turned round; the estate just couldn't be that big. Jess turned and started to make her way back along the path, resigned to the fact that she'd either have to phone her mum to get her when she reached civilisation, or grab a taxi. She only realised she'd finally escaped the maze of walkways when the car's horn blared out as she stepped out onto the road. Jess lobbed the driver the V's as she ran to safety.

The three girls sat on the wall outside of the shop giggling. It sounded spiteful to Jess. She wondered what it was they were laughing at, whether it was her? They hadn't even looked up at the sound of the squealing tires. Their heads still down. Pressed together, their fingers fidgeted with something that they cradled in front of them.

As Jess got closer, she could see that the girls were braiding friendships bracelets. Jess watched as their fingers twined the multicoloured threads, folding each one into another. They didn't look up. Jess wondered if their hair was braided together the same way. Whether they walked around like some weird human-made set of conjoined triplets. Giggles still emanated from them. Not waiting to see if the laughter was aimed at her, Jess pushed open the door to the shop and hurried in.

Jess had expected to see a rack of glossy mags, chocolate, papers, milk, veg. But instead, she was assaulted by the smells of spices; and although there was veg in the rack by the front door, she didn't recognise any of it. Slowly she made her way round the store, picking up packets and boxes of foods she'd never heard of. An array of what she presumed were sweets, stood sticky in the sun's rays that made their way through the window and settled golden on the counter.

The man behind the counter watched her. His hand beneath the counter. Jess wondered if he had a button under there. A silent alarm to call the police. Or maybe his hand held a bat or a gun. Taking a deep breath Jess gathered herself. It wasn't the ghettos; she wasn't going to get shot just for browsing. Even so Jess quickly grabbed the milk from the fridge and made her way back towards the checkout. She'd been meaning to ask the man if he knew of any taxis that would come pick her up, but now it seemed like a bad idea. As if it would cement her status as a stranger even more.

The man picked up the carton and held his hand out, Jess pulled the debit card from her wallet and held it out. "Do you take cards?"

"Five pound minimum."

"Oh, sorry." Jess reached over meaning to put the milk back, but the man stayed her hand, slipping the carton from beneath her fingers

177

and deftly placing it in a bag. He pushed the card reader over towards Jess and waited, the bag held aloft. Jess tapped her card and grabbed at the bag, looking forward to being out of the stuffy and smelly store.

"Did he diddle yeah?"

Jess stared at the girls. She didn't understand why the hell they were asking her that. She'd only been in there a moment. Why on Earth would they think she'd been in and shagged him.

"No, he fucking didn't."

Jess pulled her phone out of her pocket trying to refresh the map, but even here, away from the suffocating claustrophobia of the tower blocks' narrow walkways, she was unable to get a signal.

"Okay no need to get so defensive about it. He does it to all the newbies."

It took a moment for Jess to put her mind in gear. Luckily, she managed to stop her mouth running away with itself before she embarrassed herself even further. They weren't asking if he'd shagged her, just if he'd ripped her off.

"What's yer name newbie?" The girl in the middle looked her in the eye. The other two still concentrated on the ropes in their hands, their fingers deftly twining and knotting the strings. Their thumbs hooked into a loop at the end to hold the braids steady. "Yer name. You do have one dontcha?"

"Jess."

The two other girls looked up at her then across at the one who had spoken. The girl nodded. "This one's spoken for." She indicated at the braid in her hand. "But if you come back tomorrow, we can start one for you. Now we know your name."

"Thanks."

The two girls went back to braiding the threads in their hands. Their leader still staring at her, as if waiting for more. Jess wasn't sure what to say. She didn't really want a friendship bracelet, had grown out of them a couple of years back. She wasn't even sure if she wanted to be friends with these three girls. What if she befriended them only to find out that they were losers? That wouldn't do her streetcred any good. Jess looked up and down the road; except for the cars that whizzed past there was no sign of anyone else. She supposed there would be other hangouts that she might find, but at the moment these three looked like the only options she had for any company. She could always ditch them when she started college. "What's your name?"

There was no answer, all three girls were back engrossed in their handiwork.

Jess stepped closer. "I said what's your names?"

"Tomorrow."

Jess stared at them, her mouth open. She snapped it shut against the exasperated invectives that were trying to force their way out. Instead, she asked "Which way is Barrett Tower?"

The girl who had spoken raised her hand and pointed down the road. "Turn left at the tree."

Jess headed down the road, putting the girls behind her.

The tree stood in the middle of the roundabout, incongruous in its isolation. Its ageing limbs stretching out casting the surrounding area in shadows. Jess had no idea how old it might be, but the rest of the road ran straight, with traffic lights to allow for the occasional car joining from the estates that ran either side of the road. Jess wondered why on Earth this one tree had been spared. Casting a look both ways down the road she sprinted across to the parched and cracked ground that the tree stood upon. She supposed once there might have been grass beneath, but now the canopy, heavy with leaves, blocked any sign of the sun, leaving the ground beneath barren. Jess shivered, she hadn't expected the shade to be that cold, but stepping beneath the tree was like stepping into winter. Jess walked round the tree, running her fingers across its rough bark, but there was no plaque or sign, nothing to indicate why this tree should have been spared when the sprawling concrete mass of London had crept into this part of the countryside. If this tree had been in her old village, the bark would have been scoured and scarred with graffiti. Names and proclamations of love and life. Back home there were so many trees that each new name gouged into the bark could have had its own tree. But even as kids they'd known, a whole wood to choose from but still people had added their names to the growing roster on the old tree that had held the rope swing. Her mum said it held a special place in people's hearts. But Jess and her friends knew it was just special. She'd watched as Seth cut theirs in the night before she left. Sneaking back later she'd used her nail file to enclose their names in a heart.

Jess circled the tree once more, shoes scuffing in the dry dirt between the roots. The ground barren beneath the verdancy above. Strange that there were no birds in the tree. Even in the city birds found places to roost. The balcony of their flat was covered with bird shit, the stench enough to make her eyes water the only time she'd been out there. She'd have expected the only tree for miles to be full of them, a haven, an oasis, but the tree stood silent. No bird song, no sound of scampering squirrels, not even a whisper of leaves, the breeze too mild to stir the heavily laden branches. The ground beneath bore no signs of life either. No bird or animal droppings, no fallen nests of eggs or bones. There wasn't even a Maccy's bag, chucked out of a passing car, nestled between the tree's roots.

Jess moved away from the tree, not knowing if it was the correct direction, just wanting to put it behind her. Sweat prickling her skin as she stepped back out into the hot summer's sun. Across the road stood one of the many carparks scattered between the towers. With relief Jess spied her mum's car. How hadn't she noticed it as she approached the tree? Or how hadn't she noticed the tree yesterday when they were parking up? Maybe it hadn't seemed so special yesterday. Just another tree, before she realised that there were no other trees here. At least it gave her a landmark to find her block of flats she supposed. Crossing the road Jess made her way back to her new home.

Pulling up the search engine on her laptop Jess realised she'd not really got any idea where to start. She could type in, "Big Tree London". But she was pretty sure that wasn't going to get her anywhere. She wasn't even sure where she actually lived, other than in London. People talked about Camden or Spitalfields, Mayfair and Regent Street. Jess had even seen the names of some of them on the Underground map when she'd come down with her mum a few years ago to go to the theatre. She'd practically begged her mum to take her to see the Elephant in the Castle, and her mum had had to explain that there wasn't one. It was just the name of the area. Jess left her room to ask her mum but she was nodding along to her laptop.

Holding her finger up to quiet Jess as she soon as she'd stepped through from the hallway and into the lounge.

Jess made her way to the kitchen. If there'd been a door, she'd probably have slammed it. It was bad enough that her mum had moved her across the country with false promises of days out and city life, just to basically trap her in this shithole. But it was worse that she couldn't even exist in her own home. Jess debated putting the kettle on, but she didn't want to make one for her mum and couldn't deal with the repercussions if she only made herself one. Her mum would probably say that the kettle was too loud anyway. Jess looked in the fridge but the only drink in there except for milk was the bottle of Champagne that her mum's new bosses had left on the kitchen side along with her new work laptop and the *welcome to your new home* card.

Jess ran herself a glass of water, taking a deep gulp, she gagged at the metallic taste. Spitting it out Jess ran the tap until the water felt ice-cold on her hand before filling the glass once more. It still had a slight minerally taste, like that time Seth had gotten a bit too amorous and had bitten her lip when they were making out. But at least it no longer tasted like it was going to poison her. Jess picked up the card that sat perched on the windowsill above the sink. The missive inside typed rather than written, *Welcome to Barrett Tower*, the signature looked as if it was printed. There was no sign of her mum's name, just a generic card that the company sent out. Jess wondered how many people they'd relocated that they needed to print out cards, rather than just pop to the shop for one. Jess stared at the words, *Barrett Tower*. There were probably several of them, but at least it narrowed her search down from "Big Tree London".

Still not much for "Big Tree", but there was a surprisingly large amount about the tower block she lived in. Apparently, it was named after a Michael Barrett who'd been hung there years ago. There were some old newspaper articles about the uproar around them building the tower blocks. Old scanned images of leaflets protesting about the destruction of the area and its history. A crude drawing of a tree on one of them stated *If a tree dies, another must replace it.* Jess wondered if they'd hung Barrett from the tree, was that the kind of thing they conserved trees for? But no, looking into it a bit deeper it appeared that Barrett had been hung from a gallows.

*

"Jess." The familiar voices of Seth and Emily echoed down the corridor. The floor lay strewn with flyers. The doorways to either side of Jess stood open, the flats within black. The only light that shone anywhere was the eerie, green glow from the emergency exit signs that stood either end of the corridor. Jess wondered if there'd been a power cut. She reached down to pick up one of the flyers, in the dim light its words appeared gibberish. Stepping towards the emergency exit Jess held the flyer aloft trying to read it in the putrescent light, 'If one dies, another must replace it'. The words writhed in the light that played across the cheap shiny cardboard. Jess dropped the flyer on top of the others that lay like leaves across the corridor. A moment before there'd only been a handful, now they lay in drifts around her. Jess waded through them towards the doorway and made her way up to the next floor. But when she reached the landing, the voices still called to her from above. Jess continued to make her way up and up. Her path becoming more treacherous, her legs becoming leaden as she fought her way through the ever-deepening drifts. Jess turned a corner and found the stairwell packed with flyers, those at the bottom dried and desiccated. Her hand reached forwards. Her fingers riffling the surface. A smell of decomposition erupted in a cloud of spores that enveloped her as she felt the mass shift beneath her fingertips. Her breath catching as she inhaled spores and dust, before the barrier collapsed, burying her beneath its weight.

For a moment Jess still couldn't breathe; the stale air of her room refusing to enter her lungs as she lay swathed in sweat. Each attempted breath caused her body to spasm, the burning in her throat and lungs intensifying. Jess tried to call out for her mum. But as sure as no breath could get in, no words could escape either. Jess grasped at her neck, pulling at what was wrapped there. The sheet came away easily, its twisted fabric dropping onto the bare mattress. Jess wasn't sure if her tossing and turning had trapped her within it because of her nightmare, or whether it was her own suffocation that had pulled those dreams from her mind. She threw the sweat-soaked sheet to the floor and reached over to silence her alarm before her mum came in and shouted at her to be quiet.

The three girls had told her to meet them today. She wasn't sure if she wanted to meet them again. They seemed weird – if she was being truthful, a bit retarded – but so far, other than the shopkeeper, they were the only other people she'd met. The block of flats seemed empty, even with her window open she hadn't seen or heard anyone come or go since they'd arrived two days ago.

Jess made her way down the stairs and pushed open the heavy entrance door, letting it slam closed behind her, the sound echoing off the heavy air. Jess saw her mum's face appear at the lounge window, before her hand reached out and pulled the window shut. Only Jess's bedroom window now stood open, all the others were shut. Jess wandered round the flats but on each side it was the same. The windows shut even in the summer sun. Jess made her way towards the shop and the girls, who she only half-hoped were there waiting for her on the wall. Her pace speeding up as she passed through the shadows cast on the pavement by the tree.

"Hi." Jess stood awkwardly in front of the girls. None of them looked up. They just sat there. The two on the edges just watching their hands as the thread flowed through them to the girl in the centre – her own thread coiled around her neck like a snake – her hands binding the three strands deftly into the braid that fell between her legs. The weavings were much longer than Jess had expected. She'd thought they were making friendship bracelets, but already it reached the ankles of the girl in the middle and there was still masses of it left to be woven.

"Hi." Jess uttered a second time. She stared transfixed at the ever-growing rope. She wondered what would happen if she grabbed it and pulled. Images of the girls tumbling from the wall, unravelling in a pile on the floor. Or of the cord around the middle girl's neck getting tighter. Her face turning gradually redder until it matched the colour of the thread that they wove. Jess stepped forward her hands reaching out towards the braid. She only wanted to look, to see the patterns within.

"Not yet." The girl's voice stopped Jess.

Jess didn't know if they meant her or the cord.

"You can't touch something that's not yours."

Jess's eyes flickered to the left. She was sure that the words had been spoke by the girl who sat there, but the girl still stared down at the thread that ran through her hands.

183

"You'll know once it's yours."

Jess turned towards the words, but the girl on the right also stared at the threads in her lap. Only the girl in the middle looked at Jess.

"You told me to come back." Jess stared defiantly at the girl, wishing that her voice didn't sound quite so needy. If she'd been entertaining the thought of being friends with them, their behaviour today had made her decision for her. "But I can see you're busy." Jess hoped that the sarcasm was evident and they didn't think she was just being polite.

The girl in the middle slid from the wall. The cord hanging from her neck swinging as she stepped towards Jess. Her hands shot out and were around Jess's neck before she could step out of range. "We just needed to measure your worth."

Jess pulled away easily from the girl's grip. "Fucking weirdos!" The three girls were back on the wall as if they'd never moved, not even a turn of their heads towards her shout. Only their fingers continued to move, to dance, to weave.

She turned and fled down the street. Only turning back once she had reached the tree. "Fuck you." Jess held her finger up to them before turning round and making her way back towards Barrett Tower.

"Jess."

"What Mum?" Jess sat up in bed. The room lit only by the distant glow of the street lights below.

"Jess."

The voice wasn't her mum's. Jess slipped out of bed and made her way across to the window. Even with the window as far open as it would go, Jess couldn't see anyone below. "Who's there?" she hissed, hoping that she wouldn't wake her mum up. Jess leaned out further, peering down at the paths below. In the shadows, she saw movement, a girl stepping around the corner. Another movement, Jess watched as another girl came round the other corner, both stepping into the rays of the security light at the tower block's entrance.

"Jess."

The two girls from the wall looked up at her

184

"Jess."

Leaning out still further Jess craned her neck left and right, searching the night for the final girl.

"Jess." The voice now came from above. The two girls below giggled as Jess felt the noose slip around her neck. Reaching to loosen it, she let go of the windowsill, forgetting in the moment how far out she'd was leaning, forgetting how far away the ground was, as she tried to evade the rope's embrace. The momentum enough to send her tumbling through the window.

Jess wasn't going to stay trapped in her room, where the suffocating heat reminded her of the feel of the rope tightening around her neck in her dream. Her mum had once again taken over the living room for her work, engrossed with something on her laptop, her head nodding to whoever was speaking to her through her headphones.

Jess hadn't intended to walk back towards the shop and the three girls who sat on the wall. She'd intended to head the other way down the road and see if she could find anything actually resembling the city life her mum had promised her. But as she made her way to the kitchen to make a cup of tea, her mum waved her over, passing her a shopping list and a twenty-pound note.

Overnight someone had decorated the tree. She saw it as she stepped down from the curb. The sudden drop on her body reminding her of her dream the night before. The branches were festooned with braids. Some hung small and delicate like children's bracelets, others thick and heavy and long, winding their way along the branches, their lengths pooling on the floor beneath the drooping boughs. Each braid ended in a loop, as if this was only the first step to decorating the tree and that soon someone would come along and hook baubles and bells from them. Making her way round the tree Jess discovered that one branch remained empty. Below it on the trunk someone had carved J + S 4 EVA in a heart before crossing it out, the scratches gouged deep, sap weeping out of the damaged bark.

"Jess."

Jess turned.

"We're finished."

The three girls closed in, the braid in their hands the longest of all. Jess watched as with expert ease they threw it over the empty branch. As they pulled, the loop on the end rose higher, until Jess could almost convince herself that she was looking at a rope swing.

A Pinch Of Salt

Joanna Corrance

David had been a salt spreader ever since he left school at sixteen. There were always plenty of jobs going, and since it didn't require any particular qualifications other than the standard health and safety training and policy signoffs, David was able to jump straight into work and rent his own place in the city.

Despite all the regulations and the hefty textbook of policies, the rules of the job were actually very simple. When on a job, note every entrance to the property and ensure to line every inch of every door or window with salt; and finally, always make it home before dark. In cases of emergency, his company had supplied him with a cheap tent and an additional bag of salt. If, for whatever reason, he couldn't make it home, he was to pitch his tent and draw a circle of salt around him. He wasn't to emerge from the tent until morning. Fortunately, he had never found himself in that position before. It had happened to a few of his colleagues; most of them resigned shortly after the experience.

Slinging his pack over his shoulders, David straightened his back and steadied himself against the considerable weight of it. A number of his colleagues left the industry due to the physical burden that the job placed on them, but David didn't mind, he liked the fact that it helped him maintain a certain physique.

The city was alive with rumbling engines on busy roads and clusters of impatient shoppers eager to delve into the January sales. Great metallic structures glinted against the pale yellow of the winter sun, reflecting the light over wet streets. Wedged between them, some of the original architecture had survived, the warm sandstone and dull, sunken windows sat in stark contrast to their glittering counterparts.

David waited by the bus stop, doing his best not to bump people with his pack. When he did inevitably knock someone, they would open their mouths to swear at him before noticing the logo and realising what he did for a living. It wasn't a good idea to upset a salt spreader since there was a good chance they could be allocated to their property one day, and it was vital that the salt spreaders did a good job.

"Morning." David flashed his bus pass to the driver who waved him on without response. He sat near the front, placing his pack on the seat beside him. He felt bad taking up an additional space, but the driver had shouted at him the last time he placed his pack on the floor. A trip hazard. The final person in the queue was refused a place on the bus and they glowered in David's direction. The buses were always full.

The journey commenced and the bus rumbled through the city past the neon lights of shop fronts. Pubs and clubs were mostly obsolete since people couldn't go out at night, but in their place were rows of trendy cafes and bakeries. The restaurants only stayed open for lunch. All the old inner-city townhouses had been converted into affordable housing, floors of flats with small rooms, thin partitions dividing the previously sprawling spaces. On the steps outside, there used to be tall iron railings, but they had all been pulled out, leaving stumps in the stone. A gathering of teenagers lurked near one door, sharing a cigarette between them and looking furtively from side to side. One of them made a crude gesture at the bus as it passed and the rest of them giggled.

Continuing beyond the shops, cafés and flats, the bus emerged from the city into the more gentrified suburbs. In the past, it had been the other way around; the wealthy folk lived in the city and the rest had to tolerate the commute. All that had changed. The roads in the suburbs were wide and clean with rows of trees that lined immaculate pavements. David waited for his stop before stepping off the bus and walking the fifteen minutes to one of the many gated communities circling the city. The housing association of Elder Tree Park had specifically requested that David do their salting every week. Once, when he took a holiday and someone stood in for him, there was a disgruntled call to management about it. They insisted that David was a 'nice chap', which translated into 'the kind we can bring ourselves to tolerate'. David didn't mind too much; they tipped well and were generally pleasant.

Through the gate and beyond the perfectly pruned shrubbery, David walked past the tennis courts which were always swept clean of leaves and any debris caught in the wind. Despite the cold, he felt the perspiration run down his face from the walk with the weight of his pack.

"Good morning, David!"

He glanced up to see Mrs McNeil, one of the members of the homeowner's association, jogging toward him in her pale blue lycra. Her ponytail bobbed behind her and her face had been injected free of any lines betraying age.

"Good morning, Mrs McNeil." David replied, not unaware of the way she paused to appreciate his muscular frame.

"Gosh," she breathed. "Carrying that bag about all the time must keep you very fit."

"It certainly does."

"Well don't you be working too hard." She leaned over and patted his bicep. "If you need to stop for a drink or anything, you just let me know and I can get you something from the residents' bar."

"Thank you, Mrs McNeil."

"Oh, please David. I've told you a dozen times – call me Shirley."

Being familiar with the layout of the complex, David finished the job quickly. The doorways and windows were sprinkled with a fine layer of salt that would ensure the residents of Elder Tree Park were safe at night. Once he was done, he hurried back to the bus stop, eager to catch the earliest bus possible. When he was back in the city, with an hour to spare until nightfall, he stopped in at one of the corner shops and picked up a crate of beer to take home with him. By the time he reached his flat, the sky had turned a warning pink colour as the sun descended behind the buildings. Before he locked up for the night, he sprinkled a line of salt across the entrance to his flat. Pausing, he glanced to the unsalted door of his adjacent neighbour and sprinkled a little over theirs as well. The salt spreaders in his area were supposed to salt the entrance to each building of flats, but David considered it

189

prudent to do the flat doors as well. There had been an incident just a few years back when there was a mix up in shifts, resulting in an entire street of flats going unsalted. The gruesome pictures were all over the news for weeks afterwards.

The city belonged to the fairies at night. When David was young and shielded from the truth, he imagined that fairies were delicate little winged creatures filled with good intentions. That wasn't the case. His mother told him they were the angry spirits of the trees cut down to make way for the city, making themselves known when the last green belt was eradicated from the city; meanwhile, the men who drank in one of the last standing pubs near the bus stop theorised that during the last industrial revolution, people dug too deep and released something long forgotten. Before David's time, the city council once dug up an entire cemetery to check that the dead hadn't arisen. The theory was proved false, but it did result in a spike in cremations for a period of time.

When darkness descended over the city, the fairies would clamber out of nooks and crannies in roofs, the narrow spaces between buildings and even from the ground and the ponds in the parks. They never came from the sewers since the iron of the manhole covers repelled them; even as they crept through the streets at night, David would watch them hiss and swerve round them. People who had found themselves trapped at nightfall with no way of making it to the emergency night shelter in time had sought sanctuary in the sewers, protected by the iron shield.

For the most part, everyone got on with their lives. As long as the right measures were taken, the two could co-exist. The fairies stayed away from the daylight and instead claimed the darkness. David had always wanted to see one of them up close, but he didn't dare, choosing instead to sit by his window at night and observe them as they wandered the streets, blind to all the doors and windows that were sealed with salt. Sometimes they shrieked in rage, not ignorant to their restrictions.

"Fuck off!" Someone hollered from an adjacent flat as a man threw a bottle at one of the creatures on the street. It paused to watch the explosion of glass that glittered as it bounced over the icy cobblestones.

*

David arrived at Elder Tree Park at his usual time and was greeted with a flurry of flashing blue lights and emergency vehicles. Residents looked flustered as they buzzed about the outskirts of the commotion; some of them were still in their dressing gowns. David's eyes widened as he looked to the tennis court where, in the centre, there was the body of a young man, still and sprawled at unnatural angles. There was a clean slice across his throat and a pool of blood congealing beneath him. David instinctively raised his hand to his own throat.

"They must have chased him into the court to trap him."

David glanced round to see Mr Nicholson, another member of the homeowner's association.

"Dreadful way to go," he continued, shaking his head, his morning paper still clutched in one hand.

"Who is he?" David asked.

"Not one of us, thank goodness." Mr Nicholson squinted in the direction of the courts, having forgotten to take his glasses outside with him. "An opportunist – I'd put money on him being a burglar from the city. Must have been desperate to risk coming out at night."

"Yes," David nodded. "Must have been."

"There will always be some." Mr Nicholson opened his mouth to say something else, but found himself interrupted by Mrs McNeil who rushed over, her silk dressing gown billowing behind her. She paused at the sight of David.

"Isn't it awful!" She declared after a moment's hesitation.

"Yes." David agreed, hand still touching his throat.

"Roger," she turned her attention to Mr Nicholson. "I think we need to arrange a homeowners association meeting. The residents are rightly concerned about a burglar getting through the gates – I had Mrs Adie questioning me about the level of management fees if we're not able to keep security up to standard. Everyone needs a bit of reassurance that this was just a one-off."

"Of course," Mr Nicholson nodded in agreement. "We'll get right to it once they've cleared," he hesitated and pointed in the vague direction of the tennis court, "*that*."

191

David received a call from work with a last-minute job on an old estate on the edge of the city. Apparently it was home to an aristocratic family whose funds had depleted over the decades and the only person remaining in the house was the elderly mother of the adult children who had left some time ago to make their money elsewhere.

As it was outside of the bus routes, David had to ask his company to provide him with a taxi, which they begrudgingly did. The grounds were a sprawling mass of tangled roots and weeds, with foliage left to extend over paths and disguise any definition in the gardens. It felt strange to David that the city was only a short drive away, it was like another world. The house itself stood proud in spite of its crumbling edges and cracked windows. It boasted what would once have been a grand greenhouse, but some of the glass panels were shattered and weeds coiled round the original greenhouse residents.

"Hello!" He called out in all directions as he wandered through the grounds. "Salt spreader!"

A barking cough came from a nearby shed and an elderly woman appeared, her breath forming a cloud of condensation against the cold air. Her long, bony body was wrapped in old tweeds and a battered wax jacket that hung off her. Admiring the definition of her face, David reasoned that she must have been beautiful once. She stared at him with strikingly violet eyes.

"A what?" she snapped.

"A salt spreader." David smiled in an attempt to thaw her a little. "I spread the salt."

"*Really.*" She walked past him, ensuring he saw her eyes roll before her back was to him. "Go away, I don't need that."

"Your son booked our services."

"You tell my son that what I need is a chimney sweep. This place is freezing, and my chimneys are full of birds' nests." She waved a hand. "Go and give that salt to someone who needs it."

"But you *do* need it." David insisted. "It'll keep you safe from the fairies. Every property needs to be salted at least once a fortnight, ideally weekly. You've been lucky to survive this long."

The woman laughed, turning back to face him.

"Yes, I have." she agreed. "But that's got nothing to do with fairies. My children just want to spend the bare minimum easing their consciences."

"They do care." David continued. "The fairies could kill you."

"The fairies aren't going to kill me. Not this far out of the city. My children are perfectly aware of this." Narrowing her eyes at David, the old woman gestured for him to follow. Wordlessly, he wandered behind her, frozen ground crunching beneath his boots. After a few minutes of walking, she stopped near the stone wall of the estate and kicked a solid lump in the ground that was surrounded by wiry shrubs.

"The fairies aren't going to hurt me just as long as I don't step over *this.*"

David frowned.

"What is it?"

Bending down with surprising agility, the woman dug at the ground with her gardening gloves and exposed a dull metal edge. She patted it triumphantly.

"You see."

David approached carefully, leaning down beside her and removing his glove to touch the cold metal. He pushed the surrounding dirt to the side to reveal what appeared to be some kind of track.

"A train track?"

"Not just any train track." Her eyes glinted. "An *iron* train track. My grandfather thought he would make his fortune building a railway line around the city, back when it was still mostly forest – he invested just about everything he had in it. Freight trains, for transporting goods and materials." She sighed. "But iron is no good for railway tracks. It's not durable – erodes too quickly under the weight of the trains." She laughed bitterly. "So, they were declared unfit for purpose and abandoned."

"But iron is so valuable these days," David brushed off his hands. "Why just leave it here?"

The woman began walking slowly back in the direction of her house.

"What's more valuable than an iron ring around the city? Built prior to the emergence of those things," her magnificent eyes

193

glittered, "a cage to keep the monsters inside, not that my grandfather was ever aware that it would serve such a crucial purpose – one, I ought to add, that my family was never compensated for. It's so overgrown now that nobody will ever come across it and only the people we want to know will ever know about it." She cackled between coughs. "There was a time when the suburbs were cheap."

"No," David shook his head. "It can't surround the city; the fairies must have found a way through it. They're still killing people in the suburbs." He paused, shuddering internally as he visualised the young man sprawled across the tennis court.

The old woman shrugged, the hint of a smile on her lips.

"But imagine you *could* keep them out, you could put iron rings round whole communities and keep them safe." David paused thoughtfully.

"And you'd be out of a job." She coughed into her glove. "Anyway, you can go. Pass the message on that I need a chimney sweep – or a gardener. Ideally both."

David waited for the old woman to return to the house before lining her doors and windows with a fine sprinkling of salt that she would barely notice.

When David woke up, there was a woman in bed beside him. It took him a moment to recall the previous night, his date who had invited herself in for a drink and then declared that it was too far to walk home with night closing in. He hadn't planned on seeing her again, the date itself had been uninspiring, and he had found her conversation vacuous. She spoke of friends he had never met as though she expected him to be interested in their lives and showed him videos on her phone which she found funny. David had pretended to laugh. He only agreed to the drink back at his because he was too polite to say no.

He hadn't slept well that night, he never did sleep well when he shared a bed. Every sharp intake of breath or small movement woke him, and he would startle, glancing from side to side in the darkness, questioning whether he had remembered to salt his doors that night.

She got herself ready at a painfully slow pace while David tried his best to emphasise how late he was for work. Out of politeness, he nipped into a café and got them both a coffee and a bacon roll. She lingered by his stop and leaned in to kiss him as he got on the bus. He deflected the kiss with a hug, wondering how he could sensitively let her down.

David finished his bacon roll just as the bus came to a halt at the stop nearest Elder Tree Park and he jumped off, jogging the rest of the journey in an attempt to make up time. The temperature had dropped significantly so that each gasp was visible in the air. Making a point not to look at the tennis court when he arrived, he got to work salting the doors and windows as quickly as possible. However, in his rush he realised that he hadn't counted properly which resulted in him going over everything again, by which point he was flustered and checking his watch anxiously. Flakes of snow drifted past his face and eventually gave way to a violent flurry that swirled round him and rested on the frozen ground. He shivered, wishing his work jacket was better quality. Once he had finished up, he made his way back to the bus stop just as the bus he was supposed to catch pulled away. Cursing loudly, he dropped his pack into the snow with a dull thud and sat on the plastic bench to wait for the next bus, the last bus until tomorrow. He waited for nearly half an hour.

"*Oi!*" Someone shouted from across the street and David squinted at them through the snow. "Buses are cancelled because of the weather! You'll need to find another way home."

Before David could say anything back, the stranger had vanished round the street corner, leaving him alone by the stop. Looking nervously around, David knew he could never walk the distance home and none of the taxis would risk being out that late. He had his tent, but given the freezing temperature, he wasn't convinced that his company would have provided him with anything suitable for these conditions. If he asked nicely, he was certain that the residents of Elder Tree Park would take pity on him and let him sleep on a floor. Mrs McNeil might even give him a sofa for the night.

Breaking into a run which was easier than he expected, he made his way back to Elder Tree Park just as the sky was darkening. The gate was shut by that point, but he clambered over it with relative ease.

"Hello!" He banged on several doors but received no response. "It's David, your salt spreader – I'm stuck! Can anyone help me?"

The sky was a threatening navy as the sun descended entirely. Realising he was out of time, David reached for his pack to pitch his tent and risk the elements. However, when his hand touched his back, there was nothing there. To his horror, he realised that he had left his pack with his tent and the salt at the bus stop. Night had fallen and there was no way he would make it back to his pack in time.

He stopped, frozen in fear. Due to the flurry of snow, he could barely see several feet ahead of him, but as he listened more closely, he could hear the crunch of approaching footsteps. He realised that nobody was going to help him and if he remained still, he was going to die a horrible death. Moving blindly forward, he bumped into parked Range Rovers and tripped on potted plants that were now completely covered by the snow. He recalled that the residents' bar sold food and if that was still the case, he bet that there would be salt in one of the cupboards. Breaking into a sprint, he raced towards the residents' leisure building and kicked at the backdoor entrance which wasn't even locked. It swung open with ease, and he barrelled down the corridor to the small bar, leaping over the polished mahogany surface and shattering several glasses that had been left lying out.

Breathlessly, he swung open the cupboard doors, pushing aside bottles, jars of coffee, crisps and nuts. He stopped at the sight of a tiny paper packet, like the ones takeaways offered. It had barely anything inside, but he figured if he was careful, there might be enough to form a very sparse circle around himself. Sitting down, he tucked his knees into his chest and tore open the packet. The salt ran out just as it completed the circle. He cried out in relief and buried his head in his hands just as the bar door creaked open. Shutting his eyes tightly, he listened to the floorboards groan as the monsters shuffled around the bar, the sound of their breath filled the silence between creaks. Despite a lifetime of curiosity, he couldn't bring himself to open his eyes and look. When he could no longer hear their breath or movement, he exhaled a heavy gasp, opening his eyes and looking at the empty space around him. A tear of relief rolled down his cheek and he brushed it aside. To his surprise, there was a stickiness to the tip of his index finger. Curious, he touched it to his tongue and let the sweetness linger in his mouth. He frowned and reached for the salt packet, holding it close to his face to read the small

196

print in the darkness. It was sugar. That meant he hadn't been invisible to the fairies, they had walked around him and chosen not to attack. He stepped out of the circle, confused as he crept tentatively to the door, peering from side to side down the corridor. There was the faint whisper of voices nearby which he followed to the entrance of the leisure building. As he hid behind a decorative pillar, he made out a cluster of shadowy figures. Leaning in, he listened carefully.

"Well at least we know it wasn't another burglar." He made out Mr Nicholson's voice above the storm. "It's that idiot salt spreader. He must have missed his bus. I heard public transport was cancelled because of the storm."

"His name's David," Mrs McNeil's voice was instantly recognisable. "He's actually very nice."

David opened his mouth to tell them he was there, but a little voice inside told him to wait and listen just a little longer.

"Well, no harm done." Another voice from the homeowner's association. "To be perfectly honest, I'm relieved."

"Oh, me too." Mrs McNeil agreed. "Nasty business with that last boy."

"I did suggest we just call the police."

"Well, you know they wouldn't have done anything, he'd have been in and out of here with most of our valuables by the time they arrived and then gone and spread the message to all his city friends that we were easy pickings. How long do you think it would be before they figured out that nothing gets beyond those railway tracks?"

"On the plus side, property prices would go up even more."

"Everyone we want to know already knows."

There was a flurry of muffled agreement.

"Thank goodness you realised it was the salt spreader," another voice interjected. "Roger was just about to stick him with his kitchen knife! Can you imagine?"

"You really must stop using a knife if you want people to believe it's the fairies, Roger." A sniff of disapproval. "It's too clean a cut."

David's eyes widened as he continued to watch them from the shadows, suppressing the urge to run at them in a blind rage.

Mr Nicholson cleared his throat in obvious indignance.

"It's a good thing really," he insisted. "That boy will go home and tell all his city friends how he narrowly escaped the fairies in the suburbs, and they'll think twice about travelling any distance to bother us. You're all a hell of a lot younger than me, but I recall the days when we had to lock our doors every night." He cleared his throat. "The more people too scared to go out at night the better."

There was another murmur of agreement.

"It's all quite exciting actually." Mrs McNeil giggled. "I haven't been out this late in a while. You get used to an early bedtime, don't you?"

"Nothing wrong with an early bedtime, Shirley," Mr Nicholson said firmly. "This is a nice neighbourhood; we all value our peace. Let's keep it that way."

"Good morning, David!" Mrs McNeil waved as she jogged by.

"Good morning, Mrs McNeil." David smiled politely, stepping carefully over a cluster of snowdrops that had appeared as the temperature rose. "Beautiful day, isn't it?"

"Isn't it just – it's lovely to see you smile again, the cold weather really can make folk a bit blue."

David's smile didn't falter as he continued to look at her. For a while, he hadn't been able to look at any of the residents of Elder Tree Park for fear of betraying the hatred and anger that he felt for them. Instead, he kept his head down and offered only monosyllabic answers. However, he didn't feel any anger towards them any more, not since he had told his friends back in the city about the iron railway. Together, they had unearthed the tracks, and whilst David was at work that day, they were in the process of dismantling them. After all, iron was worth a fortune. The savviest amongst them had made a valid point about the property market once the fairies had free reign. City properties would once again become coveted and their value would soar.

"Well," Mrs McNeil continued. "You have a glorious day."

"You too, Shirley."

As Shirley jogged away down the immaculate footpath, David approached the front door of Mr Nicholson's house. Bending down by the doorstep, he opened his pack and sprinkled the entrance to the house with a fine dusting of sugar.

~*~

With thanks to my lovely friend Nicki for sharing your knowledge of railways and for your invaluable feedback.

198

A Body's Got To Have Hope

Angela Slatter

Today, the god is late.

Muriel hopes, perhaps a little foolishly, that it's okay. That nothing's happened to it. Not because she thinks it has any finer feelings for her – she's not *that* cracked – and knows that, in a pinch, it'll eat her as soon as look at her if there's nothing else around. In her favour, she's just skin and bones like most of the remaining population (not at all tempting). There are the exceptions, of course, there always are.

But she really hopes nothing's happened to the god because she's gone to a lot of trouble today, given that it's an anniversary of sorts even if not many will remember it, not after everything else. She even left her very own patch in the wasteland, where the Imperial War Museum used to be (still is, really, just repurposed), picked her way through the landmines that were sown in the last days when England's remaining royals were trying to hang on, holed up in the Lord Ashcroft Gallery, hoping beyond hope that, somehow, they'd survive. But… well, a surprising amount of its holdings were still quite explodey, to everyone's collective amazement. Muriel's learned the safe ways through it all, knows what to avoid, where to tread light as a faerie. Has made a nice little home for herself in Lambeth she has, foraged furniture, boobytrapped the entrance hall, and has a lifetime's worth of canned goods and teabags in the old museum café.

Some days, though, she does get a bit sick of spam and jam.

Yet she's not going to give up or take silly risks (even though some might argue that even breathing nowadays is a silly risk). Nope. All efforts are aimed at survival; no intention of going any sooner than she has to. Wants to stick around and see what happens next. Maybe make a difference, big or small.

She doesn't like to wander too far these days, mind, what with the Tube mostly flooded, buses and cars all burnt out, roads and tunnels impassible, but scavenging runs are necessary. She hears the National Gallery is still going though, that's where the last of the London curators and librarians gathered, after well… everything. A weird little community now, militant about their remaining charges, some entirely devoted to the portraits in the NPG, little cults springing up in rival wings and rooms, some coming to blows over Gainsboroughs and Reynolds and the provenance of a couple of Picassos. Rumours of the Ditchley Portrait shifting around at night all on its own. Muriel would bet a tenner that it's sprites, having fun. If she had a tenner that is; if anyone did any more. Humans don't really have time for such frivolity now – either betting or pranks; take everything very seriously since the well-you-know. But there's definitely been a notable rise in sightings of formerly hidden creatures, things that no longer bother to stay in the shadows or below ground or in those spaces between breaths. Pixies and hobgoblins and the like. A legion of Jenny Greenteeth along the Thames, and all her once-buried sisters now back in the light, Bazalgette's careful work undone. At least one barghest per park or green or common.

Yeah, she went to a lot of trouble today and now the bloody sack's moving, and she's not sure she's got the strength to drag it back home, so she'll wait a bit longer. All that wriggling, though, just won't do so Muriel aims her battered Doc Martens at it, gives a couple of satisfying kicks; the squirming subsides. She's tired but pleased; never undertook to wait patiently.

The minutes pass, the sun peeks out from behind the blasted grey sky every so often – more often than it ever did before the well-you-know – and she stretches, enjoys the brief warmth. A November treat, a fortunate day. The longer she waits, the lower her mood dips; all that work, all for nothing –

The sound startles her even though she's been expecting it, the terrible scrape and scratch, an industrial kind of a shriek. She breathes a sigh of relief. Recognises the noise made by the front end of a

London bus that forms part of the left leg, a thunderous step, then the grate and grind of a limb dragged ever so slightly.

"Thank feck." She prods the sack, elicits a groan. "The wait's over."

Muriel's been feeding it for almost a year now, and it's grown, yes it has, on a diet of small dogs and errant children. Not cats, though. Never cats. Cats are something different, probably closer to the god in nature, Muriel's quite sure, and there's no point upsetting it. Or them – last thing she needs is a feline attack on the IWM, not when those furry fuckers move so lightly they'd never trigger any of the traps. But right now, she's got other things to consider as the god heaves into view.

It's made of metal and glass and just a little bit of shit.

Well, there's brown stuff at least that appears to leak from its joints – the places where metal and glass meet, the poorly melded hinges of shoulders, elbows, hips and knees. Industrial and organic. Looks like a fawn, only larger-larger, long arms and legs, those cloven hoofs, hands-or-paws like satellite dishes, turbine blade shoulders. And the head…

The head shaped vaguely like a pot plant, vines and flowers growing down, curling around horns of spiralling wood – almost, she thinks, like someone took them from a statue in a church, an art gallery, a museum, even those old very private libraries, places like that. Places fallen into disuse and ruin – the Tate drowned, the Tate Modern too (thankfully, some say). Muriel considers, as she watches the god lurch toward her, all those buildings blown to pieces, all the things that rained down afterwards, a precipitation of smaller and larger chunks, sometimes nothing more than dust molecules, sometimes the side of a house, sometimes the foundation stones from the Houses of Parliament. Thinks of all those crushed beneath the unexpected weight of a strange storm. All the blood in the cracks, all the blood in the bricks…

"Hello," she calls to the god, casually, respectfully. A fond familiarity, reverential. "Something special for you today."

Muriel unties the neck of the sack, the spiky fibres of the rope can't penetrate the toughened skin of her hands and fingertips. Pulls the hessian back and hears the contents take a gasping breath,

201

prematurely relieved. "Nothing new for you, thinking you're special, eh? Right Honourable Member for Whatever-the-fuck-it-was."

He's still in a pinstriped suit, of all things, like he'll be called back in for the afternoon sitting at Westminster, waiting for the sound of Big Ben to tell him where to be, when to come and go. Some of them still live in big houses in Mayfair, Knightsbridge and the like, with survival shelters built beneath, deeper down than the houses are built up, designed to keep the rich safe and sound for years to come. Until it's "safe" to come out, until all the folk they failed to protect from taxes and plagues, bombs and rapes and themselves, were at last *gone*.

But Muriel's noticed on her scavenging runs that sometimes there are lights on in the houses, and bodies moving about in the day – maybe they think they're less likely to be noticed – as if they've come up for air or out of boredom. Whatever, she's been watching, and this was her reward. Can't believe he's wearing that fucking suit. Only missing his bowler hat.

"I can –" he gasps.

"You really can't." She shakes her head. "You're not special, not to me, but maybe you'll make a difference this way."

Muriel steps back, holds her hands palm-out, spreads her arms wide. A gesture that says, *He's all yours*. The god's huge head nods, sways, the foliage swings forward and back. "But something better might come, with enough blood in the bricks, the right sort of blood," she says. "A body's got to have hope."

The Call

James Everington

He didn't quite mean to end up alone, but somehow it happened. It was the end of term, and the last of his freshers' year exams was delayed by some bureaucratic cock up, giving him a few extra weeks revision time with Kafka, Canetti, and the rest of the European Moderns. All of his housemates had finished their exams and gone back home for the summer break. He considered doing the same, to revise in company. But funds were tight at term's end and besides, surely he didn't mind some solitude? Introvert, bookworm – he spent a lot of time alone anyway. He had his books, his tapes and CDs, had his revision to do – he could cope with a fortnight alone.

After four days of seeing no one, of talking to no one but himself (and then so loudly and unnaturally that he soon stopped) he thought he might have made a mistake. Not a serious, life-changing one, admittedly, but one that would fortify his already deep-set shyness and the intermittent loneliness that accompanied it. Truth was, he had few friends, finding it hard to talk to people. Thrown into a house with three strangers at the start of uni life he'd become friends with them by default, by their efforts more than his. But he'd made few other friends, certainly no one he could just call and ask if they were still in town and wanted to meet up.

One evening the sense of itchy, cooped up dissatisfaction forced him from the house. The door shut on the latch behind him with a loud click and he nervously checked his keys were in his pockets, for what would he do if locked out? They were. One of the neighbourhood cats sauntered towards him, stopped purring when he stooped to pet it, sauntered away with the disinterest of a well-fed feline. He sighed, checked his keys again, started walking towards the city centre. It was a short walk from where he lived if you used the canal towpath. He felt somewhat anxious doing so, it was always busy with people unsteadily drunk and bunched together, obliviously pushing past on the uneven path, edging him towards the still and stinking water.

There was a pub where he knew, by repute if not by experience, that students from his course went. Most of them would have had their last exam delayed too, so were more likely to still be in town. The pub was crowded, but although that increased the odds of seeing someone he recognised, it made him more tense. He walked with his head down to the bar, flushed with a shame no one else noticed when he got IDed ordering a lager. He walked quickly towards a free table, cursing as his over-full pint glass spilt beer over his hand, left a trail behind him like he'd pissed himself. The table was unsteady and as he set his drink down he spilt even more, flushed even more. He didn't look up from the damp and beer-sticky table until he was three quarters through his drink.

After his days of silence in the house, the pub seemed deafening and crazed with the noise of people talking. It took him a while to readjust, to shed his face-blindness and to distinguish individual voices in the din trapped under the low ceiling of the pub. When he did so, he saw three people he knew over in the far corner.

Well, 'knew' was a strong word. The two boys and one girl were in the same Contemporary Writing tutor group as he was. Lots of the students studying English Lit appeared to be doing so despite having no great love for or interest in books, but these three he remembered because while they were obviously cooler and more outgoing than he was, they spoke confidently and passionately about the assigned texts too. His own love of reading had always made him feel geeky; they made theirs seem all of a piece with the fact they liked all the right bands, wore the latest trainers, espoused the right student politics. Once, their tutor had told the class to write and read aloud a contemporary urban haiku; voice fluttering he'd done so and one of the boys had said it was "really good". Looking over gratefully to their group, he saw the girl (who was a redhead with a nose stud and who he thought was very pretty and assumed was seeing one of the boys) had given him a thumbs up.

None of the three were looking his way now. He remembered as they'd left the tutor group the other week they'd been talking about going to see a band at one of the local venues he'd never dared enter. He went to get another pint and checked the pub jukebox; flushing again he put in a pound he could ill afford and selected three songs by that band, then scuttled back to his seat. He stared into his beer; he wasn't expecting them to come over all smiles, wasn't expecting to be invited to their table or wherever they were going later... but maybe when he looked up, a nod of recognition. A smile, a thumbs up from the girl. "Hey look, that guy from our tutor group, the one who wrote...".

When he did raise his head, he saw they were standing and pulling on their coats, laughing at some in-joke, drunkenly, voices blurred in with everyone else's. They didn't appear to have recognised him or the song that was playing. He sank lower in his chair, face flamed, hoping now they wouldn't look his way, hoping they wouldn't remember him at all. He closed his eyes. He smelt cigarette smoke, BO, the gents toilets. Did he even *like* the song that was playing? When he opened his eyes the pub seemed so crowded with people he'd never dare speak to that he couldn't tell if the three students had actually left yet or not.

He spent the next two days alone in the house, revising and revising the same meaningless page from Eagelton's *Literary Theory* over and over again.

Early the next evening, the phone rang.

The sound of the rotary phone made him physically jump, so loud it seemed in the silent house, in his silent life. He approached it slowly, cautiously, half-hoping whoever it was would hang up before he answered. He hated speaking on the phone and normally let his housemates answer. After all, it was never for *him*, and this call wouldn't be either.

When he said hello into the receiver, lack of use made his voice sound both clumsy and more eager than he'd intended.

"So, how are you?" a voice said briskly, as if the two of them were already mid-conversation. He had the odd sensation of both recognising it and not knowing who it was. "Thought I'd give you a

205

call," the voice continued, "see how you were doing all shut up on your own."

"I'm, uh, all right," he said, for what else could you say when someone asked you how you were? Can't complain. "So, uh, I…"

"*Are* you though?" the voice said, cutting off his attempt to ask who was calling him. "Are you all right?"

"Yes, I, um, am," he said. Mustn't grumble. "I'm all right with my own company," he added.

"Well of course you are!" the voice said, enthusiastically convinced. "That's why I called! Why don't we meet up tonight? I won't take no for an answer!"

He didn't know how to respond, and when talking on the phone he always wanted to end the conversation quickly. So he heard himself making a wordless noise that was nonetheless affirmative.

"I knew it," the voice said, softer now, so it sounded more intimate, closer. Sounded like someone else. "So I'll see you there," it said.

"Where?" he said, but only after whoever had called had hung up.

He held the phone to his ear a few seconds longer, until the flush and tension faded from his face. Not that they did entirely. The house was silent around him. You could call 1471, see who called, he thought. Dial them back. Find out.

But he didn't.

He went upstairs, showered and changed, brushed his teeth. He left the house, checked his keys, took the shortcut towards the city. He smelt canal water, cut grass from the verges, BBQ on the wind. He thought the city centre busy, but then he always thought places were busy. He walked without destination but without hesitation: down this road, cross this street, left at the end. It was hot, people were sitting outside drinking cocktails or tall glasses of beer at tables out in the streets. It made the streets feel different, narrower, foreign, and he felt a vague disquiet that he might become lost in his home town. But it *isn't* your home, is it? he thought bitterly. You left home, came here, and you've barely explored it except when chaperoned by your housemates. All the people crowding the unfamiliar, sweltering streets – it was their home not his. He wiped sweat from his brow, wishing he could just as easily wipe the blush from his face.

When he reached the bar, whose name he didn't know, on a road he didn't recognise, there were bouncers framing the steps down below street level that led to the door. He prepared to fumble out his student ID card, but they stepped aside to let him pass before he could do so, moving smoothly and symmetrically apart like heavy gates opening. He descended the stairs carefully; there was a wooden door at the bottom. When he opened it and stepped inside he didn't know whether he felt *déjà vu* or a drunken freshers' week memory. The place was packed, people at every table, dancing between the tables, thronging the understaffed bar. He normally would have run a mile; but he felt further away from home than that. Instead he walked straight towards a table near the back. People brushed against him, dancing to a song he recognised but couldn't say if he liked. He sat down at the table, took a sip from the cold and welcome beer already in front of him.

"Hey, you made it," the person sat opposite said.

He nodded, not sure what to say. But then, he never did. Nervously, he ran his forefinger through some spilt beer on the table, stopped suddenly and flushed when he realised what he was doing. The person sat opposite just watched, smiling.

Then they leant forward and did the same. Watching, he couldn't help but think that they weren't just copying his actions but the exact shapes he had traced in the foamy beer.

They leant back, licked the beer from their fingertip. "What is it?" they said, grimacing like a child at the taste.

How was he supposed to know what type of lager they'd bought both of them? "Beer," he said nervously, attempting a joke.

"Beer," they repeated, as if tasting the word, and then they drank deeply from the untouched glass in front of them. As if awaiting permission, he did the same, mirroring them. The person opposite was dressed oddly, a faded padded jacket with fake brass buttons, a crop top underneath, and a headband looking like it was fresh from the 80s. In the shadows the person's age was similarly vague; there were clues but they were all over the place: baby smooth cheeks, lank hair, crow's feet... even one hand looked younger – less gnarled and wrinkled – than the other rested next to it on the table. Chipped nail polish on both, in different colours.

"So how you been?" they said, accenting oddly. "All alone like you said and wanted?"

"Can't complain," he said. He smelt stale beer, dry-ice, menthol cigarettes. "Mustn't grumble."

"I thought so," they said, as if his answer had been different. "That's why I called you. You," they repeated.

"Uh, thanks," he said. "Genuinely, I mean…" But could he tell them that he hadn't been coping as well as he'd anticipated? "I've not been here before," he said instead, gesturing around the bar, although he wasn't sure if that was true. There were lots of people dancing in the bar, still to *that* band, like he'd chosen here and now as well as before. There was obviously some dance to the song that he wasn't cool enough to know, for everyone in the bar was making the same shapes as they moved, making the same convoluted and ritualised hand movements. But then, crowds always make him feel excluded.

"I know you don't like talking on that thing, that telephone," the person opposite was saying. "But how else was I meant to get you here? It's not like I could just pop round." They laughed raucously, and he laughed too, not getting the joke. They suddenly stopped laughing mid-breath, leaving his own laugher to sound lonely and misplaced until he too stopped.

"I don't like this," they said. "'Beer'. You have it." They pushed the still mostly full pint of lager across the table to him.

"Um, cheers," he said. "But I mean, it's my round, do you want a, uh, wine instead or coke or?"

They looked him like they didn't know what he was talking about, and he flushed like it was his fault.

"When you finish that," they said. "We'll go. Time's a tickin'"

They watched him with no sign of impatience or thirst as he finished his own beer, started on theirs. The lager was room-temperature and gassy but he didn't want to look ungrateful by not finishing it. They looked on unblinking. He felt sweaty and unattractive and tongue-tied, but that was hardly uncommon enough to blame on their gaze. They asked him occasional questions which they must have known the answers to ("at university," he answered; "English Lit," he answered; "music," he answered; "dancing, they're dancing," he answered gesturing towards the swaying synchronised crowd). They were obviously making small-talk to break the silence, although it was seemingly he who felt awkward about the silence not them. It seemed to take him an age to finish the second beer, although when he did that same bloody song was still playing so it couldn't have; the people in the bar were still dancing in unison and placing their hands steeple-like together as they did so.

"Yes," the person opposite said. "Let's go and make a call." They stood briskly and he followed suit. They picked up a carrier bag that must have been by their side the whole time; it looked distended and close to bursting with whatever was inside. He saw what looked like stakes and offcuts of painted wood sticking from the top of it. He smelt tar, super glue, cardamom. He'd read smells were one of the surest ways to evoke memory, evoke emotion, but he felt nothing, his head pleasantly blank as though the beer had been much stronger. The music suddenly ceased playing mid-that song – how could it be closing time? – but no one else made a move to leave other than them. As they left, the others all stood quiet and straight-backed and sober, avoiding eye-contact like a bride or a dignitary or a coffin was passing by. The bouncers similarly stood aside and framed their exit from the underground bar.

"This way," the person said and he followed. After the hubbub of the bar, the streets seemed emptied, the bars and cafes shut up, darkened. They were leading him down side-streets then alleyways, away from where people might be. The only sounds he could hear were the rustle of the carrier bag his companion held and the awkward noise of their footsteps as they walked: their shoes were unlaced and seemed several sizes too big. There was also – was there? – a soft ambient hiss that, when he paused to try and identify its source, seemed to be both coming from the close black sky above and not to be there at all.

Wordlessly, he was led down red-brick-sided alleys and cut-throughs, losing what little sense of direction and location had remained to him, although surely he couldn't be as far from recognisable landmarks as he felt. The air was unusually humid, and steam was rising from vents in the streets, something he thought only happened in movies or other cities. He started to notice the alleys were widening and foreign seeming: this one was lined with small empty bamboo cages, white feathers stuck to the sides twitching in a breeze he couldn't feel. Wooden barrels, stacked corded wood, scorch marks in the road from burnt out fires seemingly lit right here in the street...

They stopped. "Here," they said in an accent that bore scant resemblance to the one they had spoken with before (just as their voice in the bar had not been the same as that on the phone earlier). "Here, now."

"Um, okay... what?" he said, coughing from a throat parched dry despite the beers he had sunk. They didn't answer, they put down their carrier bag and rummaged inside it. He smelt leaded petrol, honeysuckle, manure. They stood, a bundle of painted sticks, old tent pegs, snapped bamboo canes in their hands. They looked up to the hissing, fizzing night sky as though it were something they might stretch up to and tear down, closed their eyes, held out their burdened arms (which he saw now were both tattooed and scarred), licked their lips, and let all they were holding drop and scatter across the uneven and muck-stained alley.

They remained in the same pose: head up neck bared eyes closed arms out. They licked their lips. "What do you see?" they said, and it was the first he'd heard a hesitation, a *need* in their voice. Suddenly he felt like he was going to be very, very sick, and he had a massive and painful erection. The sky sounded like spitting, shivering, smoking oil and looked like it was sinking down and he'd soon need to stoop.

"Wh... what?" he said.

"What do you *see?*" they demanded. "Quickly, before... What shapes do you see? What words? What places? Do you see people? See... friends?"

"P... people?" he said, aware he wanted to say something else. He looked down at the jumble of detritus they had thrown to the street, looked away, stopped, looked closer. The sky *boiled*.

"I see..." he started.

He wasn't hungover as such the next morning, but listless and lacking focus; his memories of the previous night were groggy and nebulous and lacked separation from the strange dreams he'd endured. The house was too, too quiet. Yet he didn't put the TV or one of his CDs on – he was waiting for a call, he realised.

He brushed his teeth and winced, some of his teeth feeling loose and his gums enflamed. When he spat out his spit was brown, stringy with something he couldn't identify, but which smelt bad. There was something stuck between two of his teeth; when he probed it with his tongue it felt like a splinter of wood. He showered, scrubbed whatever the hell was under his fingernails away, shampooed the bonfire smell from his hair.

He opened his revision notes but they seemed incomprehensible to his itchy and red-raw eyes. Still, the way he scanned the shapes of his handwriting for meaning reminded him of something, dreamt or half-forgotten, which made him uneasy. One day not revising wouldn't hurt – he just sat in the empty lounge, talking to himself. Eventually, he did turn the TV on, but it was obviously broken for the screen displayed only static and the speaker only hissed and he was again reminded of something opaque from the night that made him want to nervously hunch down. He'd let one of his flatmates call the TV rental company; he didn't like speaking on the phone. And besides wasn't he waiting for it to ring?

Later, it did.

"Yes," he said. "Yes, I'll see you there."

He left the house, didn't bother to check his pockets for his keys. The neighbour's cat rushed straight over to him, mewing and winding around his legs as if starving. He set off towards the city. He wasn't wearing a coat, the day didn't seem hot or cold, it just was, an ambient thing around him. The sky was empty of clouds; he told himself it was just his dreams making him think it was empty of more than that. There was a faint hiss to it, but that was his ears still ringing from the loud music in the bar last night.

The cobbled path besides the slow waters of the canal didn't seem to be busy at this time of day (not that he was sure what time it actually was) and without having to worry about dodging or stepping aside for other people he walked distracted in his own thoughts.

When he next realised where he was, he saw there was steam rising in the streets; there was shit and spilt paint and the contents of overturned dustbins on the pavements. He smelt burnt sugar, wood

211

smoke, spunk. His temples throbbed, the sky hissed and wavered in his vision like something ill-defined yet falling, and none of the words he saw on the shop signs, advertising hoardings, pages of newspaper and scraps of pornography blowing in the windless streets against his legs like something weak pawing at him... None of the words made the slightest bit of sense. He went left, crossed a wide road without looking, turned right, ducked down a backstreet. Was this the way they'd led him, last night? He thought so, although the day's grey, wavering light made it hard to be sure.

Left, out of the alley to cross another road, down another side street, into an adjoining alleyway. He smelt cinnamon and silage and rendered fat and gas leaks; he was hunched under the dead static locust sizzling meat sound of a blank and cloudless sky slung too low. Right, left – he doubted he could find his way back if he tried. Had he fallen and not realised? For he was rubbing mud and shit and oil from his hands.

And yes: a shadow outstretched as if flung from a bigger, lower sun than the anaemic one already falling; a shadow made strange by the outlines of eccentric and ill-matched clothing; the rustling sound of a carrier bag.

They were still head up neck bared eyes closed arms out. Filth and rot and small bones and old maps and stakes like those used to kill monsters permanently were spread out incomprehensibly in front of them. He told himself he wasn't going to look, especially as he thought (*hands dashing and scattering the shapes the shapes among the sticks and stakes and dry dog shit and not just seeing but*) that he'd done more than look, previously.

"There you are," they said in a voice he didn't recognise, "are you there?" They looked exhausted, as if they'd been in this pose all this time, which was impossible. He'd been called, hadn't he? They licked their lips. They opened their eyes.

"What did you see?" they said.

"P... people?" he said, and again he wanted to say something else. Again, he *wanted* something else, even as he shrank from it.

He stared at them, not sure if they recognised him or he them. But he hoped to God he did, for as he'd walked here he'd realised: other than this still and absurd figure in front of him, the entire city under its collapsed tent static scarred sky had been as quiet and empty of people as his house had been for days.

Fulfilment
Harvey Welles and Phil Raines

"Ally, you won't believe what he's done this time."

Ally didn't say anything. She could probably guess, but since Donna tracking her all the way to the break room to tell her might well be the best thing in the whole of Donna's working day, Ally indulged her colleague. "Okay, what?"

"Milverine."

"That some kind of drug?"

"No, *Milverine*. Milwaukee's very own Wolverine."

Ally still looked blank. Donna shook her head – Ally was renowned for having nothing to do with social media. "The guy who walks around everywhere without his shirt? Stacked like Hugh Jackman? Sideburns and all?"

"A Marvel movie guy?"

"A god-damned celebrity guy, Ally."

"Working here?"

Her co-worker winced. "Of course not. We can't hire anyone for shit and suddenly we have an X-Men lookalike working as a packer?"

"I don't get it."

"Come on, not the real Milverine. He's got an *imposter* into the packing team."

"So – someone who looks like someone who looks like someone else?"

"It's batshit, Ally. But packers are still lining up for his autograph. Got their own little cult down in the packing hall."

Now Ally got it, and she whistled. "He's really getting desperate this time."

Ally didn't want to think about this. If the packers were distracted, with the knock-on, just about every team in the warehouse would be

213

fucked. And everyone's performance would dive – again. And that would mean supervisor Gene would bring more shit to Quality's doorstep, and Ally, Donna and Rafal would have to pull more overtime and – Jesus, they were tired enough already. Twice this week, Donna had had to call her mother to pick up Natalie, and Ally could smell the fortifying swigs on Rafal's breath every morning now.

She could almost get why *he* kept doing this. He was just looking out for the other packers, maybe the whole warehouse workforce, trying to get them all to bond together or something. Ally understood about looking out for your colleagues – she didn't think she could count the number of times she'd stepped forward for Donna and Rafal – but dammit, it was just work.

Ally was still considering her next move, when Rafal returned from his rotation around the warehouse. "*Mierda*, have you heard?"

"About the knock-off superhero?"

"What?" His face showed he didn't know anything about that. "Nah, I mean the accident."

Ally and Donna sat down. This was serious.

The loading bay – someone slipped on a ramp, someone hadn't braced a refrigerator properly, someone's foot was crushed. Donna and Rafal talked back and forth about how loading had to stop treating their safety for shit and how someone was going to get really hurt, one day, certainly worse, and if it wasn't loading, it would be some mechanical failure with the pallets or shelves or somewhere else in this deathtrap of a warehouse.

Ally was only half listening. "That'll work."

Rafal and Donna stopped talking – their esteem for her was still disconcerting. "Ally?"

"Follow me."

Ally didn't like going into the packing hall – it felt like ground zero of everything that was going wrong in the warehouse. Even more so today when she saw a *Packers Welcome Milverine!* banner over the metal detector and creepy packs of what she took to be toy Milverine bobble-heads all around the entrance to the hall. Inside she could hear the froth of activity, people taking selfies, ranking their favourite Marvel movies, bonding shit.

Ally felt bad about getting Donna and Rafal to do her dirty work, but she couldn't bring herself to go in. Anyway, they were better at the gossiping thing – picking a few packers on their own, casually telling them about the accident in loading, wondering how long before the distraction of Milverine would cause one in Packing and what Gene would do if there were *two* accidents in this shift.

A few well-placed words, and it would spread through the whole crew down here. Give it an hour, she reckoned. She didn't even have to come down here, but she just wanted to see if *he* was here.

But there was no sign of Pep.

The next morning, even before Donna bounded up to her with the news, Ally knew. She'd seen the trashcans filled with bobble-head toys.

This week's inspiration: *Make time for your family at home, but make a family for your time at work*

Team performance on previous cycle:
Packing A B C D E decline
Picking A B C D E decline
Boxing A B C D E decline
Loading A B C decline
Stocking A B C decline
Housekeeping A B decline
Quality A B no change

Days without an accident: 11

Both Donna and Rafal came to fetch her, but Ally had already guessed. "Sweet Jesus, you can hear it all the way over here."

Only fifteen minutes left in the break – Ally could tell them to fuck off, she was bone weary and her shoulder was sore again. But when had she ever done that to these two? So she put away her sigh and her Yolanda Arroyo Pizarro paperback and followed them out to the parking lot.

Rafal licked his lips the same way he did when talking about the Bucks blowing away the Lakers or the Heat. "Corporate will really fry some ass now."

Ally pointed to Gene, standing at the edge of the lot, eating a buffalo sandwich and frybread. He was already wearing an Oneida Nation cap, enjoying it all.

There were stalls with cooking and clothing and leaflets to clubs and associations, other stalls with baskets with weird symbols and totem poles that Ally knew would pop up all over the warehouse. A dozen stalls, and just as many Native American nations represented. A big flag announcing the Indian Summer Festival affiliated them with the city-wide event. Ally recognised a few of the workers there – especially the Fox picker with threaded braids, one of the cleaners who always wore a Potowatomi casino t shirt – but the majority were outsiders.

Ally calculated quickly. It wouldn't look good for Gene to close down a festival offshoot celebrating local roots and traditions, but he couldn't tolerate warehouse staff drinking beer during working hours, not with performance the way it was, according to the official posters all over the walls. A supervisor would clock what was happening, revel in it for ten minutes, then report back. Eventually they would all feel the punishment – little extensions to their working time that might mean missing an hourly bus home, less regular re-stocking of the snack machine, something. A few might say fuck this place and jump to the new Amazon facility in Oak Creek, but most would just stay and simmer, like frogs in a pan of water over a stove.

"Hey Nuna."

"Ladies and gentlemen, we are blessed with Wonder Woman!" The Fox cleaner hooked fingers with Ally, flipped her braids. "Wonder Woman is owed a free taco for persuading Gene to give us those fine new uniforms."

"Well, if it comes with that hot sauce I'm hearing about…"

"Only the best for the best."

"Ah, this is tasty. So when we getting that broken toilet fixed?"

Nuna put her head in her hands – that toilet down the south end of the warehouse was a sore point. "I'm lighting candles and saying prayers to management."

Ally smiled. "You praying for our jobs?"

"I'm praying they give Housekeeping a third team. Great Wisaka isn't listening."

"Si Dios quiere. Nuna, your sister still works at the casino?"

"Yeah, cleaning like me. Pay's worse, but she likes the people."

Later, Ally recognised his friend, Abraham at the Potowatomi stall and went over to him. "You're going to tell me this is full of shit."

"You? Full of shit? Ally, Ally – and what next, you start a book on the Brewers taking the Series?"

"Abraham, I know you're going to say it just ain't true what I heard. You know, about those blocked toilets in your casino."

"Talking shit about shit?"

"Talking shit about sabotage. Just I heard. Some tribal thing going on?"

Abraham snorted, but then he saw Ally pointedly looking across the parking at Nuna.

"Just not saying what someone's sister might be capable of."

When a fight broke out, Gene finally acted and security separated the groups and cleared the stalls out.

As the workers dispersed, Ally saw that Pep had been there all along, watching with a few of what Donna called *his groupies*. He stared at her a long time, but Ally just took that in and held it, before giving him a tip of the Oneida Nation hat she'd picked up from the ground.

```
This week's inspiration: Your best self is right here,
right now

Team performance on previous cycle:
Packing A B C D E decline
Picking A B C D E decline
Boxing A B C D E decline
Loading A B C decline
Stocking A B C decline
Housekeeping A B decline
Quality A B no change

Days without an accident: 2
```

Ally was beginning to accept that she was never going to get a whole lunch break to herself. Usually it was Donna or Rafal coming to report another accident, and Jesus, they were lucky it wasn't a fatality yet.

But it was Pep himself this time.

"I figure we should be introduced." He made the announcement grinning back to his retinue at the break room doorway. "I'm what they call your nemesis."

A few of the other tables looked up. Ally didn't look up from her bowl of sancocho. "That's not what they call you round here."

"Oh, I know what they call me. *Dark lord.*" He enunciated with glee. *"Master of the nether arts."*

Ally thought about the small bookshelf of fantasy paperbacks Pep had donated to the break room back when he first started, hoping to start a reading club. "They don't call you those things either."

Pep was wearing huge movie-star sunglasses as usual. Up close, she saw he wasn't much in the flesh – not even as tall as Donna and a lot chubbier than Rafal. He always wore a different sweatshirt to work. Today was *Milwaukee – The Well-Kept Secret!* Ally was pretty sure he wasn't from Milwaukee. She was pretty sure Pep wasn't from anywhere.

But he was right – this was the first time they'd ever spoken. How long had he been in the warehouse – a year? Two?

"But we don't have to be nemeses." He gripped the table top. "We could work together."

"You're a packer. I'm Quality."

"We can transcend such distinctions. We can build a community!"

She remembered him wearing that t-shirt as well.

Pep pulled up the chair and leaned forward. A fog of unwashed excitement enveloped Ally. "Do you know what people need to bring them together?"

"Someone annoying to hate."

Pep's conspiratorial whisper could be heard across the break room. "Festivals."

"We were lucky the police didn't get called the last time you tried that."

"I admit that was an error of judgement."

"So was getting someone to pretend to be a local TikTok legend."

"Life is trial and error. I realise now you can't bring people together artificially like that. If you're going to reap a sense of belonging, you need to sow what's really important to people here."

"Right. And what's really important to people here?"

"Their roots, of course! And that's why you could help." He paused, looking very pleased with what he was going to say next. "Three Kings."

"Three Kings the karaoke bar?"

"No. Three Kings the festival." Pep's voice got a little louder, addressing the whole audience in the break room. "Okay, it's not till January, but plenty of time for planning. I thought we could do some kind of procession in the parking lot. And cakes with – I don't know, gift tokens baked in? Little boxes with free wishes? And pop-up shrines – maybe use that decommissioned toilet?"

He leaned back, hands making a flourish like a bow. "But you and the others will know the kind of thing, right, Alanis?"

Ally took a few deep breaths. She hated the way Pep had used her full name.

"Because there are a few here?" Pep looked around. "Luis in Admin? And Jean, the new associate? All you Puerto Ricans?"

Ally squirmed. She only shared a bus route with Luis and couldn't tell you what Jean looked like.

"But you know, doesn't have to be Three Kings." Pep was talking quicker, sensing he was losing her. "What about – Bad Bunny? He's playing Detroit next year. We could hire a van, organise a trip. *Saluden a Titi*, right? *A ti te gusta lo malo, irte a fuego conmigo!*"

She spoke slowly and carefully. "Not every Puerto Rican likes Bad Bunny."

Not every Puerto Rican likes being Puerto Rican, she wanted to add.

"Don't worry, I'm not trying to single your people out! This is just the start. We'll move onto other groups. We'll have a whole calendar of community events."

"If people wanted a community they wouldn't work here."

Pep looked genuinely perplexed. "But – communities make people feel strong. It gives them *power.*"

"And the last time someone tried to start a union it didn't go well."

"Oh, I'm not talking about that kind of power. I'm talking about something more awesome than that. I'm talking *magic.* The magic of celebrating something bigger than yourself. Not union, but *communion.*"

"You got that from a sociology night class? Pep, stop."

"*Communion* plus *ritual* plus *faith* equals – *boom!* That's fulfilment. That's always been serious power."

"I said –"

219

"People come together, they act in unison, they believe, and who knows what they can —"

"*I. Said. Stop.*"

She didn't have to raise her voice. Finally Pep understood he was on the far side of a line he'd had no idea existed.

"So this is how you spend your time dreaming?" Then turning to his acolytes in the doorway, "All of you?"

The look on Pep's face, the way he struggled to keep it from collapsing into itself.

Ally came in for the kill. "That's not what brings people together here. We clock in, we do the line for ten hours, we take a shit if the toilet's not busted and we go home. It's not *communion* to cheer the Brewers for the ten minutes they get a sniff of the pennant. It's not *ritual* to read the same book together. It's not *faith* to go to some local folk festival, or any of the other stupid things you've tried. People have the line and their teams and their work. That's all that will ever matter here."

Her turn to lean forward. If he wanted that sense of belonging so badly, let him get the whiff of beef and cabbage from her lunchbox. "We check our roots at the door. This is company soil. And if you don't want them to shut this place, you'd better think about that and nothing else."

Pep was paralysed, processing.

"*Performance* is the only magic here, Pep."

She stood up and walked straight out. She felt the other tables watching. One of Pep's followers did a strange warding sign as she passed, but Ally didn't care. No bigger curse than getting back to the line late.

This week's inspiration: *A team is a family is a community is a new world waiting to happen*

Team performance on previous cycle:
Packing B **improved** A C D E no change
Picking A C D E decline B no change
Boxing A B D E decline C no change
Loading A B C decline
Stocking B C decline A no change
Housekeeping A B decline
Quality A B no change

Days without an accident: 19

"*Improved?*"

"No kidding, Ally."

Rafal didn't crack a smile so Ally knew Donna wasn't making this up. "I'm talking about Packing B."

Rafal muttered, "And you know whose team –"

Donna grunted. "That's right."

Ally shook her head. But as long as there was one positive number in the stats, Gene would stop fretting.

That afternoon, she saw workers standing in small groups around the new posters with the stats, murmuring. Ally recognised a few of the packers who worked with Pep, handing out small boxes. It almost looked like they'd been lifted from the line, but she could see that these were reject boxes: tape diagonal rather than straight edge, cardboard corners crumpled. Names had been written on in black felt capitals. Some of the workers took the boxes and laughed at what the packers whispered to them. Some carried the boxes away with shaking hands.

Afterwards, Housekeeping complained about having to clear up empty boxes all over the warehouse. Ally spotted a few of the workers who'd taken the boxes on the bus home, keeping to themselves, very quiet as they stared out the window. Others she found out later had requested double shifts and worked through the night.

Next morning, she went to Gene. "What's going on with those boxes? Aren't you supposed to be worried about stealing?"

Gene raised an eyebrow.

"Come on, Gene, you're not throwing that Donna episode back at me. And yes, I still owe you for that favour. This is different."

"You want different, look at the numbers, Ally. A few boxes go missing? Small numbers. Packing B's performance improvement? *Big* numbers."

A few days later, Ally started seeing pages from the company guide for packers cut out and put up on the walls. The cartoons of the different steps in the packing process were coloured over in gold and silver highlighters. It reminded Ally of the icons in her mother's church, back when she could stomach going there.

She found Gene again.

"What you see is an, ah, unorthodox poster." Gene's eyes were twinkling as he talked. "What management sees is an employee initiative to innovate our training materials. A little more of that thinking, maybe there wouldn't be an axe hanging over this place."

At the end of the week, when Ally heard that the toilet at her end of the warehouse had finally, miraculously, mysteriously been fixed, she wanted to go back and confront Gene again: *now will you accept something weird is going on?* But there wasn't any point – Gene wouldn't believe her. And Ally wasn't sure she believed herself, even as she stood inside the cubicle, flushing once, twice, over and over.

So she went looking for Pep.

It took her three packers to find one who didn't answer with some weird cult nonsense like *he's everywhere*. The third one confirmed: Pep was in the packing hall. He hadn't left there in weeks.

Ally stood by the metal detector at the entrance to the hall. It was now decorated with old payslips, linked into paper chains that looped around the metal framework like overgrown foliage. On one of the large cardboard boxes someone had written, *All welcome within!*

She wanted to go in. She would go in.

Beyond, the packing hall was quiet. Even as packers filed in, past her, smiling but saying nothing, only the distant drone of the ramps could be heard inside.

Okay. Maybe not today.

But when she turned to leave at last, Ally yelled back. *"Damn right I'm your nemesis!"*

```
This week's inspiration: Some companies care about
vacations - we care about vocations

Team performance on previous cycle:
Packing A B C D E improved
Picking A C D improved B E no change
Boxing A B C E improved D no change
Loading A B C no change
Stocking A B C no change
Housekeeping A B no change
Quality A B no change

Days without an accident: 29
```

Ally followed a group of them to a candy vending machine outside the toilets. She never came across packers in the break room any more.

"Helmut. Feng. Marta."

They looked at each other, looked down, didn't say anything for a long while. At least one of them was embarrassed, which Helmut damned well should have been after Ally had covered his shift that time his boy needed his Covid jab.

Finally, Helmut managed to speak. "Ah, Quality – we don't like using personal names in here any more. We prefer you just call us by our title."

"Packers."

"If you've got to distinguish, you could just point."

The one who used to be Marta addressed the other two. "Maybe that's not so fair on Quality though. Maybe we could use, like, badges with numbers. Packer 1, Packer 2. Or colours."

"Or letters!"

"Or you could just use names." But they weren't listening to Ally.

"There aren't enough letters. Have you seen how many are lining up in the parking lot to work here?"

Packer Marta was right: there were dozens of applicants out there. Donna had been redirected to help with processing them.

"I didn't know we were advertising."

"I don't think we did." Donna pointed at the first person in the line, what he was holding in a death grip. A small cardboard box. Ally saw the printed name of the company with a date. She also saw the address label, and how it was replicated on all the boxes right up the line.

"An *invitation?*" Ally couldn't believe it.

"The Packers call it a summons."

"You mean Pep calls it a summons." Ally spat away a sudden sourness in her mouth. "Of course he does."

Ally tried to engage the newcomers. One of them started to say something, but was shushed by the others. The rest turned their backs.

223

Only a small girl holding an older woman's hand – her mother, Ally guessed – answered her. "They're wish boxes." Her voice was all hush.

Ally knelt. "Did your mami make a wish for a job?"

The girl bent forward to tell Ally a secret. "The job made a wish for my mom."

Then her mother noticed Ally and jerked the girl away.

Gene was avoiding her, but she caught him putting up the latest stats behind the garden equipment shelving. "Not hiding. Just wanted you to find out first before you had to hear it from me."

"Find out? About the workforce expansion? Everyone's talking about the new weekend shifts."

Gene looked vacant. Ally explained what she'd seen in the parking lot.

"Oh, that. No, I thought you were asking about Rafal."

"What about Rafal?" As far as Ally knew, it was only a second day of sick leave and a supervisor didn't get nosy until the third day.

"He's not coming back."

Ally blinked. Rafal had loan sharks to pay back. Dammit, she couldn't afford to help him out again. "Where – how did you hear that?"

"One of the Packers told me."

"Which one?"

"Um."

Ally cursed.

"I wouldn't worry too much though."

"Without Rafal, I don't have enough people for two teams!"

That wasn't what upset her – not really, even though it was the only thing that would matter to Gene. It was just – Jesus, Rafal? Not coming back? But hey, chill, it's only work, Ally told herself. No big deal.

But she wanted to scream at Gene and would have done, if he didn't then tap the poster he'd just put up. "The numbers keep going this way, we're not going to need two Quality teams. Hell, we won't need any. You might even want to think about moving to Packing. Corporate are relocating capacity there."

224

She had to talk to someone about this. Ally went to tell Donna, but she couldn't find her anywhere. She did find Donna's headphones by her regular seat in the break room, and an empty, defective packing box.

Ally knew then where Donna would be. The packing hall.

She should go in.

She really should.

```
This week's inspiration: Don't just believe. Be! Live!

Team performance on previous cycle:
Packing A B C D E F G H improved
Picking A B C D E F G H improved
Boxing A B C D E F G H improved
Loading A B C D improved
Stocking A B C D improved
Housekeeping A B C improved
Quality A no change

Days without an accident: 54
```

Ally looked at the small box on the break room table the way she imagined a bomb expert would.

Like the others, it was damaged in some way – scoring along one side, like a dog had tried to get into the cardboard, and warped and bulging on the other, like something was trying to burst out. It was big enough to hold an apple but too small for a bible. Names were no longer being written out, but were neatly printed on labels. Her Sunday name: Alanis.

It had sat undisturbed for two days. No one had taken it, Housekeeping hadn't cleared it away. No one else came in here any more.

This time Ally pocketed it like a good luck charm and strolled back to the line. She didn't have to – Gene had been right, there was no need for Quality any more – but the routine was comforting. Out in the warehouse, the teams were fast, inhumanly so.

She wanted to warn them about accidents. "Jordan? Maria? Lottie?"

The words flopped in the stillness. "Hey Pickers."

225

Across the vast, shelved space, dozens of Pickers looked up. No one smiled. Ally thought she recognised the mother of the little girl from the parking lot the other week, but she wasn't sure. None of them looked like they could be recognised any more.

They went back to working. Every step was deliberate, stylised, but still the most natural, the most inevitable thing in the world. A choreographed dance.

Each team had its own shrine, tended with fresh flowers. The toilet at this end of the warehouse was out of commission again, commandeered by Housekeeping. The three teams had constructed their own statues out of mops, buckets and spray bottles in each of the cubicles. But that was probably okay as no one seemed to need to take a piss any more.

Ally cut her rotation short and came back to the break room. Pep was waiting.

"Have you got your wish yet, Alanis?"

Ally fished out the box and lobbed it at him. "So I get to make a wish if I open the box?"

"No, you get to *take* a wish." Pep caught the box and tossed it onto the table. "It's our gift."

"The first taste always comes free, doesn't it?"

Ally pulled out a chair from the table and sat down, doing everything deliberately so she wouldn't show her nerves. Pep had changed, but not the way she expected. Long, matted beard, dread hair, crazy eyes – all of that she'd have believed. Not the trim, well-kept figure before her. A little weight lost. Upper body work out. No fat in any of his movements.

Bravado was her last defence, so Ally gestured at the poster on the wall. "Respect, I guess. Gene says the numbers don't lie."

"Oh, I'd say we're beyond performance now." Pep smiled at her. "Don't tell Gene."

Ally smiled back. "I won't tell Gene."

He gave a laugh, as mannered as any super-villain. "I've been wanting to thank you for a while."

Ally prodded the box on the table. "Ah, you didn't have to get me a gift."

"Seriously, Alanis. Quality should listen sometimes. When I told you: communion plus ritual plus faith."

Pep's hands ballooned up in a cartoon explosion.

When he leaned forward, he didn't smell of anything now. "But you were right about two things. You remember what you said? *Performance is magic.*"

His eyes glazed, looking at something else that still seemed to dazzle him. "I don't think I can explain what really happened. I don't fully – It's just, you – you focus on something. Doesn't matter what. You find the right way to do it. You get into a flow. Then the people around you, your team, they get into a flow. And at some point, everything around you just starts to flow. Everything becomes performance."

Ally didn't understand what he was talking about – but Pep didn't either. "I always tell them in the packing hall there's something special about this place. What we do in this place. There isn't – but if you stay here long enough and you tell people often enough, they believe. And at some point, they *really* believe. And they can whisper that into the boxes and send those boxes out into the world so others believe. It's like –"

He closed his eyes, wanting to find the words, wanting Ally – someone – to finally get this. "It's like – if you're going to be your best self, you've got to start with right here, right now. You've got to make the time to make a family here. Your team becomes a community becomes a new world waiting to happen. It's a step beyond believe. It's – *be*. It's –"

"Leave."

"I was going to say, *live.*"

"I know, Pep, I've read the posters. No – *leave.*"

Pep opened his eyes, saw right down into her, then right through her. He was still grinning, but he didn't pretend to laugh any more.

"No. *Come.*"

Every year, a kind of mania swept through the warehouse and the rest of the city: the Brewers would get into the playoffs and everyone would start saying maybe, just maybe this was the year, and people would gather around TVs with six-packs and plan where on Wisconsin Street they were going to watch the homecoming parade.

Weird things always happened in those giddy weeks. Crime dipped. Car engines never stalled. Bread always landed jelly side up. You could pretend that if you wanted it hard enough and there were a lot of you, reality had to give way. It just had to. And it felt like that until someone reminded everyone about the '82 World Series, the last time Milwaukee was close enough to touch baseball heaven, and they'd mention the Curse of the Brewers. And there was a crinkle of doubt, which could never be smoothed over. Even before the first playoff defeat, something tipped. Bread went back into the trash and cars choked again at the lights and you didn't walk certain streets at night. And the Brewers would slide out of the playoffs.

Little pockets of paradise only lasted so long. Ally had always known it. Her church. Her family before her mami had left. One job, the next. Like a gambler feeding a one-arm bandit in Potowatomi, you gave a place your heart, you weren't going to get it back.

Ally didn't like being the one to tell people, to spoil the party, but then she'd never had a poker face. "Thanks. I'm good."

"Yeah, I figured. Okay. Then leave. Come, or leave. There's no halfway. We can't have someone standing at the side with their arms folded, telling everyone they're being stupid. You can see that. You can see I can't guarantee that something wouldn't happen to you."

"Happen? Wait – like a threat?"

"Like one thing leads to another leads to something bad. You're Quality. You understand what happens when performance goes wrong. You get why that can't be tolerated."

When Pep saw Ally shiver, his voice softened. It made her shaking worse.

"Look, I said you got two things right. The second was – you set the scene for me, Alanis. All those little kindnesses for people? Getting folk to look out for each other? Binding them together without making a big deal about it? *You* made the company soil. All I had to do was take root."

He pushed the box back towards her. "Open the box. Join us in the packing hall."

Pep stood up, quietly, gliding out of the break room. "Or drop off your ID when you go tonight."

228

Long past the end of her break, Ally sat there, fraying the tape on the box. She tried to stop herself imagining what it was like in the packing hall. The sound of people and machines and purpose making some kind of music. The hall lit by the glow of every atom there. Joy dissolving everything.

She should go. She really –

Alanis, stop talking so loudly. The other children want to listen to the padre.

Ally pinched herself. "Yeah right."

She hurled the box as far across the room as she could. It sailed on the air for a moment before plummeting into the shadows.

She didn't have to come back tomorrow. There were other jobs, right? Why find out how much of Pep's threat was bluff?

She should. She had to.

But –

Where else would she go?

Performance on previous cycle: no change

Days without an accident: 1

Extraction

Don Redwood

Senga hardly noticed the leaky walls at first. She clocked it as condensation from a recent shower and went on cleaning her tooth, withstanding the pain – both the deep throb within it and her toothbrush's scuffles with the surrounding gum. She hadn't showered for weeks – could hardly get her bad leg over the bathside, but she thought Jim or one of the kids must have.

She was about to go on to floss, to give the exposed roots of her sore tooth a good polish. It was too little, too late – there must be rot to make it throb like that – but there was no way she was going to the dentist, paying some creep to poke about her business. She'd send Jim out to pick some nettles and paste them for her. That would do the trick.

As she popped her toothbrush back in an otherwise empty mug she realized her folly. Jim was dead five years. Fee and the boys moved out long ago.

So where was the condensation coming from?

She studied it closer. There was a wet film giving the mouldy artex a glossy sheen. What she'd first mistaken for droplets was actually bubbles – teeny tiny bubbles scattered everywhere, some patches thick with them, foaming nearly.

"What in the name…" she muttered to herself, trailing off. Damp was one thing, but this was a whole other kettle of fish. Maybe the bathroom mould was getting bigger and bolder, or maybe her upstairs had run a bubblebath and left the tap running. But no, it couldn't be either of those, because she walked through the hall and into the living room and saw the same crud covering her prized William Morris wallpaper.

Jim was going to be furious. Never mind how much it cost, she remembered the pains he was at getting the flowers lined up perfect. She nearly called out his name, then remembered there would be no response, no footsteps coming to investigate her panic.

She tightened her mouth angrily, as if that would save her from being so stupid again, and stared at the walls, clueless what to make of the stuff seeping out of them or what to do about it. She didn't want to touch it, that was for sure, but she leant closer and gave it a wee sniff. It wasn't a punch in the face, just faintly unpleasant, like bad breath.

Senga felt calmer. At least Jim wasn't here to lose his rag. She'd speak to the housing. It wasn't like they would do anything about it, mind. They'd been trying to get the tower block condemned since forever. She'd just have to get used to living in a flat with wet walls.

Her heart was still racing away though, flurries of fast beats constantly wrongfooting her. It dawned on her she was supposed to be taking tablets for it – and not supposed to as in 'the doctor said so', but supposed to as in she'd finally accepted she could no longer control even the beat of her own heart. She tried to remember when she'd last taken the doctor's prescription, but who knew what day which memory came from these days? She'd have to check, so she shuffled through to the kitchen. She was pleased to find the kitchen walls clean and dry, and her blister pack in its place above the microwave.

Something had been spilled on it at some point – tea, probably. The stained grid of crumpled, empty windows made her chuckle grimly at the resemblance to the long abandoned East block framed in her kitchen window. There was only one missed blister – a Thursday tea-time, but she didn't know what day it was now, couldn't even be sure the whole pack wasn't weeks old. So on through to the front door she went, and rummaged through the heap of unread letters for a fresh blister pack. She found one, two, three, and was surely about to find a fourth when she heard her phone ringing somewhere. She had no clue where she'd left it, and with her one good ear she couldn't easily place it. Eventually, she found it plugged into the wall by her bedside. The sockets were still dry, thank goodness.

She'd missed the call, but it was Fee. Who else would it be? Worth answering anyway. Senga knew she'd call again any second, so she sat on the edge of her bed, smoothing the knitted throw with her hand, pleased to find her bed so neatly made.

She tried to snuff her excitement. There'd be nowt but nagging from Fee, and whatever warmth she let into her cockles would leave her feeling all the colder after. But it was useless. As soon as Fee's picture reappeared on the screen, she felt giddy as a schoolgirl.

Her tablets, she remembered, as she fumbled with the phone's screen to pick up the call.

"Oh, my darling," she said as Fee's picture was replaced by a crystal clear view of her. She was in the car, seat belt on but not driving. She looked smart – make-up on for a change, hair down and straightened rather than the usual messy bun. It was nice to see her making an effort, rather than acting the frazzled mum, but it made Senga feel self-conscious. She could see her own image in the wee box in the corner, and she was ashamed at the sight of herself – all greasy haired and gaunt.

"How are you doing Mum?" Fee asked. Her voice went down at the end of the question, as if she wasn't caring about the response, which was odd as Fee was normally obsessed with just how Senga was doing.

"Aye, not too bad, plodding on. Funny thing happened though, you'll never believe it. I don't know what's going on, I think that cow upstairs must have flooded me. You should see the state of my walls!"

But Fee didn't join in in Senga's shock. She didn't quite roll her eyes, but Senga did see her nostrils flare as if she was sighing. "Mum. Please. There's no one even living upstairs."

Senga scoffed. "What, do you think I'm hearing things then? She's clattering about all hours of the day. Sometimes I swear she's following me from room to room. She wants shot of me – accuses me of poaching or poisoning her grandkids, just for feeding the wee

233

toerags. Well, stop them chapping my door, I told her, and I won't bloody have to!"

Fee full on winced at that, then took a deep breath. "Mum, for the umpteenth time, it's no your neighbours wanting shot of you, because you've not got any neighbours. It's the housing – so they can knock the flats down before they collapse with you in them."

Senga's instinct was to shrug this off as another example of Fee not taking her seriously, but actually, it did ring a bell.

"Read the Post-it notes, Mum. I can't keep going over this."

Senga nodded. "I'm sorry pet. I do remember that now. Listen, how are you anyway? Where are you off to all dressed up?"

"Just an appointment, Mum, nothing special. Listen, I need to speak to you. There's a doctor coming to see you, Dr Sharma. One of the new GPs at the health centre. Just so I can help manage your money and that. He'll be there this afternoon."

Senga was frowning. It was an odd request. "What's a doctor got to do with money then?"

Fee looked annoyed. "Never you mind, Ma. That's what they're saying – the council. If I don't do this, they will. So it's them or me, all right?"

Then, as if in response to Fee's sharp tone, which Senga would never have taken with her own parents in a million years – Senga's tooth started gnawing away at its nerve worse than ever. She winced, puckering her lips as if she could sook out the rot.

"What's wrong, Ma? It's no your chest again, is it?"

Senga shook her head, no longer wincing, annoyed with herself for having let her pain slip. "It's nothing. Just the usual aches and pains. Old age, I tell you – wouldn't wish it on my worst enemy."

Fee did roll her eyes now. "Aye, sure. Well, all the more reason to see the doctor. Let him in, Mum. I'm serious."

Senga nodded, not sure whether she was giving in to her daughter's will or the pain. "I will, I promise."

"Don't forget," Fee warned her, keeping her face all stern another few seconds before sighing. "Right, I better skidaddle. Your shopping's coming tomorrow morning. I've ordered the usual. Anything else you're needing?"

Senga didn't have a clue, but she didn't want to give that away. "Some bin bags. Maybe some flowers if you fancy treating me."

Fee shook her head. "I got you bin bags last week, ma. Listen, do me one thing. Just go and make a list the now of what all you're needing and send it to me in a wee voicemail."

Senga nodded, biting her tongue.

"Right, love you, Mum."

"Love you, sweetheart."

Sernga tried to do as she was told. She unplugged her phone and walked through to the kitchen. But then she saw the leaky walls of her hallway, how the bubbles were piling up at her skirting boards. Was she seeing things? She steadied herself on the sideboard, and reached a slipper up to the foam, and heard the faint crackling of tiny bubbles popping. So if it wasn't her upstairs – if there was no her upstairs – what in the name of the wee man was going on? Was this just what happens to condemned buildings? She couldn't phone the housing about it now – surely that would just give them more ammo to get her out of here.

She moved on to the kitchen before she forgot and started rummaging through her kitchen cupboards. She couldn't focus though. All she could think about was what on Earth was happening to her walls – that and the doctor's visit. Fee had stressed the importance of it and Senga's memory was so full of holes these days she had to hold it tight in her mind or she'd forget all about it. But more than that, she was just wondering what it was all about. Fee had just bullied her into it, rather than explaining it, trusting that daft old Senga would blindly do her bidding. But Senga wasn't daft. Forgetful, yes, but not so far gone she'd forget that people, even loved ones – especially loved ones – weren't to be trusted.

So I can manage your money… and that. Those two words, tacked on so casually, as if to suggest busy, busy Fee hadn't the time to properly understand herself what the doctor was to do.

235

Fee had never been a good liar. She'd always slipped in these little clues.

What she was hiding was obvious enough. Fee was normally like a broken record on at Senga to move. This time, she hadn't touched the subject, even after having to remind Senga she was living in a condemned building. Meanwhile, a doctor was coming to help Fee manage Senga's money – "and that".

That doctor was coming to have Senga certified.

The easiest option, of course, was to not open the door – just "forget" as Fee was clearly expecting her to. But this didn't seem a problem likely to go away, and Senga *was* forgetful – what was to stop her opening the door to the doctor one day thinking it was the Tesco man? Better to let the doctor in with eyes wide open and put on the best show she can.

That decided, she abandoned her stock check and set about making shortbread. It was a much easier task, demanding little from her brain, her hands falling into the well-worn motions, having retained how much flour, butter and sugar to mix into which bowl much better than her mind could have. As she worked the dough till it felt just right, she thought through what she'd say to the doctor.

She'd be calm, humble, insightful about how dire her situation was. Yes, she was dementing. Yes, she was isolated. Yes, her house was crumbling around her. Yes, she knew the housing would have her evicted eventually by hook or crook. But no, she didn't want to leave. Why? It was a good question. Apart from the fact she'd lived here more than half her life, since the flats were built in fact, which, by the way, were like luxury hotels compared to the tenements she'd been dragged up in – yes, even now. Apart from all that, she was an old lady now, her organs were giving up. Her heart had a mind of its own – and her mind? Pfft. More holes than the roof of the East block over there. You can't take a woman like her and expect her to live somewhere else. She'd forget who she was. She *was* this flat. And as if taking her out of here wasn't bad enough, they'd blow the place up as soon as she was out the door. They might as well be blowing *her* up, half of Glasgow watching and cheering as she comes down. Aye. The flats are condemned, but so is she. And she's no leaving. End of. Now off you pop, doc. Take some shortbread back for your wife. Have you got kids?

She smiled as she scored and pimpled the dough and dusted it with more sugar. It looked good to go, but Senga paused, doubting herself, sure she'd forgotten some vital ingredient or step, but clueless as to what it was. She shrugged – no use racking an empty brain, the proof would be in the pudding – and slid the baking sheet in the oven.

She didn't dare rest with the shortbread baking. Fee would have kittens if she knew she was still using the oven at all. Instead, she pottered about doing a bit of tidying here and there – gathered all the unread mail and shoved it into the sideboard drawers, dusted the windowsills, a quick sweep of the kitchen floor. She paused a while looking at the fridge door and its tidy grid of Post-it notes. "New pills – bin the old ones", "BBC News at 7!", "Check fridge", "Plumber next tuesday", "Phone Mary" and so on. All of them in Senga's own handwriting, but no doubt written at Fee's behest. She wasn't sure whether to chuck them or not – whether they made her look on top of her failing memory, or just drew attention to it. The sight of them annoyed her – all those luminous colours clashing with one another, and their unstuck bottom halves all flapping about and curled at the corners. In the end, she decided to chuck them all bar one – "Check fridge" – seeing as she was clueless as to what most of them were about anyway.

As she set the shortbread, perfectly golden, out to cool, she felt wonderfully smug. The house looked good. The shortbread looked great. Her plan was coming together. She still had to tidy herself up a bit, but for now she'd put her feet up and listen to some Classic FM.

She walked through to the living room, but with each step, it became harder and harder to ignore the slight squelch of her slippers on the hall carpet. She looked down and saw the liquid from the walls was now spilling over the skirting boards, foam piling up on the edges of the carpet. Senga's heart fluttered in her chest. Whatever this was, she hadn't thought it would get out of hand so quickly. The carpets would be soaking by the time the doctor got there. How would she explain it, far less her willingness to live alongside it?

She was panicking. For every few fast featherlight heartbeats, there was a heavyweight one thunking in her chest, up her throat and making her tooth feel like it was going to explode. Between the pain and the panic, she felt like she was going to pass out. She rushed to the bathroom and opened the mirror cabinet, sure she'd find just the thing there. But even if she was calmer, even if her noggin wasn't past its best, she'd have some job finding it. Dozens of wee brown bottles with long-since faded labels. Several had leaked, their crystalized contents discolouring the labels, rendering them completely illegible.

But on the top shelf sat Jim's tub, and she remembered his painkillers, the strong ones the doctor gave for his last few weeks. She'd used them before when her hip bothered her sleep – they should take the edge off the pain, maybe even the panic as well. There was a risk it might see her slurring her words for the doctor, but better that than him finding her in this state.

She flicked through the foil strips till she found the oxycodone. She took one along with another couple of tablets she was sure were antibiotics, then made her dizzy way to her armchair in the living room, using the still dry wooden door frames for support.

She turned up the radio – a lively violin piece – then sunk her tired hips into the armchair's cushion. She sighed, letting the tension out of her shoulders and waiting for her heart to calm down. Her tooth was still throbbing away like an approaching siren, but it wasn't long before the oxycodone kicked in, the pain seeming to bleed into the searing high notes of the violin, carried off, round and about, into a blissful silence.

Her last waking thought – shampoo. She'd tell the doctor she'd shampooed the carpets. Then she let her smug smile carry her off to sleep.

The first time Senga's phone rang, it made no mark on the dreams she was having – of watching fireworks night from her tenth floor flat, the grandweans pressed up against the kitchen window, elbows fighting for space among the candlestubs stuck to its cill, while Senga and Fee washed and dried the dishes. The second time its polyphonic Greensleaves ringtone started up over the choral music on the radio, she wilfully cast it out as a distant ice cream van, and let it ring out. The third time, it was her anger that properly woke her, and when she tried to re-enter the too lovely dream, she couldn't quite manage – the kids were no longer hers, their faces now pressed up outside the window looking in. She opened her eyes to deal with the stubborn intrusion.

It was Fee, of course, obviously worried about her. But Senga was still more than half asleep, and clueless as to what she'd been up to before she slept. She'd only add to Fee's worries answering the phone all confused, so she let it ring out once more while she sussed things out.

She was no further forward when she heard a knocking at the front door, then a foreign man's voice. "Mrs Boyle?" More knocking. "Hello?"

Senga was still drowsy as hell, but it was starting to come back to her. Her toothache. The walls, rotting. A visitor needing impressed.

The doctor.

She got to her feet, slowly, waiting for the usual dizziness to pass. It did, but something unusual remained. The room didn't look right. The floor didn't look flat. The carpet was swollen, domed in the middle like a giant ravioli.

The doctor knocked again. "Mrs Boyle?"

Was she seeing right? Maybe the painkillers weren't agreeing with her. She tried to cross the living room. It was like climbing a hill – steep, the thick pile carpet spongy as sphagnum moss. She reached the rounded plateau in the middle okay, but coming down was another story. She didn't have the strength to control her speed, or the balance to run, and had to lower herself to the ground and bumshuffle to the doorway.

The hallway was as bad as the living room – the floor arched from wall to wall, a lower peak but still steeper than the living room. To walk along it, she was forced to press up against the slimy wall, walking heel to toe along the foamy gutter. Her slippers were soaked through by the time she made it to the front door, and even then, she had to crawl over the hump to reach it.

She looked through the peephole and saw a brown-skinned man, his shirt collar poking out the top of a knitted, grey sweater. He wore thick-rimmed glasses and his hair was gelled neatly to the side. His hands were behind his back and he watched her door with a fixed smile. Senga's phone rang again, and she saw her visitor's eyes and smile widen at the noise. "Mrs Boyle? It's Dr Sharma here. Your daughter told you I would be visiting." He reached into his sweater's neckline, pulled out a badge and held it up to the peephole. "May I come in?"

Senga pulled back from the peephole to reject Fee's call while she figured out what to do. All the shortbread in the world wasn't going to help here – if anything it would just make her look all the more crazy, baking goodies while her flat dissolved and warped around her.

Then Senga caught sight of herself in the hallway mirror, and any remaining hope she had melted away. Her skin was beyond pale – the only colour a sickly yellow round her eyes, and a wet shine to her forehead, like sweating bone.

It was probably her tooth. The pain was less, but maybe because its pus was now moving into her bloodstream.

If she opened that door, the doctor would take one look at her, another look at her flat, then do whatever he needed to get her out of there. For a moment, Senga actually wondered if this might be for the best after all, but even if she did want to open the door now she wouldn't be able to – it would jam on the swollen carpet. She felt trapped and desperate, all too aware this might be her last best chance to get out.

But whatever nightmare was brewing in her flat, she still found herself more scared of leaving it. Leaving just seemed like death – her spirit leaving its body, to become another lost soul trudging about the corridors of some nursing home. It wasn't even a natural death at that. It was a killing. Her daughter, this doctor, the social work – they were all together, pitchforks in hand, hellbent on rooting her out.

Well, they'd met their match. Senga was as stubborn as they come.

"Sorry doc, it's not a good time. I've got a bad stomach and not long had a wee accident. Just want to get things cleaned up and rest. Could you come back tomorrow? Maybe the next day, if you want to play it safe?"

He didn't answer. Senga peeked through the peephole again, and saw him still standing there, his smile gone, his lips pursed.

"Off you fuck now."

His gaze met hers through the peephole, then he looked away and wandered back to the lift.

She stood there at the door a while, put her phone on silent, and figured out her next move, committing herself fully to a siege mentality. The doctor was away, but he'd be back with reinforcements. Meanwhile, the flat would keep doing whatever it was doing. If Senga was to go down with the ship, she had to stall the outside world however she could.

First thing was first – she couldn't open the door to anyone at all. Not the doctor, not the housing, not the Tesco man – nobody. A foot in the door could become an elbow, a shoulder, a body, two bodies.

She edged her way to the kitchen, going through her cupboards, resuming the stock check she'd abandoned earlier, but this time thinking how long it could last her. Two packets of pasta, two packets of rice, a bag of flour, a tub of broth mix – that alone should keep her going for the foreseeable.

For now, she made herself a cup of tea, and treated herself to three fingers of shortbread. It was fine after all. The doctor didn't know what he was missing. There was no need for biting – they crumbled against her tongue, and melted away. Still, her tooth tried its best to spoil it for her, throbbing away again, and after the heat of her tea – searing, as if the pus was stretching and tearing whatever tissues were trying to contain it.

It wasn't food supplies she should be worrying about, she realised. The way this pain was going, if she ran out of painkillers she'd be begging for that doctor to come back.

241

To get to the bathroom she had to get down on all fours again to traverse the hump in the hallway. It was a muckier business than before. So much fluid had pooled alongside the skirting boards she could see a horrible pink colour to it that reminded her of Jim's blood-tinged vomits when his stomach cancer announced itself. As she pushed herself back to standing, her knuckles dipped right in it and she felt the hiss of tiny bubbles popping, warm and tacky on her skin.

"For gods' sake," she cursed, keeping her hand away from her face as she got back to her feet, her elbows and knees picking up more slime as they pushed against the doorframe. She tried to dry her hand on the towel, but it too was sodden now, so she settled for the inside of her cardigan.

There was only three painkillers left. With the strongest will in the world, she'd be out this time tomorrow.

She took two, there and then.

The tooth would have to come out.

She poked it with her tongue, watching for the wobble in the cabinet mirror, wondering how the hell she was going to go about this. There was a fair bit of wiggle, limited by a wall of pain rather than any real firmness of the swollen, squidgy gum. It felt like it would come out easily enough if she managed to get enough purchase on it to lift it straight out without bending it against her gum.

She tried with her fingers first – not having a proper go yet, just seeing if it was going to be that simple once the painkillers kicked in. It wasn't.

So she found the dental floss in the mirror cabinet. It must have been years old. The label on the packet was discoloured like the medicine bottles – a swirl of pastel pink and yellow – but the floss itself was in good enough nick. She was able to wrap it twice round the exposed root of the tooth but it was too fiddly to tie it, and the whole thing just loosened and slipped free with even the teensiest bit of upwards pressure.

She remembered, vividly, doing this as a child, jealous of her school friends' winnings from the tooth fairy. It hadn't worked then either, but a crisp apple the next day had done the job.

Senga didn't have any apples, or anything for that matter that she couldn't simply sook, tongue and gum to a smooth pulp.

She could make toffee though.

Back through to the kitchen she went before the double dunt of painkillers robbed her of her ability to bake. She put a saucepan on the biggest hob, turned it up to six, and eyeballed a decent amount of sugar and butter. She stirred it until the butter bubbled and soaked up the last of the grit, then watched, shoogling it now and again, until the bubbles shrank in size and grew in number, the mixture looking almost as foamy as the substance leaking from her walls. As she tipped the lot into a casserole dish, she felt herself tipping with it, the painkillers kicking in hard, softening the pain from her tooth a little, but turning the rest of her body to jelly.

She steadied herself against the kitchen counter, the fridge, then the kitchen doorframe, making her way through to the living room to rest while the toffee cooled to a hard set. Balancing was hard when she got to the hall. The substance filling the channel was up to her ankles and it had changed again. It was proper pink now, and opaque. The bubbles were gone, except for a few bigger ones. It seemed thick, viscous, dragging at her feet enough to tire her legs and tip her forward.

She stopped to rest, leaning against the wall, letting its cool wetness seep through her cardigan. Her heart was up to its tricks again, whether from the exertion or the painkillers, probably both. She waited for it to settle, but at some point, realized that just wasn't going to happen – she'd be waiting till kingdom come. She'd just have to get on with it.

That was easier said than done though. In the time she'd rested, either her limbs had grown weaker or the substance had grown thicker. The sole of her slipper seemed to be stuck down. With effort, she could peel it off but it left her too exhausted to actually move her foot further through the pink stuff, and she just sank it back down, practically in the same spot.

She was stuck.

243

It was a scary feeling, helped a little by the painkillers. It felt like it was someone else's feet that were stuck, like she was just watching. But then there was a knocking at the door – a hard knocking, that sent vibrations singing through the hinges.

"Senga? Can you hear us? It's the police."

Senga, already stuck, froze completely. She hadn't expected it to come to this so soon.

She cleared her throat and took a deep breath, but still her voice came out wobblier than she'd hoped. "Yes, I can hear you just fine. I'm not deaf, and you must have shook the whole building with your knocking there."

"Sorry about that Senga. We were asked to do a welfare check. Your daughter's worried about you. Apparently you're not answering your phone."

Senga patted her pockets down for her phone. "Well, consider my welfare checked. I'll phone Fee the now and tell her off for wasting your time."

"Right you are, Mrs Boyle."

Silence.

She unlocked her phone. There was a whole list of messages and missed calls to scroll through, all from Fee. She was trying to figure out which one to press to call her back, when Fee's face appeared with a fresh call. When Senga stroked the green button, Fee's face was just tiny, the top left in a grid of ten.

"Mrs Boyle."

It wasn't Fee speaking, but someone else. Their faces were too small for Senga to see who.

"My name's Jackie, I'm a social worker in the Adults Support and Protection Team. This is an emergency meeting we've scheduled in response to your situation. Stakeholders present are your daughter Fiona, your housing officer Gary, his manager Theresa…"

"Are the police there, Ma?"

"Just to confirm, our officers are standing by. They have made verbal contact with Senga and she appears to be safe and well."

"What do you mean safe and well? Look at her! Does that look safe and well to you?"

"She does look pale. Does she normally have better colour than this? Senga, this is Dr Sharma, I spoke to you earlier. Are you feeling okay?"

"Why are you no talking, Ma?"

"Can I ask you all to mute yourself just until I explain to Mrs Boyle what the purpose of this meeting is?"

Senga had been overwhelmed, struggling to keep up with all the different voices chiming in, but with this last comment she finally found her way in. "Do you think I came up the Clyde on a bloody bicycle? I know fine well what you're all up to, and I tell you what, you've no bloody right to. This is my home, my body, my decision. End of. Just remember, it'll be your turn one day."

She hit the red button and threw her phone across the hall. It landed on the substance with only the faintest sound.

The substance felt solid round her feet now. She could wriggle her toes and bend her ankles in her slippers, but nothing more.

It should have been a nightmare, this being stuck business. Like sinking sand, or a snared rabbit. But, and maybe this was the painkillers talking, Senga found she quite liked it. She felt safe. Like the house was holding onto her. Taking her with it.

To hell with it, she thought, and bent forward, plunging her hands into the pink amber as hard and deep as she could. She tried her head as well but couldn't reach, only succeeding in sticking a few hairs to it which yanked at her scalp whenever she turned her head.

She was too old for yoga, but between the support the substance was giving her limbs and the painkillers, she found herself strangely comfortable.

Jim would be proud, she thought, chuckling to herself. Not actually proud, just the head shaking, eye rolling kind of proud, seeing just how stubborn a bastard she still was.

Senga knew what was coming. It had only been a matter of time. She spent what little there was left thinking just what all this flat had been through with her. Fee had been born a few yards away in the

245

living room for gods' sake. The noisy, exhausting chaos of family life. The second wind of her and Jim's sex life when Fee finally moved out. The long misery of Jim's final days. Then the dementing peace of the last few years, watching the sun sail over Glasgow, still tracking its reach, resolutely lighting candles whenever it sank into the distant glimmer of the Clyde estuary. Until even that simple ritual was beyond her. How many seasons had passed unmarked by now? It could be the equinox today, for all she knew. "Aye," she sighed, somewhat comforted by the thought.

She was expecting a battering ram, like on the telly. A wooden explosion, people flooding in. Instead, there was the buzzing of power tools. She turned her head, but there was nothing to see, yet. Just the light from her phone screen, the same grid of faces, looking up in silence.

Flip

Ray Cluley

Philip landed hard and with little grace, squatting low to keep his balance, but he *did* land it.

"Like riding a bike," he said to no one.

He kicked the skateboard up under him, hooked the deck with his toes to flip it.

And promptly fucked it up.

The skateboard made an ugly clatter and rattled away from him as he stumbled, bumping up against one of the bollards marking the end of the street.

Oh yeah, still got it, Flip.

He bent to retrieve the skateboard and looked it over as if the fault of his fall might be found there and not in the fact that he hadn't been on it in years. The deck was scuffed, over and under. Most of those scrapes were on the underside where stickers overlapped stickers, torn and peeled and rubbed into a mosaic of faded colours mostly devoid of illustration. There'd been a design there once, a crappy graphic he'd not liked, and some of it remained beneath the stickered coverup. Part of a rat's tail. Sunglasses held in a partial paw where one edge of the board was delaminating. The trucks and hangers were scarred bright from grinding. The whole baseplate, really. None of the wheels matched in colour but they were all Formula Four Spitfires. He span them. Three times for luck, as was his usual ritual – or used to be his ritual – not that he was looking to generate any good mojo here. He was just listening to the sound, trying to find some comfort in it, the same way he'd hoped standing on his old deck in his old streets would have brought some comfort when all it brought was familiarity and frustration, like seeing an actor you knew was from something you'd seen before. Too much had changed. He had changed.

The wheels keep turning, he thought. Spun the ones he could control.

He set the tail down and put his foot to it, holding the skateboard upright, then stepped the rest of it down to the pavement with his left. He felt the spring and flex of the deck under his weight, rolled forward with the momentum and kicked once, twice, three times, riding the rattle over the uneven pavement; stamped into an ollie from the kerb without even thinking about it, and rode that feeling, too. Let it carry him along like he'd never left. Like he'd never grown up.

It used to be that the open area in front of the courthouse was loud with the clackety-clack and slam of skateboards on a Saturday, but not any more. Just people walking, most of them in a hurry. The NO SKATEBOARDING sign was new, but surely that didn't deter anyone, even here.

It didn't deter Philip. He took his skateboard up the steps and sped along the top one, cloppa-cloppa-cloppa-cloppa over every paved square there as he moved towards the long zigzag of a ramp at the far end. He wasn't about to try grinding the handrail like he used to, so he slalomed, taking his time. When he saw an old man with a cane waiting for him at the bottom, he cut back to the steps instead and ollied the rest of the way down, one step at a time. A few years ago he'd have leapt the remaining lot of them, but that was then, and this was a very different now. Not that he'd ever exactly been fearless.

Philip remembered when his brother had tried to air walk from a switch stance and fumbled it, supermanning down at 45 degrees before faceplanting the last step. He'd fractured his cheekbone, broken his nose, and scraped his face from forehead to chin, but apart from a loud shout of pain and a moment of stunned bleeding, he'd simply raised his thumb to the air – I'm good, I'm fine – before getting back to his feet and grinning through a mask of blood. He'd skated himself to hospital with the whole gang in tow, whooping and laughing behind him, Philip included.

Any you can skate away from, right?

He remembered one of his brother's TikToks. Watching the videos he posted was how Philip tricked himself that they kept in

248

touch, dropping a like or commenting a thumbs up to show he'd visited. Videos of his younger brother jumping a stack of cans, sliding across the top of a bench, weaving between bins and bollards. In one of the videos he'd been at the playground in the park. Poised at the top of the tallest slide, he'd performed a perfect 360 kick turn before descending in a fakie and laughing like a fucking lunatic over the heavy thrum of the skateboard's wheels on the bowing metal, not grinding or even – ha! – sliding, but riding it down and kicking up at the bottom into a full Cab, stumble-landing it at the camera with one thumb raised and knocking his phone aside for a final chaotic shot of sky and cement and skittering sky again. From somewhere off screen, half-manic in laughter: "Any you can skate away from!"

At the last of the steps, Philip fucked his landing again, redeeming himself only slightly in picking up the skateboard as he staggered.

"Kook."

The word came at him fast and past, the Doppler effect given voice. By the time he'd looked up to see who'd spoken, they were carving across the street on a deck far newer than his to where a set of steps led down towards the train station. He had a glimpse of purple hoodie, a wide-eyed black cat on the back sticking its tongue out – 'blep' – and then they kicked up onto the handrail to ride it down, grinding, and gone.

Philip gave them the finger. A delayed reaction rather than a cowardly one, and it made him feel foolish. Immature. Saying fuck you to who? Some grom who'd already forgotten him. After all, he was just a kook, apparently. A newbie.

Nothing new about me, though. If only.

He stepped to the deck again and skated his way to the next stop on his mourning tour of his old home city, trying not to think about how much it had grown up in his absence. Trying to pretend that nothing had changed.

The carpark where he'd taught his brother to skate still loomed over the dodgier roads behind the high street, casting them into forever shadow, but it was closed now and boarded up. The barriers at the entrance and exit had been removed from their island in the middle of the turnoff, and gathered in the empty sockets left behind were crushed cans of Monster, flattened Maccy bags, and throw-away vapes. A perimeter of six-foot panels surrounded the entire carpark. A notice on each declared imminent demolition, though there'd been time enough to post fliers in ragged lines across many of these. Fliers for nightclubs he'd never heard of and gigs at venues he didn't know. There was plenty of graffiti, too. Tags sprayed over tags. Scrawled profanities. The classic SK8 OR DIE that had been old even before Philip was. Over that particular sentiment was a name he knew, and a trick, too. Ollie. It had been painted at an angle as if performing its namesake.

When Ollie had been very young, he couldn't pronounce his brother's name and had called him Flip. Philip had loved it, had seen it as far more than a fair trade considering he'd been the one to name his younger sibling (something his mother had offered, he suspected, as a way of reducing the risk of rivalry). In a sense, then, they had named each other. That this graffitied Ollie was his Ollie, Philip knew from the unsmiling smiley face of the 'O', one eye crossed out above a mouth that was mostly straight-lined but turned up at one end and down at the other. A grimacing face. A wounded face. A cartoon hand beside it raised a single thumb like everything was good, everything was fine.

SK8 OR DIE. Ollie with an X for an eye. He could have been jumping, could have been falling.

SK8 & DIE.

"What are you staring at?"

The voice startled him. No Doppler effect this time, it was just suddenly right there beside him.

It was blep-cat.

She looked about his brother's age. Not what he would be now, but back then. She was wearing her hood up – it had little cat ears – and she wore panda smudges of eye makeup, her hair coloured purple and blue. Bruise colours, same as her deck, where a black cat graphic prowled a night sky background.

Nine lives must be nice, he thought. And always landing on your feet. We should all be cats.

She was waiting for an answer.

"Did you know him or something?" she said, pointing her skateboard at Ollie, grimace-winking with his crossed-out eye as he kicked up or fell to DIE.

"I'm his brother."

"Ollie didn't have a brother."

The hurt of that was sharp, stinging like a skinned knee.

"I'm Flip" he said, as if to prove his claim, but she showed no sign of knowing the name. Nor did she give him hers.

Blep-cat it was, then.

"Did *you* know him or something?" he echoed back at her.

She shrugged, but what kind of answer was that?

"I saw you earlier," he said.

"Where?"

"Court house. Sweet rail grind."

She nodded, like, of course. Didn't judge him for sweet.

"It's a good rail," she said, "but –"

"It wobbles at the kink."

"Yeah." She reassessed him. "Not a kook, then."

"Not a kook," he admitted. "Just rusty."

"You going in there, Rusty?"

It was his turn to shrug.

"There's a board around the side that sort of comes off," she told him, then warned, "Stinks of piss in there."

"Yeah, but I like the bumps, and the top level has these concrete divides that are great for –"

"Park's better."

"The park?"

He thought of the playground and his brother's TikTok, coming down the slide.

"Yeah," the girl said. "It's got good banks if you don't want the quarters or verts, and lots of little launchers. Better than anything in there."

A *skate*park. Of course. That must've been new, too.

"Where is it?"

She pointed a vague direction for him and said, "Gets pretty busy at the weekend." She dropped the nose of her skateboard and stepped

251

to it and pushed off all in one graceful motion. She went the opposite way, without effort and without a glance back.

Philip considered checking out the skatepark, but not yet. He wanted at least one run through the multi-storey first. He'd loop his way up to where he'd once learned to blunt and grab, then do a lap and come right back down. Just a little something for old times' sake.

And then the bridge.

Maybe the skatepark after that.

Maybe.

He leant back on the tail to raise the nose and tried for a 180 kick turn, overshooting it to turn a full 360, back where he started. SK8 OR DIE and Ollie half-smiling like it was a horrible joke.

Philip tic-tacked away from that and looked closely at the boards where blep-cat had indicated. He located the loose one. A scraped arc over zigzags of tags and torn fliers showed where the neighbouring board rotated on a single fixture to create an entry point. He checked the ground for broken glass and saw only tramped dirt and weeds and stamped flat cans, more energy drinks with their gem-bright titles. Here be monsters, Philip thought, and squatted, waddling into the dark carpark with his board before him like a shield.

Spring may have been warming the rest of the city, but inside the carpark was cold. It was not entirely pitch black. Sunlight came down to the lower level from one of the ramps. There was a single car still here, tyres flat, windows smashed. A notice had been slapped across what was left to declare the police were aware. There was a pigeon in the car, sitting on the back shelf, watching Philip as he put his board to the ground and skated the gloom. He was loud in the open space, and moved through his own echoes. The pigeon sat up a little straighter, chest out, but otherwise did nothing but posture at the noise. Philip rushed at a speedbump, intending to kick up from it, reaching under to clutch his board and bone out an Indy-grab before landing, nothing burly, but it was like he was learning everything new again. The old, familiar ways were not returning to him as easily or as comfortably as he thought they should have, and he was forced to bail.

So much for muscle memory.

He heel-kicked the board into his hands and walked it up the ramp, spinning the wheels idly as he went. This time he found something soothing in the sound, the low purring hum of them like a lullaby of white noise.

He'd taught his brother how to skate here because the only people who saw you fuck up were too focused on not running you over to care how stupid you looked. They did speed runs and simple tricks at first, tic-tacs and spins and the eponymous ollie. His brother's first proper fall had been here, too, coming at a speedbump too hard and kicking up too late and hitting the ground only after colliding with a concrete pillar. That had given him a hell of a black eye.

"It's like riding a bike," Philip had told him, not because you didn't forget but because you had to fall a few times to learn.

After that, his brother's confidence had soared, as if now that he'd fallen he had less to be afraid of, and he'd been proud of that black eye. He wore it like a badge of honour. More difficult tricks followed, more dangerous ones, and he advanced much quicker than Philip could have anticipated. He fell plenty more times, of course, but that first one had made him.

Just as his last had done the opposite.

At the top of the ramp, Philip put his skateboard on its tail and nudged it to its wheels with his knee. He let it roll away from the slope.

Behind the noise of it, he heard its echo. It was louder than it should have been.

He glanced down to the lower level, crouching to peer between the concrete pillars and down the angle of the ramp.

There was no one down there.

"Ollie ollie oxen free," he said, but no one replied.

His skateboard bumped against the wall at the end of a parking space and was stilled, but as he went to retrieve it, ready for his descent, from somewhere else in the place came the smooth roll of other wheels.

A skateboard click-clicking as it crossed a ridge in the road surface or passed over the lip of a drain cover. He wondered if blep-cat had come back, but there was no movement below him that he could see.

Yet he could hear it. An unseen skateboard, picking up speed. Coming at him from behind now, from the right, then when he turned to look, at his left, and passing him. He turned with it, still looking, and –

Nothing.

He heard the kick of a trick and its landing, but –

No one.

He placed his skateboard at the top of the ramp, stepped to the deck, and let it carry him back down, away from the noise. Below, though, on the darkest level of the carpark, he saw a furtive movement. Someone crouched but gliding, easing smoothly out of sight behind the ruined car. Someone low on a skateboard. And stacked at the bottom of the ramp stood a low pyramid of drinks cans, arranged ready for a jump trick. It hadn't been there before.

"Flip," someone said.

And with no thought yet to wonder who, Philip did.

He came at it frontside and crouched to jump, bringing the board up with his heel and the tips of his toes as he cleared the cans, flipping the deck on its lengthwise axis, but when he landed he turned in a wild 360 spin and slammed against the parked car. He startled a burst of feathers from the back, the pigeon leaving a stream of shit in its wake as it took off for somewhere – anywhere – else.

Philip ducked to avoid the bird, and stepped back from any of the shit that might splatter him, letting his skateboard roll beneath the vehicle and out the other side.

Behind him, the tower of cans toppled. He heard the distinctive clatter and rattle of their collapse but there was no one there to knock them down. Monsters, tumbling in the dark, and fast laughter carried away on the quiet shush of a skateboard not his own. A flatline of noise.

"All right," Philip muttered, retrieving his skateboard. "Whatever."

He was too old for tricks.

"I'll go," he called.

Go came back to him in echo.

He walked, deck in hand so as to hear any other noises, peering left and right as if for traffic, but he heard nothing. Only the tic-tac metronome of his heartbeat restored, and the noise that came with the scrape of a wood panel sliding against its neighbour as he rotated it open and emerged squinting into the brighter, warmer light of day.

Behind him, the panel fell with a swing like an executioner's axe, and shut abruptly with the finality of a guillotine.

Philip only had one last place left to see.

He followed the streets of the city, skating pavements he knew and moving through more of his own echoes. Raised kerbs and ramp railings leading down to subways. Ledges and benches and low, perfect walls. In a few places he found his own sprayed name amongst other tags, but it was ghostly beneath coats of fresher paint, a rune without its previous power to assert who had once been here. He'd expected more memories to linger in such old haunts, but many of them had been pushed aside, evicted by a city forever changing around them. Here was a new warehouse, and there was an arts centre. This was now a fountain space, and that was now a billboard screen, a fancy gym, a whole new chain of eateries. When the old carpark was gone, would the halls of the new flats or the office aisles be haunted by the sound of skateboards? Philip didn't think so. Nature's first green was gold, and the ancient ways faded. The new held more power than the old, and so much had changed in his absence. Was still changing. Growing. Swelling, like some pregnant thing aborting the old with every new construction it pushed out to litter the city.

The bridge was still there, he was both glad and sad to see. It had changed as well, though. There were wire fences up at the railings now, caging a way never meant for pedestrians in an effort to prevent any from falling because *of course* people risked the busy traffic to walk the narrow strip of concrete that wasn't really a pavement. It saved them 10 whole minutes. Prior to the cage fencing, the only barrier on the bridge had been the low Armco crash barrier meant to keep cars from plummeting to the motorway below and if you came to it with enough speed, running low across the busy road and slipping the deck beneath your feet as you neared, it was the perfect height for an

Ollie

anchor grind. The trick, so to speak, was to ensure you came down on the right side of the barrier afterwards.

He wondered what Ollie had thought was the right side.

He wondered, for the thousandth time, if it had been an accident.

An old bouquet had been cable-tied to the Armco. Shrivelled and brown, the flowers were hanging like bowed heads. Who'd left them? Not his mother, she would have said. And his stepfather didn't give a shit, so not him, either. Philip wondered if any of the other local skateboarders came out this way to pay their respects. Maybe to try the same trick, which amounted to the same thing.

Assuming a trick had been what Ollie was doing.

Philip put his skateboard down and looked over the barrier, through the square mesh of the fence, to the crowded lanes below. Ley lines bringing power into the city, leading speeding vehicles onward in an arterial rush of fortunes and futures. He imagined the disruption of that traffic, the screech of tyres, horns blaring. Imagined the sudden crump and thump of metal, the crunch and shatter of scattered glass.

The sudden crump and thump of flesh. The crunch and shatter of broken bones. Because unlike in the carpark, the drivers here would run you over. They had no other choice.

He imagined a bloody thumb raised from the mess of it all – his younger brother's dying lie that everything was good, everything was fine, as he finally hitched a ride out of this fucking place – and he wondered, briefly, what had happened to his skateboard.

Philip knelt, reverent, and retrieved a spray can from his jacket pocket. His brother's colour. He shook it up while thinking of the old aviation motto they'd adopted and adapted, how any landing you could skate away from was a good landing, and he sprayed Ollie's name on the Armco barrier because his had not been a good landing, his had been the fucking worst. Philip scrawled the name and the crossed-eye smiley, a tag with which to paint the town

dead

red, and he hooked his skateboard by the wheels beside it. He would leave it behind. Just as he had his brother.

The sudden scream of a skateboard grinding on the Armco startled Philip. He stood up and recoiled from the shriek of a baseplate scraping metal, stepping backwards into traffic. He had a moment to think, 'As above, so below' although it was actually the

256

opposite, before lunging back to the relative safety of the tiny pavement. He felt the gust of a truck as it blasted past. Felt, as well, the displaced air of someone pass across him on the barrier at his back, grinding close enough to snatch his cap from his head had he been wearing one. He crouched as if that might happen, turning again and putting his hands to his head where there was no hat to remove, and knelt that way at the sadly gathered flowers.

He remained like that for a long moment as cars sped away behind him and below, the drone of them like giant flies clouding around the dead or dying.

After the bridge, Philip went to the park. He thought maybe the sight of the playground would cheer him because of the slide. His experience at the carpark had unsettled him, but the one on the bridge had been worse. He could still hear the metallic shriek, a banshee call he seemed to have summoned with a word in sprayed paint that was still on his hands.

He looked up from them to the playground. That temple for weekend parenting was still there, at least. The loose bark that had once littered the floor around it all was gone, replaced by a spongy kind of nuclear green asphalt. An elaborate climbing frame had been added, and a tangle of tunnels wormed themselves into a warren beneath a complex set of monkey bars, but most of it was as he remembered. There were some new spring-bottomed animals in which children could sit to rock backwards and forwards without going anywhere – a horse, a hound, a long-eared hare – but they hadn't replaced the see-saw. The swings remained, though the rubber seats had been wrapped around the overhead bar, far out of reach. The roundabout was the same too, albeit freshly painted.

And the slide was still there.

The place was dead, though. Empty. Maybe because the rest of the park had gone the same way as the rest of the city, which was to say that it had changed. Almost all of the green space – proper green, not the toxic colour of the playground – was gone. The playing field had been paved over. Instead of grass: asphalt, and the painted rectangles of a carpark, filled today with 4x4s, sedans, and minivans.

Instead of the trees that once lined the perimeter: a low wire fence; streetlights; a pay and display.

And next to this was the skatepark.

It rivalled the playground in size, with banks and mini ramps and quarter pipes, and even a tall half pipe that towered over it all, everything outlined with bright red coping. Verts dropped into an impressive bowl that sloped and curled and curved, while a flat area served as a stage for other stunts. He saw a rainbow rail and a box and a short set of steps for feigned urban skating.

He would've loved a place like this, growing up. Flip would have. Even now, Philip was drawn to it, following the footpath that snaked around the playground to this tribute built for the youth of the city. An offering to distract them, contain them. Maybe even tame them.

And the place was packed, as busy with activity as blep-cat had said it would be. Tens of children, dozens of them, dropping and riding and climbing and leaping their tricks into the air, back and forth and upside down, like it was all one grand dance to celebrate their daring. He watched them and their repetitions, their routines, the overlapping, over*looping*, figure eight patterns like it all might go on for infinity. Only, everything had to end, didn't it? That was just one of the sad truths you had to learn, growing up. Getting old.

He watched the choreography, saw them dip and circle the bowl in waves that refused to ever settle, that avoided the whirlpool pull of any plughole that might deny them the brightness of their young lives. There was something tribal in the scene, in the cooperative magic of their movements around and on and leaping from the monolithic structure meant to stave their reckless appetites. Ring a ring o' roses, but without any falling down. He saw alley-oops and air walks and handplants, Cabs and nose grabs; he saw ollies and nollies and blunts, Schwifty flips and tail slides, and grinds. Some of what he saw was switch stance, some of it goofy-foot, all of it steezy. Occasionally one of them bailed and recovered, but he saw no wipeouts, no faceplants, nary even a skinned knee.

As he watched, he saw one of them take to the air, fired up from the ramp into an aerial display that seemed to defy the laws of physics, that made gravity pause and reconsider its existence, and in that pause the kid turned once, twice, fuck, was that three times? For a moment it was gloriously and impossibly Ollie, and when the boy landed it he did so fakie and with such effortless ease and nonchalance that Philip found himself cheering with the others only after a moment of stunned awe.

The cheers of the others ceased, petering off as all of them turned to look his way. As did the boy that was not Ollie

of course he wasn't Ollie

who rolled casually up the opposite ramp and back down to the other, looking right at him. Up again, and back down to the other. A slow pendulum, decreasing. Tick, and tock... tick, and tock. But counting down to what?

All of them were staring. Every. Single. One.

Children, really, no one older than their mid-teens, but gathered together they were a pack, feral but unified in their scuffed hoodies or open plaids, their shorts and skorts and ragged jeans, their two-tone tattered shoes. Wrists were bound with bands and bracelets and beads. No one wore a helmet. No pads on the knees or elbows. The only concessions to safety were baseball caps and beanies, and the fingerless gloves some of them wore, padded at the palms.

Amongst them, poised at the top of one of the verts, stood blep-cat. She nodded at Philip, recognising him, and pulled her cat-eared hood up before descending, dropping into the curve as graceful as her totem. She purred a circle around the lad who'd just fucking 1080ed like it was nothing and said something to him.

The boy she spoke to wore a faux foxtail on a beltloop at the back of his long shorts. His hoodie – White Fox, because of course – was not white but red and brand new bright, like the wheels of his skateboard, neon bright like warning lights. He saw them flash as the kid executed a Casper flip coming over to him, out of the pipe, tossing the deck beneath his feet like it didn't need thought. At the edge of the park, he heel-kicked the deck to his hands and offered it to Philip.

"Do you wanna go?" he said.

The boy didn't appear to be mocking him. Or if he was, nobody laughed. They waited.

"No," Philip said. "Thanks."

"What's your name?"

"This is Rusty," blep-cat said for him.

259

"Philip," he corrected. And then, "Flip."

The boy smiled. "Flip," he said. "Okay."

"He knew Ollie," blep-cat said.

Fox-boy glanced at her then reassessed Philip.

"He's all right," blep-cat added.

But was he?

One of the boys in the group, his chest puffed as he postured next to fox-boy, nodded like he was agreeing, head bobbing to whatever music cooed from his earbuds. The others had gathered closer, too, forming a loose circle around fox-boy at the skatepark perimeter. One of the girls flicked her hair back, preening. A lad nearby pawed sweaty strands of it from his face. All of them watched Philip.

Fox-boy offered the skateboard again, but this time he walked it over to where Philip stood.

Closer, Philip saw the board was red ply. He saw familiar crimson grip tape. He knew, too, just *knew*, the bearings would be Bones Big Balls Reds. His brother would say, "Big Balls!" and grab his own before trying to sack-whack him.

Philip snatched the deck from fox-boy and flipped it. On the underside, a Dali clock melted over a tree branch.

"Where did you get this?"

Fox-boy shrugged.

"It isn't yours!"

The boy shook his head. "It's yours," he said. He held another board now, but Philip couldn't see who might have given it to him.

He looked at each of them, and each looked right back at him. He wondered how he appeared to them, what he might look like in their eyes, strangely grateful they even saw him at all.

He looked at the deck in his hands.

"Skate or die."

He had no idea who'd said it. All of them were nodding.

"Yeah," someone said.

"Show us," said another.

Philip looked at the skatepark behind them. Considered its verts and curves. He realised he was spinning the wheels of the board in his hands, like he might actually do it, do *something*. Like spinning his wheels wasn't all that he did these days.

One of the children pushed him. He didn't see who, only saw the one he fell into, a small boy wrinkling his rodent nose in something like disgust as he shoved Philip back the other way, into the belly of a boy who grunted and shunted Philip aside.

Philip fell, but someone caught him before he could finish the action and helped him up.

Then shoved him again.

This time as he stumbled, Philip pushed at those around him to force a way through, and when he'd cleared a space, parting the gathered crowd, he put the skateboard down and stepped to it for a quicker exit.

The others followed, and were faster, weaving easily around him as he tried to make his escape. He was knocked and nudged and shoved but he kept his course, pushing for speed on the footpath, turning abruptly to evade them through the playground.

They turned with him, seeming to anticipate – manipulate? – the direction, steering him in their murmuration, holding him within their herd. Within the boundaries of the playground they broke away, expelling him towards the swing frames and through, around the upright angle of the see-saw, to collide with one of the dividing rails of the roundabout. This he clung to, folded over, as they surrounded him once more, and within their crowd he began to spin, a clock hand turning at the merciless hands of youth passing, and passing, and passing. Round and round and round we go, and ring a ring o' roses, we all fall down. But all around him, past their leering, peering, cheering, faces, he watched the city rise, saw cranes and new buildings climbing into the sky, heard the traffic flow of its blood as cars came and trucks came and never mind who might fall in the way of their daily grind.

In the flash of faces round him, one was bloody and swollen-eyed. The forehead was broken, pushed in and pushed back and pushed impossibly down. There was a smile, though, sharp with broken teeth then suddenly slack as the fractured jaw sagged and fell away. But everything was good, everything was fine, everything was A-okay, because Ollie offered an upward thumb and aimed it right his way. Jagged it back, hitching a lift to elsewhere, out of here, come on, come with me. To the slide! Come on Flip, come on bro, let's ride!

Philip launched away from the roundabout and the gathered crowd parted around him to let him fly. Only their laughter followed, the bright laughter of the young, still alive while others were done. It carried him to the slide. He would need

Ollie

to ollie, and he stamped the tail to do so, daring a flip, though the trick with a flip was to end back where you started, and he'd done that.

He stuck it, landed on the slide's flatline and rode its slope up, up, to where the ladder on the other side climbed, pausing up there to view the ever-changing skyline of a city he no longer knew.

Any you can skate away from...

He remembered the frightened pigeon, taking off for somewhere, anywhere else, leaving a stream of shit behind, and thought, that's me.

He'd had no other choice.

Had he?

Below him, a hooded circle of hooting, howling, cooing, growling youngsters skated around the playground. Standing still amongst them, the brother he'd bailed on – who had not grown up, who would never grow up – offered the board Philip had left behind on the bridge.

You wanna go?

No.

The sun was dipping behind the new buildings and the new stadium and the new supermarkets and it set the sky alight; it flashed on roads like ploughed furrows where horns bleated instead of sheep and it shone on metal mezzanines and scaffolds and a hundred thousand windowpanes and it bathed the whole city with fire. With a defiant cry to the sky, Philip kick-turned a 360 and dropped with it, ablaze and racing, looking backwards, downward fakie. The slide thrummed under him like urban thunder while the city's children moved in synchronised loops to bind him, their wheels an incessant buzzing hum as the swarm of them called for him to skate or die, skate or die.

Philip leaped fearless into his grief and waited for them to decide.

About the Authors

James Bennett is a British Fantasy Award winning author. Raised in Sussex and South Africa, his short fiction has appeared internationally. His acclaimed debut *Chasing Embers* came out in 2016, the first of his Ben Garston novels. Other works include the well-received *The Book of Queer Saints* and his latest stories can be found in *The Dark, BFS Horizons*, and *Occult Detective*. A new collection *Preaching to the Perverted* came out from Lethe Press in September 2024. Feel free to follow him on Bluesky: @jamesbennett.bsky.social.

Ray Cluley's fiction has been published in various magazines and anthologies. He has published two short story collections, *Probably Monsters* and *All That's Lost*, and won the British Fantasy Award for Best Short Story. He holds a PhD in Creative Writing and lives in Wales with his partner and two mischievous but adorable cats.

Joanna Corrance is a lawyer and author from the Highlands of Scotland. She writes dark speculative fiction, gothic horror and science fiction; her publications include *John's Eyes* (Luna Press Publishing), *The Hamlet* (NewCon Press) and her horror novel *The Gingerbread Men* (Haunt Publishing).

Dan Coxon is a finalist for the World Fantasy Awards (*Heartwood: A Mythago Wood Anthology*) and has won two British Fantasy Awards (*Writing the Uncanny* and *Writing the Future*, both co-edited with Richard V. Hirst). He has been shortlisted for the British Fantasy Awards a total of eight times, and was a finalist for the Shirley Jackson Awards. In October 2025 his anthology of haunted house stories, *Unquiet Guests*, will be published by Dead Ink Books. His second short story collection, *Come Sing for the Harrowing*, will be reissued by CLASH Books in April 2026.

Lyndsey Croal is a Scottish author of strange and speculative fiction, with work published in over eighty magazines and anthologies, including *Apex, Analog, Shoreline of Infinity*, and *Weird Tales*. She's a Scottish Book Trust New Writers Awardee, Shirley Jackson Award and British Fantasy Award Finalist, and former Hawthornden Fellow. Her longer works include *Limelight and Other Stories* (Shortwave Publishing) and *Dark Crescent* (Luna Press). Find her on Bsky/Instagram as @lyndseycroal or via her website: www.lyndseycroal.co.uk.

James Everington mainly writes dark, supernatural fiction, although he occasionally takes a break and writes dark, non-supernatural fiction. His second collection of such tales, *Falling Over*, is out now from Infinity Plus. Other works include the novel *The Quarantined City* ("*an unsettling voice all of its own*" The Guardian) and the novellas *Paupers' Graves* and *The Shelter*. He's also co-edited the anthologies *The Hyde Hotel*, *Ebb Tides*, *Pareidolia* and the BFS Award nominated *Imposter Syndrome*. Oh, and he drinks Guinness, if anyone's asking. You can find out what James is currently up to at his Scattershot Writing site.

Tracy Fahey is an Irish author. She has won the 2025 Rubery International Book Award and the 2024 Paul Cave Prize for Literature. In 2023 she was awarded a Saari Fellowship. She is a three-time British Fantasy Award finalist and has been shortlisted for the London Independent Story Prize and the Leicester Short Story Prize. Fahey's short fiction has appeared in over 50 anthologies. Her writing is supported by residencies in Greece, Ireland, Scotland and Finland. She holds a PhD in the Gothic and lectures in Critical and Contextual Studies at the Limerick School of Art and Design.

Matthew Hopkins is a semi-professional bad boy from Derbyshire. His work has appeared in *The Nottingham Horror Collective*, *DOG TEETH*, *TOWER* and elsewhere. He is working on his first novel. linktr.ee/swearjaragain

Timothy J. Jarvis is a writer with an interest in the antic and strange. His novel, *The Wanderer*, was first released in summer 2014 by Perfect Edge Books and republished by Zagava in 2022. Short fiction has appeared in various venues and in 2023 a collection, *Treatises on Dust*, was published by Swan River Press. He lives in Bedford.

Penny Jones knew she was a writer when she started to talk about herself in the third person. Penny's debut collection, *Suffer Little Children*, published by Black Shuck Books, was shortlisted for the 2020 British Fantasy Award for Best Newcomer, and her short story, *Dendrochronology*, published by Hersham Horror was shortlisted for the 2020 British Fantasy Award for Best

Short Story. Her novella, *Matryoshka*, published by Hersham Horror was shortlisted for the 2022 British Fantasy Award for Best Novella. And her second collection, *Behind a Broken Smile*, published by Black Shuck Books was shortlisted for the 2023 British Fantasy Award for Best Collection.

A dark fantasy and science fiction author, **Kim Lakin** has published many short stories in leading genre magazines and anthologies, including Black Static and Interzone. Her novel, *Cyber Circus*, was shortlisted for the British Science Fiction Association Award and the British Fantasy Society Best Novel Award. Kim's novels and short stories reflect her dual love of history and futurism, alongside the macabre, the mythic and the mechanical. Kim lives on a farm in rural Derbyshire with her black cat, Diablo.

Tim Major's books include *Jekyll & Hyde: Consulting Detectives* and a sequel, *Jekyll & Hyde: Winter Retreat*, plus *Snakeskins, Hope Island*, three Sherlock Holmes novels and short story collection *Great Robots of History*. Tim's short stories have been selected for Best of British Science Fiction, Best of British Fantasy and The Best Horror of the Year, and his story, "The Brazen Head of Westinghouse", won the British Fantasy Award for Best Short Fiction in 2024.

Phil Raines is a member of the Glasgow Science Fiction Writers Circle and lives in Linlithgow, Scotland. **Harvey Welles** lives in Milwaukee.

Don Redwood lives in Glasgow. His short stories have previously appeared in *Daily Science Fiction, Little Blue Marble* and most recently, *Gallus – A Glasgow Science Fiction Writers Circle Anthology*. Find out more at: donredwood.com

E.Saxey is a queer Londoner who works in universities. Their first collection of short weird stories is *Lost in the Archives* (Lethe Press). *Unquiet*, their debut novel, is a Gothic tale set in Victorian London which wanders into folk horror in the West Country (Titan Books). More recent short fiction includes the novella, On the English Approach to the Study of History (*Giganotosaurus*) and Quethiock by Night, in *The Crawling Moon: Queer Tales of Inescapable Dread* (Neon Hemlock).

Angela "A.G." Slatter is the author of the gothic fantasies *All The Murmuring Bones, The Path of Thorns, The Briar Book of the Dead* and *The Crimson Road* (Titan Books). She's also the author of 12 short story collections, five novellas, two writing books, and a Hellboy Universe collaboration, *Castle*

Full of Blackbirds. She's won a World Fantasy Award, a British Fantasy Award, a Shirley Jackson, a Ditmar, three Australian Shadows Awards, eight Aurealis Awards and a Premier Ignotas Award. Her work's been translated into Bulgarian, Chinese, Russian, Italian, Spanish, Dutch, Japanese, Polish, French, Turkish, Hungarian, Czechoslovakian and Romanian. www.angelaslatter.com

Phil Sloman is a writer of dark psychological fiction. Phil is a three-time finalist at the British Fantasy Awards in the categories of Best Newcomer for his novella *Becoming David* (2017), Best Anthology for *The Woods* in 2020 as editor, and Best Collection for his second collection *No Happily Ever After* in 2024. Phil was also part of *Impostor Syndrome* from Dark Minds Press shortlisted for British Fantasy Award Best Anthology in 2018. Phil regularly appears on several reviewers' Best of Year lists. www.philsloman.com

Steve Toase lives in the Frankenwald, Bavaria, Germany. His fiction has appeared in *Nightmare Magazine, Bourbon Penn, Analog, Three Lobed Burning Eye*, and *Shimmer* amongst others. *To Drown in Dark Water* was published by Undertow Publications, and his archaeology themed horror collection *Dirt Upon My Skin* is out now from Black Shuck Books. He also likes old motorbikes and vintage cocktails.

Ian Whates is the author of ten novels (two co-written), two novellas, and some eighty short stories that have appeared in venues including *Nightmare Magazine, Galaxy's Edge, Daily Science Fiction*, the science journal *Nature* and numerous anthologies. In 2019 he received the Karl Edward Wagner Award from the British Fantasy Society and his work has been shortlisted for the Philip K. Dick Award and on three occasions for BSFA Awards, while his stories have been translated into Spanish, German, Hungarian, Czech and Greek. In 2006 Ian founded publisher NewCon Press by accident.

Neil Williamson has been a finalist as an author and an editor for British Fantasy, British Science Fiction Association and World Fantasy awards. His most recent books include *Nova Scotia vol 2: New Speculative Fiction From Scotland* (Luna Press Publishing) and the urban folk horror novella, *Charlie Says* (Black Shuck Books). His next will be *Hand-Me-Downs*, a collection of horror stories about weird inheritances, coming from PS Publishing in April 2026. Visit neilwilliamson.blog.

ALSO FROM NEWCON PRESS

ANIMALS – Geoff Ryman

A powerful new novel from the multiple award-winning author of *HIM*, *Was* and *The Child Garden* The chilling tale of a family caught at the heart of a terrifying and transformative epidemic; an astonishing fusion of beautiful writing and pure horror as the world we know falls apart.

The Hamlet – Joanna Corrance

Screens go blank, radios go silent, and the government is advising everyone to stay indoors. The residents of a rural Scottish community abandon their picnics and return home. A fabulous tale laced with horror and an added dash of weird, *The Hamlet* is a mosaic featuring the inter-linked lives of inhabitants of a very peculiar rural community when 'things got strange'.

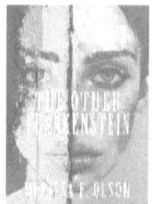

The Other Frankenstein – Melissa F. Olson

Elizabeth Frankenstein's life had been carefully planned, until that future was stolen from her. Elizabeth and Heck Saville's parallel, intersecting stories encompass murder, loss, trauma and ultimately empowerment, in this stunning feminist saga that uses the classic story of *Frankenstein* as a springboard and weaves a potent tale of horror, love, and revenge.

The Essence – Dave Hutchinson

Michael's troubles start with the breakdown he suffers following the death of his wife. He learns there's a phenomenon – a force, a spirit, a flaw in Reality – known as *the Essence*. A small group of people have been attempting to study it for centuries but are none the wiser. Now, some very powerful people believe Michael may hold the key and they will stop at nothing to claim it.

Rise – Kim Lakin

Denounced by her own father and charged with crimes against the state, Kali Titian – pilot, soldier, and engineer – is sentenced to Abbandon prison camp, the worst hellhole on the planet, where she must somehow survive among her fellow inmates, the Vary, a race she has been raised to consider sub-human; a race who until recently she was routinely murdering to order.